COMPULSION

Jonathan Kellerman is one of the world's most popular authors. He has brought his expertise as a clinical psychologist to over two dozen bestselling crime novels, including the Alex Delaware series, *The Butcher's Theater*, *Billy Straight*, *The Conspiracy Club*, and *Twisted*. With his wife, the novelist Faye Kellerman, he co-authored the bestsellers *Double Homicide* and *Capital Crimes*. He is the author of numerous essays, short stories, scientific articles, two children's books, and three volumes of psychology, including *Savage Spawn: Reflections on Violent Children*. He has won the Goldwyn, Edgar, and Anthony awards, and has been nominated for a Shamus Award.

Jonathan and Faye Kellerman live in California and New Mexico. Their four children include the novelist Jesse Kellerman.

Visit the author's website at www.jonathankellerman.com

Books by Jonathan Kellerman

JONATHAN KELLERMAN

COMPULSION

AN ALEX DELAWARE NOVEL

MICHAEL JOSEPH
an imprint of
PENGUIN BOOKS

MICHAEL JOSEPH

Published by the Penguin Group
Penguin Books Ltd, 80 Strand, London WC2R 0RL, England
Penguin Group (USA) Inc., 375 Hudson Street, New York, New York 10014, USA
Penguin Group (Canada), 90 Eglinton Avenue East, Suite 700, Toronto, Ontario, Canada M4P 2Y3
(a division of Pearson Penguin Canada Inc.)
Penguin Ireland, 25 St Stephen's Green, Dublin 2, Ireland (a division of Penguin Books Ltd)
Penguin Group (Australia), 250 Camberwell Road,
Camberwell, Victoria 3124, Australia (a division of Pearson Australia Group Pty Ltd)
Penguin Books India Pvt Ltd, 11 Community Centre,
Panchsheel Park, New Delhi – 110 017, India
Penguin Group (NZ), 67 Apollo Drive, Rosedale, North Shore 0632, New Zealand
(a division of Pearson New Zealand Ltd)
Penguin Books (South Africa) (Pty) Ltd, 24 Sturdee Avenue,
Rosebank, Johannesburg 2196, South Africa

Penguin Books Ltd, Registered Offices: 80 Strand, London WC2R 0RL, England

www.penguin.com

First published in the United States of America by Ballantine Books,
an imprint of The Random House Publishing Group 2008
First published in Great Britain by Michael Joseph 2008
1

Printed in Great Britain by Clays Ltd, St Ives plc

A CIP catalogue record for this book is available from the British Library

ISBN: 978–0–718–15408–0

www.greenpenguin.co.uk

Penguin Books is committed to a sustainable future
for our business, our readers and our planet.
The book in your hands is made from paper
certified by the Forest Stewardship Council.

To Gina Centrello

COMPULSION

CHAPTER

1

Kat loved breaking the rules.

Don't talk to strangers.

She'd talked to plenty of them tonight. Danced with a few, too. If you could call the way those losers moved dancing. The big, scary consequence: a stomped toe, courtesy of a loser in a red shirt.

Don't go crazy mixing your drinks.

Then how did you account for Long Island Iced Tea, which was basically everything tossed together and the best buzz in the world?

She'd had three tonight. Plus the tequila shots and the raspberry beer and the weed the guy in the retro bowling shirt had offered her. Not to mention . . . hard to remember. Whatever.

Don't drink and drive.

Yeah, great plan. What was she supposed to do tonight, let one of those *losers* drive her Mustang home?

The *plan* was Rianna would limit herself to two drinks and be the designated wheel-girl so Kat and Bethie could party. Only Bethie and Rianna hooked up with a couple fake-o blond guys in fake-o Brioni shirts. Brothers, some kind of surfboard business in Redondo.

We're thinking maybe we'll go party with Sean and Matt, giggle, giggle. If that's cool with you, Kat.

What was she supposed to say? Stay with me, I'm the ultimate loser?

So here she was three, four a.m., staggering out of the Light My Fire, looking for her car.

God, it was so dark, why the hell didn't they have outside lights or something . . . ?

She took three steps and one of her spike-heels caught on the asphalt and she stumbled, nearly twisting her ankle.

Fighting for balance, she righted herself.

Saved by quick reflexes, Supergirl. Also all those dancing lessons she'd been forced into. Not that she'd ever admit it to Mother, giving her fuel for more I-told-you-so bullshit.

Mother and her rules. No white after Labor Day. *That* made sense in L.A.

Kat took two more steps and one of the spaghetti straps on her plum lamé top fell off her shoulder. She left it that way, liking the kiss of the night air on her bare skin.

Feeling a little bit sexy, she flipped her hair, then remembered she'd had it cut, not much to flip.

Her vision blurred—how many Long Islands had she polished off? Maybe four.

Taking a deep cleansing breath, she felt her head clear.

Then it clouded again. And cleared. Like shutters being opened and closed. Crazy, maybe that weed was messed up . . . where was the Mustang . . . she walked faster, tripped again, and Supergirl reflexes weren't enough and she had to grab out for something—the side of a car . . . not hers, crappy little Honda or something . . . where was the *Mustang?*

With only a few cars in the lot, it should've been easy to spot. But the darkness screwed everything up . . . losers who owned the Light My Fire too damn cheap to invest in some spots, like they weren't making enough packing the bodies in, the bouncers and velvet ropes a big joke.

Cheap bastards. Like all men.

Except Royal. Would you believe that, Mother finally lucking out big-time? Who knew the old girl had it in her?

Kat laughed out loud at the image. Something *in* Mother.

Not likely, Royal was in the bathroom every ten minutes. Didn't that mean a screwed-up prostrate?

She lurched across the inky lot. The sky was so black she couldn't even see the chain-link fence surrounding the lot, or the warehouses and storage lots that made up this crappy neighborhood.

The club's Web site said it was in Brentwood. More like the hairy, stinky armpit of West L.A. . . . okay, there it was, her stupid Mustang.

She hurried toward the car, heels clacking against knobby asphalt. Each impact set off little echoes that reminded her of when she was seven and Mother forced her to take tap.

When she finally got there, she groped in her purse for her keys, found them. Dropped them.

She heard the rattle as they landed, but it was too dark to see where. Bending sharply, she teetered, braced herself with one hand to the ground, and searched with the other.

Nowhere.

Squatting, she smelled something chemical—gasoline, like when you fill up your car and no matter how many times you wash your hands afterward you can't get rid of the stink.

A fuel leak? That's all she needed.

Six thousand miles and the car was nothing but problems. She'd thought it was cool at first, but decided it was lame and stopped making payments. Hello, Re-po Man. Again.

We took care of the down payment, Katrina. All you had to do was remember on the fifteenth of each . . .

Where were the goddamn *keys*! She scraped her knuckles on the ground. A fake nail popped off and that made her feel like crying.

6 JONATHAN KELLERMAN

Ah, got it!

Struggling to her feet, she flicked the remote, dropped into the driver's seat, started up the engine. The car balked, then kicked in and *here we go Supergirl* she was driving straight into the black night—oh, yeah, put on the headlights.

Slowly, with a drunk's exaggerated care, she coasted, missed the exit, backed up, passed through. Turning south onto Corinth Avenue, she made her way to Pico. The boulevard was totally empty and she turned onto it. Oversteered, ended up on the wrong side of the road, swerved and compensated, finally got the stupid car in the lane.

At Sepulveda, she hit a red light.

No cars at the intersection. No cops.

She ran it.

Sailing north, she felt free, like the whole city—the whole *world* was hers.

Like someone had dropped a nuke and she was the last survivor.

Wouldn't *that* be cool, she could drive over to Beverly Hills, run a gazillion red lights, waltz into the Tiffany store on Rodeo and scoop up whatever she wanted.

A planet without people. She laughed.

She crossed Santa Monica and Wilshire and kept going until Sepulveda turned into the Pass. Off to her left was the 405, just a scatter of taillights. On the other side was hillside that bled into moonless sky.

No lights on in gazillion-dollar hill houses full of sleeping rich people. The same kind of idiots she had to deal with at La Femme.

Women like Mother, pretending they weren't shriveling or fat as pigs.

Thinking about work made Kat tense up and she deep-breathed. That made her burp real loud and she cracked up, drove faster.

At this rate, she'd be over the hill and at her apartment real soon.

Stupid little dump in Van Nuys, but she told everyone it was Sherman Oaks because it was on the border and who cared?

All of a sudden her eyes began to close and she had to shake herself awake. A hard shove down on the gas pedal and the car shot forward.

Saaiiiling. . . . You go, girl!

Seconds later, the Mustang sputtered, whined, stopped.

She managed to steer to the right, stop just off the road. Let the car sit for a sec and tried again.

Nothing but a whiny noise.

Two more attempts, then five.

Shit!

It took a while to find the switch for the interior lights and when she brightened the car, her head hurt and she saw little yellow things dancing in front of her eyes. When they cleared, she looked at the gas gauge.

E

Shit shit shit! How had that happened, she could swear—

Mother's voice nagged at her. She put her hands over her ears and tried to think.

Where was the nearest gas station . . . nowhere, nothing for miles.

She punched the dashboard so hard it hurt her hands. Cried, sat back, drained.

Realizing she was exposed by the interior lights, she switched them off.

Now what?

Call the Triple A! Why hadn't she thought of that?

It took what seemed like a long time to find her cell phone in her purse. Even longer to locate her Triple A card.

Tapping out the toll-free number was hard because even with the phone light the numbers were teeny and her hands were shaky.

When the operator answered, she read off her membership code. Had to do it twice because her eyes had blurred and it was hard to see what was a 3 and what was an 8.

The operator put her on hold, came back and said her membership had lapsed.

Kat said, "No way."

"Sorry, ma'am, but you haven't been active for eighteen months."

"That's frickin' impossible—"

"I'm sorry, ma'am, but—"

"Like hell you are—"

"Ma'am, there's no reason to be—"

"Like hell there isn't." Kat clicked off.

Now what?

Think, think, think—okay, plan B: Call Bethie's cell and if that interrupted something, too frickin' bad.

The phone rang five times before Bethie's voice mail kicked in.

Kat hung up. Her phone went dead.

Jabbing the *Power* button did nothing.

That brought back a vague memory of something she'd neglected.

Charging up before she went out tonight—how the *hell* had she forgotten?

Now her whole *body* was shaking and her chest was tight and she was sweating.

She double-checked to make sure the car was locked.

Maybe a highway patrol dude would come by.

What if another car did?

Don't talk to strangers.

What was her choice, sleeping here all night?

She nearly fell asleep before the first car showed up, speeding toward her, headlights startling her.

Big Range Rover; good.

Kat waved out the window. Bastard sped right by.

A couple of minutes later, headlights brightened her rearview and enlarged. This vehicle stopped right next to her.

Crappy pickup, stuff piled in the back, under a tarp.

The passenger window rolled down.

Young Mexican guy. Another Mexican sat at the wheel.

They looked at her funny.

The passenger got out. Small and scruffy.

Kat slid down low in her seat and when the Mexican came over and said something through the glass, she pretended he wasn't there.

He stood there, really freaking her out.

Kat kept making believe she was invisible and the Mexican finally returned to the pickup.

It took five minutes after the truck drove away before she was able to sit up and breathe normally. She'd wet her thong. Rolled it off her butt and down her legs and tossed it into the backseat.

Soon as the undies made contact, her luck turned.

A Bentley!

Screw you, Range Rover!

Big, black, and glossy, that aggressive grille.

And slowing down!

Oh shit, what if it was Clive?

Even if it *was* Clive, she could handle it, better than sleeping here all—

As the Bentley rolled to a halt, she opened the window, tried to get a look at who was inside.

The big black car idled, moved on.

Damn you, rich bastard!

She jumped out of the Mustang, waved frantically.

The Bentley stopped. Backed up.

Kat tried to make herself look safe by shrugging and smiling and pointing to her car.

The Bentley's window lowered silently.

Just a driver inside.

Not Clive, a woman!

Thank you, God!

Kat said, "Ma'am," in the syrupy voice she used at La Femme. "Thank you so much for stopping I ran out of gas and if you could just take me somewhere where I could maybe find a—"

"Certainly, dear," said the woman. Throaty voice, like that actress

Mother liked . . . Lauren Lauren . . . Hutton? No, Bacall. Lauren Bacall had rescued her!

Kat approached the Bentley.

The woman smiled at her. Older than Mother, with silver hair, huge pearl earrings, classy makeup, a tweed suit, some sort of silk scarf, purple, looked expensive, draped over her shoulders in that casual way that came easy to the classy ones.

What Mother pretended to be.

"Ma'am, I really appreciate this," said Kat, suddenly wanting this woman to *be* her mother.

"Get in, dear," said the woman. "We'll find you some petrol."

Petrol—a Brit.

A frickin' aristocrat in a frickin' *Bentley.*

Kat got in, beaming. What had started off as a shitty night was going to end up a cool story.

As the Bentley glided away, Kat thanked the woman again.

The woman nodded and switched on the stereo. Something classical—God what a sound system, it was like being in a concert hall.

"If there's any way I can repay you . . ."

"That won't be necessary, dear."

Big-framed woman, sturdy bejeweled hands.

Kat said, "Your car's *incredible.*"

The woman smiled and turned up the volume.

Kat sat back and closed her eyes. Thought of Rianna and Bethie with the fake-o shirts.

Telling *this* story was going to be delicious.

The Bentley cruised silently up the Pass. Cushy seats, alcohol, weed, and the adrenaline drop plunged Kat into sudden, nearly comatose sleep.

She was snoring loudly when the car made a turn, climbed smoothly into the hills.

Headed for a dark, cold place.

CHAPTER

2

I was having lunch with Milo at the Surf Line Café in Malibu when the call came in.

No reason for either of us to be here other than gorgeous weather. The restaurant's a clapboard bungalow with wall-sized windows and a wide plank deck, perched high on the west side of PCH, just south of Kanan Dume Road. At half a mile from the ocean with no view of the water, it was misnamed. But the food's fantastic and even at that distance you can smell the salt.

It was one p.m. and we were out on the deck eating barbecued yellowtail and drinking beer. Milo was back from a week in Honolulu, where he'd managed to preserve a skim-milk pallor. Bad light brings out the worst of his complexion—the lumps, the acne pits, the scowl lines, gravity tugging at mastiff jowls. Today's light was glorious but the best it could do was obscure the rough spots.

Despite that and the ugliest aloha shirt I'd ever seen, he looked good. None of the twitches and split-second winces that betray his attempt to hide the pain in his shoulder.

The shirt was a riot of puce elephants, aqua camels, and ocher monkeys on a sea of olive-green rayon that clung to his kettledrum torso.

The Hawaiian trip had followed a twenty-nine-day stay in the hospital: recuperating from a dozen shotgun pellets embedded in his left arm and shoulder.

The shooter, an obsessive psychopath, was dead, sparing everyone the nuisance of a trial. Milo had dismissed his own injuries as "a stupid goddamn flesh wound." I'd seen the X-rays. Some of the pellets had missed his heart and lung by millimeters. One chunk of deer shot was too deep to remove without causing serious muscle injury, hence the winces and twitches.

Despite all that, only a three-day hospitalization had been projected. On the second day, a staph infection set in and he ended up on antibiotic drips for nearly a month. Sequestered on the VIP floor because he lived with Dr. Rick Silverman, director of the E.R.

Bigger rooms and better food didn't help where it counted. His fever ran high and at one point his kidney function didn't look good. Eventually, he pushed through and started griping about the accommodations and the twenty-one-year-old actress in the corner suite up the hall. Her official diagnosis was "Exhaustion." The hospital's detox director had virtually moved in.

Two paparazzi had managed to breach security, only to be tossed unceremoniously by one of the starlet's private security guards.

I said, "They don't get her, maybe they'll settle for you."

"Oh, sure, *People* and *Us* can't survive a circulation war without close-ups of the vast polar tundra that is my VIP ass."

He worked his way out of the bed, stomped out into the hall, and glared at the rent-a-cop hovering near his door. The guy moved on.

"Intrusive asshole."

Definitely on the mend.

After discharge, he pretended everything was fine. Rick and Robin and I and everyone else who knew him pretended not to notice the stiffness and the loss of energy. The department physician insisted he take some downtime and his captain wouldn't debate the issue.

Milo and Rick had been talking about a tropical vacation for months but when the time came, Milo's mood suggested an impending prison sentence.

He sent me a single postcard: gargantuan Samoan sumo wrestlers tussling on white sand.

A:

Having a great blah blah blah yawn yawn yawn. These are the locals. A few more luaus and there goes my modeling contract.

Primitively yours,

M.

Now he finished his second beer and said, "What are you smirking about?"

"Didn't know I was."

"I'm a trained observer. You were."

I shrugged.

"It's the shirt, right?"

"The shirt's great."

"Lucky for you there's no polygraph around. What, you don't dig authentic island *couture*?"

"Elephants in Oahu?"

"Dr. Literal." He rolled rayon between sausage fingers. "I'da found one with Freud analyzing a mahimahi I'da brought it back for you."

"The macadamia nuts were fine."

"Yeah, yeah." He brushed black hair off his forehead, called for another beer, finished it fast. Bright green eyes took in the view of the highway below. His eyelids half lowered.

"You okay?"

"Back to work tomorrow, the leisure thing was driving me out of my mind. Problem is, once I get to the office, there's nothing to do. No new cases, period—let alone an interesting one."

"How do you know?"

"I e-mailed the captain yesterday."

I said, "Quiet time in West L.A."

"Calm before the storm, or worse."

"What would be worse?"

"No storm."

He insisted on paying and was reaching for his billfold when his cell squawked. I used the opportunity to hand the waiter my credit card.

"Sneaky." He clicked in, listened. "Okay, Sean, why not? But if a *real* crime happens, all bets are off."

As we left, I said, "Sean's got a fake crime?"

"Car theft in Brentwood. *Recovered* car theft." Like many homicide detectives, he considers anything less than the loss of human life on a par with jaywalking.

"Why'd he call you?"

"He thinks it might be more because there's blood on one of the seats."

"That sounds like more."

"Not buckets, Alex. Maybe a spoonful."

"Whose?"

"That's the big hoohah mystery. Nervy kid wants my expertise. No one told him I'm a free bird until tomorrow."

I kept my mouth shut. When he's like that, irony is wasted.

Sean Binchy was waiting in front of a vanilla-colored house, wearing his usual dark suit, blue shirt and tie, spit-polished Doc Martens. He's a young, gangly, redheaded Detective I, a former ska-punk bassist who'd found Jesus and the LAPD simultaneously. He'd been mentored by Milo, whisked away by the brass and transferred to Robbery, then moved to Auto Theft. Rumor said all that movement had something to do with his "lack of creativity."

The house behind him was one of those imposing, bland, grand dream-projects starting to dominate L.A.'s luxury districts.

This was a high-end part of Brentwood, west of Bundy, north of Sunset, where the streets narrow and sidewalks are replaced by grass. Shaggy eucalyptus hovered above much of the street. The vanilla house's immediate neighbors were one-story ranches, sitting on residential death row as they awaited the wrecking ball.

Sean pointed to a wide stone driveway leading to twin garages. A black Bentley Arnage sedan sat in front of one of the doors.

"VIP wheels," said Milo. "Just what I need."

"Hi, Loot. Hi, Dr. Delaware."

The conventional department contraction for Milo's rank is "Loo." Milo is not one to deal with the small stuff.

"How was Hawaii?"

Milo said, "I got you some macadamia nuts."

"Thanks—great shirt."

Milo's eyes shifted to the Bentley. "Someone stole that and had the nerve to leave blood?"

"Or something that looks a whole lot like blood."

"As opposed to?"

"I'm pretty sure it's blood, Loot. Haven't called for analysis because I wanted to see what you thought."

"Who recovered it?"

"The owner." Binchy thumbed his pad. ". . . Nicholas Heubel. Solid citizen, didn't have to call us in the first place."

Milo walked over to the Bentley. Unfettered sunlight bore down on a paint job so shiny it looked like molten tar. "How'd he find it?"

"Drove around and spotted it three blocks away."

"Not much of a joyride."

"If you think I should forget it, I will. I just want to make sure I wasn't missing something."

"Car unlocked?"

"Yup."

"Give me some gloves and show me this alleged blood."

CHAPTER

3

Several cows' worth of premium hides, a tree or two of burl veneer.

All of it smelling like a private club in Mayfair.

The Bentley's interior was off-white piped with black; missing the stain was impossible. The blemish in question was a smear about an inch square, on the right side of the driver's seat. Sloping down toward the welting, at its lowest point more diluted. Rundown or someone had wiped it that way.

I supposed it could have been old ketchup, but my bet was on hemoglobin.

Milo said, "Not too impressive."

Sean said, "There could be more, but with the carpet black it's hard to spot anything without an up close and personal."

"Check the trunk?"

"I popped it and did a visual scan. Looks like nothing's ever been in there. I mean literally. There's a couple umbrellas still rolled up and belted to the firewall. Owner says they were an option, cost eight hundred bucks and he hasn't used them once."

Milo stretched latex over his paws, leaned in, stuck his head close to the smear but didn't touch it. Studying and sniffing, he checked out the carpet, the door panels, an array of glass gauges. Opening a rear door, he said, "Car smells new."

"It's a year old."

"Three thousand miles on the odometer. Looks like it's not just the umbrellas the owner doesn't use."

"He has a Lexus," said Sean. "Says it's less showy and more reliable."

Milo examined the smear again. "Looks like blood but I'm seeing no impact, high or low velocity. Some asshole, probably a neighbor kid, took a joyride and cut himself on a chipped bong. Was the car taken from the garage?"

"From the driveway."

"Wheels like that, owner doesn't lock up?"

"Guess not."

"Keys left in the ignition?"

"Owner claims no. I was going to ask him more but he had to go inside and take a call."

Milo said, "They probably *were* left in, no one wants to look stupid. Boosting something this conspicuous says immaturity and impulsivity. Which fits with a neighborhood punk. So does dumping it close by. What do you think, Alex?"

"Makes sense."

He turned back to Sean. "If this was a serious case, I'd canvass the area, starting with the dump site, find out who has teenagers with behavior problems. But that's a big if."

"So I shouldn't pursue it," said Sean.

"Owner pushing you to pursue it?"

"He's rattled by the blood, but says he doesn't want to make a big deal 'cause there's no damage."

"It was me, Sean, I'd tell him to get out the Meguiar's and forget about it."

"What's that?"

"Premium leather cleaner."

"Okay, I'm good with that," said Sean.

"Have a nice day."

As we headed for the Seville, the door to the vanilla house opened and a man hurried out.

Late thirties to early forties, six feet tall, with long, loose limbs, close-cropped brown hair graying at the temples, and tiny, oval-lens eyeglasses. He wore a gray T-shirt, blue velvet sweatpants, brown boat shoes without socks. The glasses perched atop a narrow, straight nose. His lips were tight and bunched as if someone were squeezing his cheeks.

"Lieutenant?" Bypassing Sean, he headed for us, took in Milo's elephant riot shirt, then my black polo and jeans. Squinted through his glasses, trying to figure out who was in charge.

"Milo Sturgis."

A long-fingered hand shot out. "Nick Heubel."

"Pleased to meet you, sir."

Heubel hooked a thumb at his Bentley. "Bizarre, huh? I told Detective Binchy I didn't want to make a production out of it, but now I'm having second thoughts. What if the bad guy was someone in the neighborhood and they're after more than just cheap thrills?"

"More like expensive thrills," said Milo.

Heubel smiled. "Buying it was one of those what-was-I-thinking moments. Drive it for a week and you realize it's just a car and you got sucked into the whole illusion . . . Anyway, what I was getting at is what if some local delinquent with serious antisocial tendencies is running around and the theft was a symptom?"

"Of what, Mr. Heubel?"

"Taking whatever he wants." Heubel's eyes behind his glasses were light brown and active.

Milo said, "You're worried he may come back and try something else."

"I wouldn't call it worry," said Heubel. "More like . . . I guess I *am* worried. It was so blatant, just swooping in and driving away."

"Do you have any idea when it happened?"

"I told Detective Binchy it could've been anywhere between eleven p.m.—which is when I got home—and this morning, when I stepped out of the house and found it gone. I was headed for the Country Mart to get some breakfast. For a second, I wondered if I'd parked it in the garage, then I knew I couldn't have because my other car's there and the rest is taken up by storage." His eyes rolled. "Gone. I couldn't believe it."

"What time this morning did you step out, sir?"

"Seven forty-five. If you want me to narrow it down, I doubt it happened after five a.m. because by then I was up and in my office, which is in the front of the house, so I think I would've heard something. Though I can't be sure. One thing you *can* say about the darn thing, the engine's quiet."

"Five a.m.," said Milo. "Early riser."

"I like to be well prepared for the markets when they open in New York. Sometimes when I'm looking at the international bourses, I'm up even earlier than that."

"Stock trader?"

"Dabble in commodities. This morning nothing enticed me, so I figured I'd get some breakfast, make some calls."

"Must be successful dabbling."

Heubel shrugged and scratched his head. "Beats honest labor. Anyway, I reported it, by the time I heard back from Detective Binchy, I'd found it."

"Right in the neighborhood," said Milo.

"Three blocks west, on Villa Entrada."

"Any particular reason you went there?"

Heubel looked puzzled.

Milo said, "Are you aware of some delinquent living on Villa Entrada who might do something like this?"

"Oh," said Heubel. "No, not at all. I just drove up and down, can't even tell you why I did it because I wasn't really hopeful. Probably just to do *something*—you know? Trying to take back control?"

"Absolutely, sir."

"If you'd asked me to bet, I'd have said it was in East L.A., or Watts or on a flatbed to Tijuana. You can imagine how surprised I was when I spotted it, parked right at the curb, keys in the ignition."

"Speaking of the keys," said Milo. "How did—"

"I know, I know, stupid," said Heubel. "The main one's in my desk drawer but who figured someone would find the other?"

"Spare set?"

"One of those magnetic dealies, I keep it in a wheel well in case the main one gets lost." Heubel colored. "Dumb, huh?"

"Who knew it was there?"

"That's the thing," said Heubel, "no one. I'm so careful that when I go to the car wash I remove it. Guess I wasn't careful enough. Maybe someone drove by and saw me removing it. Believe me, I've learned my lesson."

"All's well that ends well," said Milo.

"Absolutely. But the blood's troublesome, isn't it, Lieutenant? It wasn't until I got home that I noticed it." Blinking. "That's what it is, right?"

"It's possible, sir, but even if that turns out to be the case, there's no evidence of violence."

"What do you mean?"

"It really isn't that much blood, and with violence you generally see what we call impact spatter—dripping or spray or sizable splotches. This looks more like someone wiped a cut on the leather."

"I see," said Heubel. "But still, someone bled in there and it wasn't me."

"You're sure about that, sir?"

"Hundred percent positive. The first thing I did was to go inside and check my legs—maybe I got a mosquito bite and didn't feel it. Not that it would bleed through my pants—I was wearing heavy jeans—my winter Diesels, they're darn sturdy." Patting his thigh. "I checked the front and the back of my legs, even used a mirror. Nothing."

"That's a lot of effort," said Milo.

"I was a bit shaken up, Lieutenant. First the car gets taken right out of my driveway, then I find it, then there's *blood*? I guess when you do the DNA and it doesn't match to any crime victims, I'll be able to put it to rest."

"There's no reason to do DNA, sir."

"No?" said Heubel. "I heard the technology's much better than back in the O.J. days. All these new tests, you can get results quickly."

Milo glanced at Sean.

Sean said, "Quick*er,* but it still takes time, sir. And DNA's a real expensive process."

"Ah," said Heubel. "This is low priority for you guys."

"It's not like we don't appreciate your situation, sir—"

"The shock," said Milo. "The feeling of violation."

"You've got that right," said Heubel. "But the main issue is what's to say he's not still out there plotting something?"

Milo gave him what he calls the Forensics Damage Control Lecture. An increasing necessity due to week after week of televised fairy tales.

The main points were: Forensic wizardry made for good entertainment but crime scene minutiae were relevant in less than 10 percent of crimes, the DNA logjam at the Department of Justice was so severe the department contracted with a lab in New Jersey for the overflow, and the backup was so bad only homicides and violent sexual assaults merited analysis.

"Even with a serious felony, Mr. Heubel, it can take months."

"Wow. How in the world do you ever solve any crimes, Lieutenant?"

Milo smiled. "We bumble around and sometimes we get lucky."

"I'm sorry, I didn't mean to—ten percent, that's all?"

"At best."

"Okay, I hear you . . . It's just that one lives in a specific neighborhood in the belief that one can be relatively insulated from—I suppose that's also a fantasy."

"This *is* a safe neighborhood, sir. One of the safest in our division." Holding back the nasty little Westside secret: Violence in the high-priced zip codes is rare but burglaries, including grand theft auto, aren't. Because as one captured burglar put it, "That's where the cool stuff is."

Nicholas Heubel said, "So I should just calm down and forget it ever happened."

"I'll tell you what, sir. If Detective Binchy has time, he can call for technical assistance and get a scraping, at least verify that it is blood. If the crime scene specialists have time, they can also inspect the rest of the car. If that's your desire."

"What would they be looking for?"

"More blood, anything out of the ordinary. It might take some time."

"So I'd lose the car for a few days."

"Could happen."

"Well," said Heubel, "I didn't see anything anywhere else—" He flashed a sick smile. "I looked around with a flashlight. Guess I messed up forensically."

"Have you vacuumed the car, sir?"

"No, but my fingerprints—"

"Your prints are going to be all over the vehicle because you're the driver. If you haven't vacuumed and some sort of notable stain or fiber was transferred, it can be found."

Heubel poked a finger under an eyeglass lens. "Ten percent, huh? I'd have bet ninety. Guess I'm really out of my element."

"That's why we're here, sir. Would you like Detective Binchy to call for tech support?"

"Would they need to take off the door panels?"

"No, sir. They'll use swabs, maybe do some superficial scraping, wet whatever they get in saline solution, toss in various reagents—chemicals that react with body fluids. They can do an on-spot analysis for human protein, and if it is blood, obtain an ABO typing. We're talking a few minutes but waiting for the techs could take a whole lot longer, maybe days, so it would be best if you didn't drive the car. In the meantime, Detective Binchy can take all your information and write a comprehensive report for our files."

Sean kicked one shoe with the other.

Heubel said, "I do have another car to drive. Let me think about it."

"Your choice, sir."

"Nice to have choices," said Heubel. "Or the illusion of such."

As we drove away, I said, "Comprehensive report? What's that, Sean's punishment for wasting your time?"

"I acknowledge no such vindictiveness."

"Planning to follow up by grounding him and taking away his Game Boy?"

He laughed. "What I *will* cop to is butt-covering. Guy like Heubel just might know the mayor. Last thing I need—last thing *Sean* needs*—is cocktail chatter about how the police don't give a crap."

"Ah," I said. "You were protecting the kid."

"That's what Uncle Milo do."

"And who knows," I said. "The stain could lead somewhere."

He swiveled his head toward me. "Appeasing the rich is one thing, Alex. Conjuring up retro-Goth-neo-Mansonite vampires roaming the streets of Brentwood to butcher commodity traders is another."

"The original Mansonites roamed Beverly Hills and Los Feliz and butchered all kinds of rich people."

"This is a no-damage car theft perpetrated by a joyrider considerate enough to park where the owner was likely to find the damn thing."

"Okay," I said.

He said, "Don't use that tone of voice with me, young man."

CHAPTER

4

If Sean called in the crime scene techs to scour the Bentley, he never notified Milo.

For one week, no new murders were reported in West L.A. Cursing whatever psycho-economic-social factors were causing a peaceful autumn, Milo got to work on some old unsolveds. The murder books he looked for were missing or sketchy to the point of uselessness and he dead-ended.

On his eighth day back on the job, I phoned to see how he was doing. His captain had just relayed a directive from the police chief's office. A rapist-killer named Cozman "Cuz" Jackson, awaiting execution in Texas, was scrambling to avoid the needle by confessing murders all over the country and promising to pinpoint the graves.

Before Texas agreed to investigate, they wanted local cops to produce some facts.

Cuz Jackson's claimed victim in California was Antoine Beverly, a fifteen-year-old boy from South L.A. who'd vanished in Culver City sixteen years ago while selling magazine subscriptions door-to-door.

Jackson had been living nearby at the time, in Venice, and had worked ten miles from Antoine's magazine route, as a handyman at a Westchester animal shelter.

No sign of the Beverly file in Central Records, either. Downtown wanted Milo to search for it in West L.A. and, if he found it, recontact witnesses.

No success, so far. He said, "Time to put a fatwa on the Great Bureaucratic Satan. Let me tell you how this went down: Normally this would go to the Homicide Special boys, but they love high-profile guts and glory and this ain't either so they lobbed a pass to West L.A. Captain figures at this point I'll be happy with anything and tosses it to me."

"Well," I said, "at least there's the novelty factor."

"Which is?"

"A captain who takes pity."

"Gotta go, Alex."

The gray cloud hovering over him hadn't cleared a bit. Maybe it was lead in his arm and residual pain.

Or spiritual erosion after two decades as a gay detective in LAPD.

That whole concept had changed, perhaps at a rate so slow it never registered in his head as progress.

As a rookie, he took pains to hide his orientation. The truth emerged anyway, leading to smirks, whispers, bursts of outright hostility. He stopped hiding but didn't flaunt. Opened his locker more than once to find hate mail. The teamwork that forms the core of homicide work eluded him as a succession of partners heeded the whispers and requested transfers.

Making the best of the isolation, he piled up overtime and racked up one of the highest solve rates in the department. Unsure what to do with him, the department dithered to the point where civil rights advances and a jacketful of grateful letters from victims' families made him tough to persecute.

Then an old murder brought him back to his rookie days, digging up indiscretions by the police chief, and earning him a deal: In return for not going public, he'd be promoted to lieutenant, allowed to avoid that rank's desk duties and continue to work murders.

Shuffled out of the detectives' room, he was stashed in a closet-sized office that had once *been* a storage closet, given a balky computer, the occasional assistance of untested D I's, if no one else needed them, and told to pick his cases.

Translation: *Stay out of our way and we'll return the favor.*

Another man might've withered. Milo took well to the arrangement, establishing a second office at a nearby Indian restaurant and closing cases with dyspeptic reliability. All the while indulging his only hobby: complaining.

His solve rate caught the eye of the new chief, a man obsessed with crime stats.

A new captain named Raymonda Grant didn't care who anyone slept with.

Milo got a better computer, more access to backup, and continuing job flexibility.

Invitations to division barbecues never showed up in his box, but he'd never been one for socializing and it was all he could do to find time for Rick.

If life had gotten easier, he wasn't showing it.

No doubt Antoine Beverly's family considered their son's case as vital as the day the boy had disappeared, but Milo's pessimism was well founded: Sixteen years is long enough to obscure any evidence and confession-cramming's a common death row ploy that usually leads nowhere.

Still, he should've been happy to work.

Or could be I was projecting because my own work, this year, was proving satisfying. Several child custody cases had actually turned out the way they should, with parents making honest attempts *not* to eat their young, and attorneys restraining the impulse to destroy. Sometimes my reports even ended up on the desks of intelligent judges who took the time to read them.

I fantasized about a kinder gentler world, maybe in reaction to all the brutality on the front page.

When I raised the possibility with Robin, she smiled and stroked the dog and said, "Could be one of the positive side effects of global warming. We blame it for everything bad."

She and I were back together after our second breakup in ten years, living in the house above Beverly Glen that she'd designed and I'd found tomb-like in her absence. She'd received a six-figure commission from a dot-com mogul to build a quartet of hand-carved instruments—guitar, mandolin, mandola, mandocello—a project that would occupy her for the best part of the year.

Dream gig, when she didn't think about the mogul being tone-deaf and unable to play a note.

The koi in our pond had spawned a dozen baby fish, ample rain had juiced up the plants in the garden, and we had *The Dog Who Smiled and Meant It:* a one-year-old French bulldog named Blanche, a warm, soft little blond thing so bright, amiable, and mellow that I'd considered donating her chromosomes for research on the Biology of Nice.

Not that anyone was studying the topic. Dog doesn't bite man is no story at all.

Milo's ninth day back on the job, someone got bit.

It took place on one of those streets where that kind of thing doesn't happen.

At six thirty-two a.m. on a quiet Sunday in a South Westwood neighborhood where small, tidy houses are dominated by the spire of the Mormon temple on Santa Monica Boulevard, a seventy-three-year-old retired schoolteacher named Ella Mancusi opened the door to her mint-green stucco bungalow, walked ten feet to pick up her newspaper, and came face-to-face with a man and a knife.

The sole witness, an insomniac advertising copywriter named Edward Moskow, was drinking coffee and reading his own paper in his living room, two houses south. By chance, he looked out the window, saw what he thought was a man punching Ella Mancusi, watched in horror as the old woman crumpled into a pool of blood.

By the time Moskow reached Ella, she was dead and her murderer was fleeing the scene.

The coroner's investigator counted nine stab wounds, four of them fatal. From the depth and width of the cuts, the on-the-scene guess was a hefty, nonserrated, single-edged blade, consistent with some kind of hunting knife.

Most remarkable was Moskow's description of the killer: a tall, heavyset, white-haired man wearing dark, baggy clothes and a blue plaid cap.

"One of those old-guy caps, he was a geezer. When he walked to his car, he moved stiffly, like old guys do."

The car had been left idling at the curb, driver's door open, as the man in the cap butchered his victim. Once finished, he wiped the blade on a trouser leg, got back behind the wheel, and drove off at a moderate rate of speed.

Moskow's eagle eye extended to the vehicle.

"Late-model Mercedes S600, black, shiny and clean. It's their top-of-the-line four-door if you don't count the Maybach. I'm sure of it because I'm a car freak. We're talking a bill and a half. I only caught part of the license plate."

One letter, three digits. Milo put a trace on the vehicle before he went out to inspect the scene. By the time he called me, a hit had come through.

"Lifted from the Prestige Rent-A-Car lot in Beverly Hills, returned before they opened at nine. Company didn't even know it was missing till I called. Odometer says forty-three miles were put on."

"Was the lot locked?"

"Supposedly there's a chain."

"Six thirty homicide, back in place two and a half hours later," I said.

"Talk about gall."

"Big black luxury car boosted and returned," I said.

He frowned. "That, too."

"Sean follow through on the Bentley?"

"All Heubel authorized was a swab of the stain, no fancy tech stuff. Sean got a kit and did it himself. Human blood, type O-positive. But we're a long way from tying the Bentley into this mess. And no cracks about thousand-to-one odds."

"God forbid."

"I do the forbidding when He's busy. Want to have a look at this scene?"

"Sure."

"See you in twenty."

Ella Mancusi's body had been taken to the crypt. What remained was blood-drenched brick and syrupy lawn.

Harder to make out patterns on the uneven surface and I'm no expert, but I'd seen enough over the years to guess at arterial spatter and slow leakage.

The old woman's body shutting down as blood volume dropped and her heart stopped and her soul washed away.

Milo, standing straighter than I'd seen in a long time, was talking to Sean Binchy. Black strands of hair blew into his face and he slapped them away without success. A hurricane would've been required to budge Sean's cropped, gelled do.

I left the blood and walked over to them.

Sean looked pale. "An old lady. A *teacher.*"

Milo said, "The Benz is on its way to the auto lab. Sean will talk to Mr. Heubel about voluntarily relinquishing the Bentley for further analysis. If Heubel doesn't agree, we're out of luck, according to the hardest-ass A.D.A. I know."

Sean said, "Maybe if I tell him about this, he'll be cool. He seemed like a nice guy."

"Or just the opposite."

"What do you mean?"

"Rich folk avoid messes." Milo started to walk away.

"Um, Loot, I'm still officially on GTA."

"Want me to talk to someone?"

Sean chewed his lip. "I'm not sure Lieutenant Escudo would be thrilled and I'll need him for my performance rating."

Milo's eyes narrowed. "What are you saying, Sean?"

Sean looked back at the blood. "Whatever I can do to help I will."

I waited for Milo to bark at him but he said, "See how far you can get with Heubel, then we'll talk."

Sean saluted and marched away.

I said, "When does he get his bedtime extended?"

"When his grades improve." Milo turned and faced the little green house. "Any spontaneous insights?"

"Elderly victim, same for the murderer, all that overkill, it's probably personal. I'd check out boyfriends, ex-husbands, romantic entanglements gone bad."

"Geritol lover's spat? My witness says she was a widow and the only visitor he ever saw is a guy in his forties he assumed was her son. Techies are inside. When they're finished, I'll start digging through her personal effects."

A man came out of a Spanish bungalow two doors up. Rubbing his eyes, he looked away from the blood.

"That's him," said Milo. "Why don't you have a chat while I see how the house-toss is going."

Edward Moskow was in his mid- to late fifties, bald with a frizzy gray beard. His *Swarthmore* sweatshirt was frayed at the cuffs and a size too large. Khaki pants had faded to off-white, nearly as pallid as his bare feet.

I introduced myself, leaving out the title.

Moskow nodded.

I said, "Terrible thing to see."

"I'll never forget it." He touched his forehead. "Etched right here."

"If there's anything else you remember . . ."

"Old bastard." His voice was soft and hoarse. "Unbelievable. You'd think by that age they'd lose the urge."

"Often they do."

He looked at me, as if he'd just realized we were having a conversation.

I said, "It's called criminal burnout. Otherwise known as too pooped to pop."

Small nod.

"Mr. Moskow, how old would you say this man was?"

"Only saw him for a few seconds." Moskow's face screwed up and his beard bristled. "Mostly I was looking at his arm." He raised his own limb, mimed a downward thrust. "I thought he was hitting her with his hand, ran out to confront him. By the time I got there, he was walking back to his car and I saw the blood under Mrs. Mancusi. Spreading . . . a flood . . . I've never seen anything like it . . ." He shuddered.

"In terms of his age—"

"Oh, yeah, sorry . . . Seventy? Sixty-five? Seventy-five? I really can't say, all I know is he *moved* like an old guy. No limp or anything like that, just stiff. Like his body was all bound up."

"Slow."

He thought. "He didn't run, but he wasn't halting. All I really saw was his back. Heading for his car. I guess I'd call it a medium pace. Normal walking. Like he'd just delivered a package or something. And he didn't look back. I'm screaming at him and it's like I'm not there. Bastard doesn't even bother to turn, just keeps going, gets in the car, drives off. That's what gets me. How *normal* he acted."

"Business as usual."

He played with a loose thread at the sweatshirt's neckline.

I said, "So you never saw his face."

"Nope. It was crazy. I'm screaming at the top of my lungs, hoping someone will come out, but no one did." He looked up the block. "Ghost town. Pure L.A."

"What did you scream at him?"

"Who remembers . . . probably something like 'Stop, you ass-hole!' " Moskow plinked the hem of his sweatshirt with a thumbnail. "Mrs. Mancusi's lying there, covered in blood, and this bastard is sauntering away like nothing happened. I started after him, which in retrospect was idiotic. But you don't think. Then I saw the knife and stopped in my tracks."

Moisture collected at the bottom of his eyes.

"How'd you see the knife?"

"He wiped it on the front of his pants. Above the knee. Casually, like it was a natural thing to do."

"Then what?" I said.

"Then he pocketed it and got into his car and drove off. The whole thing took seconds."

"The car was idling."

"I don't remember him starting it up, so probably. Don't remember any engine noise at all but maybe I was blocking it out. That particular model's pretty quiet."

"Which way did he drive?"

He pointed south. "Right past my house."

I knew the neighborhood from my grad student days at the U., had roamed these same streets searching for shortcuts home to my dismal little single on Overland. "It's a bit of a maze. All those dead ends."

Moskow stiffened. "You're thinking he's from *around* here?"

"No, but he may have planned his escape route."

"Well, I've never seen him in the neighborhood. Same for the car. This isn't exactly S600 territory."

"Not a lot of Benzes?"

"Plenty of Benzes, but not 600s."

"You're into cars."

"I've owned a few junkers that I fixed up." He managed a half smile. "Owned a DeLorean. That was an experience. So what are we talking about, some old Mafioso?"

"What makes you say that?"

"Big black car, execution-style killing, guy that age. What came to mind is maybe he's an old goombah hit man who *didn't* burn out."

He pulled the thread loose, rubbed it between forefinger and thumb. "That stupid cap."

"Would there be any reason for Mrs. Mancusi to be involved with an old Mafioso?"

"Wouldn't have thought so. Then again, who'd imagine this?"

"How well did you know her?"

"Not well at all. She was quiet, seemed nice enough. We'd say hi, good-bye, that's about it."

"Any social life?"

"Just that guy I told the lieutenant about."

"How often was he here?"

"Maybe every month, that why I assumed he was her son. Could've been more often, it's not like I kept my eyes fixed on her house."

"Anything more you can say about him?"

"Forties, blond, sloppy-looking. Now that I think about it, I never actually saw them together. He'd knock on the door and she'd let him in. When he left, she never walked him out."

"Was walking hard for her?"

"On the contrary, hale and healthy."

"Anything else you can tell me about the blond guy?"

"Kind of thickset, when I say sloppy I mean he didn't seem to care about his appearance."

"Any idea what his name is?"

"Never heard her call him anything. Like I said, never saw them actually together. He never looked happy to be here, so maybe there was tension between them. And the last time he visited, a month or so ago, he stayed outside, talking to Mrs. Mancusi through the open door. I assume it was her, because no one else lives there. I couldn't hear what they were saying, but from the looks of it they could've been arguing. Then he did this."

Slapping a hand on one hip, he bent one leg and grimaced.

"It was a little . . . theatrical, know what I mean? It seemed funny, a grown man who wasn't particularly gay looking, vamping like that. It struck me as an odd thing to do. Especially when you're talking to your mother. *If* she *is* his mother."

"You think they could've been arguing."

"Look, I'm not trying to get anyone in trouble," said Moskow, "and it's nothing I'd swear to. Just my impression."

"Because of his body language."

"The way he positioned himself—he looked a little . . ."

"Aggressive?"

"More like defensive," said Moskow. "Like Mrs. Mancusi told him something he didn't want to hear."

CHAPTER

5

Mafia hit because her name was Mancusi?" said Milo.

We were in Café Moghul, around the corner from the station. The restaurant's owners view him as a human rottweiler and are all too happy to create personal buffets. I watched him make his way through plates of lamb curry, tandoori lobster, spicy okra, lentils and rice. A pitcher of iced clove tea sat at his elbow.

After all that blood in Ella Mancusi's driveway, the mental pictures I'd drawn of the murder, it was all I could do to pour myself a glass.

I said, "Moskow didn't say so but that was probably part of it. But maybe he's on to something. The setup—knowing when she came out to get her paper, leaving the car idling, planning the escape route— smells of pro. So does the killer's demeanor: brutally methodical, no hurried escape."

"Grampa bad guy," he said. "Doing her in broad daylight and giving himself less than three hours to get the car cleaned up and back in place is professional? Not to mention driving it back to Beverly Hills in full view?"

"Where's the rent-a-car lot?"

"Alden Drive near Foothill."

"B.H. industrial zone," I said. "Pretty quiet on Sunday morning."

"It's also five minutes from the B.H. Police Department."

"But a black Mercedes wouldn't attract anyone's attention. Neither would a car *entering* the lot. Any blood in the Benz?"

"At first glance, no. Let's see what the lab turns up."

"He wiped the knife on the front of his pants, careful not to make a mess. Two and a half hours was enough time to clean the car before he returned it. Maybe he's got a safe place, somewhere between the crime scene and the drop-off."

"That's half the Westside," he said. "Think I'm gonna get some media coverage on this one. Geriatric knife man, how many of those can there be?" Forking lobster, chewing, swallowing. "Nervy knife man, doing it in broad daylight."

"Maybe in his mind a daytime hit was safer because a night-prowl would've meant breaking into her house. Did she have an alarm system?"

"Dinky. Front and back doors, no windows."

"For an old guy, climbing through windows could be a problem," I said. "He figured that early on Sunday, most people are sleeping. We're also talking a victim unlikely to put up serious resistance, and a silent weapon. He blitzed her so fast she never had time to scream. If Moskow hadn't forgotten to take his Ambien last night, the whole thing might've gone unnoticed. Any other neighbors have information?"

He covered his ears with his hands, repeated the gesture with his eyes and mouth.

"Moskow come up clean?"

"Spotless." He pushed his plate away. "Wiping the blade on his pants. What's *that* all about?"

"Could be an expression of contempt," I said.

"Those arterial wounds, no way he'd avoid leaving some trace in the car."

"He cleans up the obvious, the Benz gets steamed by the company, he's home free."

"I'm definitely buying contempt," he said. "Lotta rage, here. The question is what did a seventy-three-year-old retired schoolteacher do to incite that."

"People have secrets."

"Well, none of hers have turned up, so far. The house was neat, clean, real grandmotherly."

He drew his plate closer, began bolting his food.

I said, "Hot rage but cool planning. Maybe he wasn't quite so careful last time."

"What do you mean?"

"The stain in the Bentley."

"No body associated with the Bentley, Alex. I'm not ready to connect the two."

I kept quiet.

"Yeah, yeah, there are parallels," he said. "Now give me another homicide that ties it together and explain to me how such a careful guy could leave a stain in full view."

"It was dark when he brought the Bentley back and he missed it. Or something made him nervous and he left quickly."

"That's weak, Doctor."

"Another possibility is he left it there on purpose."

"Another contempt message?"

"*Look what I got away with.* Maybe the Bentley was a rehearsal for today."

"A senior-citizen psychopath who likes to play games." He drummed the table with his fork. "Or the Bentley has nothing to do with Ella."

"Or that."

"You don't believe it."

"Do you?"

He sighed. "I've got Records checking violent crime reports during the hours the Bentley was missing. Nothing so far."

Spooning lentils into his mouth, he said, "Someone that old. Weird."

"You know what they say. Seventy's the new fifty."

He reached for a lobster claw. "And up is down and low is high."

I said, "If we are talking some kind of organized crime link, that could mean teamwork. One person steals the car, passes it along to the killer, and is available to help scrub it down afterward, maybe drive it back. Combine all that with the killer making sure to limit his contact to the front seats, and the time pressure would reduce."

"Homicidal pit crew," he said. Cracking the claw along the joint, he sat motionless, as if taking in the sound. "The goodfellas haven't been a major factor since Mickey Cohen, but there are some loan sharks floating around the Valley and over in that arcade on Canon Drive in Beverly Hills."

"Canon's also close to the rental lot."

"So it is." He pulled a tube of meat from the claw, ate, repeated the process with another leg. "So what, our nice little retired school-teacher has a dark past as a moll?"

"Or a hidden vice. Like gambling."

"She managed to rack up a big enough debt on her pension to get sliced and diced? Make no sense, Alex. The last thing a shark wants to do is snuff the minnow and end any hope of getting paid."

"Unless the shark has given up on collecting," I said. "Or she wasn't the gambler, someone else was, and they used her as an example."

I described the unhappy exchange Moskow had witnessed between Ella and the blond man he assumed was her son.

"Arguing," he said.

"Nothing causes conflict like money. Maybe Junior asked Mom for money and she turned him down."

"What I don't see is even a big-time shark butchering an old lady just to strike terror into her mope kid's heart."

"You're probably right," I said. "But it is a new, cruel age."

"Meaning?"

"Turn on the news at random."

He dove back into his food.

I said, "Here's another way to spin it: The blond man's not her son, he's the collector."

Removing a blue plastic binder from his attaché, he handed it over. Inside was a prelim crime report form yet to be filled out, a few of what looked to be Ella Mancusi's personal papers, and an envelope that held a three-by-five color photo.

In the snapshot, a tiny white-haired woman in a belted floral dress and high heels stood next to a flabby-looking fair-haired man in his forties. Behind them was mint-green stucco. Ella Mancusi had a bird-face and sparkling dark eyes. Her lips were rouged and her nails were polished. Smiling, but something was missing from the upturn of lip.

The blond man stood with his arms at his sides. Tight around the shoulders, as if posing for the picture had been an imposition.

I said, "Fits the guy Moskow described."

"Read the back."

I flipped the photo.

Anthony and me, my birthday. I baked a chocolate cake. The writing was elegant cursive. The date was December, two years ago.

"Devoted son lets her bake her own birthday cake," I said.

I studied Ella Mancusi's smile some more and realized what was missing. Maternal pride.

Milo said, "I'm figuring he's an only child because the few photos in the house were all of him, mostly when he was a kid, all the way back to grade school. She held on to his birth certificate and twelve years of report cards. C minus student when he applied himself. There's one Anthony Mancusi in the county and the only thing on his record is a DUI six years ago, pled down to misdemeanor. If he's got a drinking problem, doesn't look to be genetic. The only booze Ella had was a bottle of sherry, unopened, dust all over it."

He rubbed his face. "She didn't own much, Alex. All her important papers were in three cigar boxes near her bed. Eighteen years ago she retired from L.A. Unified. Her last job was teaching social studies at Louis Pasteur Junior High, they wrote her a nice letter. She was widowed way before that—when Anthony was a teenager. Husband was Anthony Senior, supervisor at a dairy in Santa Fe Springs, died on the job of a heart attack. The house has been paid off for eleven years, between her pension and Senior's she did okay. Your basic upstanding, middle-class lady living out her days in a low-crime neighborhood. Why the hell would she end up this way?"

I took another look at the photo. "It's his mother's birthday but he wants to be anywhere else. Toss in Moskow's account of the irate conversation and there's some kind of issue here. Was there a will in the box?"

He thought. "No. Junior bumps her off to inherit?"

"It's been known to happen."

"Sure, it has, but what kind of beast would have his mother carved like a holiday roast?" He motioned for the check. The smiling, bespectacled woman who always serves him hurried over and asked how the meal was.

"Everything was delicious," he said, slipping her some bills. "Keep the change."

"This is far too much, Lieutenant."

"Don't worry about it."

"I give you credit," she said. "For next time."

"Don't bother."

"I bother."

Outside the restaurant, he hitched up his trousers and looked at his watch. "Time to talk to Tony Mancusi Junior, our misdemeanor drunk."

"The lack of a serious record says nothing about a gambling problem," I said.

"Yeah, but why get involved with living, breathing sharks when you can boot up and use PayPal?"

"Why would a movie star staying at the Four Seasons go trolling for thirty-dollar streetwalkers on Sunset when he'd have access to call girls who look better than his leading ladies? Sometimes dirty and dangerous is part of the thrill."

"Games," he said. "All right, let's talk to this joker. At the very least, I'll be the bearer of really bad news."

Anthony James Mancusi Jr.'s phone was disconnected, which made Milo more intent on finding him.

The papers on his eight-year-old Toyota listed a residence on Olympic, four blocks east of Fairfax. The address matched a pink neo-Regency six-plex built around a compact, green courtyard. Vintage charm, blooming flowers, spotless pathways. If you discounted the brain-sapping traffic roar, not bad at all.

The landlord, a sixtyish Asian man named William Park, lived in one of the ground-floor units. He came to the door holding a copy of *Smithsonian* magazine.

"Tony?" he said. "He moved out three months ago."

"How come?" said Milo.

"His lease was up and he wanted something less expensive."

"Money problems?"

William Park said, "The units are two-bedrooms. Maybe Tony felt he didn't need so much."

"In other words, money problems."

Park smiled.

Milo said, "How long did he live here, sir?"

"He was already here when I bought the building. That was three years ago. Before that, I don't know."

"Easy tenant?"

"Mostly," said Park. "Is he in trouble?"

"His mother just passed away and we need to find him."

"Passed away . . . oh." Park studied us. "Something . . . unnatural?"

"Afraid so, Mr. Park."

"That's *terrible* . . . hold on, I've got Tony's forwarding address. Sometimes I still get mail for him."

"Have any of his mail now?"

"No, I mark it *forward* and the mailman takes it away." Park disappeared into his apartment, leaving an open view of a neat white room.

Milo said, "The observant Mr. Moskow, now him. Law enforcement and the citizenry, working hand in hand. Maybe the world ain't so mean, after all."

Strange thing to say after viewing Ella Mancusi lying in a quart of her own blood. Still, it was nice to hear him positive.

I said, "Global warming."

"Huh?"

"Nothing."

Park returned and handed Milo a scrap of paper.

Post office box, L.A. 90027.

East Hollywood. Good chance it was a mail drop. Milo smiled through his disappointment and thanked Park.

"Anything I can do to help. Poor Tony."

"So he was a good tenant," said Milo. *"Mostly."*

Park said, "Sometimes he was late with the rent, but he always paid the extra fee without griping."

"What does he do for a living?"

"He told me he used to work for the studios—a grip, moving scenery. A few years ago, he hurt his back and had to live on disability. His mother helped him out. Sometimes, the rent check was hers. Someone *killed* her?"

"How well did you know her, Mr. Park?"

"Me? I didn't know her at all, just cashed her check."

"Did Tony talk about her?"

"Never. Tony didn't talk much."

"Quiet guy."

"Really quiet," said Park.

"How often did his mother pay his rent?"

"Hmm . . . I'd say about half the time. Maybe more the last few months."

"How much more?"

"I believe out of the last six months, she paid four."

"Did she mail you the checks?"

"No, Tony gave them to me."

"What was the nature of Tony's disability?"

"You mean was he crippled or something like that? No, he looked normal. But that doesn't mean anything. A few years ago I had a ruptured disk. It was painful but I kept it to myself."

"Tony suffered in silence."

"You don't suspect him, do you?" said Park. "He was never violent."

Uncomfortable with the notion that he might've rented to a killer.

Milo said, "These are just basic questions, sir."

"I hope so. He was really no trouble at all."

The mail drop was in a litter-strewn strip mall on Vermont just above Sunset, one of those metallic-smelling mini-vaults lined with brass boxes, where the renters get keys and twenty-four-hour access.

A sign in the window said, *In case of problems check with Avakian Dry Cleaners next door.*

At the cleaners, a man unraveled a pile of crumpled shirts and said, "Yes," without looking up. William Saroyan mustache, quick hands.

"Police. We're looking for one of your box holders. Anthony Mancusi."

Time to look up. "Tony? He brings his bulk laundry here. With the price of water and soap, we can do it just as cheap and you don't need your own machine. What's up with Tony?"

"His mother died, Mr. . . . ."

"Bedros Avakian." Tongue click. "Died, huh? Too bad. So how come the police are here?"

"It wasn't a natural death."

"Oh . . . that's real bad."

"Could we have that address, please?"

"Yah, yeah, hold on, I get it for you."

Avakian walked to a small desk and clicked a laptop. "Got a pen? Give Tony my condolences."

Anthony Mancusi Jr.'s new digs were in a grubby three-story box on Rodney Drive, not far from the strip mall. No landscaping, no charm, inquiries to be directed to a real estate firm in Downey.

The front door was key-locked. The directory listed eighteen tenants, each with a mail slot. No one answered at *A. Mancusi*'s unit.

I said "Bit of a step-down from his last place. That and his mother taking on more of his rent says money issues."

Milo tried the button again, pulled out a business card, and dropped it into Mancusi's mail slot. "Let's get over to the rental lot."

As we headed for the car, movement up the block caught my eye. A man in a short-sleeved white shirt and brown pants shambled toward us.

Less hair than two years ago, the blond tint was peroxide, and he'd put on weight in all the predictable places. But this was the man not thrilled to pose with his mother.

Milo told me to wait there and went up to greet him. The glint of the gold shield caused Tony Mancusi's head to retract, as if he'd been slapped.

Milo said something.

Mancusi clapped both sides of his own head.

His mouth opened and the mewling that emerged filled my head with an image: animals shackled in the slaughterhouse.

The end of hope.

CHAPTER

6

Tony Mancusi's hands shook as he fought to get his key into the lock. When he dropped it the second time, I took over. Once we were inside the grimy little room he called home, he braced himself against a wall and wailed.

Milo watched him, impassive as a garden gnome.

Some detectives put a lot of stock in people's initial reactions to bad news, suspecting the too-stoic loved one, as well as the scenery-chewing hysteric.

I reserve judgment because I've seen rape victims blasé to the point of flippancy, innocent bystanders twitching with what *had* to be guilt, psychopaths offering renditions of shock and grief so convincing you wanted to cuddle them and feed them soup.

But it was hard not to be impressed with the heaving of Mancusi's rounded shoulders and the racking squalls that nearly lifted him off a threadbare ottoman. Behind him was a wall fitted with a Murphy bed.

Ella Mancusi had baked her own birthday cake. Maybe her son was remembering.

When he stopped for breath, Milo said, "We're sorry for your loss, sir."

Mancusi worked himself to his feet. The change in his complexion was sudden and convincing.

From indoor pallor to green around the edges.

He hurtled six feet to a shabby kitchenette and vomited into the sink.

When the heaves stopped, he splashed water onto his face, returned to the ottoman with raw eyes and strands of pale hair plastered to a greasy forehead. A fleck of vomit had landed on his shirt, just beneath a wrinkled collar.

Milo said, "I know this is a hard time to talk, but if there's anything you can tell us—"

"What could I *tell* you!"

"Is there anyone—anyone at all—who'd want to hurt your mother?"

"*Who?*"

"That's what we're—"

"She was a *teacher*!" said Mancusi.

"She retired—"

"They gave her an *award*! She was tough, but fair, everyone loved her." He wagged a finger. "Want the *grade*? Do your *work*! That was her motto."

I wondered how that had meshed with a son who lived on disability and borrowed rent money.

C student, if he applied himself.

Milo said, "So there's no one you can think of."

"No. This is . . . this is insane."

The vomit fleck fell to the carpet, inches from Milo's desert boot.

"Insane nightmare." Mancusi lowered his head. Gasped.

"You okay, sir?"

"Little short of breath." He sat up, breathed slowly. "I get that way when I'm stressed."

Milo said, "If you don't mind, we've got a few more questions."

Mancusi said, "What?"

"After your father passed, did your mother have any romantic relationships?"

"Romantic? She liked books. Watched a few soap operas. That was her romantic." He flipped his hair, cocked his head, smoothed a peroxide strand from a sweat-soaked brow.

Effete symphony of movements that recalled the posturing Ed Moskow had observed.

"Any close friends, male or female?"

Mancusi shook his head, noticed the vomit fleck on the floor, and raised his eyebrows. The carpet was grease-stained, fuzzed by crumbs and dust bunnies. Some sort of beige, darkened to the hue of a smoker's teeth.

"No social life at all?" said Milo.

"Nothing. After she retired, Mom liked to be by herself. All the L.A. Unified bullshit. She put up with it for thirty years."

"So she became a private person."

"She was *always* a private person. Now she could be *herself*." Mancusi stifled a sob. "Oh, Mom . . ."

"It's a tough thing to deal with," said Milo.

Silence.

"Did your mother have any hobbies?"

"What?"

Milo repeated the question.

"Why?"

"I'm trying to know her."

"Hobbies," said Mancusi. "She liked puzzles—crosswords, Sudoku. Sudoku was her favorite, she liked numbers. She had a math certificate but they had her teaching social studies."

"Any other games?"

"What do you mean? She was a teacher. She didn't get . . . this didn't happen because of her hobbies. This was a . . . a . . . a *lunatic*."

"So no hobbies or interests that might have gotten her into debt?"

Mancusi's watery brown eyes drifted to Milo's face. "What are you *talking* about?"

"These are questions we need to ask, Mr. Mancusi. Did your mom buy lottery tickets, do online poker, anything of that nature?"

"She didn't even own a computer. Neither do I."

"Not into the Internet?"

"Why are you *asking* this? You said she wasn't robbed."

"Sorry," said Milo. "We need to be thorough."

"My mother did not gamble."

"Was she a person of regular habits?"

"What do you mean?"

"Did she have routines—like coming out the same time each morning to collect the paper."

Mancusi sat there, eyes glazed, not moving.

"Sir?"

"She got up early." He clutched his belly. "Ohh . . . here we go again."

Another rush to the sink. This time, dry heaves left him coughing and panting. He opened a space-saver fridge, took out a bottle of something clear that he uncapped, and swigged. Returned with the liquid still in hand.

Diet tonic water.

Grabbing a section of his own gut, he squeezed hard, rolled the adipose. "Too fat. Used to drink G and T's, now it's just sugarless T." He drank from the bottle, failed to suppress a belch. "Mom never gained a pound from the day she was married."

"She watched her diet?" said Milo.

Mancusi smiled. "Never had to, she could eat pasta, sugar, anything. I get it from Dad. He died of a heart attack. I need to watch myself."

"The old cholesterol."

Mancusi shook his head. "Mom—did they hurt her?"

"They?"

"Whoever. Was it bad? Did she suffer? Tell me she *didn't*."

"It was quick," said Milo.

"Oh, God." More tears.

Milo handed him a tissue from the mini-pack he always brings to notifications. "Mr. Mancusi, the reason I asked about your mother's social life is we do have an eyewitness who describes the assailant as around her age."

Mancusi's fingers flexed. The tissue dropped. *"What?"*

Milo repeated Edward Moskow's description of the killer, including the blue plaid cap.

Mancusi said, "That's nuts."

"Doesn't ring a bell?"

Mancusi flipped his hair again. "Of course not. Dad had a bunch of caps like that. After he went bald and didn't want sun on his head. This is totally *insane.*"

Milo said, "What about a black Mercedes S600? That ring any bells?"

"Don't know anything about cars," said Mancusi.

"It's a big four-door sedan," said Milo. "Top-of-the-line model."

"Mom wouldn't know anyone with a car like that. She was a *teacher,* for God's sake!"

"Please don't be offended by this next question, Mr. Mancusi, but did your mother know anyone associated—even remotely—with organized crime?"

Mancusi laughed. Kicked the vomit fleck. "Because we're Italian?"

"It's something we need to look into—"

"Well, guess what, Lieutenant: Mom *wasn't* Italian. She was German, her maiden name was Hochswelder. Italian was Dad's side, he grew up in New York, claimed when he was a kid he knew all kinds of Mafia guys. Had all these stories."

"What kind of stories?"

"Bodies tossed out of cars, guys getting shot in barber chairs. But no way, no, that's nuts, those were just stories and Mom *hated* them, called them 'coarse.' Her idea of suspense was *Murder, She Wrote,* not *The Sopranos.*"

He returned to the kitchen, placed the tonic water bottle on a counter. "Gambling, gangsters—this is ridiculous."

"I'm sure it seems that way, but—"

"There's no reason for her to be dead, *okay?* No *reason,* no *fucking* reason. It's stupid, insane, shouldn't have happened—could you stand up?"

"Pardon?"

"Stand up," said Mancusi. "Please."

After Milo obliged, Mancusi slipped behind him and yanked down on the Murphy bed. Halfway through, he breathed in sharply, slammed a palm into the small of his back, and straightened. "Disk."

Milo finished the job, revealing a wafer-thin mattress, gray sheets once white.

Mancusi began easing himself down toward the bed. Sweat rolled down his cheeks.

Milo reached out to help him.

"No, no, I'm fine."

We watched as he lowered himself in stages. He ended up curled on the bed, knees drawn to his chest, still breathing hard. "I can't *tell* you anything. I don't *know* anything."

Milo asked him about other family members.

Mancusi's rapid head shake rocked the flimsy mattress. "Mom had a miscarriage after me and that was it."

"What about aunts, uncles—"

"No one she's close to."

Milo waited.

Mancusi said, "Nobody."

"No one to help you?"

"With what?"

"Getting through this."

"G and T used to be a big help. Maybe I'll get back into that. Think that's okay?" Harsh laughter.

Milo didn't answer.

Mancusi said, "Maybe fuck everything, I should eat and drink what I want. Maybe I should stop trying to impress anyone." Tears flowed down his cheeks. "Who's to impress?"

He turned onto his back. "Could you get me some Aleve—it's in the cabinet by the stove."

I found the bottle, shook out a pill, filled a water glass from the tap.

Mancusi said, "I need two." When I returned, he snatched both tablets from my hand, waved away the water. "I swallow dry." He demonstrated. "My big talent . . . I need to rest."

He rolled away from us.

Milo said, "So sorry for your loss. If you think of anything, call."

No answer.

As we made it to the door, Mancusi said, "Mom always hated those caps."

Outside the building, Milo said, "Think that was a performance?"

"Moskow described him as theatrical, but who knows?"

"Theatrical how?"

I recounted the hand-on-hip hair toss.

He frowned. "Did a bit of that just now. But he did barf right-eously."

"People get sick for all sorts of reasons," I said. "Including guilt."

"Symbolic catharsis? Or whatever you guys call it."

"I call it throwing up. He's an only child with no close relatives. I'd really like to know if there was a will."

"Agreed," he said. "The question is how to find it."

"Maybe those relatives she wasn't close to can tell you."

"Tony minimizing the relationships because he didn't want me talking to them?"

"Family values," I said. "It's where it all starts."

He drove three blocks, popped the unmarked's trunk, gloved up, and rifled through the box of personal effects he'd taken from Ella Mancusi's bedroom.

No mention of any relatives other than Tony, but an attorney's card in a rubber-bound stack elicited a hand-pump.

Jean Barone, Esq. Wilshire Boulevard, Santa Monica.

The other cards were for plumbers, electricians, A.C. and heating repair, a grocery delivery service.

Men coming in and out of the house, maybe getting to know Ella Mancusi's routine. If no other leads surfaced soon, they'd all need to be checked out.

Milo phoned Jean Barone and after she got over the shock, she said yes, she'd drawn up Mrs. Mancusi's will, preferred not to discuss client matters over the phone.

As we headed for Santa Monica, Milo said, "Maybe it's me, but she sounded eager."

Jean Barone met us in the cramped, empty lobby of her building, a two-story structure just west of Yale. The space needed freshening. She looked as if she'd just renewed her makeup.

She was a middle-aged, wavy-haired brunette packed tightly into a peacock-blue knockoff Chanel suit. After checking Milo's I.D., she took us up in the elevator to her two-room suite. No name on the plain white door but hers. Below her degree, supplementary credentials as a Notary Public and Certified Tax Preparer.

Her office smelled of Shalimar. She took a seat behind a dark, wood-like desk. "So horrible about Mrs. Mancusi. Any idea who did this?"

"Not yet. Is there anything you can tell us about her, ma'am?"

"Not really. The only thing I did for her was draw up the will, and that was five years ago."

"Who referred her to you?"

"The yellow pages. I'd just graduated, had no referral base yet. She was one of my only clients in six months. It was easy, basically boilerplate."

She opened a drawer and drew out a single sheet of paper. "Here's your copy. No confidentiality for deceased individuals."

"There was no copy in Mrs. Mancusi's house."

"She didn't want one," said Barone. "Said I should keep it."

"How come?"

Barone shrugged. "Maybe she didn't want anyone finding it."

Milo scanned the will. "This is all of it?"

"Given her situation, there was no need to get fancy. The estate was her house, plus a pension, a little cash in the bank. No liens, no encumbrances, no attachments."

"Only one heir listed."

"Her son," said Barone. "I did suggest there were steps she could take to reduce the estate tax burden on him. Like putting the house into a joint trust with a lifetime usage clause for her. She wasn't interested."

"Why not?"

"She wouldn't tell me and I didn't pry. She was more interested in my hourly rate, clearly didn't want to spend an extra dime."

Milo handed me the will. In the event of Anthony Mancusi Jr.'s pre-deceasing his mother, everything was willed to the Salvation Army.

Milo said, "She talk at all about the son?"

"Is he a suspect?"

"We're looking into everyone close to her."

"Bet that's not a huge crowd."

"Why do you say that?"

"She was polite," said Jean Barone, "but a little . . . I got the feeling she wasn't too sociable. No interest in small talk, cut to the chase. Or maybe she was just minimizing the billable hours. You know that generation. Careful with a buck."

"Unlike today's generation," said Milo.

"My two kids have great jobs but they're overdrawn on their credit cards."

"Maybe Mrs. Mancusi thought her son was irresponsible and that's why she didn't want to give him the house."

"She wouldn't have actually been giving it to him, just—" Barone smiled. "Functionally, it's the same thing, so maybe you've got a point. But if she didn't trust him, she didn't tell me. I can't overemphasize how reserved she was. But polite. Ladylike. It's so strange to think of her being murdered. Was it a robbery?"

"Doesn't seem to be."

"You're thinking the son wanted to push things along?"

"We're not thinking anything yet."

"Whatever you say." Barone batted her lashes.

Milo got up. "Thanks for the copy. And for the nonbillable time."

"Sure," she said, touching his hand. "You're the most interesting thing that's happened all week."

During the ride down I said, "Must be the uniform—oops, you're not wearing one."

He said, "Nah, my cologne. Eau de schmo."

It was four p.m. by the time we headed for the Prestige Rent-A-Car lot in Beverly Hills. During the drive, Milo called the motor lab. A couple of errant hairs and various wool, cotton, and linen fibers had showed up in the Mercedes, but no blood or body fluids. The car had been vacuumed recently by someone who'd taken care not to leave prints. The lab would be removing the door panels tomorrow but the tech cautioned Milo not to expect too much.

He said, "Story of my life," and drove faster. "Ella's estate was mostly her house. What do you think it's worth?"

I said, "That part of Westwood? Million three, minimum."

"That's what I was thinking. Nice windfall for a loser like Tony."

I said, "Ella wasn't interested in reducing his tax burden and she stood by as he lost the apartment on Olympic and ended up in that dive."

"Mommy thinks he's a loser and he knows it."

"Nothing like self-loathing to stoke rage," I said. "And this was a healthy, youthful seventy-three-year-old who planned to be around for a while. Meaning extended poverty for Tony."

The unmarked's radio kicked in with a message to call the station.

"Sturgis, I'm on my way to a . . . who? Okay, tell them . . . tomorrow. Afternoon. I'll call them in the morning to set up a time . . . handle them with care."

Click.

"Antoine Beverly's parents dropped by the station. Downtown told them I'm on the case, they want to meet me. Feel like sitting in? It could turn out to be a situation where psychological sensitivity is called for."

"Sure, just give me a couple hours' notice."

He said, "Thanks—oh, man, look at all that chrome."

Prestige Automotive Executive Services amounted to a cracked concrete lot covered by a canvas awning. Small-print signage, two dozen vehicles crowded nose-to-bumper, and a shed-like office to one side.

"All that chrome" was a mass of Porsches, Ferraris, Lamborghinis, a mammoth Rolls-Royce Phantom, a pair of Bentley GT coupes— smaller cousins to Nicholas Heubel's stately sedan. Up in front, three Mercedes S600s.

Two silver, one black. A vacant slot next to the black car.

Iron posts marked both edges of the driveway. Between them, a limp length of chain snaked across the cement. A key lock was looped to a ring that passed through the right-hand post. Shiny, but cheap.

Milo's laughter lacked amusement. "A gazillion worth of wheels and they use drugstore crap. I could pick this under the influence of any number of mind-altering substances."

In the office, a small man around thirty sat next to a folding card table and listened to reggaeton. The tag on his blue shirt said *Gil.* The tattoos brocading his neck and arms said his pain threshold was high. His black hair was perfectly combed, his soul patch squared to the size of a Scrabble tile. On the wall were a tool-company calendar and *Playboy* centerfolds that made me feel like a ten-year-old kid.

Milo flashed the badge. The man switched off the radio. "Yeah, they told me you were coming."

Milo said, "You're off the beaten path, Mr. . . ."

"Gilbert Chacon."

"How do customers find you, Mr. Chacon?"

"We don't rent to no customers. The rental lot's on La Cienega. This is the ultra-luxury lot. We do calls from hotels, it's all delivery."

"Guest wants a car, you bring it to them."

"Yeah," said Chacon, "but we don't deal with no guests, just the hotels, everything goes on the hotel bill."

"So not much traffic here."

"Nobody comes here."

"Someone came here last night."

Chacon's mouth screwed up. "Never happened before."

"What's your security setup?"

"Chain and a lock," said Chacon.

"That's it?"

Chacon shrugged. "The police is what, a minute away? Beverly Hills, you got cops all over the place."

"Is there a night watchman?"

"Nope."

"Alarm system?"

"Nope."

"All those fancy wheels?" said Milo.

Chacon reached back. His fingers grazed a clapboard wall. He must've liked the feel because he began stroking the wood. "The cars got alarms."

"Including the Mercedes that got lifted?"

"It come with a system," said Chacon. "They all do."

"Was the system activated?"

Chacon's hand left the wall and rested on the desk. His eyes floated up to the low plasterboard ceiling. "Supposed to be."

Milo smiled. "In a perfect world?"

Gilbert Chacon said, "I'm the day supervisor, come at nine, leave at four thirty. At night, it's up to the main lot what happens."

"On La Cienega."

"Yup."

"Who has the key to the lock?"

"Me." Chacon reached into his pocket and brought out a key-chain.

"Who else?"

"The main lot. Maybe other people, I dunno. I just started working here a couple months ago."

"So there could be copies of the key floating around?"

"That would be stupid," said Chacon.

I said, "The lock looks new."

Chacon said, "So?"

Milo said, "Someone did manage to unlock the chain. Boosted the Benz, put forty-three miles on it, cleaned it up, brought it back before nine, and laid the chain back in place—if it was in place when you got here."

"It was."

"What time was that?"

"Like I said, they want me here at nine." Chacon's eyes rose to the ceiling again.

"Maybe you were a little late?"

"That would be stupid."

"So you arrived on time."

"Yeah."

"When you got here at nine, nothing unusual made you look twice."

"Nope."

"Who's responsible for locking the chain at four thirty?"

"Me." Chacon licked his lips. "And I did it."

"What if a car comes back after four thirty?"

"If it's from the main lot, they unlock and put it in."

"That happen often?"

"Sometimes."

"What about last night?"

Chacon got up and opened a file cabinet next to a watercooler. Miss January smiled down as he leafed through folders.

"Yesterday was no bring-backs. Right now, we only got one car out, period. Black Phantom over to the L'Ermitage on Burton. Some Arab sheik and his driver are using it for three weeks."

"Business is slow?"

"It comes and goes." Chacon's eyes took another ride, this time from side to side.

Milo said, "Anyone come by recently, show interest in the cars?"

"Nope."

"Know why we're asking these questions, sir?"

"Nope. Sir."

"The car was used in a murder."

Chacon blinked twice. "You're kidding. Who got murdered?"

"A nice old lady."

"That's bad."

"Real bad," said Milo. "She mighta been killed by a not-so-nice old man." He described the blue-capped killer.

"No way," said Chacon, over the music.

"You think it's impossible an old guy would do something like that?"

"No, what I'm saying is I never saw no one like that."

"How about anyone walking around the lot, checking out the wheels?"

Chacon shook his head. "It's real quiet here, the only time someone comes is when a car's broke and the main lot sends a mechanic."

Milo turned off the music. The silence made Chacon blink repeatedly.

"No one loitered. Or just hung around? Anyone, even a homeless guy?"

"For sure no."

"For sure?"

"There was someone I'd tell you." Chacon reached for the radio dial. Thought better of it.

Milo said, " 'Cause you want to cooperate."

"Yeah."

We returned to the car. Running Chacon's name through the system brought up a Boyle Heights address, no outstanding wants or warrants. Three arrests ten years ago.

Two gang-related assaults and a burglary pled down to petty theft, all in Rampart Division.

"Old gangbanger," I said.

"That's who they put in charge of hot wheels."

"He moved to a new neighborhood, works a straight job."

"Reformed?"

"It happens."

"But you think not," he said.

"What do you mean?"

"That question about the new lock. You're wondering if he forgot to bolt up, found the chain down this morning, bought a replacement."

"Mind reader," I said. "Also, his eyes moved a lot."

"Goddamn pinball machine. Maybe it's worse and someone paid him to leave the chain off last night."

"Or the killer picked it," I said. "Cheap drugstore crap."

He looked over at the shack. "A guy with Chacon's past is wise to the drill, he's got no motivation to give anything up. I get closer to the bad guy, I can come back with leverage, offer him a break on aiding and abetting."

Once, not *if.*

Nice to see him thinking about the future.

7

The meeting with Antoine Beverly's parents was set for noon the following day.

When I got to Milo's office, a note on the door said *A: Rm. 6.*

Largest room, at the end of the corridor. An *Interview in Progress: Do Not Disturb* sign dangled from the doorknob.

I knocked once and went in.

A middle-aged black couple sat across the table from Milo. A wallet-sized photo of a boy was placed in front of the woman and after she appraised me, her attention returned to the image.

The man next to her wore a stiff brown suit, a white shirt, and a gold tie secured by a silver clip. An American flag pin rode his lapel. His gray hair was tight; in front it faded to skin. Under a white thread of a mustache, his smile was obligatory.

The woman had on a charcoal pantsuit. High waved hair was one shade darker than her clothes. She drew away from the photo with reluctance and placed her hands flat on the table.

Milo said, "Mr. and Mrs. Beverly, this is our psychologist, Dr. Delaware. Doctor, Gordon and Sharna Beverly."

Gordon Beverly half stood and sat back down. His wife said, "Pleased to meet you, Doctor."

The pressing of cool dry flesh. I sat next to Milo.

He said, "Mr. and Mrs. Beverly brought me this picture of Antoine."

I studied the picture, maybe longer than I needed to. Smiling, clear-eyed boy with a space between his incisors. Short hair, blue shirt, plaid tie.

"Doctor, I was just explaining that you were involved because of the complexities."

Sharna Beverly said, "We could use a psychiatrist because if it wasn't that maniac in Texas, it was *some* kind of maniac. I knew it from the beginning, kept telling those other detectives." A silver-nailed finger touched the edge of the photo. "It's been so long. No one *did* anything."

"They tried," said her husband. "But there were no leads."

Sharna Beverly's stare said he'd blasphemed. She turned to me. "I'm here to tell you what Antoine was like, so you'll understand he didn't run away."

Milo said, "No one suspects that, ma'am."

"They sure did sixteen years ago. Kept telling me he'd run away, run away. Antoine liked his practical jokes but he was a good boy. Our other boys went to college and that was Antoine's plan. He especially looked up to his biggest brother, Brent. Brent has a degree in sound engineering and works on motion pictures. Gordon Junior is an accountant at the Water and Power."

Gordon Beverly said, "Antoine wanted to be a doctor."

"You probably heard this a million times," said his wife, "but not knowing is the worst. Doctor, be honest with me. Knowing what you know about maniacs, what chance is there this devil in Texas is telling the truth?"

I said, "I wish I could give you a solid answer, Mrs. Beverly. But there's no way to know. His story's certainly worth pursuing. Every angle is."

"There you go," she said. "*Every* angle. That's what I told those detectives sixteen years ago. They said there was nothing more to do."

I glanced at the picture. A boy frozen in time.

Sharna Beverly said, "They should've had the courtesy to answer our phone calls."

Gordon said, "They answered them at first, then they stopped."

"They stopped pretty quickly." Daring her husband to argue.

Milo said, "I'm really sorry."

"No need to be sorry, Lieutenant. Let's do something *now.*"

Milo said, "Getting back to what we were talking about, ma'am, how exactly did Antoine get that magazine job?"

"Magazine subscriptions," said Gordon Beverly. "Nice white neighborhood, supposed to be safe."

His wife said, "He's not asking *what,* he's asking *how.* Antoine found out at school. Someone put a flyer up on the bulletin board just before summer break. Antoine loved to work."

"Antoine had ambitions," said her husband. "Talked about being a surgical doctor. He liked anything scientific."

Sharna Beverly said, "The flyer made it sound like easy money, magazines selling themselves, just jumping into people's hands. I told Antoine that was foolish but he couldn't be convinced. He copied down the number and went to a meeting on a Saturday. Took two friends, all of them agreed to do it. They got sent to Culver City, which in those days was all white. They worked five days steady and Antoine sold the most subscriptions. The following Monday is when Antoine never came home."

I said, "Did Antoine or the other boys have any unpleasant experiences on the job?"

Sharna said, "Antoine said a couple of people called him nasty names and slammed the door in his face."

Gordon said, "The N word. Other things along those lines."

"Why they sent those boys into a white neighborhood," said Sharna, "I'll never understand. People in Crenshaw read magazines, too."

"Supposed to be safer," said her husband.

"Apparently it wasn't," she snapped.

He touched her elbow. She shifted away from contact. Ran a hand over the snapshot. "They threw those children in with strangers."

Milo said, "Did the detectives sixteen years ago canvass the neighborhood where Antoine delivered?"

"They claimed they talked to everyone," said Sharna. "If they didn't, are they going to admit it?"

She folded her arms across her chest.

Milo said, "What was the name of the company that hired Antoine?"

Sharna said, "Youth In Action. They closed down after Antoine disappeared. At least in L.A."

"Because of Antoine's disappearance?"

"After Antoine, the schools wouldn't let them advertise. I went to the library, used a computer to look them up, couldn't find any mention of them. Did that yesterday, when I found out we were coming here. The only person I remember was a Mr. Zint, called to tell me how sorry he was. Sounded to me like he was worried we were going to sue him. Didn't know anything helpful."

I said, "Antoine worked with two friends."

"Will and Bradley," she said. "Wilson Good and Bradley Maisonette. Friends since kindergarten. They helped carry the coffin and cried like babies. Said Antoine was selling the most." Reluctant smile. "Antoine had a way of talking you into anything."

Milo wrote down the names.

Sharna Beverly picked up the photo and held it to her breast. Her fingers covered the top of Antoine's face. His eternal smile made my eyes ache.

I said, "Did Brad or Will report anything unusual those five days?"

She said, "No, and I asked them. The van dropped them off one by one in Culver City. Antoine got off first and was supposed to be picked up last. When the time came, he wasn't there. The van waited an hour, then drove around looking for Antoine. Then Mr. Zint took Bradley and Will back to the school, which is where he always picked them up. Then he called the police. Bradley and Will were shook up, Bradley especially. He already lived through a drive-by."

Gordon said, "Not in our neighborhood. Visiting a cousin in Compton."

Sharna said, "It was me, I'd go straight to Texas, put hot pokers on that devil, run one of those electrocuting lie detectors they use on the al-Qaidas at Guantánamo. That'd clear it up soon enough."

She glared at her husband.

He fingered his flag pin.

"Lieutenant," she said, "do *you* have any feeling about that story that devil's telling?"

Milo said, "I wish I did, Mrs. Beverly. The sad truth is these lowlifes lie as easily as they breathe and they'll do anything to get out of dying."

"So what's the plan?"

"This is gonna sound frustrating, ma'am, but I'm really starting at the beginning. Seeing as Bradley Masionette and Will Good were close to Antoine and the last people to see him, let's start with them. Any idea where I can locate them?"

"It's not in the file?"

"The file, ma'am, is rather incomplete."

"Hmm. Well, Will coaches football at a Catholic school, don't know which one."

Gordon Beverly said, "St. Xavier."

She stared at him.

"It was in the *Sentinel,* Shar. Few years back, he was coaching down in Riverside, moved here. I called him up, asked if he remembered anything more about Antoine. He said no."

"Well, look at that," she said. "What else don't you tell me about?"

"No sense telling when there's nothing to tell."

Sharna Beverly said, "Bradley Maisonette did not turn out well.

From what I hear, he's spent most of his life in prison. Never did have a good family life."

Gordon said, "We're a tight-knit family. Antoine comes home all excited about all the big money he's going to make, I was happy for him."

Sharna said, "Magazines sell *themselves,* people love magazines more than *life* itself. I told him, 'Antoine, what sounds too good to be true, is.' I told him I needed to meet the people involved, make sure they weren't taking advantage. Antoine threw a fit, jumping up and down, begging, pleading, '*Trust* me, Mom. Don't *embarrass* me, Mom, no one else's parents are putting their noses in.' I said, 'Everyone else is stupid so I should be?' Antoine begs some more, turns on that smile of his." Sidelong peek at the photo. She folded her lips inward.

"I told Antoine, 'That's the trouble today, no one gets involved.' But the boy kept working at me, saying if I showed up Will and Brad and everyone else would be dissing him all summer. Then he brings out his report card, half A's, half B's, perfect in Conduct. Claiming that proved he was smart, could be trusted."

She slumped. "So I gave in. Biggest mistake I ever made and I've been paying for it for sixteen years."

Gordon said, "Honey, I keep telling you, there's no reason to—"

Her eyes blazed. "You keep telling me and you keep telling me." She got up, walked to the door, took care to close it silently.

Projecting more rage than if she'd slammed it.

Gordon Beverly said, "Sorry."

"Nothing to be sorry for, sir," said Milo.

"She's a good wife and mother. She didn't deserve what she got."

"What both of you got."

Gordon Beverly's face trembled. "Maybe it's worse for a mother."

"Well, that was fun," said Milo, when we were alone in his office. "Now I got little fishhooks sticking into my heart and decent people tugging on them. Time to check out this Youth In Action, on the off chance they're still in business and Mrs. B. missed it."

She hadn't. He got to work locating Antoine's friends.

Wilson Good's name pulled up several references to varsity football games at St. Xavier Preparatory High in South L.A. In addition to coaching, Good was head of the Physical Education Department.

Bradley Maisonette's criminal record was extensive. Over a dozen narcotics convictions, plus the predictable larcenies that fed a life of addiction.

Maisonette's last parole was eleven months ago. His downtown address was a government-financed SRO. Milo phoned his probation officer, got voice mail, left a message.

Pulling a panatela out of a shirt pocket, he peeled off the plastic and wet the tip but kept the cigar in his hand. "Something else you think I should do?"

"Why doesn't Texas just send Jackson out here and dare him to point out the graves?"

"Because he's a serious escape risk—tried four times, nearly succeeded once and injured a guard in the process. No way are they gonna let him out of their custody until some local department comes up with serious corroboration. So far, three of Jackson's claims have turned out to be bogus—crimes he didn't know were already solved. Bastard probably scans the Internet searching for open horrors he can cop to. Unfortunately, he can't be written off yet because the stakes are high. If I could find Antoine's damn file it might lead me somewhere."

"Where are the detectives who worked it originally?"

"One's dead, the other's living somewhere in Idaho. At least that's where his pension check goes. But he hasn't answered my calls. Meanwhile, there's Ella Mancusi, with a body barely cold. Why do I think I'm gonna break the Beverlys' hearts?"

He placed the beginnings of Antoine's new murder book in a drawer. Changed his mind and laid it next to his computer. "I've started surveillance on Tony Mancusi, got three brand-new uniforms who think they like plainclothes. Still no violent crime reports the night the Bentley got boosted and Mr. Heubel had the car washed and detailed the day Sean scraped it, so the chance of finding anything new is sub-nil. I'm putting *that* at the bottom of the drawer."

"Any luck getting Ella some media exposure?"

"You know the *Times*—maybe yes, maybe no. Public Affairs say there should be something on the six o'clock news tonight."

His phone rang. He listened, wrote something down, clicked off. "That was a message from one of Ella's allegedly noninvolved cousins, wants to talk to me. He's close, works at a lamp store on Olympic and Barrington. Maybe the gods are smiling."

Brilliant Crystal and Lighting was a thousand square feet of glare.

Aaron Hochswelder met us at the door and announced that he owned the place, had sent his employees on a coffee break. He walked us to the rear of his showroom. Heat from scores of chandeliers seared the back of my neck. Blinding light evoked a near-death experience.

Hochswelder was in his sixties but still dark-haired, tall and gaunt with a horse-face and fox-eyes. He wore a green short-sleeved shirt, pleated khakis, spit-shined oxfords.

He said, "Thanks for coming quickly. I could be out of line here but I felt I should talk to you. I still can't believe what happened to Ella."

Milo said, "She was your cousin."

"First cousin. Her father was my father's older brother. She used to babysit me." His attention was snagged by an unlit bulb in a Venetian chandelier. He reached up, twisted, brought forth a twinkle. "You have any idea who did it?"

"Not yet. Anything you can tell us would be helpful, sir."

Aaron Hochswelder chewed his cheek. "I'm not really sure I should be saying this but have you met her son, Tony?"

"We have."

"What do you think?"

"About what?"

"His . . . personality."

"He seems to be down on his luck."

"That assumes he ever had any luck."

"Tough life?" said Milo.

"Self-imposed." Hochswelder's bony forearms tightened. "I don't want to stir anything up, but . . ."

"Something about Tony bothers you?"

"It's hard to talk about family this way but you might want to look at him."

"As the killer?"

"It's a painful thought. I'm not saying he'd actually do anything like that . . ."

"But," said Milo.

"He might *know* someone bad? I'm not saying he *does*. It's just . . . this is really tough. I feel like a turncoat." Hochswelder inhaled through his nose, breathed out through his mouth. "All I'm saying is Tony is the only one I can think of. In the family."

"Tony told us there wasn't much family, period."

"Because he chooses to have nothing to do with anyone."

"Who's anyone?"

"Me and my wife and our kids, my brother Len and his wife and their kids. My brother's a dentist, lives in Palos Verdes. None of the kids are close to Tony. Which, frankly, was okay."

"Bad influence?"

Hochswelder cracked his knuckles. "I don't want you to think I've got some kind of vendetta against Tony. It's just . . . he called me this morning to tell me about his mother. That's how I found out. First time I've heard from him in years. He said he had no energy to call anyone else, I should do it. Shunting responsibility. He also hinted that he wanted me to take care of the funeral. Financially and otherwise."

"What was his demeanor when he called?"

"Not crying or weeping. More like . . . off."

"Off, how?"

"Off in space."

"Does Tony have a drug history?"

"He did as a kid," said Hochswelder. "According to *my* kids. I also think—the family thinks—he might be gay, so there's all sorts of issues here."

"Why does the family think that?"

"He never dated any girls we ever heard about, never got married. And sometimes he—he's not a sissy but he can get—I don't know how to say it—all of a sudden he'll do something pansyish, you know? A mannerism? We used to talk about it. How one second Tony would do one of those things—throw his hair, bat his eyelashes. And then *bam* he'd be just like a normal person."

"When's the last time you saw him?"

"That would have to be Thanksgiving four years ago. My brother had a family get-together and Tony showed up with Ella. He looked like he didn't wash his clothes regularly. Put on quite a bit of weight. Maybe he ate before because he didn't eat much at Len's table. He got up before dessert, went to the bathroom, came back announcing he'd called a cab, was going to wait outside. Ella was so embarrassed. We all pretended it never happened, just went on normally with the meal."

"Any reason he left early?"

"That's the thing, there was no conflict or anything. *Boom,* he just gets up and announces. Like he was mad at something, but for the life of me nothing happened to make him mad."

"Tony have a temper?" said Milo.

Hochswelder scratched a temple. "Not really, I couldn't say that, no. Just the opposite, he's always been kind of quiet. No one understands him."

"Being effeminate and all that."

"That and just being strange—like getting up before dessert, no warning, and leaving. Like always keeping to himself. His father was like that, too, but Tony Senior would at least go to family gatherings and pretend to be social. Though, frankly, most of the time he'd sit outside and smoke—big smoker, that's what caused his heart attack. He worked for a milk company, they delivered to the studios and Tony got Tony Junior a job at one of them. Paramount, I think. Basically a janitor job, moving stuff around, but those people pay well, lots of union pressure. Tony Junior would've been set up financially but he claimed he hurt his back and quit and since then he's been doing nothing."

"Claimed?"

"I'm sure he's got some pain. We all do."

"Let's talk about his drug use."

"All I know is what the kids said."

"Your kids?"

"Mine and my brother Len's. Not that Tony was a big topic of conversation, it just came up. We talk about everything in our family."

"What did Tony's cousins say he used?"

"It was never specific. More like Tony was stoned all the time, that's why he bombed out in school. Which was hard for Ella, I'm sure. Education was important to her."

"She ever mention being disappointed?"

"Ella wasn't one to share her feelings. But everyone had a sense Tony was a *big* disappointment to her. Also, I think he gambles. In fact, I know he does. My boy Arnold saw him at one of the Indian casinos near Palm Springs. Arnold and his family were vacationing and he and Rita—Arnold's wife—were playing the slots, just fooling around, they're not gamblers. When they went to get the kids at the day care the casino has, Arnold spotted Tony at the blackjack table. Arnold was going to say hi, even though he and Tony weren't close, just to be friendly. But then Tony played a hand and lost all his money and stomped away from the table cursing. Arnold didn't think it was a good time to be social."

"Do you have any other examples of Tony's gambling?"

"No, but Arnold said from the way Tony was sitting—all hunched over, hiding his cards—it looked like he was used to it."

"Drugs and gambling," said Milo. "Anything else?"

"And gay," Hoschswelder reminded him. "But I'm not accusing, just passing the information along. Don't want you to think I've got something against Tony. I don't, I feel sorry for him. Frankly, Tony Senior couldn't have been easy to live with. That one *had* a bad temper, the Italian hot blood. But with what happened to Ella . . . I just thought I should talk to you."

Milo said, "Let's be theoretical, Mr. Hochswelder, and assume Tony does have some connection to Ella's murder. What motive would you say he'd have?"

"Oh, no, Lieutenant, I couldn't go that far."

"Theoretically," said Milo. "Just between us, right now, with nothing on the record."

Hochswelder gnawed his upper lip. "Knowing Ella, she probably left everything to Tony. No reason she shouldn't, he was her only child. Though, in my opinion, giving money to someone who doesn't work is like flushing it down the toilet."

"You don't buy Tony's injury."

"Who knows?" said Hochswelder. "It's between him and God."

"How would you describe Tony's relationship with his mother?"

"Like I said, Ella didn't talk about her personal life."

"Ever see any animosity between them?"

"No, I can't say that. Except for that time at Thanksgiving."

"Ella got mad at him?"

"They both looked tense when they arrived. Ella wore kind of a frozen smile, like she was pretending to be happy."

"What about Tony?"

"Off in his own world."

"Any idea what would've made them tense?"

"None whatsoever."

Milo said, "Let's switch gears for a second. Who were Ella's friends?"

"I never saw that she had any," said Hochswelder. "She and Tony Senior tended to keep to themselves. Every year we invited her to Christmas, told her to bring Tony Junior. Every year she showed up with a nice fruit basket. He never showed up. Frankly, we wondered if she even told him."

"Why wouldn't she?"

"She knew he was antisocial. And after that scene at Thanksgiving four years ago, maybe she was embarrassed."

"Leaving before dessert."

Hochswelder adjusted a bulb. "Trust me, Lieutenant, our desserts are worth sticking around for. My wife bakes and so does my brother's wife. That year we had six kinds of pies, as well as bread pudding and compote. From the way Tony looked at the spread the girls put out, you'd think we were trying to serve him garbage."

8

We left the lighting store and stepped out into a mild evening.

Milo said, "Place is Dante's Inferno. Charming fellow, huh?"

"Not that he wants to bad-mouth Tony."

We got back in the unmarked and he began driving. "Close-knit clan except when they're not. Any ideas from what he said?"

"His description of the Mancusis is interesting. Asocial father with a bad temper, isolated family. Abusers are great at corralling the herd, so Tony may have had a rough childhood."

"You see that as grounds for Junior hating Mom bad enough to have her carved?"

"Abused kids can resent the parent who didn't save them. Moskow said when Tony did visit, Ella never walked him out, so there were issues."

"He wasn't worth getting off her chair for but the morning paper was."

"And that's when she got it," I said. "Interesting."

"Bit of a reach?"

"Maybe not. Getting symbolic can lead to all sorts of dark places."

"Ol' Tony's sitting on a whole lot of primal anger and chronic pain doesn't improve his disposition?"

I said, "As long as Ella helped him financially, he was able to keep his feelings under control. She turns off the tap, he views it as yet another abandonment. Comes to see her, pleads his case, she says no. He argues. She gets mad. If she really lost her cool and threatened to change the will, leave it all to the Salvation Army, that could've done it."

"She told Barone she didn't want a copy of the will at home. Maybe to shield it from Tony."

"A million three for that house," I said. "More than tempting. If he does have a gambling problem, he could know bad guys who'd take on the job."

He drove for a while. "It's as logical as any scenario, but Hochswelder labeled Tony a compulsive gambler based on a second-hand account of a single episode. And he doesn't like Tony, so anything he says is suspect."

A block later: "A slovenly fat guy who's not a decorator or a florist or a choreographer being gay? Impossible."

I laughed. "You see his sexuality as relevant?"

"You don't?"

"What do you mean?"

"Something else for Mama to disapprove of," he said. "Parents can get picky that way."

Back at the station, he checked in with the plainclothes officer surveilling Tony Mancusi. The subject had left his apartment once to get a burrito and a soda at a stand on Sunset near Hillhurst. Walking distance but Mancusi had taken his car, which he'd used as his dining room, munching in the parking lot.

"Officer Ruiz also observed that subject tossed his junk out the car window onto the ground, rather than use a trash basket ten feet away. Officer Ruiz began a violation roster on the subject. When I pointed out to Officer Ruiz that littering private property was bad behavior but nothing citable, he was conspicuously disappointed."

"Eager," I said.

"Twenty-one years old, six months out of the academy. The other two are just as green. I feel like I'm running a day care center, but at least they're motivated."

"Mancusi go anywhere after lunch?"

"Right back home and he's still there. I'd love to have grounds for his phone records."

Shuffling through the message slips on his desk, he tossed the first four, read the fifth, and said, "Wonders never cease. Sean got creative."

Binchy, though still on Auto Theft, had continued combing the crime reports for incidents coinciding with the time period the Bentley had been missing. Coming up empty on homicides, rapes, and assaults just as Milo had. But the young detective had gone further and a missing person had surfaced.

Milo phoned him, grunted approval, got the details.

"Katrina Shonsky, twenty-eight-year-old female Caucasian, blond and brown, five four, one hundred ten. Out partying that night with friends, drove home alone, hasn't been heard from since. Mother reported it three days later. Took this long to make it into the computer."

"Go Sean," I said. "You run a good day care, Papa Sturgis."

Mr. and Mrs. Royal Hedges lived in a vast, loft-like condo on the fourteenth floor of a luxury building on the Wilshire Corridor. Walls of glass opened to a southward view that avoided the ocean and stared down at Inglewood, Baldwin Hills, LAX flight paths. Altitude and a starless night transformed miles of tract housing into a light show.

Royal and Monica Hedges sat on a low, black Roche-Bobois sofa, smoking in unison. The condo's floors were black granite, the walls white diamond plaster that threw off its own glints, the artwork big and blotchy with an emphasis on gray.

Monica Hedges was somewhere between fifty and sixty. Tiny and blond and skinny to the point of desiccation, she had heavily lined brown eyes, a face stretched past the point of reason, and great legs displayed by a little black dress.

Royal Hedges looked to be seventy, minimum, sported a red-brown toupee nearly good enough to pull off the illusion, and a Vandyke dyed to match. He wore a red silk shirt, white slacks, pink suede loafers without socks. Hid his fourth yawn behind liver-spotted hands and flicked ashes into a chrome tray.

Monica said, "Katrina's my only child. From my second marriage. Her father's long gone."

"Disappeared?" said Milo.

"Dead." Her tone said no loss.

Her third husband's body language said this was *her* ordeal.

She said, "I'm not panicking, Lieutenant, but I am getting a little nervous. Katrina's done stupid things before, but not like this, a week and counting. I can't help worrying because that's what a mother does. Though I fully expect her to walk right in with one of her *stupid* excuses."

Royal said, "I'll be back," patted her knee, left the room.

"Men and their plumbing," said Monica Hedges. "He'll be up and down the whole time. We've been married two years, he doesn't really know Katrina."

Milo said, "Is there any friend or relative Katrina might've gone to visit?"

"You mean her father's family? Never. Norm Shonsky wasn't in her life and neither is his clan."

Airy wave. Showing no curiosity about why someone of Milo's rank would be doing a house call on a missing person.

At her income level, probably used to service.

"Besides," she said, "Katrina doesn't *visit*. She picks up impulsively and leaves."

"Where does she go, ma'am?"

Another wave. "Wherever. Mexico, Europe. Once she even made it to Tahiti. That's what I meant by stupid. She'll find a cheap flight on the Internet, do no planning whatsoever, and just fly off in gay abandon."

"By herself."

Silence.

"Mrs. Hedges?"

"There are men, I suppose," she said. "If she doesn't travel with them, she's certainly capable of finding them along the way. She makes a point of telling me when she comes back."

"Telling you what?"

"That she behaved in a way I wouldn't approve. She does it purely to rile me. The exceptions are those times when she neglects to take enough money for expenses and calls me in desperation. When that happens, she's like someone from the Travel Channel. Going on about the sights, museums, quaint old churches."

She smoked greedily. "I love my daughter, Lieutenant, but she can be trying."

"How long has it been since you last saw her?"

Hesitation. "A month give or take. We weren't fighting, nothing like that. But Katrina had convinced herself she needed to be *independent*. In other words, no contact with Mother until finances deem otherwise. I'd never have known she was gone if her friend hadn't called to ask if Katrina was with me."

"Which friend?"

"A girl named Beth Holloway. Never met her. She was out with Katrina at that club, they split up, she hasn't heard from Katrina since."

He read off the Van Nuys address on Katrina Shonsky's driver's license. "Is that current, ma'am?"

"It is."

"Does Katrina live alone?"

"Yes. In a dump."

"Any current men in her life?"

"Not that I know," said Monica Hedges. Losing volume by the end of the sentence, as if she doubted her own veracity. "Katrina tends to guard her privacy."

"How long has she been at this address?"

"Fifteen months." She stubbed out her cigarette, watched the diminishing trail of smoke.

"In terms of guarding—"

"She kept me out of her private life."

"Don't be offended, ma'am, but do you think she was hiding something?"

"Could be, Lieutenant. If she was dating someone high-caliber I have no doubt she'd be showing him off just to show me I'm wrong."

"Wrong about what?"

"She's a gorgeous girl, I keep telling her she needs to elevate herself, run in a different circle. Royal and I are members of the Riviera Country Club. There are socials all the time. When I call Katrina to inform her of an event, she laughs and then her mood turns ugly."

"She prefers doing things her own way."

Her eyes shifted toward the front door. "I just know she's going to run out of cash and come waltzing in any minute."

"Do you have a recent photo we could keep?"

Reaching for a new cigarette, she marched across the living room, turned a corner. Muffled voices filtered back. Inflections that suggested tension.

She returned alone, carrying the cold cigarette in one hand, a three-by-five glossy in the other.

"This is about four years old, but Katrina hasn't aged appreciatively." Touching her own cheek. "Good genes. It was taken at a cousin's wedding. Katrina served as a bridesmaid. After much complaining about the dress."

Pretty girl with a heart-shaped face wearing a big-shouldered sateen gown the color of mortified flesh. Ill-fitting cap sleeves rode too high on smooth arms. A high, square bodice kept its promise to flatter no one. Katrina Shonsky's fair hair was upswept and tasseled by curls that resembled brass sausages. Her lips were shaped into something resembling a smile but the rest of her face radiated disdain.

"So," said Milo, "you're pretty confident she's off on one of her trips but you reported her missing just to be safe."

"I know she didn't travel far, because she didn't take her passport."

"You've been to her apartment?"

"Talked my way past the landlord and went through the entire place. Straightened up, while I was there, Lord knows the dump needed it. Her passport was right in a dresser drawer. If she took clothes, she didn't take many, Lieutenant. But Katrina's capable of hopping off with nothing but her purse and a credit card."

"Do you co-sign for her card?"

"I do *not*. No more of that, Katrina abused my credit limit. She now has a Visa with a one-thousand-dollar-a-month maximum and is expected to pay her own bills. And I have to say for the most part, she's done so." Crossing her fingers.

"No passport, no clothes," said Milo. "Doesn't sound like much of a vacation."

"Some of those places she goes to," said Monica Hedges, "all you need is a bikini and a wineglass. It's also possible she used her employee discount for a wardrobe."

"She works in fashion?"

"She sells clothing at La Femme Boutique in Brentwood. Overpriced tacky, if you ask me. I told her I could probably get her a position at Harari or one of the places on Rodeo through Royal. He was in garment manufacturing. Owned a huge company that did contract work for some pretty big couture names."

She played with her unlit cigarette, reached for a white onyx lighter. Milo got there first.

"Katrina's job," she said, between puffs, "is a dead-end position. Like every other job she's held. If you ask me, down deep she thinks she deserves no better because she lacks formal education. She dropped out of high school, finally got her GED, did a semester at Santa Monica Community. The *plan* was to finish two years and transfer to a UC. Instead she dropped out and worked selling shoes at Fred Segal. They fired her for poor work habits. I told her to make lemonade out of lemons and return to SMC, all she needed was one and a half more years. No go."

I said, "Sounds like Katrina's a bit of a rebel."

"A bit?" Raspy laughter. "Gentlemen, I love my daughter dearly but I do believe that she thinks bucking me is the key to her identity. She was always a difficult child. Colicky baby—face cute as a button but screaming twenty-four hours a day. When that finally ended, she began walking early, was into everything. She *always* hated school. Even though she's smart. She can sing, but wouldn't go out for chorus. Has a lovely figure, could've gone out for cheerleading." She sighed. "Maybe eventually she'll mature."

Milo said, "Let's go back to that night. Katrina went out clubbing with two friends. Beth Holloway and . . ."

"Rianna something foreign."

"Which club did they go to?"

"Some dive in West L.A., more like a barn than a bona fide nightclub."

"You've been there?"

"I went over yesterday and talked to some monstrous men—bouncers. Ugly industrial area off Pico—one of those side streets. I also talked to the manager. No one was helpful. They said the place was packed, they have no memory of Katrina or any other specific individual, and there are no security cameras on the premises. Isn't *that* stupid, Lieutenant?"

"Not the way I'd run things," said Milo. "What's the name of the club?"

"The Light My Fire."

"As in the song."

"Pardon?"

"Do you have phone numbers for Beth and Rianna?"

"No, but I can tell you where to find them both. Beth said she sells jewelry at a place near La Femme and Rianna works the cosmetics counter at Barneys."

"Do you have the name of the jewelry store?"

"Somewhere near Katrina's work—San Vicente near Barrington. I'd be concerned if this was anyone but Katrina. Even with it *being* Katrina, I'm getting a bit nervous. What will you do for me, Lieutenant?"

Milo said, "What's the longest she's ever been gone?"

"Ten days. Hawaii—she visited all the islands, never called once, came back with the deepest tan I've ever seen, you'd think she was a Mexican or something. Another time she spent nine days in Cozumel, some sort of discount special."

"So this is within her usual pattern."

"Does that mean you won't do anything?"

"No, I'll look into it, ma'am. Did Beth Holloway say how Katrina happened to be separated from her friends?"

"She did after I asked twice. The plan was for Rianna to be the designated driver but they went in Katrina's car because this Rianna girl's car was broken. Rianna and Beth got picked up by two men and asked Katrina if it was okay for them to go their separate ways. They claim Katrina was fine with that. That's the last time they saw her."

"You have doubts that Katrina was fine with the change?"

"My daughter does not take well to disappointment, Lieutenant. Low frustration tolerance her teachers called it. What concerns me is that she decided to do them one better by meeting a man herself. Then ran off to God-knows-where."

"Without her passport."

"If you're out for fun, you can find it anywhere," said Monica Hedges. Relaxing her posture for a second, as if reminiscing.

Milo said, "Rianna being the designated driver meant Katrina was drinking that night."

"And Katrina loves her Long Island Iced Teas. Which is a hodge-podge cocktail, just a kitchen-sink mess that does God-knows-what to your brain. I always tell her stick with the classics, they won't pollute your mind. Martini or Manhattan, never on the rocks. That way you know how much you're getting. But try telling Katrina that. To her, anything with fruit liquor and a kick is a Martini."

"Has she been known to overindulge?"

Monica Hedges shifted her weight. "That has happened from time to time."

"You're concerned she might have driven home intoxicated."

"What if God forbid she had an accident? But I called the highway patrol and they reported nothing on the freeway that night."

"Is the 405 her customary route home?"

"I don't know," she said. "Easiest way to get to the Valley, isn't it?" Frowning. "She used to have a place near the U. that she shared with another girl—some Indian student who hit the books all the time. Which isn't Katrina's style, it didn't last long. Katrina complained that everyone in the building was a student and it made her feel old. I suspect her own lack of education embarrassed her. I was hoping that might motivate her but it didn't. She wanted her own place, said the rent this side of the hill was too steep. I told her I'd help. She never took me up on my offer, just picked up and moved to Van Nuys. Though she keeps insisting it's Sherman Oaks. Is that logical, Lieutenant? Turning down a sincere offer?"

"Kids," said Milo.

Monica Hedges puffed manically. "You didn't answer my question. What *exactly* are you going to do for me?"

"What would you like us to do, Mrs. Hedges?"

That startled her. Ashes dropped to the granite floor. "I'd like you to *detect* where my daughter is. Use that computer you've got—tracking airline tickets, credit card receipts, phone usage. Put out one of those APBs."

"Ma'am, without evidence of a crime, that would be an invasion of Katrina's privacy."

"Oh, *puleeze,*" said Monica Hedges.

"Sorry, ma'am, but that's the way it is. If she were a minor, it would be different."

"Psychologically, she's about fourteen."

Milo smiled.

"You're telling me there's *nothing* you can do?"

"We'll do everything we can, legally. That means talking to her friends, stopping by the club—"

"I already did all that."

"Sometimes repetition helps, ma'am. We'll also look for her car. Is she still driving the yellow Mustang that's currently registered to her?"

"Yes, but not for long. I just got a notice that she's missed the last two payments. That loan I *did* co-sign for. The agreement was I made the down payment and the payments were to be her responsibility."

"Give me the finance company data and I'll see if it's been picked up."

"I did that myself, and no, it hasn't."

"Sounds like you've accomplished a lot."

"Want something done well, do it yourself. So that's all you're going to do? It doesn't sound very promising."

"Let's start and see where it leads, Mrs. Hedges. Call me anytime if you think of something."

"Oh, I will, you'd better believe I will."

She got to her feet, hurried to the door, held it open.

Milo said, "I'm going to ask you one more question that might alarm you, but it's only routine, in case we do come across accident reports."

Monica Hedges straightened and sucked on her cigarette. "What?"

"Do you know Katrina's blood type?"

"That is . . . eerie."

"Just routine, ma'am."

"Some routine you people have," said Monica Hedges. "I certainly wouldn't want *your* job."

Milo smiled. "Most people don't."

"And I'm one of them . . . her type is the same as mine. O-positive. It's the most popular."

She smoked and watched us walk to the elevator. As we stepped into the lift, I heard her say, "*There* you are, *darling*. Is everything *working*?"

The door slammed.

Milo had asked the condo valet to keep the unmarked close. When we got to the front of the building it was gone and the valet was poking a BlackBerry.

A high-decibel throat clear made the man look up.

"The Crown Victoria?"

"Had to move it, too crowded."

No other cars in sight.

Milo said, "Could you get it?" Adding a "Please" that made the valet flinch.

The guy ambled off toward the subterranean parking lot.

Milo said, "The Shonsky girl's been missing over a week, Mommie Dearest sees it as playing hooky, wants me to be her personal truant officer."

"Or she's in deep denial."

"She says she's nervous but all I heard was anger."

"Anger can mask anxiety," I said.

He looked at his Timex. "Where'd the hell he park it, Chula

Vista . . . First Tony and his mom and Hochswelder, now this harmonious bunch. Any happy families left?"

"With our jobs we're not going to meet them."

"So what do you think of our missing girl? With her history of cutting town on impulse, how far do I take it?"

"O-positive," I said. "Same as in the Bentley."

"Didn't you hear Mom? It's the most *popular* type. Like it's a contest. Growing up with someone like that, I can see needing to escape."

"That kind of rivalry could also make Katrina vulnerable."

"To what?"

"Bling. Mom marries rich but Katrina works a low-paying job. If she left the club woozy and feeling abandoned by her pals, two hundred grand worth of car rolling up would've seemed heaven-sent. Talk about something to one-up Mommy."

"*If* she was picked up, I don't see it happening at the Light My Fire. I was there last year, chasing a dead lead on a drug murder. The male clientele's acrylic shirts, too much hair gel, and dance moves worse than mine. Someone drives up in Heubel's Bentley, the bouncers and everyone else would've noticed, and by the time the guy hit the floor, fifty women woulda been all over him."

He phoned the club, asked to speak to the manager, looked at his watch again, scowled. The line clicked in. A brief conversation followed.

"Guy laughed, said what do you think this is, the Playboy Mansion? He also said nothing unusual happened at the club that night, he already said so to the 'nosy mother.' "

"If Katrina was upset about being ditched by her friends, she could've hit another club, tried to redeem the night. Or she drove home drunk, had some sort of mechanical problem. We just heard she's impulsive. And she'd stopped making payments on the Mustang. Both of which raise the chance of poor maintenance. For all we know, she simply ran out of gas, got stranded somewhere."

"Drunk girl, alone late at night, Mr. Moneybags cruises by and says hop in. Or she's in Hawaii."

"She guarded her privacy with her mother," I said, "but her friend worried enough to call Mom."

"Breaking down on the 405, even late, someone would've seen her."

"With several drinks in her, she could've been intimidated by the freeway, chose an alternate route."

"Or she got totally lost and headed south, Alex. Which could've put her in some seriously nasty territory."

"Why not start with the simplest assumption? When I'm heading north and want to avoid the freeway, I take the Sepulveda Pass. Late at night, once you get north of Sunset, it's a fast ride, pretty much empty. But that also means breaking down in an isolated area."

Engine noise sounded from the mouth of the sub-lot. The same valet rolled up in a baby-blue Jaguar sedan, got out and stood by the driver's door.

Milo walked over to him. "If you insist."

The valet said, "Huh?"

"I'll take it in trade if you throw in the extended warranty."

The valet gaped. Milo got an inch from his face. "Where's the Crown Vic, friend?"

"I got a call from a resident."

Milo took out his cell phone. "Want me to call you, too? What's your number, pal. And while you're at it, show me some I.D. for an official police investigation."

The valet didn't answer.

Milo flashed his shield. "Get it now."

"Mr. and Mrs. Lazarus are coming out in a—"

"I'll help 'em. Go."

The valet hazarded eye contact. Whatever he saw made him scurry off.

Milo eyed the Jaguar. "Budget wheels, pshaw. If Katrina did break down and got picked up, think Mr. Bentley Thief was stalking her?"

"Or cruising for a victim and she fit his appetite."

"Sexual psychopath," he said. "What's the link with Ella Mancusi?"

I said, "Thrill of the hunt."

"Guess so. Normally, I'd kiss Katrina off as not worth my time. But with two big black cars boosted and blood in the damn Bentley . . ." He shook his head. "Let's try to find the Mustang."

An elderly couple exited the condo, saw him standing next to the Jag. Stopped.

He grinned. "Evening, Mr. and Mrs. Lazarus." Opening both doors with a flourish, he said, "Have a great time."

The couple approached the car nervously. Got in, sped off.

Seconds later, the valet roared up in the unmarked and screeched to a stop. Milo took his hand, opened it, and slapped a five in his palm.

"Not necessary," said the valet.

"Nor deserved. Have a nice life."

We drove the Sepulveda Pass north all the way to the Valley's southern border just shy of Ventura Boulevard, continued a few miles beyond. North of Wilshire was the low, flat stretch of veterans' cemetery, then small businesses and apartments. After that, rolling hillside topped by lights. Traffic was thin. No sign of Katrina Shonsky's car.

As we returned to the city, Milo said, "Oh, well. If I liked the simple life, I'd be a farmer."

"There's always south," I said.

"A hundred and fifty miles' worth to Mexico."

I looked up at the foothills to the east. "Plenty of side streets to explore."

"What a fun guy," he growled, turning right and cruising several dark, winding roads.

An hour later: "I'll have patrol follow up tomorrow, try to get hold of Katrina's girlfriends. For all we know, they'll tell us a whole different story. Like she's with some bum Mommy wouldn't approve of. And don't bring up O-positive anymore. I'm not feeling popular."

Light butterscotched the windows of Robin's studio out back. I walked past the pond, stopped to check out the baby koi. The antique iron pagoda lights reached down to the floor, giving an easy view of the fish. Three, four inches long, now. Bobbing merrily in the current set off by the waterfall.

I'd first spotted them as larva-sized hatchlings. A dozen little scraps of fishy filament, swimming fearlessly among two-foot-long adults. Koi will eat their own eggs but once the young are born, they'll never inflict harm. Unlike other fish, they don't harass sick or dying cohorts. Maybe that's why they can live over a century.

I continued to the studio, rapped the window. Robin looked up from her bench and smiled. Placed a white rectangle of Alpine spruce to her ear and tapped. Searching for the tones that told her the wood might be suitable as a soundboard. From the size of the plank, a mandolin board.

Her expression as she placed it to the side said no such luck. By the time I entered, she had another piece in hand. Blanche nestled in her lap, serene as ever.

Robin said, "Hi." Blanche let out a wheezy bulldog welcome.

When Robin kissed me, Blanche turned her head sideways in that bulldog way and nuzzled my hand.

I said, "A blonde and a redhead."

"Aren't you the lucky one."

I eyed the discarded spruce. "No music in there?"

"Even though *he'd* never know the difference." She eyed a FedEx box in the corner. "Learn anything about that poor old woman?"

"The working assumption is the son had something to do with it but there's nothing even close to proof."

"A son doing that to his mother," she said. "Beyond belief."

She eyed the box in the corner again.

I said, "New tools?"

"Collection of DVDs. From Dot-com. Ten Audrey Hepburn movies and a note that said I remind him of her."

Hepburn had been five seven and built like a human clothes hanger. Robin's five three on a good day, curvy everywhere you look.

"You're both gorgeous."

She flexed her fingers, the way she does when she's edgy.

"Has he ever been inappropriate?"

"Not really."

"Not really?"

"When I met him at the luthiery show he was a little touchy, but nothing you could say was out of line."

"Well, then," I said. "Audrey Hepburn made some good flicks."

"I'm overreacting, huh?"

"He could be working on a few fantasies. Happens all the time."

"What do you mean?"

"Men are always looking at you. You've got the X factor—pheromones, whatever."

"Oh, sure."

"It's true. You never notice because you're not a flirt."

"Because I'm a space cadet?"

"Sometimes that, too."

"Alex," she said, "I've never come *close* to dropping a hint that this was anything other than business."

"It needn't have anything to do with you."

"Great."

"Hey," I said, "what's the worst that can happen? He makes a move and you gently deter him. Meanwhile you can e-mail him a friendly but formal thank-you note for the movies and tell him you and I are going to enjoy watching them."

She stroked Blanche. "You're right, I'm being silly. As they used to say in seventh grade, *conceited.*" She touched a hoop earring. Tossed her hair. Much better from her than from Tony Mancusi.

I played with the top button of her shirt.

She said, "Factor X, huh? Does that make you Mr. Y?"

We picked out two movies and watched from bed. *Roman Holiday* had held up beautifully over half a century. *Breakfast at Tiffany's* hadn't and when *The End* finally arrived, we were half asleep.

Cutting the lights, we touched fingertips. I murmured something I'm pretty sure was affectionate.

Robin said, "Audrey Hepburn was beautiful but I'm nothing like her," and was out.

At ten the next morning, I picked Milo up at the station and drove to Barneys in Beverly Hills.

The ground floor was skinny girls hawking cosmetics. A blonde specializing in nail polish pointed out Rianna Ijanovic.

Tall, narrow brunette, one station down.

She smiled at us through a fragrant cloud. An array of sample atomizers adorned the counter. Shoppers and shopgirls chattered. Everyone chasing the next big thing in self-improvement. Milo identified himself and Rianna responded with the blank, frightened look of a toddler thrown off course.

She was thirty or so, pale and square-shouldered with hard, black eyes, optimistic breasts, and a face rescued from beauty by an off-kilter nose and a too-sharp chin.

"Police? I don't understand."

Milo said, "We're here about Katrina Shonsky."

"Oh, oh." It came out *aw, aw.* Faint accent, barely audible over the magpie chorus.

"Could we talk somewhere quiet?"

Rianna Ijanovic tapped another perfume sprayer on the shoulder. "*Cawver* for me, okay?"

We left the department store through the front door on Wilshire, walked around the corner to Camden Drive, passed the entrance to the parking lot.

Milo said, "Ijanovic. Czech?"

"Croatian. I'm legal."

"Even if you weren't, it wouldn't matter. We're here about Katrina, that's all."

"I only know Katrina through another girl."

"Beth Holloway?"

"Yes."

"We tried Beth first, but she's not working today and we don't have a home number."

"You wouldn't find her at home," said Rianna Ijanovic.

"Where is she?"

"Torrance. She met a man." Sticking out her tongue.

"You don't approve?" said Milo.

"I have an opinion, she has an opinion."

"Are we talking about the same guy she met the night you two went clubbing with Katrina?"

"Yes."

Milo said, "I heard you met a guy, too."

Rianna Ijanovic's black eyes narrowed. "Who told you?"

"Katrina's mother. Beth told her."

"Beth talk talk talk." Folding a hand into a silhouette duck, she flapped her thumb against her index finger.

Milo said, "If Katrina's hiding something from her mother, we couldn't care less. Knowing right at the outset would save a lot of hassle."

"I don't know about secrets."

"What'd you just mean about Beth talking too much?"

"I am private person," said Rianna. "Beth is very American—no offense. Share everything."

"Any reason Beth shouldn't have been open with Katrina's mother?"

"Maybe," she said, gazing past us.

"What's that?"

"Katrina hates her mother."

"Katrina said that?"

"Many times."

"Rianna, do you have any idea where Katrina is?"

"Uh-uh, sorry, no."

"And the last time you saw her was . . ."

"That night."

"At the Light My Fire."

"Yes."

"Tell us about that night."

"We went to the club, I was the driver, not to drink. Beth met Sean. Sean's brother is Matt. Beth wanted to be with Sean so I had to be with Matt."

"Had to."

"She's a friend."

"Where are Sean and Matt from?"

"Torrance," she said. "They are brothers. Say they own surfboard business. What they own is nothing. Sean make surfboards in a factory. Matt want to be an actor." She hooked a thumb at the department store. "Everybody here gonna be movie star or model."

"You, too?"

"No, no, no. I want to *work*."

"What'd you do in Croatia?"

"Architecture student."

"So you and Beth left with Sean and Matt. And went . . ."

"To Torrance." Another tongue-stick. "I call cab to go home, cost so much money."

"What time was this?"

"Four in the morning."

"And Beth?"

"She stay there," said Rianna. "She mostly there now."

"With Sean."

"Yes."

"True love," said Milo.

"American love."

"How did Katrina feel about the change in plans?"

"She didn't yell."

"But not happy."

"I was unhappy, too. She was more unhappy."

"How did she express being unhappy?"

"Pardon?"

"What did she say, Rianna?"

"Nothing. She turn her back, walk away."

"Where'd she walk?"

"Into the action."

"The dance floor."

"Yes."

"Did you notice her dancing with someone in particular?"

"I didn't see."

"At any time that night did she concentrate on one guy?"

"I didn't see, no."

"No one, the whole night?"

"Lots of people," said Rianna. "I was busy."

"With Matt."

"With Matt here and here and here and here." Grimacing and slapping her neck, shoulder, breast, rear.

Milo said, "Pesky guy, Matt."

"Pesty, yes. Mr. Surfer-dude." *Meester sorfer-doood.*

"What time did you and Beth tell Katrina you were going with Sean and Matt?"

"Honest answer? I don't know."

"Take a guess."

"Maybe one thirty, two. They want to get out of there."

"Beth and Sean."

"American love," she said.

"What can you tell us about Katrina—the kind of person she is."

"Kat, we call her Kat. After the big damage, never Katrina."

"She doesn't like being associated with a hurricane."

"All the damage?" said Rianna Ijanovic. "It's like being . . . a bad, wild-animal name."

"Katrina's not a wild girl."

"An animal? No."

"Is she wild in another way?"

"What do you mean?"

"Does she like to party?"

"Very much."

"What else does she like?"

"Clothes."

"Sounds like she found the perfect job."

"Pardon?"

"La Femme Boutique."

"Too expensive," said Rianna. "Even with employee discount. She make fun of the fat ladies in the big sizes."

"Katrina doesn't like the customers."

"Old, fat, rich," she singsonged. "Maybe remind her of Mother?"

"You ever meet her mother?"

"Never."

"She's skinny."

"Okay."

"Does Katrina have a thing about money?"

Confusion in the black eyes.

Milo said, "Is money really important to her?"

"Not to you?" said Rianna.

"I mean especially important. More than most people. Like, would she be impressed by a man with money?"

Rianna's smiled spread slowly. "She should be impressed with losers?"

"Did she ever date anyone rich?"

"All the time I know her she never date anyone."

"How long is that?"

"Two, three months."

"How come no social life?"

"She says she never meet the right guys."

"What about cars?"

"What about?"

"Did she have a special interest in cars?"

"Special . . . no. In the beginning she like her Mustang. Paid for by the rich stepdaddy."

"She have something to say about him?"

Head shake. "Rich."

"Why'd she stop liking the Mustang?"

Shrug. "Maybe she tired of it."

"Katrina bores easily?"

"She move around—from thing to thing. Like a butterfly. ADD, you know? She say she have ADD in school. Lots of ADD in America, no? Lady customers talk to me about kids jumping like kangaroos. Everyone seeing psychiatrist."

"Does Kat have a psychiatrist?"

"Don't know—you ask these questions because her mother hire you to find her?"

"We work for the city, Rianna."

"The city wants to find Kat?"

"If she's been hurt."

"I think not."

"Why not?"

"ADD. Always like this." Black irises zipped from side to side, bobbed up and down. "Jumping."

"Restless," said Milo.

"Not happy," said Rianna Ijanovic. "Sometimes when she drinks, she talks about moving somewhere."

"She drink a lot?"

"She like to drink."

"Where does she talk about moving?"

"She never say, just somewhere. Not a happy girl. I don't like being with her all the time. She . . . sometimes you can catch un-happy—like a cold, yes? She is Beth's friend, I hang out."

"Could we have Beth's cell phone number, please?"

Rianna recited the digits. "Can I go back to work? I need this job."

"Sure," said Milo. "Thanks for your time. Here's my card. If you hear from Kat, please let me know."

"Yes. But I will not hear."

"Why not?"

"If she call anyone, she call Beth."

We walked her back to the front of the store. Before we reached the door, Milo said, "Did Kat ever talk about someone who owned really expensive cars—like a Ferrari, a Rolls-Royce—a Bentley."

"She talk about a Bentley, but not a rich guy."

"Who?"

"Some guy she used to date. Big loser, dirty hands."

"A mechanic."

"Greased-monkey she call him." Rianna Ijanovic laughed.

"What's funny?" said Milo.

"Greasy little *monkey*." Her hands climbed the air in front of her. "It sound funny."

"What's this grease-monkey's name?"

"Maybe . . . Clyde? I don't know for sure."

"Clyde what?"

"Clyde Greased-monkey." Laughing louder, she swung the door open and hurried back to the world of cover-up.

I drove out of the Barneys lot and Milo worked the phone. "Clyde the Bentley boy, shouldn't be a feat of detection."

He started with the main dealership on the Westside. O'Malley Premium Motors was on the east end of Beverly Hills but the service facility was on Pico, in Santa Monica.

Minutes from the Light My Fire.

Milo called, asked for Clyde, said, "Yeah, that's him—is he in? Thanks. No, not necessary."

Click.

"Not Clyde, *Clive*. Probably a chips and ale and darts kinda guy. And tinkering with high-priced British metal as we speak."

10

O'Malley Premium Motors Service and Maintenance was a gray wedge of front office glued onto a taller brick garage. A few nondescript cars were parked in the employee lot, soaking up sun and pollution. Off to the left in a covered *Customers Only!* area sat a few million bucks' worth of status symbol.

Milo said, "Pull in next to that blue Rolls."

"Don't I need to be preapproved?"

He slapped the Seville's vinyl dash. "How many miles on this masterpiece?"

"Sixty thou on the second engine."

"Endurance beats flash anytime, son. You are officially a classic."

The waiting area was a sliver of space facing an empty coffeemaker. No chairs, no reading material, no one waiting. Behind a glass partition, a black woman wearing reading glasses moved columns of numbers around a computer screen.

Milo rapped on the glass. The partition slid open. "How can I help you?"

He introduced himself and asked for Clive.

"Clive Hatfield? Why?"

"We'd just like to talk to him."

She pushed a button on an intercom. "Clive to front desk. Front desk for Clive."

Milo said, "Not too many customers today."

"We call them clients," she said. "They rarely come here."

"Pickup and delivery?"

"Those people expect it. We used to do it free. Now we charge a hundred dollars a trip and no one complains."

"The age of lowered expectations."

"Pardon?"

"The cost of gas, huh?"

"That's what the bosses say."

"Who does the pickup and delivery?"

"The same guys who detail the cars."

"Not the mechanics?"

"With what they get paid? I don't think so."

"Skilled job."

"That's what they say."

"How long's Clive been working here?"

She edged closer to the glass. "You suspect him of something?"

"Not at all."

"Routine questions," she said. "Like on TV."

"You got it."

"If you say so." She returned to her computer.

We waited five minutes before Milo asked her to page Hatfield again.

She said, "Maybe he's doing something noisy and didn't hear."

"We can go back and look for him."

"No, that's okay." She repeated the page. Before the announcement faded, the door opened behind us and a reedy voice said, "I heard you the first time, Esther."

Definite accent, but not chips and ale. Maybe Sweet Home Alabama.

Esther muttered, "He's all yours."

Clive Hatfield wiped blackened hands on a rag not much cleaner than his skin. Early thirties, tall and bowlegged in gray pin-striped coveralls, he had long, lank brown hair tinted brass at the tips, bushy sideburns, a tiny crushed nose. Squinty eyes looked us over while he worked at the grease. As some of the grime relented, I noticed a pallid band of flesh circling his left ring finger.

"Yeah?"

Esther said, "These are the police, here to see you."

"The police—what the . . . this is for real?"

Milo said, "Let's talk outside." Hatfield hesitated, then followed.

We passed near a bright red Continental GT coupe that Hatfield regarded with distaste.

Milo said, "Kind of garish."

Shrug. "It's their money. Where are y'all taking me?"

"Here," said Milo, stopping at the Seville.

Hatfield's face tightened as he checked out my car. "This is a cop drive? What, some sort of undercover thing?" He ran a finger along the top of the Seville's hood, left a gray trail. "GM used a Chevy Two chassis on these, gussied it up and quadrupled the price."

Milo said, "I hear the Bentley Continental's an Audi with interior decorating."

Hatfield stashed the rag in a rear pocket. "You're into wheels? What do y'all drive when you're not working?"

"Porsche 928."

"Not bad for what it was. But give me a Carrera any day."

"Clive, we're here about Katrina Shonsky."

Hatfield brushed hair from his eyes. Grazed his nubby nose in the process, left a greasy dot on the tip. "What about her?"

"When's the last time you saw her?"

"What, she's in trouble?"

"If you could just answer the question."

"The last time . . . so she did get herself in trouble, figures." Hatfield pulled a hard pack of Salems from a side pocket, blew smoke toward the scoop-mouth of a black Aston Martin. "The last time was when she got all dramatic and kicked my ass out of her crib . . . I'd have to say . . . three months ago."

"Lovers' spat?"

"There was never no love," said Hatfield, smiling. "Only you-know-what."

"Physical relationship."

"Just physical, no relationship," said Hatfield. "I picked her up in a bar, we went out a few times. The girl knows how to put on an act. In bed, I mean. Goes all crazy like she's gonna explode. I finally figured out she was faking and told her so. That's when she kicked me out."

"Which bar?"

"Which bar . . ." Hatfield scratched his head.

"Doesn't seem like a real tough question, Clive."

"Me and her went to a bunch a them, can't remember right off. I live in North Hollywood, she's in Van Nuys, but she wanted to drink in Sherman Oaks, Studio City, said it was upscale . . . the first time I'd have to say was at . . . nope, not a bar-bar, the first time was a restaurant, this French-type place . . . Chez Maurice. I was eating a steak and she was at the bar and when I went to the bathroom I saw her ass on the stool and moseyed back. Good-looking girl, the light shined on her hair, making it look all goldy. Small but a great bod. We talked real easy, she went along real easy and just like that we're at her place. A few days later I called her and we started hanging out. But nothing serious."

"How long did you date her?"

"How long . . . I'd have to say two and a half, three months. Then it got you-know-what."

"What?"

"Complicated," said Hatfield. "Lotsa drama, like with all girls. So what'd she do to get herself in trouble?"

"Why would she do anything?"

"The girl has no discipline."

"About what?"

"She drinks too much—crazy Long Island Teas, taste like iced piss. Sometimes she smokes too much you-know-what. Sometimes she packs her nose with too much you-know-what. For me it's one beer, maybe two. I don't get next to that shit."

"Drama and dope," said Milo.

"Y'all would be surprised how many of them are like that." He smoked, waited for a comment that never arrived. "I keep it real. Used to do some racing back in Pass Christian. Gotta keep the reflexes sharp."

"Where's Pass Christian?"

"Mississippi."

"NASCAR?"

"Some Pro Street, some Dixie Sportsman. I can drive in my sleep."

"Katrina overindulges," said Milo. "So maybe her reflexes aren't that great."

"For her," said Hatfield, "it's all about fun. I'm working extra shifts to make my child support and she wants steak and lobster. She thought I was a hillbilly, we never really got along. She's a shitty driver. One time I let her drive my Vette, she nearly stripped the gears, after that no way was she getting near it. When I told her, she got pissed off. What, she get into a smashup in that Mustang of hers and hurt someone?"

"Did she ever visit you here?"

Hatfield removed the filthy rag and passed it from one hand to another. "Maybe."

"Maybe?"

"Yeah, she did."

"How many times?"

"Maybe . . . twice. Yeah, twice, the second time she got me in trouble, marching back into the service bay like she owns it, asking for me. No one goes back there except us specialists."

"Like an operating room," said Milo.

"What?"

"You guys are like doctors working on patients, bosses want to keep it under control."

"You got that, I *am* like a doctor," said Hatfield, holding up blackened hands. "Some of the other guys are more like butchers." Crooked smile. "If the clients knew what went on back there."

"So Katrina dropped in twice."

"Dropped in is exactly right, I never invited her, she just dropped in. The second time she brought me lunch. Some sort of vegan shit, noodles, whatever. I told her forget it."

"By then the relationship was fading."

"There *was* no relationship. Too much drama."

I said, "But for two, three months you put up with it."

"That was 'cause of all the you-know-what. And no way there was ever gonna *be* any relationship because I was married." Massaging the band of pale skin.

I said, "Did your divorce have anything to do with Kat?"

Hatfield laughed. "Hell, no. It had to do with we got married when we were seventeen, had four kids in four years, and got sick as shit of each other. She took 'em all and went back to Columbus."

"She know about Kat?"

"None a her business." He grinned and rubbed a knuckle. "It ain't like Kat was the one and only."

Milo said, "You're a player."

"I work hard, she got nothing to complain," said Hatfield. "Support her and the kids and bust my ass to do it. If I want a little play, no one's gonna tell me different."

"Did you ever meet any of Kat's friends?"

"Nope, and she never met any of mine. It was all—"

"You-know-what."

" 'Zactly." Hatfield dropped his cigarette to the asphalt, ground it out slowly. "You ain't gonna tell me what she did?"

"She's missing."

"Missing? So what? She was always missing."

"What do you mean?"

"I'd booty-call her and she'd be nowhere. Few days later, she'd booty-call me, brag about how she was in Mexico, Hawaii, whatever. Brag about how she met some rich guy and he paid her bills while she was there, she's eating lobster and snow crab and filet mignon and not paying a dime for any of it. When she got like that, I knew it was gonna be trouble."

"How so?"

"She'd be *expecting* shit. Y'all really think something happened to her?"

"She's been gone over a week."

"Big deal. She just gets up and goes."

I said, "Do you ever get to drive the cars?"

"Huh—yeah, all the time, for testing."

"Short spins around the block?"

"Depends on the problem. If the client's claiming there's a brake squeak after he drives it for ten minutes, you got to drive it for ten minutes. Why, y'all want a ride?"

"Did Kat ever ask for a ride?"

Hatfield scratched his head. "Why would she do that?"

I said, "Goes with lobster and filet mignon."

He didn't answer.

I said, "Did she nag you?"

"Why you asking this?"

"She told her friend you drove her around in one of the Bentleys."

Smooth lie; sometimes I surprise myself. Milo turned his head, so Hatfield couldn't see his lips turn up.

Hatfield's squinty eyes showed a little white. "She said that?"

"She sure did."

"Who says she's telling the truth?"

I said, "A girl starts nagging, it can be a pain."

No answer.

Milo said, "Clive?"

Hatfield said, "Why would I admit to that?"

Milo said, "Clive, we couldn't care less about your bosses, we're just trying to get a feel for the type of girl Kat is."

"The type of girl? She's pushy, is what she is. Yeah, she kept nagging on me, pushing that bod against me, telling me what she'd do if I gave her just a little ride pretty please." Raising his voice to an alto whine. "There was one I had to test anyway, so I took her along."

Milo said, "What kind of car was it?"

"Rolls Phantom."

"Not an Arnage?"

"I know the difference, man."

"Was that first time she dropped in or the second?"

"The first time," said Hatfield. "That's why she came *back* the second time."

"Figuring you'd do it again."

"Figuring she owns the place now. Walking straight back and saying where's Clive. Running straight into the service manager."

"The first time she waited out in front?"

"Paged me. Like y'all did. I was busy, took my time getting out. She got pissed. We're alone for a second, she's nagging on me."

I said, "Ever take her for a spin in a Bentley?"

"No, just the Roller."

"Who owned it?"

"They don't tell us that."

"She enjoy the ride?"

"Sure," said Hatfield. "She's all about the green, hooking up with a rich guy, showing up her mother. 'Cause she hates her mother. That's her word, not mine. Stupid."

"What is?"

"Thinking someone's smart because a their drive. Let me tell you what it is: Rich assholes spend all that money to show off and then they get scared and never take the shit outta their garage. It's like I got money and I'm shoving it all up in your face but *uh-oh* now I'm chickenshit someone's gonna notice me and take everything away from my chickenshit self."

Milo laughed.

Hatfield said, "You bet it's funny." He lit up another cigarette. "Y'all find Kat, tell her she can call me if she wants, I'll even pretend she ain't faking it. Been married most of my life so I know about faking."

He moved to leave but Milo held him back, asked the kind of loose, follow-up questions designed to relax. Hatfield got a bit more amiable, told a filthy joke about a woman, a raccoon, and an exhaust pipe. But he had nothing more to say about Kat Shonsky. When Milo asked him where he'd been the night she disappeared, he said, "Usually, I couldn't tell y'all shit about where I am. But lucky for me, this one I know. I was back in Columbus. My older daughter had a birthday."

"When'd you arrive and leave?"

"Y'all don't believe me?"

"Routine question," said Milo. "Help us clear it up and we're outta your hair."

"Awright, awright . . . when'd I arrive . . . hmm . . . got to be the Thursday before y'all say she went partying. Stayed in Columbus for four days and drove to Biloxi to visit my mother. She's in a nursing home, when I'm there I take her to the casino, wheel her chair in front of a machine till she loses all her quarters. Two days after that, I came back here. I'd say check my time card but I don't want no trouble with the bosses so don't screw me, okay? I'm being straight with you."

"Fair enough. Did you happen to hold on to your airline tickets?"

"Why would I?"

"What's your ex's name and phone number?"

"Y'all are serious?"

"Dead serious, Clive."

"Oh, man."

"Do you send cars back with three wheels?"

Hatfield smoothed back his hair, favored us with a gap-toothed grin. "Sure, ask her, she got no reason to lie. Then y'all can tell her how good I'm looking."

"Will do, Clive."

"Make her squirm," said Hatfield. "Tell her y'all saw me with some actress."

"Name and number, Clive."

"Brittany Louise Hatfield. Hold the phone far away from your ear, that girl can get loud."

Milo copied down the information and watched him go. We returned to the front office and showed a picture of Kat Shonsky to Esther.

She studied it for a while. "Can't swear to it but she could be one of them who comes by to see him." Holding the photo closer. "Not bad. Better than some of the others."

"Clive's popular?"

"You wouldn't believe," she said. "They bring him lunch. Guy must have something going on but I don't see it."

I said, "Doesn't appear to be charm."

"Clean hands, either."

I said, "This kind of work, be hard to stay clean."

"Exactly, that's why I'm dating a teacher."

Milo said, "Clive ever ask you out?"

"You've got to be kidding." She returned the photo. "You think he did something to her?"

Milo said, "You see him as capable of that?"

"To me, he's an oaf with a sour personality but he's never lost his temper or done anything aggressive. But I guess anyone's capable of anything. So you do suspect him."

"We're nowhere near that, ma'am. It would be best to keep this conversation under the hat."

She removed her glasses. "I wasn't *planning* on spreading rumors."

"Of course not. So, Clive—"

"Clive's fine," she said. "Everyone here is fine. I'm really busy."

The glass partition slid shut.

11

As I backed out of the lot, a Bentley turned in and blocked my way.

Another black one. Red interior.

I rolled forward.

The Bentley didn't budge.

Milo stuck his head out and said, "Give us some space."

The driver's window opened and a blue-shirted man stuck his head out and shouted, "Can't you read? Customers only, dude!"

Milo said, "Ah the travails of the alpha male," got out, had a thirty-second chat with the shouter. By the time he was back in the Seville, the stunned driver had given me plenty of room.

I said, "Making friends and influencing people," and turned onto Pico.

"If I had Clive's natural charm, I could've gotten a free lunch. How do you figure?"

"I guess there could be a certain rough appeal."

"Rough enough for him to hurt Kat Shonsky?"

"He doesn't like women," I said, "and this particular woman dumped him."

"With his wife and kids gone, he's lonely, maybe gets horny and remembers how driving around in fancy wheels was a big thrill for Kat, why not try it again?"

I said, "He claims he doesn't know the customers but all he'd have to do is read a work order to learn Heubel's address. And if he actually tinkered with Heubel's car, he could've known about the spare key in the wheel well."

"Hell," he said, "he could have a master key. So you like him."

"On the negative side, he bears no resemblance to Ella Mancusi's killer. And there is the matter of that alibi."

He found Brittany Hatfield's number in Mississippi and punched it. "Hi, is your mom there? A friend from California. Yes, Cali—Mrs. Hatfield? This is Lieutenant Sturgis of the Los Angeles Police Department. No, I'm sorry, it's not about that . . . I see. I'll do what I can but, first off, could you tell me . . ."

He did a lot of listening, ended up holding the phone away from his ear. "Clive was right about her being surround sound. And she's got reason to yell, seems the prince has a bad-check problem. As in three straight months of child support bouncing. She put in for a wage garnish, that's what she thought I was calling about. Unfortunately, she does verify that he was in Mississippi when he says he was. Stayed with her and the kids until he 'went off to Biloxi to see that *insane bitch mother of his.*' "

He stretched his legs. "Back to nowhere at warp speed."

Memos and message slips blanketed his desk. Public Affairs had called to inform him that Ella Mancusi's murder might be on the news tonight, he needed to be available for comments if necessary. Sean Binchy had phoned twice, no message. Gordon Beverly wanted to know if any progress had been made on Antoine.

I said, "Sixteen years, it's still fresh for them. But Tony, with a brand-new loss, hasn't called to ask about Mom."

"Funny thing 'bout that?" He phoned the cop watching Mancusi, confirmed a clear pattern: The subject stayed in his apartment all day, emerged late afternoon for the brief drive to the same food stand, ate a burrito in his car, littered, returned home.

Sean had taken the initiative to canvass the block of Villa Entrada where the Bentley had been abandoned. No neighbor had seen or heard a thing, no one was aware of any juvenile delinquents in the neighborhood prone to GTA.

No sign of Kat Shonsky's Mustang.

He played with Gordon Beverly's slip. "I'm starting to feel like a family counselor. At least Kat's mother hasn't gotten past her denial yet."

"She might if you asked her for a blood sample."

"Mitochondrial match to the blood in the Bentley? Let's see how the initial request is doing."

He logged on to the New Jersey lab's site. "Still way at the back of the line and without a confirmed felony, it's gonna stay there. Okay, time to disappoint the Beverlys."

I said, "I still don't understand why Texas doesn't pressure Jackson to be specific before you waste all this time."

"Because it's not about logical or ethical, Alex. It's politics." He swung a big foot onto the desk. Papers scattered and fell to the floor. He made no attempt to pick them up. Unwrapped a cigarillo and bit down hard. Wood splintered. He inspected the shattered tip, tossed the whole thing into the trash. Yanking a drawer open, he pulled out a thin blue folder. "Let's give Antoine's buddies another try."

Repeat call to Bradley Maisonette's parole officer, same voice mail, same message. St. Xavier High informed him that Mr. Good was out ill. Rather than try to wheedle Good's personal data out of the receptionist, he ran a vehicle check.

"Two-year-old gray Ford Explorer, address on North Broadmoor Terrace." He thumbed through his Thomas Guide. "Up in the hills, near the Bowl. Time to pay a sick call."

His desk phone jangled. What he heard on the other end made him button his jacket and tighten the knot of his tie. Checked his shoelaces, rolled his shoulders, gave off the tiniest wince, stood.

I said, "Sudden meeting downtown?"

He stared at me.

"You went all appearance-conscious."

"Mr. Wizard. Yeah, yeah, the chief wants to schmooze, I'm to be at his office before it's physically feasible."

"What's the topic?"

"Pending cases," he said. "His Righteousness probably got media calls on Mancusi or Beverly or both, doesn't want to sound uninformed."

"Have fun," I said.

"Real chuckle-fest . . . you have a problem talking to Wilson Good by yourself?"

"Not unless it violates procedure."

"Psychologically sensitive case like Antoine?" he said. "A shrink's deft touch is clearly called for. Also, the chief likes you, so he'd approve."

"When did that come up?"

"Last time he summoned me. Seems he read that paper you published last spring, agrees that most profiling is bullshit."

"The chief reads psych journals?"

"The chief has a master's in psych. He suggested you should be on the payroll. I told him the department wasn't economically competitive."

He quoted the pay scale.

I said, "Thank you, sir."

"Always looking out for your interests. Say hi to Coach Good. Maybe you can get tips on passing and rushing."

"I played baseball in high school."

"What position?"

"Utility outfielder," I said. "Wherever they needed me."

. . .

Wilson Good's house was one of five crisp one-stories edging a dead-end street above the Hollywood Bowl's cheap seats. What brokers call "midcentury architectural," as if the fifties is a leper decade.

Close enough to the amphitheater to hear music on warm summer nights. The rest of the view was trees and brush and ozone-depleted sky.

Good's house was peach stucco where it wasn't redwood siding. The gray Explorer and a green VW Passat sat on a pebble-grain slab behind a full-width electric mesh gate.

I pushed the button on the call box, listened to the doorbell chime the first few notes of Pachelbel's Canon. A mockingbird hopped from a bottlebrush tree onto a honeysuckle hedge. Off in the distance, ravens played politics. And always, the auto hum; the freeway was the real L.A. philharmonic.

Before setting out I'd found a picture of Wilson Good on the Web. Victory party after a title game. Thick-necked, good-looking man with sad eyes that seemed at odds with the celebration.

Maybe a sensitive guy. Maybe he wouldn't mind my waking him from a sickbed.

I rang again, was contemplating a third attempt when a woman came walking up Broadmoor trailing something tiny and brown. The animal tugged and leaped and strained a spaghetti-strap leash. The woman trotted to catch up.

I guessed Chihuahua and I was wrong; this was the smallest dachshund I'd ever seen, surging and charging, head-down, like a bratwurst on a mission.

The woman was brown-haired and freckled, wore a green top the same color as the Passat, skinny black pants, black shoes. Thirties, five five, with long legs and commodious hips.

The dog surged to the end of a long leash. Developed an instant lust for my left shoe.

The woman said, "Stop, Indy," without much conviction, got her wrist yanked, fought to hold her ground.

I said, "Indy as in the big race?"

"His engine never turns off." She scooped the dog into her arms, wrestled with the squirming bundle. When Indy finally calmed, the woman looked at Wilson Good's house. Moss-green eyes. Soft color, hard appraisal.

She said, "Anything I can help you with?"

I brought out my LAPD consultant's badge. Long expired and pretty dinky, but few people bother to check. The freckled woman remained too far back to read the details, though Indy was itching for a try.

"I'm looking for Mr. Good."

"I'm Andrea. His wife." As if she wasn't sure. "What do you need with Will?"

"Fifteen years ago he had a friend named Antoine Beverly who—"

"Of course. Antoine." Indy began making gremlin noises, renewed his battle against confinement. Andrea Good gave up and lowered him to the ground. "Will and Antoine were friends since preschool. What happened to Antoine is the saddest thing Will's ever experienced. But he doesn't know anything that would help the police."

"You're sure of that."

"Of course I am. Have the police finally learned something?"

"The case has just been reopened. Could you ask your husband if he can spare me a few minutes?"

"The police send psychologists out on old cases?"

"On specific cases. If I—"

"I'm sure Will would love to help," she said, "but it's not a good time. He's got a nasty flu and a couple of big games coming up. Leave me your number."

"The detective on the case has already called—"

"Has he? I'll have to check the machine. Will's been pretty out of it. High fever, not like him at all, but there's stuff going around the school."

Choking protest from below caught our attention.

Indy reared on his hind legs, forelegs pumping air, eyes bulging.

Semi-suspended, with the leash pulling up on his throat. Andrea Good's hand had drawn up on the cord.

She said, "Oh, no!" and relaxed her grip. Indy dropped down, panting. She kneeled. "I'm so sorry, baby."

Indy gave out one last yelp of protest and kissed her face.

Unconditional faith and love; maybe one day the Vatican will start canonizing canines.

"Anyway," said Andrea Good, rising to her feet.

I said, "We'd appreciate hearing from your husband. Hope he heals up quickly."

"Oh, he will. He's a tough guy."

CHAPTER

12

Ella Mancusi's murder didn't make the six o'clock news but it was the final segment at eleven p.m., complete with pompous baritone narration and close-ups of a blood-soaked knife blade taken from stock footage.

The toll-free tip line flashed for a second, but that was enough. When I called Milo's office the next morning, I got a brand-new message.

"This is Lieutenant Sturgis. If you're calling about the Mancusi homicide, please leave your name and phone number. Talk slowly and clearly. Thank you."

I phoned Wilson Good, hoping a chat with his wife, bed rest, and civic duty might have loosened his tongue. No one answered.

Blanche was up for a walk and bounced along happily as we headed down the glen. Squirrels, birds, and cars amused her. Trees amused her. Rocks were hilarious.

A sinewy woman jogger paused to pet her. "That's the prettiest dog I've ever seen."

Blanche agreed.

At one p.m., Robin and I drove to Sherman Oaks and ate spaghetti at Antonio's. Afterward, I asked if she could spare some time and we headed over to Katrina Shonsky's address in Van Nuys.

Big-box complex on a treeless block. The air smelled of construction dust though no projects were in sight. All the charm of a heat rash.

Robin said, "I can see why she'd want to get away from this. Not that living in thirty rooms on twenty acres helps, if you're lonely."

"Thinking of someone in particular?"

She nodded. "He's coming to town on business in a week or so. In between appointments, he intends to drop by to 'visit my commission.' It's not that big of a deal but if you could be there, I wouldn't mind."

"He was inappropriate?"

"No, but when he talks to me he sounds so needy. Like he wants to get close—know what I mean?"

"An agenda behind the commission."

"Maybe it's silly," she said.

"Conceited girl."

She smiled. "So you'll be there?"

She returned to her studio and I thought awhile about Ella Mancusi and Kat Shonsky. Could see no solid link beyond big black stolen cars.

I played with search engines, pairing variants of *homicide* and *luxury car.* When that came up empty, I substituted *murder.* Still, zero.

I began combining *murder* with specific automobile marques, went through *Jaguar, Rolls-Royce, Ferrari,* and *BMW,* with no luck.

Lamborghini and *Cadillac* pulled up a pair of shootings, one in L.A., the other in New York. Two gangsta rappers gunned down leaving late-night recording sessions, one alone in his Murciélago, the other caravanning with an entourage in a tricked-out Escalade. Officially, both cases were unsolved. But everyone in the hip-hop world knew whodunit.

Bentley and *Aston Martin* came up empty. *Mercedes* elicited nothing about Ella Mancusi, probably because of the lack of media coverage—and that made me question the value of the search. *Benz* produced photos of Hitler in both of his massive 770Ks and a rant from a Qatar-based blogger who believed *Der Fuhrer* had been a misunderstood "cool guy everyone thinks is a murder."

I typed in *Lincoln,* not expecting much.

So much for my powers of prediction.

Double homicide, nine years ago, in Ojo Negro, a struggling agricultural hamlet north and inland of Santa Barbara. The case had been logged on DarkVisions.net, a borderline-literate Web site that delighted in listing gruesome, unsolved killings and posted crude cartoons and grainy photos cribbed from true-crime books.

The facts, as recounted by the site's "*soal author and webmaster, DV Zapper,*" were spare and brutal: Leonora Bright, owner of the only beauty parlor in Ojo Negro, and Vicki Tranh, her resident manicurist, had been murdered sometime after closing the shop, their bodies found the following morning "*multipally stabbed,*" and "*maybe disamenbered.*"

A black Lincoln Town Car had been parked near the shop just before dusk. A tall man in a floor-length canvas duster and ten-gallon hat had been seen earlier in the day. Exiting the car, walking past the salon, driving off.

The car was later identified as a rental, stolen from a hotel parking lot in Santa Barbara.

Cowboys were no novelty in Ojo Negro; several nearby cattle ranches struggled against Big Agribusiness. But the stranger's swagger and the costume-like getup attracted glances.

"*Pale Rider,*" the site tagged him. "*And in Wilde West days, the Detroit beast could probably a been a cole-black stalleon.*"

The morning after the sighting, a parcel-service driver delivering nail polish and "*other cosmetic items made a stomach chorning discovery.*"

"*What I wonder,*" mused DV Zapper, "*is was Leona was married and maybe Vicki also and if yeah why didn't there husbands go looking for them the hole time?"*

I ran a search using the victims' names.

Only one story, printed in *The Santa Barbara Express* a week after the murder. Two new facts: The car had been stolen at the Wharf Inn. And: "Sheriff Wendell Salmey is currently talking to Santa Barbara detectives."

Googling *Salmey* evoked zero hits and the computer's suggestion that I really meant *Wendell Salmon.* Just to be safe, I said I did and got connected to the Web site of a Washington State Fish and Game booklet for children.

I printed the newspaper text, returned to DarkVisions, clicked the bloody knife *contact* icon, and inquired if anything new had come up on the case.

Within seconds, I had a reply.

hey alex jason blasco here aka DV ZAPPER aka the mannnn. no
there is shit the cops don't wanna talk maybe its prejustice or something tranh was veetnamise you know????? if you hear something
you can post with me

Googling *Jason Blasco* brought up a similarly misspelled MySpace page.

I'd just corresponded with a gawky, dark-haired, fourteen-year-old, self-described *"genius wizard gore-geek"* who lived in Minneapolis and liked AC/DC *"even tho theyr older then anteeks and have shit drumming."*

I asked him how he'd heard about the Ojo Negro case.

they were in a magzine one a those thrilling detectives or some shit
    is in a big pile
ebay???
don do that shit this is slo lets im
sorry no buddy list

kidding

sorry

sucks dude

so that magazine . . .

you like that shit????

if the stories are good

i like it when they find the guy and xecute

yeah that's better

got tons a that shit you can buy it if you want thrilling det shocking
    det

how much

five bucks each

think about it

take or leaf

take

send cash dude no paypal yet

I asked for an address. He was ready with a P.O.B.
Ah, enterprising youth.

where are you alex geographic i mean

l.a.

cool manson nightstalker original and ramirez skid row slasher
    maybe even zodiac went down there not just san francsco

yeah hows minnesota

sucks send cash if you want fedex give me a number

snail mails ok

if you don mine slime trail gotta go

Milo phoned at seven p.m.

"Lots of tips?" I said.

"Think Noah looking out the window of the ark. One anonymous caller claims Tony Mancusi is 'kinky.' The rest is psychics and psychotics. I'm halfway through the pile and Gordon Beverly drops by.

Nice man, he tried the friends himself, no luck. You do any better with Good?"

I described my meeting with Andrea and Indy.

He said, "Gets rattled and nearly strangles the dog. Interesting."

"I thought so."

"So now we have to look at respectable Mr. Good more closely." He laughed. "You'd think people would get smart. Open the door, smile, lie pleasantly, we all move on."

"Criminals think that way," I said. "Average folk can get spooked."

"Average folk with something to hide. Okay, I'll pursue Mr. Good once I make some headway on Mancusi."

"Want me to go back to Good's house tonight?"

"No, big game coming up, guy's not going anywhere. Let him simmer for a while. Even if I wanted to bug him, my night's spoken for. One of my rookies was pulled off surveillance, I'll be the one eyeballing Tony Mancusi in an hour."

"Time for strong coffee."

"Strong and bitter. Like *moi*. Talk to you tomorrow, Alex."

"One more thing."

"Is this gonna make me smile or cringe?"

"Could go either way." I told him about the Ojo Negro murders and the DarkVisions Web site.

He said, "Fourteen-year-old gore freak. And a child shall lead."

"Maybe this child led us to something serious. Stolen black luxury wheels lifted from a rental lot, a suspect in cowboy gear. Which is all anyone noticed about him. Dusting your hair with white powder, wearing a garish plaid cap, and shuffling would accomplish the same thing. So would driving a flashy car, for that matter."

"Costumes," he said. "Art of the misdirect. Ojo Negro, huh? Never heard of the place. Nine years ago . . . talk about your extended run, you know what I'm thinking."

"If it's connected, there could be more in between. No other black-car murders came up but Ella's not logged in, so the Web's far from perfect."

"True. I'm not sure what this does for my mood . . . okay, first things first, gotta pack my mule, get over to 7-Eleven, stock up on grub and caffeine. You up for some bucolic travel? With time and mileage reimbursed, as granted by The Supreme Being?"

"God wants to pay me?"

"The chief," he said. "Same difference."

"How'd your meeting go?"

"Steely eyes, firm grip, he pumped me for progress, pretended not to be pissed when I told him there was none. But that Irish face of his gets all rosy around the edges. Then, out of the blue, he asks me if you're consulting to any of it. I say all of it, when you've got time. He says what does that mean. I say given what the department pays, you've got other fish to fry. He goes *real* rosy. Embarks on a tirade about how the department's stuck somewhere between Mesozoic and Jurassic, it's time to modernize, we need serious psychological input not whore-shrinks out to stigmatize officers. I try to get a word in edgewise about the financial end but when he gets like that, there's no interrupting. So basically, the meeting ended up being about you."

"Gee," I said. "Better soak my head in ice before it swells out of control."

"For that, all you need is to see the salary scale he proposed. Thirty percent additional allowance for gas and mileage but the hourly's still penury. I'm supposed to set up a billing account, you're supposed to keep meticulous records. Neither of which will be done because we've got real work. But can you see clear to hit the road anyway?"

"Hmm," I said.

"Thanks. And don't forget to eat. Thirty percent more gets you to 1965 prices."

"Twinkies and Flavo-straws it is."

"There you go," he said. "Brain food."

13

The Santa Ynez Valley lolls between two mountain ranges, soaking up sun and grace. Blessed with shirtsleeve temperatures and vine-coated slopes, the region's been mistaken for Eden. Where grapes don't grow, apples flourish. Hills are soft-focus and gentle and so is the ocean breeze that tempers the morning. Tourists flock to the valley for wine, food, antiques, horses, and fantasies of what could be if only.

Most of the towns that dot the region—Solvang, Buellton, Ballard, Los Olivos—flourish under the attention.

Then there's Ojo Negro, named after a ragged-edged black eye of abandoned lime quarry.

Set on an inhospitable triangle of aquifer-neglected dirt just south of where the 101 aims for Los Alamos, Ojo Negro once served as a highway rest stop. Prosperity had its drawbacks: pedestrians pulverized by semis, the kind of mischief inspired by transience. But people made a living. When the highway was rerouted a few miles north, Ojo Negro died.

So had Wendell Salmey, the sheriff who'd investigated the Bright-

Tranh murders nine years ago. Milo had found out by checking a law enforcement database. He'd also set up an eleven a.m. appointment for me with George Cardenas, the new sheriff.

"Don't expect too much, Alex. Guy's been on the job eighteen months. If you can nose around, great. Maybe you'll find some lonely soul who craves conversation."

Ojo Negro didn't show up on any of my road maps so I turned to an online service. The route summary warned of an unmarked exit 4.3 miles past Baca Station Road.

At ten p.m., Milo called again. Sitting in his car, three hours into surveillance, watching nothing happen at Tony Mancusi's apartment.

I said, "Craving conversation?"

"Craving my own pulse. I just got hold of the Santa Barbara Sheriff's detective who worked Bright-Tranh with Salmey. He told me the case was an unclosable whodunit from day one. But he's retired and bored so he'll do you a favor and meet with you. Donald Bragen, lives in Buellton. Used to be a sergeant, sounds like a guy who still digs the title. He's flying up this afternoon to Seattle, catching a puddle-jumper to Alaska for a fishing trip. If you get to Santa Barbara by nine, he'll have breakfast with you at Moby Dick on Stearn's Wharf."

"I'll bring my harpoon."

"Ciao. Back to my Red Bull and burrito."

"You and Tony dig the same cuisine?"

"Not only that, the same greasy spoon," he said.

"Empathy?"

"Cultured palates."

I set out the following morning at seven a.m., endured the commuter crush from Encino to Thousand Oaks, got a little careless with speed limits when I cleared Camarillo, and was nearing Santa Barbara by eight forty. A few miles before the Cabrillo exit, Milo phoned to let me know Donald Bragen had caught an earlier flight and canceled breakfast.

I said, "No desire to talk about old failures?"

"Or the salmon decided to show up early, self-deluded bastards."

"The fish?"

"Leaping upstream as if someone's gonna be impressed."

Now I was thirty miles beyond the beach town's city limits, past where the 101 hooks inland and north and any notion of blue water vanishes. The Baca Station Road exit wasn't much of anything. The unmarked turnoff was closer to six miles up. A bloodhound could've missed it.

Bumping along a carelessly maintained road, I sped through a cottonwood grove that ended as abruptly as a Hollywood marriage. The view on both sides was straw-colored, waist-high wild grass and a scattering of gray, twisted tree trunks. To the north, the Santa Ynez range showed a bit of skin but kept its distance, like an ambivalent starlet.

The old lime pit came into view and I slowed to have a look. Chain link hung with warped panels of corrugated plastic concealed most of the excavation but through gaps in the plastic I could see a dark maw. Skull-and-crossbones warning signs established a friendly ambience. As I started to drive away, movement caught my eye.

A mangy coyote slinked off into the grass, ruffling the blades, then disappearing.

It took a few cottonwood clumps and a lot more nothing before the grass gave way to an unattended junkyard and a bird-specked green sign proclaiming Ojo Negro to be ALT. 231 FT. POP. 927.

Half a mile later, I spotted a thin, black-haired woman walking along the side of the road, carrying a large metal cage. Using both hands to lug and keeping her back to me. The wrong way to do it.

The sound of my engine made her turn but she kept going toward an old brown jeep parked ten yards up.

I rolled to a stop and lowered the passenger window. She turned sharply, held the cage in front of her. Spring-latched animal trap, heavy enough to drag at her shoulders. Brown stains coated the bottom grid.

"You need something?" Early twenties, Latina, wearing a white western shirt, jeans, boots. Thick, shiny hair was tied back tight from a wide, smooth brow. She had gold-brown eyes, a strong nose, thin lips. Exceptionally pretty woman; all angles, like a raptor.

"I'm looking for Sheriff Cardenas."

The trap lowered a bit. "Just keep going. He's in town."

"How far's town?"

"Right around the first turn."

"Thanks."

"Are you that doctor from L.A.?"

"Alex Delaware."

She said, "He's expecting you."

"You work for him?"

She smiled. "I'm his sister, Ricki."

I held out my hand.

"You don't want to touch me after I touched this."

"What'd you catch?"

"Another ca-yote. One of the senior citizens George looks after has them messing with her garbage but she still won't get cans that shut tight. She's eighty-nine, so when she hears noise or finds scat, she calls George. It's animal reg's job, but try getting them out here."

"You volunteer?"

"I'm visiting for a week, nothing much else to do." She hefted the trap. "It was a little baby ca-yote, real scared, made pathetic noises."

"I just saw a larger one near the lime pit."

"They're all over the place."

"We get 'em in L.A.," I said. "Clever little rascals."

"Not so clever they won't walk into a trap full of cat food. George gets everything here. Bobcats, raccoons, rattlesnakes. He's had reports of mountain lions but hasn't seen one yet. Anyway, I need to clean up. George is in his office. You can follow me."

Stashing the trap in the jeep, she drove off. The turn was half a mile up. Rounding it revealed a main drag named Ojo Negro Avenue, fishboned by diagonal parking spaces. Four vehicles for two dozen slots. Three pickups and a white Bronco with a cherry on top.

Ricki pointed to the left and kept driving. The road swooped upward toward a hill of dirt and a couple of struggling sycamores. I pulled in next to the Bronco.

The sidewalks were cracked and sunken, weeds taking advantage of loose seams. Most of the storefronts were dark. Some were boarded.

The active businesses were a white cinderblock cube painted with *Ojo Negro Sheriff* in block lettering that tried too hard, a parrot-green stucco bar tagged *The Limelite,* a dry-goods/grocery store doing additional duty as an insurance broker and a U.S. post office, a beauty salon/barbershop with faded headshots in the window, and the O.N. Feed Bin graced by a *Support Our Troops* banner.

The weekly specials at the bin were oats and hay and live breeder rabbits from "Belgium, Europe."

In the sheriff's office, a young, completely bald man in khakis sat at a PC keyboard. Behind him was a one-room jail as clean as his head. The walls were papered with the usual wanted posters, bulletins, and safety pitches. Cinderblock made an inhospitable bed for tape, and some of the papers had curled loose.

"Dr. Delaware? George Cardenas."

"Morning, Sheriff."

This sibling shook heartily and smiled without reservation. His skin was clear like his sister's, his eyes the same gold-brown. But his face was round and soft, with none of that falcon-alertness. Baby-face; the lack of head hair did little to age him. "Coffee?"

"Black, thanks."

Cardenas poured both of us Styrofoam cups, dosed his with Coffee-mate, and motioned me to sit. "You're a little early."

"My previous appointment canceled."

"Detective Bragen changed his mind, huh?"

"You know him?"

"Talked to him for the first time this morning. I figured he might do that."

"Why's that?"

"Talking about the case made him kind of annoyed. He called it a loser from the git-go, like he didn't want to churn it up."

Beside his computer was a short stack of paper. He peeled off the top sheet and handed it over.

Sheriff Wendell Salmey's summary of the Bright-Tranh murders.

I learned a few facts DV Zapper hadn't reported: The name of Leonora Bright's salon had been Stylish Lady. She'd been thirty-three at the time of her death. Vicki Tranh, a recent arrival from Anaheim, had been only nineteen. No disruption of the store, other than two dead bodies and lots of blood. Both women were left with jewelry on their persons, and a day's worth of cash remained in the register, ruling out robbery.

Salmey's spelling was better than the kid's, but not by much.

George Cardenas said, "That's all there is."

He brushed imaginary dust from his trousers. "When I took the job, all of Sheriff Salmey's files were in boxes in a storage facility in Los Alamos. I started going through them, trying to get a feel for the town. Mostly, he dealt with small stuff—apples stripped from a tree, lost dog, once in a while a domestic. He was in favor of diplomacy rather than enforcement."

"Going easy on the locals?"

Cardenas's thumb hooked at the jail cell. "Folks tell me about the only time that got used was if a transient needed to sleep off a drunk. Sheriff's wife died eleven years ago, then his son a year after, traffic accident on the 101 near Buellton. Sheriff pretty much curled up after that."

"Ten years ago is right before the murders," I said. "You're thinking he wasn't in high gear."

Cardenas sat back and crossed his legs. "I don't want to talk ill of the dead, everyone says Sheriff was a great guy. But Ojo Negro since the highway moved is pretty much an oil painting. I don't mind, but it's not for everyone."

"You like the quiet."

"Sometimes I do get a little antsy and call my sister, ask her to drop in for a spell—we're twins, she's a nurse at Cottage Hospital in S.B., gets good vacation time. But mostly I'm working, so the quiet's perfect."

"Working on cases?"

He eyed his computer. "This is gonna sound stupid, but I write. Or at least try to."

"Fiction?"

Averting his face, he talked to a fire alert poster. "Started with short stories then I read in some writer's magazine that there's no market for them, so I'm trying a novel. Haven't started yet, still working on finding what they call my point of view."

"Police novel?"

"Depends what comes out once I get the story set in my head," he said. "I was a double major at U. New Mexico. English and criminal justice, couldn't figure out what I liked more, so I decided to get some police experience, maybe I'd have something to say in a book. Did a couple years with the state police, then Ojo Negro came up, they hadn't had a sheriff in five years, got a two-year state grant to fund one. My sister and her kids aren't too far and she's divorced and her ex is out of the picture. I figured maybe I could be a good influence." Shrug. "Seemed like a good opportunity."

"I've talked to a couple of detectives at Santa Fe P.D. Steve Katz and Darrell Two Moons."

"Know 'em by sight but never worked with 'em. Mostly I was in Albuquerque, doing gang suppression. That got me close to a couple of homicides, I watched the pros, learned it's not my cup of tea. Unfortunately, I'm not going to be able to help you much on this one. That one sheet's all I found."

"Is there anyone I could speak to who was here nine years ago?"

"Just about everyone still living in Ojo Negro was here nine years ago. Most of my people are seniors who don't want to or can't afford to leave. The grocery store brews fresh soup when there's enough demand and the big day is when the Social Security checks come in."

"Anyone you'd recommend to start with?"

His legs uncrossed. "Lieutenant Sturgis really thinks this could be related to an L.A. case?"

"Hard to say. The main link is a stolen black car."

"Mercedes and Bentley, yeah, he told me. The original GTA filing on the Lincoln is under Santa Barbara's jurisdiction 'cause the car was taken there. I checked and it's archived. All I could find is a basic theft-recovery report. By the time the tags were linked to that Clint Eastwood–type loiterer, the vehicle had been cleaned and rerented, had over a hundred new miles on it. No probable cause to examine it, so that was that. In terms of people who might remember, I asked around, and, sure, anyone with a working memory recalls the case. This was the first homicide in forty years. But no one has any details about the loiterer beyond tall white male, long coat, cowboy hat. And I can't find anyone who actually saw him."

"Mysterious stranger."

"We don't get too many visitors and I doubt nine years ago was any different 'cause that's still after the highway reroute. There's nothing really connecting this individual to the crime other than his hanging around and no one knowing him."

"The coat and the hat could've been a disguise," I said.

"I guess."

"Any way he could've been a local?"

"No way, Doctor. This is a real small town."

He sipped his coffee. "Hate to say it, but the whole thing sounds pretty frozen to me. Maybe I'll make up an ending and put it in my book."

"Beats reality," I said.

He tapped his keyboard. "What *you* do sounds interesting. Maybe I could pick your brain sometime."

"Sure. I noticed a salon on this side of the street. Was that originally Leonora Bright's place?"

"Nope, Cozy Coiffure replaced something else—restaurant, I think. The Ramirez family runs that place. Estella and Ramon, no kids. They moved here from Ventura three years after Leonora got murdered. Took that long for the town to get anyone, running ads in other towns' papers. Before that, folks had to drive to Los Alamos to get trimmed. The crime scene was the last store as you leave town. Want to have a look? I could use a stretch."

We left the office and crossed the street. I asked him about Ojo Negro local government.

He said, "No mayor, no city council, we just rely on the county. Basically our issues are county issues, we're kind of a stepchild to Los Alamos or anyone else who'll have us."

"How many residents?"

"Sign says a thousand but it's much less. I'd guess two hundred, tops. The way we're going, soon there'll be nothing left—okay, here we are."

He'd stopped in front of one of the boarded storefronts. Original pink stucco peeked through the flaking cocoa-brown repaint, patchy and florid, like a skin disease.

"Who owns it?"

"Condemned by the county, county never got around to auctioning it, no one seems to want it."

A key lock slotted the doorknob. Cardenas turned the knob and the door swung open.

I said, "It's never locked?"

"Sure it is," he said. "But it's not much of a lock. I got it open this morning with a nail file. Go ahead in."

What remained of Stylish Lady was vacant space walled in warped panels of fake rosewood tongue-and-groove, darkened by the plywood window and filthy oilcloth shades concealing a high rear window.

Cardenas stayed in front, propping the door open with his body. "Otherwise it shuts and you're in a cave."

I thanked him and explored. Below the high window, the back door was hollow and flimsy. My footsteps were soft pads. Concrete floors created a great sound baffle. I thought of two woman savaged, their cries unheard.

In bad movies, detective savants learn volumes revisiting long-dormant crime scenes. This was dim, dead space and I wasn't producing a single syllable.

"Where does the back door lead?"

"Kind of an alley. Go look."

Behind the shop was a ribbon of rocky dirt that paralleled Ojo Negro Avenue, barely wide enough for one car. Dead end to the south, exit to the north.

I went back inside and returned to Cardenas. "The assumption was that Leonora had closed for the day, was cleaning up."

"Makes sense," he said.

"With the town being so quiet, she'd have no reason to lock up until she left."

"People still don't lock up, Doctor. Last year, right after I got here, a bobcat waltzed right into Mrs. Wembley's house, managed to get in her fridge and ate a whole bunch of tuna salad. She's eighty-nine, try changing her."

"She the lady with the coyote?"

"How do you know about that?"

"Met your sister driving in. She'd just released a coyote trapped on an eighty-nine-year-old woman's property."

"Where'd Ricki release the darn thing?"

"Couple of miles out of town."

"Meaning it'll come right back." He shrugged. "Up to me, I'd shoot it. Ricki's one of those animal rights activists. Yeah, that's Mrs. Wembley. Critters like her 'cause she's always got open food around."

"Is she one of the people you talked to this morning?"

"Nope, she was napping on her porch when I came by to get the trap and that woman can sleep. We can go over to her place, if you like. Lady's got opinions on just about everything."

"My kind of gal."

"My ex was like that," he said. "First you think it's challenging. Then you get tired of being challenged."

I laughed.

He said, "Ricki and I got divorced three months apart. Our parents split up when we were nine and now our younger brother's making sounds like he's about had it. Guess marrying's not our talent—if there's nothing else, I'm gonna close up, Doctor."

We got into his Bronco; he U-turned and headed up the road his sister had taken past the town's center. We came to a scatter of residences, mostly prefabs and trailers set on blocks.

No one in sight but Cardenas drove slowly, looking everywhere, the way cops do.

"So," he said, "any ideas from seeing the scene?"

"Just how easy it would've been, especially after dark."

"How so?"

"The killer could've come in through either door and gone out the back. Anyone develop a theory about who the main target was?"

"You mean Bright versus Tranh? Not that I heard. I've been assuming it was Bright, because the stranger was white, not Asian, and most nuts kill within their race. But maybe that's limited thinking."

"Any idea why Vicki moved here?"

He smiled. "You mean of all the godforsaken places how'd she find Ojo Negro? I couldn't tell you. We do get immigrants from time to time, mostly Spanish. With all the surrounding ranches and vineyards, it's kind of perfect for someone who wants to work hard and doesn't want to be looked at too closely."

"By who?"

"The INS, for one. Take the Ramirezes. When they got here, they barely spoke English but is anyone checking their El Salvador visas or whichever? They cut hair real well, everyone's happy they're here." Cupping smooth, bronze cranial skin. "Not that I'm an expert."

He turned the wheel easily, drove up a packed-earth driveway, pointed to a double-wide set well back from the road and preceded by an acre of weeds. "This is Mrs. Wembley's place—and there she is, looking bright-eyed and bushy-tailed."

CHAPTER

14

The trailer was shaded by an aluminum awning. As we rolled
forward, a rotund pink form in an armchair looked up. At
ten feet away, a mouth opened in a strawberry-pudding face and a
magazine waved.

"Put some speed on, George. You're the law, no one's going to
cite you."

Cardenas said, "Don't want to churn up your dirt, Mrs. Wembley."

"Churn away," she said. "Maybe something'll grow."

We parked, made our way through dead brush. Mrs. Wembley remained in her chair. A pink *Las Vegas: Fun Fun Fun!!!* sweatshirt
matched her complexion. Gray sweatpants strained to package her
thighs. Her feet dangled an inch above the porch boards. The rest of
her body overflowed the confines of the chair.

As Cardenas began the introductions, she broke in, flashing a
denture grin. "I'm Mavis, Missus was my mother-in-law and we don't
want to remember her with anything but unpleasantness."

Pudgy fingers gripped mine and squeezed hard.

She said, "You're a cute one."

"Thank you, ma'am."

"George is cute, too. That's why I make sure critters visit, so I get to see my knight in khaki armor—this time you sent your sister, George. Is it my breath?"

"Ricki had some time—"

"Just kidding, Galahad. So serious. So tell me, that ca-yote was something, huh? Vicious teeth. Where'd she let it go?"

"Far enough."

"I think she resents me for calling you all the time."

She smoothed pleated white hair, tweaked a bulbous nose. Her cheeks glowed, smooth as a child's. Fat's a great wrinkle filler.

Cardenas said, "Of course she doesn't."

Mavis Wembley said, "She most *certainly* does," and massaged an arm of her throne. The chair was slip-covered in blue-and-white duck cloth, like something from a Hamptons pictorial. Everything else on the porch was tubular aluminum and plastic straps.

"New upholstery?" said Cardenas.

Mavis Wembley slapped her magazine against a dimpled knee. "Like it?"

"Very pretty."

"Pottery Barn, George. Love those catalogs, the whole world opens up to you. Especially suited for living in a metropolis like this one."

Another slap of the magazine. *The New Yorker.*

Cardenas said, "Didn't know you subscribe."

"I don't," she said. "They sent me one of those special offers. Four free months and then you can cancel, no charge. I figured to cancel but now I'm not sure. They tend to go on too long—don't you be like that when you write your book, George, the key is to communicate not to pontificate. But they do have some interesting tidbits. This one has a story about a New York Jew who sews fur coats for those Negro rappers. All those agitators screaming about cruelty to critters but this Jew keeps making ermine sweatshirts and the like. A man with *backbone.*"

Cardenas said, "Keep leaving food out, Mavis, and we can send him a bunch of skins."

"Nice little ca-yote coat for the rappers." She cackled. "Wouldn't that be cute. Who's your cute friend? Another policeman or another writer?"

"He's a psychologist, Mavis."

She gazed up at me. "I've known some people who could use one of those. As in mother-in-laws. What brings you here?"

"I'm looking into the murders of Leonora Bright and Vicki—"

"Tranh. Well, you came to the right place because I know who did it."

Cardenas hitched his trousers. His holstered gun wobbled. "Really."

"Really, George. And I told that to Wendell Salmey right in the beginning. Not that he did a darn thing about it." To me: "Chronic depression, that one. And lazier than a welfare cheat. Always in a low mood, walking with his eyes down, like anything worth discovering was on the ground."

She fanned herself with the magazine. "After that son of his got drunk and smashed himself up on the highway, he got even worse, just sat around all day doing nothing. Before I got married, I did some teaching and Wendell was one of my students. One of those who'd rather coast than drive. Only reason he took the sheriff job was he figured there'd be nothing to do—no offense, George." More denture display. "One advantage to being ninety is you say what you want and get away with it."

"Didn't know you had a birthday, Mavis."

"So I'm pushing it a little. The big day's next month, on the sixteenth in case you intend to send me flowers, George. Wendell Salmey died young. Bleeding ulcer at fifty-nine. By the way, what's a psychologist got to do with Leonora and the Oriental girl?"

"Their murders might be related to a current case in L.A."

"Doesn't answer my question."

"I sometimes consult to the police."

"One of those mind readers, like on TV?"

"Not really—"

"I'm kidding. I know what a psychologist does. Geez, everyone in this generation's so doggone *serious*. So, he killed someone else, huh?"

"Who?"

"Leonora's brother. Half brother. That's who killed her and the nail girl. George, would you be real nice and get me a Fresca and a slice of American cheese from the kitchen? Make it two slices, got the packet laid out on the counter along with a cute little cutting tool from The Sharper Image."

Cardenas went to fill the order.

I pulled up a chair.

Mavis Wembley nibbled her cheese and swigged from the can of soda. Handing the empty to Cardenas, she wiped her mouth and looked out at her weedy plot with satisfaction. "I know the brother did it because Leonora confided in me a few weeks before that she was deathly afraid of him. They had different mothers but the same father and it was the father who had money and he died a few months before she confided in me that she was scared."

I said, "Worried about an inheritance conflict?"

"Not worried, scared. That's the word she used."

"What's the brother's name?" said Cardenas.

"Don't know, she never mentioned it, always referred to him as 'my half brother.' Emphasis on *half*. Making it clear there was no closeness there."

I said, "How'd the topic come up?"

"She was color-rinsing me and kept dropping stuff, real butterfingered. Which wasn't like Leonora, she'd always been a real coordinated girl. Magic hands, I used to call her. Sometimes she'd toss in a neck-and-scalp massage and that was better than . . . anyway, when she moved here from Frisco, all the gals were happy because of her skills. Before that we had Sarah Burkhardt who grew up here, borderline retarded if you ask me, taught herself from books, about as stylish as roadkill. We put up with her because she was all we had. Thank God she married a truck driver and moved away and we got Leonora. Who learned her trade in Frisco from a top homosexual stylist."

"Magic hands," I said, "but not that day."

"Fumbly fingers. I asked her what was wrong. She said nothing. I said, Come on, don't be holding back, there's no one else here. Which there wasn't. Just me and Leonora in the salon. She was good but there wasn't that much call for her services, our local females believing they could do just as well with a box of Toni. If you saw them, you'd find that laughable."

She asked Cardenas for another soda.

When he returned to the house, she said, "We'll wait for George. So I don't have to repeat myself."

"Sure. I appreciate this."

"So you think it's a good clue—the brother?"

"Best we've got so far."

Cardenas came back and popped the top.

"Thank you, George. Back to Leonora that day. I could tell she really wanted to talk so I pushed her until she did. She said her father had left a sizable estate, her mother was already dead, and her stepmother was sick. So the money was going to be split two ways between her and her half brother, which was fine with her, there was enough for everyone. But she knew *he* wouldn't be satisfied with just half. I said, What, he's a selfish type? That's when she broke down and cried. Said, Oh, Mavis, if you only knew. He comes across the nicest person, always wanting to do favors for people, feeds the homeless, smiles at little kids and gives 'em candy but it's a façade. Down deep, it's all about him, always was, I just know he's going to cause me serious troubles over that money and it scares me."

She sipped. Soda dribbled onto her chin and she wiped it quickly. "I said, What kind of serious troubles? She said, I don't know, that's what scares me, you don't know what he's capable of. I told her if she was scared to call the police. She said they'd laugh at her because she had no evidence, just feelings. I said, At least talk to a lawyer. You pay them upfront, they won't laugh. But it was like she wasn't hearing me, just kept going on about how this half brother was going to start troubles, no one knew what he was really like. Finally I said, If you're going to accuse, at least tell me what you mean. She said, You don't want to know, Mavis. I said if I didn't I wouldn't ask."

She handed Cardenas the second soda can. "Now I'm full. You can spill that out, George, or finish it yourself." Merriment tugged at her eyes. "Don't worry, I don't have cooties."

Cardenas said, "I'm not leaving again, Mavis. This story's too good."

"It's not a story, George. It's a factual account."

"Even better."

"It's going to get way better once I tell you what she said. She said he taught himself to pick locks, she just knew it was to break in somewhere. Top of that, he tortured and killed animals. First bugs, then little critters, then who-knows-what. Had been doing that kind of nastiness since he was little. Leonora loved animals. Had two little Bichon Freezes or whatever you call them, would do anything for those dogs. After she was killed, they *disappeared*. So you tell me."

I said, "Did she keep them in the shop with her?"

"Sometimes she brought them, sometimes she left them at home. But the point is, no one saw them again. I brought that up with Wendell when it was clear he wasn't taking me seriously. That's what I mean by lazy. Woman gets butchered up and she's got dogs and they're not in the house, wouldn't that make you curious, George?"

"Absolutely."

"Wendell lacked a shred of curiosity. Depression does that, right, Doctor?"

I nodded.

She said, "I know curiosity can kill cats, maybe even dogs. But satisfaction can also bring 'em all back. Wendell just didn't care and neither did that Santa Barbara detective they sent down."

"Donald Bragen," I said.

"Him," she said. "All macho, like Broderick Crawford on *Highway Patrol*—before both your times. 'Yes, ma'am, thank you, ma'am,' writing everything down in a little notebook. But Broderick listened. Bragen was an idiot, didn't have time for anyone. You tell me: a prime suspect with a money motive who tortures animals and two dogs go missing. What would you think?"

"What, indeed," I said.

Mavis Wembley placed a hand on my knee. "I like your style."

Cardenas and I stayed with her for another half an hour and I did most of the talking, trying to tease out additional details about Leonora Bright's dreaded half brother.

What I got was thin soup: either older or younger than Leonora and probably from San Francisco "because that's where Leonora hailed from and she never said he didn't."

I thanked her and got up to leave.

She said, "Nice meeting you," and took hold of Cardenas's sleeve. "George, last night, I heard raccoons scratching out back near the garbage. Let's set out some traps for them, as well."

"She's something, no?" said Cardenas, backing out the dirt driveway. "Shuffling cards is her idea of aerobics but she's never sick. Claims her mother lived to a hundred and four."

"Good DNA," I said. "The rest of us jog and pretend."

"You've got that right. Think the brother angle's worth pursuing?"

"It's all we've got."

"What she said about Wendell does conform to what other people have told me. Didn't want to get into that out of respect for the dead."

"No reason. He's not the issue."

"So where are you heading now?"

"Back to L.A. unless you've got a suggestion."

"Sorry, no. Want me to do anything?"

"If you've got the time to run background on Leonora's addresses in San Francisco, that would be great."

"Sure," he said. "I was also thinking we should try to find the father's death certificate, see if the brother's name appears anywhere. Leonora being scared of an inheritance mess right before she died probably narrows the time frame on his passing."

"Good point. An obituary search might be the easiest way to go. Was Bright her maiden name?"

"Think so." He sat up straighter and pressed down on the gas. "This is different."

"How so?"

"I'm working."

CHAPTER

15

I stopped in Santa Barbara for a late lunch on Stearn's Wharf, the site of my aborted meeting with Donald Bragen.

The tourist stream was skimpy but enthusiastic-smiling, gorging people believing in immortality. Ducks and seagulls followed the food stream, content with the leavings. Out in the harbor, big gray pelicans floated, biding their time as they scanned the surface for prey. Their smaller brown cousins swooped and dove and sometimes came up with wriggle.

All kinds of ways to hunt.

I finished and continued up the pier, passing the breakfast place where Bragen said he'd meet me. Maybe he'd paid closer attention to Mavis Wembley's lead than she believed but had come up empty. Or she was right and he had ignored her. Either way, flashbacks wouldn't be as much fun as fishing.

Leaning over the railing and sucking in salt air, I phoned Milo's cell.

Rick answered. "Hey, Alex. His phone ran out of charge so we exchanged. He told me if you called to tell you he'll be tied up until ten or so, maybe later."

"Any idea where?"

"Out on the job is all he said. I had the day off so we managed to schedule lunch. Soon as we ordered, he got a call and left. Something about finding a car. Made him grumpy."

"Missing a meal does that."

"He doggie-bagged."

No one answered Rick's cell. Milo sometimes switches off when he's concentrating. I got back on the highway, tried a few miles later.

This time, his bellow rattled the little bones in my ear. "Found Kat Shonsky's goddamn Mustang."

"Yet, you are not happy."

"Guess where the hell it's been all this time? Department contract tow yard. Called in as an abandoned vehicle at five a.m. the same damn night she disappeared. Found midway up the Pass, just like you guessed."

I said, "Any idea who called it in?"

"No record," he growled. "They treated it as a routine nuisance call, sent a tow driver. Genius shows up, there's no reg or insurance in the car and the plates are gone. He hooks it up anyway and dumps it in the yard. Where it's been sitting."

"What about the VIN?" I said.

"They got around to logging the VIN a few days later, filed and forgot. All this time, I'm checking bulletins, wasting my time on the phone, and the damn thing's in plain sight, blocks from my office, accumulating birdshit and storage fees. If I hadn't been nagging every yard the department does business with, it probably would've ended up at a police auction. As is, I just spent an hour untangling the paperwork to get it to the motor lab. Eyeballed it, first. No obvious blood or sign of mischief. And here's another good guess for you, Professor: Gas tank was bone-dry, talk about wrong place, wrong time."

"Or someone siphoned it in the club parking lot and followed her until she shut down."

"There you go," he said. "That's why we're buddies."

"I have a suspicious mind?"

"You know how to think like a really evil person. Let's see what the motorheads turn up, but with the tow driver and Lord-knows-who-else pawing it and a suspect careful enough to strip I.D., I'm not expecting much. I'm on my way back to where it was found right now. After that I'll be driving the hillside roads again, narrowing it down to the immediate vicinity. If I can get K-9 to help, we'll do a sniffathon tomorrow. So what's up in Toonerville?"

I told him about Mavis Wembley's tip.

"Scary brother," he said.

"A lock picker could've fooled with the chain at the rental lot, freed the Mercedes. Toss in Mancusi and we've got two crimes featuring stolen black luxury cars, bloody knifework, and a possible inheritance motive."

"Unfortunately, Tony's a homebody leading us nowhere and the tips have dried up. In terms of his being 'kinky,' I wouldn't be surprised if that was Lamp Guy—Hochswelder—or one of the other loving relatives finking on him for being gay just in case we didn't get it the first time. With the Mustang showing up I'm gonna concentrate on Shonsky as a possible corollary homicide, and that gives me cause for a warrant on her apartment. Judge Feldman's at a fundraiser, said if I meet him at his house at ten, he'll sign the papers. Hopefully Kat's mother didn't straighten up too much. Speaking of which, if I have time, I am gonna ask her for that cheek scrape 'cause if the chief meant what he said, he'll get the mitochondrial prioritized. But even if we get a match to the stain, it just tells us what we know anyway."

"Kat's dead."

"I wouldn't sell her life insurance. Lord, I'm busy."

Not the time to remind him of his lament last week. "If the chief meant what he said, maybe you can get more help watching Tony."

"Hard to see Tony having anything to do with Shonsky."

I said, "The link doesn't need to be direct. If Tony contracted his mother's murder, someone could've hired the same killer to do Kat. And the women in Ojo Negro."

"Traveling pro with a taste for stolen wheels?" he said. "What kind of money motive could there be for Kat? She wasn't exactly an heiress."

"From what we've heard she could be abrasive. Maybe that one was personal."

"She blew the wrong guy off so he pays for an elaborate scheme to do her?"

"Or she blew the killer himself off," I said. "Clive picked her up in a bar and there's no reason to believe he was the only one."

"Even really bad guys have feelings."

"Everyone has feelings. Depends what you do with them."

Big-rig mishaps and the usual Cal Trans idiocy stretched the drive back to L.A. and it was dark when I got home. I drank Chivas out by the pond, put Blanche in my lap, and tossed food to the fish. She wanted to watch them eat so we kneeled by the rock rim. The babies were almost big enough to swallow the pellets, kept worrying the bobbing circles until they disintegrated. The adults indulged their attempts and managed not to pull a Jonah.

Robin came out and joined us, chopsticking leftovers and forgoing her glass of wine because she was thinking of working some more.

Quieter than usual.

I said, "Mr. Dot-com call again?"

She shook her head. "There's a wolf-note somewhere on the mandolin fretboard. If I don't fix it, I won't sleep."

"My soul mate." I kissed her, walked her to her studio, carried a now sleeping Blanche back to the house.

My e-mail was the usual blather and one message that interested me, sent a few minutes ago.

dr. delaware: found leonora bright's brother's name in the obit on their father. nothing criminal on him so far and it was too late to access s.f. property rolls to see if he owns a house there. see what i can do tomorrow.

george cardenas

I sent back a thanks and downloaded the e-mail attachment.

San Francisco Chronicle obituary section. Someone important enough to merit a piece with a byline.

The late Dr. Whittaker Bright, a New York native, trained at Cornell and Columbia, had been a professor of engineering at UC Berkeley with an expertise in transformers and a patent for a now obsolete switching device that had paid him royalties for over a decade. Death had come after a protracted illness. Widowed and remarried, "Whit" Bright was survived by his second wife, Bonnie, a daughter, Leonora, of Ojo Negro, and a son, Ansell, of San Francisco. In lieu of flowers, donations were to be sent to the American Heart Society.

What caught my eye was the date of death. Eight days before the butchery in Ojo Negro. Mavis Wembley's story was looking better and better.

Just as I prepared to run a search on *Ansell Bright,* my phone rang.

"Doctor, this is Amber from your service. I had a Mr. Bragen calling from Alaska. He didn't want to hold, said you can call him if you want. Didn't sound like he cared one way or the other."

Bragen's number had an 805 prefix. Fishing up north but using a cell phone with a Ventura–Santa Barbara code.

A gruff voice said, "Yeah?"

"Sergeant Bragen? Alex Delaware."

"The psychologist," he said, as if the title amused him. "An earlier flight came up. Weather changes are quick up here, the connectors get iffy. I've spent too many days in the airport waiting for storms to pass."

"Makes sense."

"You want to know about Bright and Tranh. There's not much to know. Big loser whodunit from day one and if there was anything forensically worthwhile the moron they hired as sheriff screwed it up. We had one suspect but he didn't pan out."

"Who's that?"

"Bright's ex-husband," he said. "Ironclad alibi and he passed a poly."

"Why'd you suspect him?"

" 'Cause he was the ex. But forget it, it's not him."

"Could I have his name, just for the record?"

"Jose something. Mexican, probably illegal, in those days we weren't allowed to ask. He worked at the feed store, unloading hay and whatnot. Claimed he was a big-time chef back in Guadalajara or wherever, but they all claim that."

"Immigrants."

"If everyone was so better off, why do they come here? Anyway, he's not your guy, that woulda been nice. He and Bright were married six months, got divorced, he moved to Oxnard, got a job cooking at one of the hotels. Which is where twenty people saw him during the entire time frame of the murders. We also had witnesses eyeballing before and after. At his apartment complex, then at a bar that night dancing with his new girlfriend, so no way. I asked him to take a poly anyway, he agreed. Passed with flying colors. Claimed he and Leonora parted friendly, had a Christmas card from her to prove it. Also, he seemed real broken up about her dying. And for all I know, Bright wasn't even the target, maybe Tranh was. Not that I ever found anyone who'd talk about her. Took the time to visit her family—big clan, down in Anaheim. Everyone crying and weeping and lighting candles to Buddha. Listening to them, Vicki was a nun, had no enemies."

"You had reason to doubt that?"

"No," he said. "But I'm not a trusting guy, by nature. You get up there today?"

"Sure did."

"Still a one-horse town?"

"Maybe half a horse."

"Place that rinky-dink, you'd think someone would've known something. But all those hicks could say was how nice they both were." Harsh laughter. "Nice people is the bane of a detective's existence."

"While I was there, I met a woman named Mavis Wembley—"

"Oh, that one," said Bragen. "Old Fatso. Stuck her nose into everything, couldn't shut her up. But she had nothing to say, either."

"You don't buy her story about Leonora's brother?"

"Yeah, right. You want to work that, good luck, pal. Can't believe she's still alive. Big as a cow. Like that alien in *Star Wars*—Jabba the whatever. She used to *summon* me. Her word. 'Detective Bragen, may I *summon* you for a little talk?' You're working a case, you can't close off anything, so I'd get over to her place and she'd sit in her chair and try to pump me for information. But like I said, you've got to follow up on everything so I talked to the brother. He also had an alibi—working, some gay job—we're talking featherlight here. Even more emotional than Jose . . . Castro, that's what it was. Jose Castro, like Fidel."

"So much for Ansell," I said.

"Ansell?"

"That's his name, according to the father's obituary."

"Guy I spoke to called himself Dale. And that's what his mother called him, too, and I'd expect she'd know. She's the one I got his number from in the first place. And don't waste your time with her, she died a few months after Leonora. Cancer, the father was heart problems I think. Bad-luck family. Dale was taking care of her, he was at her place when I called."

"Maybe Dale's his nickname," I said.

"Whatever. Guy *fluttered* over the phone. It was like talking to a girl. This is not the caliber person who could overpower two healthy women and do what was done to them. You want to lose your lunch, get hold of those autopsy photos."

Over the phone. He'd never met Ansell "Dale" Bright in person, had no inkling of the man's size and strength.

I said, "I see what you mean."

"I put it all in the file, Doctor."

"Where is the file?"

"Probably storage," he said. "They moved everything a few years ago, lots of stuff managed to fall off the truck. Not my problem. Shouldn't be yours, either. This is a dead one."

Mavis Wembley hadn't mentioned Jose Castro. I found her number in my notes.

It was nearly ten p.m. I bet on her being a night owl.

She picked up on the first ring. "Cutie! Have you solved anything?"

"Far from it. But I have learned that Leonora was married—"

"To Jose. You talked to Bragen, right? That fool fixed on Jose even before setting eyes on him because you-know-why."

"Why?"

"Jose was a Mexican. There was lots of loose talk about it being a Mexican murder—all this gossip about drugs, gangs."

"Any reason for that?"

"Back then we were a downright racist town. Most of the people are Mexican now, so no one opens a mouth except some of the older cowboys when they come into town and have a few too many. My second husband was half Mexican and you should've seen the looks I got. Jose was a nice young fellow."

"Younger than Leonora."

"In his twenties. Handsome, too."

"You never thought he was responsible?"

"Nicest young man you'd ever meet, Doctor. Muscles out to here. After they broke up, Leonora said she still liked him as a friend, it just didn't work out as a marriage. You want to know my opinion? They were *never* more than friends, the whole marriage was a put-up so he could get immigration status."

"Leonora would do that for a friend?"

"That's the kind of person she was. And Jose did get his papers, Leonora told me, she was all thrilled about it. Shortly after that, they broke up and Jose moved down south, somewhere, and it didn't seem to trouble her. Besides, what motive would Jose have to hurt her? Neither of them had any money to speak of. Unlike Leonora's family. Who had plenty. I'm telling you the brother's where to look. Bragen probably said I was a meddling old nut but anytime he wants to have an IQ contest, I'm ready."

I laughed.

She said, "You think I'm kidding?"

16

At noon the following day, I met Milo up in the hills above the Sepulveda Pass.

Vacant lot, a mile or so above the spot where Kat Shonsky's car had been found. Two K-9 handlers worked the brush between a pair of sleek, contemporary stilt-houses, running a chocolate Lab and a border collie.

Sharp-eyed dogs, beautifully groomed. Both with a thing for dead flesh.

Milo said, "In answer to your unasked question, this is one of the few open, unfenced spots around here. Which means nothing, she could be in Alhambra. But early this morning we gave a pack of tracking dogs a whiff of her clothing and ran them all over the neighborhood. Zilch for the first hour, then one of them raced up here and got somewhat excited."

"Somewhat?"

"He changed his mind and got distracted. Happens more than you think. Still, better to be careful. So now it's the cadaver mutts."

"Who owns the property?"

"It's shared by the two neighboring houses. Couple of sisters married to lawyers, they've got plans to build a joint swimming pool. Currently cruising together in South America for the last two weeks."

"There's your happy family," I said.

"Not so happy if Lassie and Rin Tin Tin find something with maggots in it." His skin sagged and his clothes were distorted beyond wrinkles, as if he'd wrestled with an intruder.

I said, "All-nighter?"

"Coma-time watching Tony's place, went over to Kat's apartment at seven a.m. Place looked like Martha Stewart had just filmed there."

"Mom's artful hand."

"I called for techies anyway. No evidence of any violence or struggle but one thing Mom didn't find was a Baggie of weed at the bottom of a tampon box. No credit card receipts, which would fit with ol' Monica cutting her off. No phone records or tax returns, either, but Kat didn't keep paper around, period. Not a single book in the place and the only magazines were old copies of *Us* and *Elle*. She did hold on to a few travel souvenirs—cheap crap from Hawaii, Tahiti, Cozumel. Snapshots, too. Her in bikinis, too-big smiles, no men friends. Like she got someone to take her picture to prove she was happy."

"Sounds like a lonely girl."

He yawned. "Anyway, I got the blouse."

We returned to watching the dogs. The retriever was circling the lot with the intensity of a sprinter training for the big race. It stopped. Resumed circling. The border collie had lost interest and its handler led it back to the K-9 car.

"Dog's life," said Milo. "If nothing happens soon, I'm on my way to the boutique where Kat worked. Someone's got to know something about her personal life."

I said, "I've been thinking about the Ojo Negro killings. Leonora Bright was murdered only eight days after her father died. Her stepmother was terminally ill, making the sibs heirs sooner rather than

later. A boilerplate will would split everything fifty–fifty with rever-
sion to the survivor. Leonora was in her thirties, so there's a good
chance she never wrote a will of her own."

"Scary brother gets rid of her to make sure she never sees a
lawyer."

"It's a motive. And not that different from the one we've suggested for Tony Mancusi: Kill Mom before she changes *her* will."

"There's a specialty hit man out there fixing inheritance problems
and both Ansell and Tony just happened to find him?"

I said, "I know it sounds remote but think about stolen black cars
and costumes."

"Theatrical traveling hit man . . . can't dismiss it, but before I get
historical, I need to focus on the here and now. If we can find some
kind of link between Tony and Ansell, I might start breathing hard."

"Donald Bragen thought Ansell was incapable of that level of violence because he sounded effeminate over the phone."

"And Tony vamps. Okay, a theatrically gay specialty hit man. Bragen look into Ansell beyond his vocal qualities?"

"He didn't even know Ansell's real name because Ansell called
himself Dale. And alibied himself for the time of the murder—working. Bragen accepted it."

"Oh, Lord."

"Sheriff Cardenas said he'd look into Ansell's background. I ran a
basic search last night, got no hits on that name. The Dale Brights I
found were a fourteen-year-old girl who plays field hockey at a prep
school in Florida, a sixty-year-old female insurance agent in Ohio, and
a Nebraska churchman and farmer who wrote a book about wheat
and died in 1876."

"My bet's on the girl . . . okay, let's make sure we've buttoned
down everything—"

He stopped midsentence.

The retriever sat down.

Stayed.

. . .

The head showed first.

Kat Shonsky had been buried three feet deep, stripped of her clothing, stretched out on her back with her legs slightly parted. Her skin was greenish gray, marbled, slipping loose from its skeletal underpinning. White-blond hair served as a nest for worms. Where putrefaction hadn't taken over, black hyphens were evident.

Probable stab wounds. I stopped counting at twenty-three.

In the grave was a purple silk scarf, placed diagonally across the abdomen and upper thighs. Removing it revealed Katrina Shonsky's driver's license. Wedged between her labia.

"There's a statement for you," said Diana Ponce, the C.I. kneeling above the body.

Milo said, "Look what I did."

"And I want the whole world to know it."

Ponce bagged the license and called for a large envelope for the scarf. While she waited, she inspected Katrina Shonsky's neck. No obvious ligature marks but there wasn't much neck left and the final say would be the coroner's.

Placing the scarf back on the body, she cupped the remains of the head gently in one hand and probed with the other. "There's bone breakage at the back, Milo. Want to feel it?"

Milo got down next to her, and she guided his gloved hand.

"Oh, yeah," he said. "Like cracked eggshell."

"Someone bopped her good," said Ponce. "Maybe to knock her out before he cut her?" She looked up at the twin houses. "This close to private property, you'd want to keep things quiet."

Milo stood. "You should be a detective, Diana."

She grinned. "According to the tube, I already am."

The envelope arrived. Setting the head down with reverence, Ponce removed the scarf and unfurled it. Diaphonous thing; it waved in the breeze.

"Louis Vuitton label."

Milo said, "I thought they did luggage."

"They do everything, Lieutenant." Ponce admired the silk. The

blew harder and a few granules of dirt slid off the garment and
attered the body. Ponce handed the scarf off and used tweezers to
recover them.

Milo said, "Costs a fortune but it was left here."

Perfect opening for one of those jokes cops and techs sometimes
tell to buffer the horror.

This time, no one did.

Crypt attendants wrapped the body in plastic and took it away. Moments later Diana Ponce left and the criminalists got to work.

Milo said, "Time to get over to Monica Hedges. You can meet me
there if you want."

"Sure."

I followed him to Wilshire, turned left. At Warner he pulled over,
motioned me to do the same.

"Aborted mission. No answer at the Hedges, not exactly the time
to leave a message. Let's check out the place where Kat worked.
You're a fashionable guy."

"Not really."

"Too bad," he said. "I was hoping you could interpret."

La Femme Boutique was on San Vicente west of Barrington, squeezed
between a coffee emporium specializing in Indonesian brew and a
hair salon crowded with beautiful heads.

The shop was high, narrow, and white, hung with vintage absinthe
posters and floored in weathered, wine-colored marble. The few
pieces of furniture were heavy and Victorian, the clothes in the window frothy and fitted to malnourished mannequins.

No shoppers in sight. Milo and I passed through a narrow aisle
walled by double-high racks. Some of the dresses and tops were
marked *Sale,* which put them into three figures.

Edith Piaf on the stereo, *Made in France* on the labels.

Designers I'd never heard of, but that meant nothing.

He said, "I didn't look that closely at the stuff in Kat's pad but it wasn't like this. She didn't have any scarves, either—hey, how's it going?"

Addressing a hollow-cheeked brunette in a black lace top, sitting behind the sales counter, drinking Evian and reading *InStyle*. Behind her was a high shelf of bath toys, fruit-shaped candles, pastes and gels that wouldn't get past airport security.

She got up and glided around the counter, head back, hips leading, like a runway model. Thirty, give or take, with deeply shadowed dark eyes. Makeup thick as cake frosting worked at masking a complexion not much better than Milo's. The black top was tucked tight into cream calfskin jeans.

"Hey, guys. Someone buying a guilt gift or are we talking birthday?"

Milo tugged his lapel to one side and revealed his shield. "Police. Katrina Shonsky's body was just found a few miles away. She was murdered."

Hollow cheeks puffed. Eyelids vibrated. "Omigod, omigod—Kat!"

She bent at the knees. I caught her elbow, walked her to a puce velvet divan. Milo fetched her water bottle and dribbled some between her lips.

She gulped. Started to hyperventilate. I returned to the counter and got a shopping bag printed with the store's name. By the time I got back, she was breathing normally and talking to Milo.

Her name was Amy Koutsakas but she called herself Amelie, had been working with Kat Shonsky for just over a year. At first she sang the dead woman's praises. We sat that out and let the shock wear off and soon she was confiding that she and Kat hadn't been close. "Not that I'm bad-mouthing her. God forbid."

Milo said, "You guys just didn't hit it off."

"We never fought, but to be honest, Lieutenant, we had different professional views."

"Of what?"

"This job. Kat could be tactless."

"With you or the customers?"

"Both," said Amelie. "I'm not saying she went out of her way to be mean, it just . . . I don't know what I'm really saying. Sorry. I can't believe this . . ."

I said, "Kat was sharp-tongued."

"She was—sometimes it was what she *didn't* say. To the customers."

"Not good at stroking egos."

She sat up straight. "To be honest, guys, this business is all about fear. Most of our clientele is mature, who else can afford the prices? We're talking about used-to-be size eights who are now fourteens. When you get older your body changes. I know, because my mom was a dancer and that happened to her."

Stroking her own flat-plane abdomen.

Milo said, "Kat didn't understand that."

"We get lots of women coming in for special occasions. Wanting to look really fabulous and ready to pay for it. Sometimes it's a challenge but you need to work with the customer. You examine her assets and liabilities without being obvious, guide her toward stuff that'll minimize her issues. If she tries on something and it turns out horrible, you say something nice and ease her toward something else."

"Applied psychology," said Milo.

"I was a psych major in college and believe me, it helps."

I said, "Kat didn't take that approach."

"Kat thought her job was to help carry garments to the dressing room and stand around examining her nails during the try-on. She'd never volunteer an opinion. Never. Even when the client was obviously needy—crying out for validation. I tried to tell her we were more than attendants. Her answer was 'These are grown-ups, they can make their own choices.' But that's not fair. People need support, right? Even if something looked *good* Kat would just stand there and say nothing. She gave no *guidance* and that led to customers bringing a lot of her sales back. Returns come straight off the commission."

Milo said, "Do you guys split commission?"

"That's the way it used to be but I told the owners no way would I split with someone like Kat. They value me so they agreed and I ended up making around three times as much as Kat."

"Is commission a big part of your salary?"

"Seventy percent."

"So Kat wasn't exactly raking it in."

"And boy did she complain about that. Constantly. It made no sense. All she had to do was be nice." She bit her lip. "I know it sounds like I'm putting her down but that's the way it was. That's why after she stopped coming in and didn't return calls, the owners figured she'd flaked out. After three days, they fired her."

"Who are the owners?" said Milo.

"Mr. and Mrs. Leibowitz," she said. "They made money in the florist business and retired. It started as a hobby for Laura—Mrs. L. They'd travel to Paris each year and she'd bring back great stuff that her friends adored."

"We talking absentee owners?"

"For the most part. I'm the manager and Kat is—was the assistant manager." Past tense made her flinch. "Do you have any idea who did it?"

"Not yet," said Milo. "That's why we're here."

"I can't imagine who would do something like that."

"Kat ever get into an altercation with a customer? Or anyone else?"

"No, no, our clientele is sophisticated. *Nice* women."

"What about the men in Kat's life?"

"Never met any of them," she said, "but from what she said she'd been through plenty of losers and was swearing off men."

"Anyone in particular?"

"Uh-uh, we never got to the name level. She'd just make remarks. She was a big one for remarks."

"About men?"

"Men, her job, life in general. Her mother—she talked about her mother a lot. Said there was all kinds of pressure to conform and she hated it. From what I could tell, she had an unhappy childhood. Basically, she struck me as an unhappy person. That's probably why she drank."

"On the job?"

Silence.

"Amelie?"

"Sometimes she'd come in with way too much mint on her breath. A couple of times she forgot the mint and I smelled the alcohol. I started keeping mouthwash for her."

"Partying hard?"

"I guess," she said. "You know who can answer these questions better than me? Her friend Beth. She works at a jewelry store up the block. She's the one who told Kat about the job opening."

"Thanks for the tip," said Milo.

"Anything I can do to help."

She walked us to the door, straightening garments along the way.

Before Milo's hand touched the knob, she said, "This is probably nothing, but maybe there is something I should tell you. About a customer."

We stopped.

"It's not really an altercation, but—I'm sure it's nothing."

"Everything's helpful, Amelie."

"Okay . . . About a month ago, maybe five, six weeks, I was off for the morning and came in after lunch and found Kat was in a real goofy mood. All giggly, which wasn't like her. I said what's up and she said the most hilarious thing had happened. A customer—a man—had just come in and started pawing through the sale items. Kat assumed, just like I did with you guys, that he was looking for a gift. Kat ignored him like she always does. The guy kept examining the goods, concentrating on the larger sizes. After a while, it made Kat nervous and she finally went over and asked if he needed help."

"What made her nervous?"

"Being alone with him, how long he was taking. We're not some huge department store, how much time does it take to go through the merchandise? And most guys have no patience at all, they're in and out or asking for help. Anyway, this guy said he was fine and Kat returned to the counter. But something gave her a funny feeling and she checked him out again. Couldn't see him, but heard him behind one of the double racks and she went over and peeked. The guy had taken out a dress and was holding it up against his own body. Stroking it— like fitting it on himself. Kat said she couldn't control herself, she just broke up and the guy heard it and nearly fell over himself putting the dress back. But instead of apologizing, Kat just stood there. And instead of rushing out, the guy turned and stared at her. Being . . . blatant. Like he needed to show he wasn't ashamed. Kat told me that really pissed her off, she wasn't going to take shit from a weirdo, so she stared back. I guess you could call that conflict."

"Sounds like an assertive weirdo," said Milo.

"Kat thought it was hilarious," said Amelie. "I was appalled. Everyone's got their secrets, why make them feel stupid?"

"Then what happened?"

"The guy stared some more, finally gave in and left quickly. Kat said she made sure to laugh some more. So he could hear her as he slunk away. It's probably nothing, but you asked about problems."

"Did Kat describe this guy?"

Black-rimmed eyes rounded. "You think it *could* be him? Oh, no, what if he comes back?"

"I'm sure there's no connection, Amelie. We just need to collect as many facts as possible."

"That would really freak me out," she said. "The thought of being here with—"

"You'll be fine, Amelie. Did Kat describe him?"

"No, no. She just told the story and laughed. It kept her giggly the whole rest of the day."

CHAPTER

17

A jewelry store named Cachet was visible at the end of the block.

Milo said, "Being a big-time hoohah detective, I'm willing to guess that's where Beth Holloway works. But first, blood sugar therapy."

I followed him into the coffee store. The place was nearly empty but it took a while to get the attention of the iPod-wearing kid hiding behind the espresso machine.

Milo bought two Frisbee-sized bagels smeared with crème fraîche, filled a small paper cup with free water, brought his bounty to a corner stool.

One bagel down. He wiped his chin. "Been a while since I worked a case with *overtones*."

Years ago, he'd reported to a captain who'd made sure to assign him every homicide with "unconventional overtones" that came through the division. Meaning anything but male on female, the more lurid the better.

Kat Shonsky's body bore the signs of a lust homicide—blitz-attack head wound, overkill knifework, sexual positioning, the contemptuous placement of the driver's license. But nothing suggested it was anything but male on female.

"I'm not sure I see overtones, Big Guy."

He smiled.

"What's funny?"

"Wherever it leads."

Glitter and temptation filled the jewelry store's windows. A spade-faced young man in a dark suit studied us before buzzing us in. Once we entered, he kept his hands beneath the counter.

Milo identified himself and asked for Beth Holloway and the guy relaxed.

"That's Beth." Eyeing a petite honey blonde showing a gray velvet tray of cocktail rings to a stooped white-haired man around eighty.

Beth Holloway had large pale eyes, flawless skin, smooth, bronze arms. A mini-collection of bangles circled delicate wrists. She wore a clingy, low-cut taupe dress, enjoyed frequent bends that flashed a freckled wealth of cleavage. The customer's attention kept shifting between all that skin and the toys on the tray.

She said, "Pretty gorgeous, Mr. Wein. No?"

The old man sighed. "This is always difficult."

Beth touched his wrist. "You always know what to do, Mr. Wein."

"If you say so . . ." He held up a platinum-and-sapphire piece. "What do you think?"

"Perfect, she'll love it."

Wein held the ring to the light and turned it.

"Would you like a loupe, sir?"

"Like I know what I'm looking at."

Beth laughed. "Take it from me, Mr. Wein, these are really great stones. And those are teeny baguettes, not chips."

A few more turns. "Okay, this is fine."

"Great! I'll have it sized and ready for Mrs. Wein in two days. Would you like me to deliver it to your house?"

"No, not this time, I'm going to give it to her at dinner."

Beth clapped her hands. "So romantic! She's a lucky woman, Mr. Wein."

"Depends what day you ask her."

He left and she turned to us, smoothing her dress. "Hi!"

Milo introduced himself and told her why we were there.

She froze.

Burst into tears. Covered her face with one hand and pressed the other against the countertop.

The man in the dark suit took the tray of rings, locked it up, and looked on curiously.

Milo said, "Sorry to have to tell you."

Beth Holloway ran toward the rear of the store, threw a door open, and disappeared.

The dark-suited man said, "We're talking Kat, from La Femme?"

"You know her?"

"Wow," he said.

Milo repeated the question.

"I went in there a couple of times, maybe get my wife something."

"Kat waited on you?"

"She was there, but she didn't do much," said the man. "It's her, huh? Weird."

"What is?"

"Knowing someone who got killed."

"What can you tell us about her?"

"Nothing. I'm just saying."

"Saying what?"

The man's lips screwed up.

I said, "She wasn't a helpful salesperson."

"Yeah, but it didn't bother me," said the man. "I like to do my own thing. With jewelry, you've got to guide them. But clothes, it's whatever works for you."

Beth Holloway reemerged wearing a chocolate-brown sweater over her dress. Her eyes were puffy. Her lips looked bruised.

"What happened to Kat?" she asked.

Milo said, "We don't know much yet. Can you spare some time?"

"You bet. Whatever it takes to find the animal who did this."

"Any candidates come to mind?"

The man in the dark suit had sidled closer.

Beth Holloway said, "I wish, but no."

Milo said, "Let's take a walk."

When the three of us were outside, he pointed to the coffee emporium.

Beth Holloway said, "I'd throw up. Let's just walk."

She took off, arms swinging. "What I really need is a ten-mile run."

Milo said, "We'd need the EMT rescue van for me."

"You should get into it. It's therapeutic."

"Kat into exercise?"

"Not a lick. And I tried." She slowed down, picked up speed again. We hustled past storefronts, dodged pedestrians. Beth Holloway forged through the crowd like a woman with a plan.

Milo let her dissipate energy for a block and a half. "Anything you want to tell us before we start asking questions?"

"Kat had a thing for losers but I can't imagine anyone that evil."

"How about some names?"

"There was Rory—Rory Cline. With a C. Works in the mailroom at the CRP agency, thinks he's going to be a big-shot agent. Must be forty but he tries to look younger. Kat met him at a club, I don't know where. She was attracted to him but he had no interest in sex, just wanted to hold hands and listen to music. That made her feel unattractive."

Milo wrote down the name. "Next?"

"Next was Michael . . . what was his last name . . ." Tapping her hair. "Sorry, it's escaping me. Michael . . . unlike Rory, he *loved* sex. All the time. Kat said he was a stud but turned out he was married. An accountant or something . . . Michael Browning, there you go."

"Did Kat stop seeing him when she found out?"

"Nope. But she got bored. With him *and* the sex. All quantity, no quality, she said. The third one was a real asshole—some hick who worked on Rolls-Royces."

Milo said, "Clive Hatfield."

Her shoulders tightened. "You suspect him?"

"Riana gave us his name so we went over to talk to him."

"And?"

"No Prince Charming. Unfortunately, he's got a tight alibi. Any others?"

"No," she said. "Rory, Michael, and Clive, the loser brigade."

Milo had her recount the last night of Kat Shonsky's life. She was forthcoming about her "growing serious" relationship with Sean the surfboard sander. "It's a real connection, you know? I mean I'm sorry Kat had to drive home alone, but that's not my fault, right?"

"Of course not."

"She was p.o.'d. Did what happened to her relate to drunk driving or something?"

"Doesn't seem that way."

"Thank God, I'd feel terrible about that."

"Beth, is there anyone besides Rory Cline and Michael Browning we should know about?"

"No one I can think of."

"No one Kat met at the club that night?"

"She didn't meet anyone. That was what p.o.'d her. We thought of inviting her but figured it would be uncomfortable." She walked faster, gritted her teeth, cried silently.

"Beth, did Kat ever talk to you about problems with anyone?"

"Just her mother. They didn't get along."

"What about people at work?"

"She hated her job, thought the girl she worked with was a suck-up. That made me feel a little bad because I was the one who told her about it."

"What'd she hate about the job?"

"Lousy money, boring, you name it. Kat had a tough life. Her real dad died when she was young. Her mother was a slut, had men coming and going all the time. Finally, she found a rich guy."

"How'd Kat get along with the rich guy?"

"She actually liked him better than her mother. Said he was more laid-back, didn't pressure her. With her mother it was always criticism." She sucked in breath, took a long time to exhale. "Kat was beautiful but didn't know it. The truth is—I'm realizing this now—I've never seen her really happy."

"How'd she deal with her unhappiness?"

"What do you mean?"

"Sometimes people escape."

"Oh," she said. "Her drinking. Yeah, it could get out of hand. But you just said DUI had nothing to do with it."

"It didn't. So there's no one she had conflict with recently?"

"I can't think of anyone."

"Someone told us a strange story, Beth."

"What's that?"

He repeated the incident with the cross-dresser.

She said, "Oh, that."

"Kat told you."

"She thought it was *hilarious*." A trace of a smile said Beth had agreed.

"She describe this guy?"

"Omigod—you think *he* could be—"

"We're just collecting facts, Beth."

"Did she describe him . . . just that he didn't look queer-y on the outside, you'd never know."

"Masculine."

"I guess."

"Let me ask you something else, Beth. Would Kat have been impressed by money?"

"Isn't everyone?"

"How about a special attraction?"

The pretty face went slack with confusion.

"Fancy houses, expense accounts—real nice cars. Any of that float her boat?"

"Sure, all of the above," said Beth Holloway. "That just makes her normal."

18

Milo ran backgrounds on Rory Cline and Michael Browning.

Cline was easy—one motorist with that name in L.A. County. Studio City apartment, no criminal record, wants, or warrants, eleven-year-old Audi.

Sixteen Michael Brownings. Narrowing the search to the three who lived in the Valley and cross-checking business listings turned up one accountant: Michael J. Browning, office on Lankershim, near Universal Studios.

One-year-old Saab, another clean record.

"A mailroom flunky and a number cruncher," said Milo. "No reason for either of them to have car-boosting skills, but let's talk to them anyway."

Creative Representation and Promotion occupied a travertine-and-green-glass fortress near the intersection of Wilshire and Santa Monica. Inside was more of the same beige stone. A mural of stiff people watching a movie dominated the three-story, skylit lobby. A milky skylight aimed for an indoor-outdoor effect but missed. Mussolini loved travertine but got strung up before he could remodel Rome.

A pair of male receptionists in gunmetal silk shirts hid themselves behind a high counter and whispered into tiny phones suspended from their ears. A beefy black man in a bad suit stood to their side.

Milo strode up to one of the gray-shirts and held out his badge. The security man smiled and remained in place. The receptionist kept talking. From the sound of it a personal chat.

Milo waited, slapped a hand on the counter. The security guy smiled wider as the receptionist jumped.

"Hold on." Sudden smile, as sincere as silicon. "Are you here for a meeting?"

"We're here to see Rory Cline."

"Who might that be?"

"He works in the mailroom."

"The mailroom doesn't take calls."

"It's taking this one."

"Uh-uh-uh. Working hours are—"

"Irrelevant. Call him."

Grayshirt shrank back. Glanced at the security guard. Saw a broad back.

"Look, I don't even know how to get anyone there."

Milo said, "Time to learn."

It took several calls delivered in a perplexed whisper, and frantic repetition of the word "police" before Grayshirt said, "He's on his way, you can wait over there."

We hung by the brown chairs. Five minutes later an elevator slid open and a narrow, round-shouldered, dark-haired man strode toward us.

Rory Cline looked every minute of forty and then some, with hollow cheeks and eyes to match. His spiky do fit him like lipstick fits a goldfish. His white shirt was wrinkled and limp as a used Kleenex. A skinny black tie dangled below the cinched belt line of gray pipe-stem trousers.

He pointed to the front doors, hurried past us, left the building.

We found him half a block down on Linden Drive, hands jammed in his pockets, pacing.

"Mr. Cline?"

"What are you doing to me? Now everyone'll think I'm a felon!"

Milo said, "In your business, maybe that could be career-enhancing."

Cline's eyes bugged. "Funny funny funny. I can't believe she sent you here. I already gave you guys my version and they believed me that her story was total bullshit. Now you're back? Why, because she's got beaucoup bucks, that's the way you guys do it, like that Eddie Murphy movie? What, I'm living a fucking Beverly Hills *comedy*?"

Herky-jerk movements, rat-a-tat speech, constricted pupils.

"She," said Milo.

"Her, she, whatever," said Rory Cline. "Let me cue you in: The only reason she's pursuing this is she probably heard I'm due to move up and she wants to get in on the gravy train."

Milo said, "Congrats on the promotion."

"Yeah, it's happening. Or *was* going to until you guys showed up and maybe fucked everything up. I'm being considered for an assis-tantship to Ed La*Moca. Get* it?"

"Big-time guy."

"As *in,*" said Cline, rattling off a list of movie stars. "Everyone wants to work for him, it's taken me shit-all *years* to get in position, and now you show up and they're going to think—how could you *do* this just because those *assholes* tell you to? They're fucking lying, the whole thing is a fucking put-up."

The pace of his speech had ratcheted from frantic to nearly unin-telligible. I wondered if the building was vast enough to conceal a meth lab.

Milo said, "Who do you think called us, Mr. Cline?"

"Who do I *think*? *Them.* Persian *bitch* and her *fucking* Persian husband. No matter how they're spinning it, *she* hit *me,* fucked up *my* bumper, fucked up *my* trunk, fucked up a *taillight.* I was in front, she was behind me, and there's no fucking way I rolled backward, it wasn't even uphill. I didn't call you guys because there were no injuries and she admitted it was her fault, promised to pay A-sap. Then she goes home, tells her rich fucking asshole rug merchant husband, he starts spinning. Fine, they wanna fight, I'll fight. What I don't get is you wasting your time when I already gave a statement to her insurance and they said they believed me, it's obvious I didn't roll back into her. The only reason I didn't have my own insurance was it lapsed after I moved here from ICM and if you read the insurance reports you'd know that."

He embarked on a ten-step march, came back. "May I go back to *work* and try not to get fucked *up*?"

Milo said, "This isn't about your fender-bender."

"Then *what*? I'm *busy*!"

"Calm down, sir."

"Don't tell me that. You probably just ruined my life, so don't—"

"Stop—"

"You stop—"

"Be quiet. *Now.*"

Something in Milo's voice killed the tirade. Cline wrung his hands.

"Let's start over—"

"What now? Oh, man," said Cline, "I haven't slept in I don't know—"

"Then we have something in common, Mr. Cline. I'm investigating a homicide."

"Homi-who? Someone got *killed*? *Who*?"

"Kat Shonsky."

Cline's posture loosened as if he'd been shot up with Valium. "You're kidding." He smiled.

"You think it's funny?"

"No, no, it's—that's—totally bizarre. You really came at me from left fucking field. Who killed her?"

"That's what we're trying to find out. What's bizarre?"

"Someone getting killed." Cline's mouth got hard. "Why are you talking to *me* about it?"

"We're talking to everyone she dated."

"Count me out, we never dated. She picked me up in a club, we had sex for a few months, then we both realized we were faking and said why bother."

"Hard for a man to fake," said Milo.

"You're being literal," said Cline. "Don't tell me it hasn't happened to you. I'm not talking losing it, I'm talking being there without *being* there."

Milo didn't answer.

"Fine," said Cline, "you're macho mellow, can do it with a can of liver. For me, it got empty. Because she was never *there*. We decided to be friends, just hang out. That didn't work either."

"How come?"

" 'Cause we didn't like each other." Cline drew back, maybe realizing the implication. "Listen, the last time I saw her was maybe half a year. I've had two girlfriends since then, you want to talk to them, be my guest, they'll tell you I'm safe as milk."

Cline fired off names. Milo wrote them down.

"You're actually going to call them? Unreal. Fine, do it, why not, could work for me with Lori, maybe she'll get interested again."

"Why?"

"Making me look dangerous and all that," said Cline. "Being safe is my issue. Lori thought I was average to nothing. Mostly I feel like nothing. Don't eat, don't sleep, and now you've fucked up my career." Shrill laughter. "Hell, maybe I'll cut my wrists." Rubbing his arms. "And it'll be your fault."

Milo said nothing.

Rory Cline said, "I know, I know, get some rest, do yoga, take my vitamins. Sorry, Charlie, it's like the ad for that gym. 'I'll rest when I'm dead.' "

Milo said, "Then I guess Kat's resting."

Cline shut his mouth. Tried to stand still and settled for rocking on his heels. "Unbelievable."

Milo asked where he'd been when Kat Shonsky left the club.

Cline said, "Here."

"In L.A.?"

"Here," said Cline. "Working. Down in the bowels, eating shit."

"Working over the weekend."

"What's a weekend? You want to check with the security logs, I can't stop you, but please don't, it's only going to fuck me up further."

"You do that a lot?" said Milo.

"Do what?"

"Work weekends."

"Fuck, yeah. Sometimes I don't go home for days. Ed LaMoca set the record twenty years ago, ten days without bathing. Dominated the droobs with radioactive ambition and cosmic body odor. They fade easily, the droobs, mostly Ivy League brats thinking they're gonna waltz from Harvard to repping Brad Pitt. I went to Cal State Northridge. Hunger gives me the edge."

Milo said, "Anything you can tell us about Kat Shonsky?"

"Big faker," said Cline. "Not just about *that,* about everything. Like she wanted to live someone else's life."

"Whose life?"

"Someone lazy and rich. She had half of it down."

"You didn't like her."

"I already told you that."

We asked a few more questions, slipping in cues about fancy cars and sexual kinks. All of that went right past Cline as he talked about himself.

When we turned to leave, he stood there.

Milo said, "You can go back to work."

Cline didn't move. "Listen, if it does turn out to be a story, let me know. If it's something Brad or Will or Russell can use, I'll make sure you're in it in a way that pays off big."

"Gee, thanks," said Milo.

"Excellent." Cline pumped air, ran back inside.

As Milo drove to the Valley, I reached one of Rory Cline's past girl-friends, a lawyer named Lori Bonhardt. She described Cline as "a wimp and a dishrag," denied ever witnessing a violent side.

"What's he done?"

"He knows someone who got hurt."

"Knows someone?" She laughed. "If that's all it is, forget it. Aggression would take effort and Rory's hobbies are drinking and sleeping. I used to tell him he should get on speed or something. Might give him some ambition. My Lhasa apso used to hump his leg and Chi never does that to anyone else. Know what that means?"

"Submissive personality," I said.

"Beta male. Pure vice president."

Michael Browning's eyes got moist when he heard about Kat.

He was a barrel-chested, rust-bearded fireplug, five six in thick-soled shoes, with sturdy, hirsute wrists and lumberjack hands. He wore a yellow-and-blue windowpane shirt, a big-knotted red tie of gleaming silk brocade, leather knit suspenders. The shoes were mocha suede wingtips, maintained impeccably.

The stylish duds of a full partner at Kaufler, Mandelbaum and Schlesinger, but Browning's office was a cubicle on the ground floor, one of two dozen in a fluorescent warren.

He spoke freely. Kat had stopped seeing him four months ago after learning he was married.

"I wasn't cheating. My wife and I were having problems. Debbie was doing her own thing and so was I. I met Kat at Leonardo's—the one on Ventura that closed down. Kat found out about Debbie when Debbie called my cell at Kat's place. Debbie was cool with the whole thing but Kat told me she didn't want to be space-filler and kicked me out. I didn't blame her." A curling thumb brushed a tear duct. "This is so incredibly sad. She was a nice girl."

First time anyone had used that adjective to describe Kat.

I said, "You parted on friendly terms."

"Of course," said Browning. "Kat was right about not wanting to be used. I told her I was sorry. She said she forgave me but we both knew it could never be the same."

"Did you see her after that?"

Tucking bristly beard hairs into his mouth, he chewed. His eyes shifted to the left. "Not often."

Milo and I waited.

"Don't tell my wife, okay?" said Browning.

"She's not cool with it anymore."

"We're back together. Expecting our first in two months."

"Congrats," said Milo. "How often did you and Kat see each other after the breakup?"

"We didn't really *see* each other," said Browning. "Not in the sense of a consistent relationship."

"But . . ."

Browning flashed what he considered a charming smile. "There were a couple weekends—retreats thrown by the firm." He glanced around the warren. The symphony of computer clicks hadn't slowed when we entered and no one was watching us now.

Milo said, "Where were the weekends and when did they take place?"

"Palm Springs and Mission Bay. As for the when . . ." Browning consulted his day planner. Read off dates.

Nine weeks ago and less than a month ago.

"Did she drive down and meet you or did you travel together?"

"Palm Springs she drove herself. San Diego, we went together. Please don't tell Debbie. We're happy now, it would be disruptive."

"No doubt," said Milo.

"Look," said Michael Browning, "I'm being totally open with

you. Even if I had reason to lie, I wouldn't because I'm no good at it. Debbie says I'm one big poker tell."

Milo asked where he'd been the night Kat disappeared.

Another page flip through the planner. The color leached from Browning's cheeks. Milo took the book. "Says here 'meeting, year-end deductions, TL.' What's that stand for?"

"Code," said Browning.

"For what?"

"Is it really important?" Browning asked.

"Now it is," said Milo.

"Sir, I'd never hurt Kat. Nothing but affection ever passed between us."

"Until she booted you out."

"When we were together it was always loving. I swear. Even if I wanted to, I couldn't lie and I have no reason to. A part of me might've *loved* Kat. I certainly wouldn't hurt her."

Milo said, "TL."

Browning leaned on his low-backed swivel chair. The seat creaked. "As long as Debbie doesn't get involved."

"Another woman."

"Nothing serious," said Browning. "A fling. Do you really need the details?"

"You bet, Mr. Browning. And we'll get them one way or the other."

"Okay, okay. Tenecia Lawrence. She was an intern from Valley College, spent a summer working for me and came in for a recommendation letter to the business school at the U. One thing led to another."

"You wanted to review her qualifications."

"It was mutual," said Browning. "If all she wanted was the letter, she could have just called."

Milo smiled. "First date for you and Ms. Lawrence."

Browning said, "Strictly speaking, no. We hung out a bit when she interned." Touching the rim of his desk. "She's black."

The irrelevancy hung in the air.

Browning said, "She's twenty, gorgeous, legs to infinity. I'm not going to make excuses. It's the way I'm wired."

"Let's have her phone number," said Milo.

"How about I just give you the facts? Tenecia and I spent that entire weekend together, I can produce hotel receipts. Debbie was at her mom's. She's hormonal. It leads to changes."

"The number."

"Receipts aren't enough?"

"If Ms. Lawrence confirms your story, they may be."

"*May?*" Sweat beaded Browning's flat, ruddy brow. "I have no anxiety about Kat, but Debbie—"

"If you didn't kill Kat, Debbie will never know we were here."

Browning exhaled. "Thanks. Thanks so much, I really appreciate it."

"Don't call Ms. Lawrence before we do," said Milo. "We'll know."

"Of course not, that never entered my mind." Browning held out a hand for a shake.

Milo pretended not to see it.

I said, "The last time you saw Kat, did she mention anything about an encounter with a customer?"

"A customer?"

"At her workplace."

"Oh, that," said Browning. "If you're talking about what I think you are."

We waited.

Browning said, "The freak, right? Transvestite, whatever."

"Tell us what Kat told you."

"A guy came into the store, checked out the goods. Kat figured out it was for himself."

"How?"

"She said he looked sneaky and nervous. She thought it was hilarious. Kind of faced off with the guy, like 'What do you think you're doing?' Kat could be like that."

"Like what?"

"Aggressive." Another shrug. "It had its benefits."

"How did the man react to being confronted?"

"She said he got ticked off and left and she felt good about handling him."

"How'd she describe him?"

"Um," said Browning. "She really didn't."

"Nothing at all?"

"She did say he was big, looking at plus sizes. That really cracked her up. Guy in a size sixteen cocktail dress."

"What else did she tell you?"

"That's it," said Browning. "It wasn't like I wanted to continue the discussion."

"Why not?"

"We were having a good time. Last thing I wanted was to talk about perverted stuff."

"Put her out of the mood," I said.

"Put *me* out of the mood," said Browning. "Kat was always ready. Made a lot of noise. Sometimes it got so loud you could almost think she was faking it but she wasn't."

"How could you tell?"

"No one fakes it with me. No need to."

"Mr. Speedfreak and Mr. Amoral Cretin," said Milo. "She did know how to pick 'em."

He sped back to the city, fighting the curves on Coldwater Canyon. "Good thinking bringing up the cross-dresser."

"Browning's her most recent lover, I figured it might come up."

"Pillow talk . . . sounds like she told everyone who'd listen."

"Proud of herself," I said. "For handling him."

"Aggressive with the wrong guy. But putting that aside, do either of these jokers bear further attention?"

I said, "Cline's got the anger and the dope-fed impulsiveness to do damage to Kat if she caught him at the wrong time. But he's got no obvious motive and he seems way too wired to pull off something so well planned. My guess is the agency security logs will back up his alibi but I'd definitely try to get them. Browning comes across agreeable but to my mind, he's scarier. He lies easily and lives to manipulate and I have no doubt he'd eliminate Kat, or anyone else who got in his way. His alibi's even simpler to verify."

"Tenecia Lawrence," Milo said, digging his notepad out of his pocket. "Let's do it before Browning preps her. Your turn, I need two hands on the wheel."

I put my cell on speaker and called the number he'd written down. A female voice answered with a high, chirpy "This is Neesh."

When I told her the reason for the call, she dropped from soprano to alto. "Am I in trouble?"

I cited the date. "We need to know if you were with Michael—"

"He told you?" Her voice broke. "It was supposed to be totally secret."

"It can stay that way," I said.

"Please," she said. "My parents."

"True or not, Tenecia?"

"Um . . . how do I know you're the police?"

"If you'd like we can drop by in person."

"No, no, that's okay."

"Were you with Michael?"

Silence.

"Tenecia?"

A scared little girl's voice said, "Yes, I was. My dad's a fire captain and that weekend he took my mom to a reunion at Lake Arrowhead, all the battalions that had fought the big Laguna fire. Michael wanted to come to the house but I wouldn't let him, no way. He would've stood out."

"Why?"

"We live in Ladera Heights," she said.

Prosperous black suburb.

I said, "Where did you and Michael go?"

"You'll really keep this secret?"

"If you're truthful, there's no reason for it to get out."

"Okay, um—Michael picked me up at school and we drove to a hotel."

"Which one?"

"Dayside Inn."

"Where is that?"

"Near the airport, I don't know the street. We stayed in all day. Watched movies. *The Wedding Planner* and *Prime* with Uma Thurman and Meryl Streep 'cause it's one of my favorites. Michael was okay with it, he likes chick flicks."

"Then what?"

"Then the next day we went to Long Beach, visited the aquarium. I'd never been there."

Silence.

"It's really pretty," she said. "The aquarium."

"What happened after that, Tenecia?"

"Nothing."

"You stayed in Long Beach."

"I—this is going to sound . . . we were just having fun."

"Where'd you go?"

Audible sigh. "Another hotel. Best Western, near the aquarium. The next day, we came home. I mean, not right away. First we went to dinner at Sizzler, then we drove through Palos Verdes to see the ocean. Then we went to Michael's house in Granada Hills. I was nervous to go there but it was dark and Michael said it was okay. The next morning, he drove me back to school. I didn't have a class until one p.m., so we had breakfast on campus, hung out, then he drove to work. Am I in trouble?"

"Not if you've been truthful."

"I have been, I swear."

"So you were definitely with Mr. Browning the entire weekend."

"I won't see him anymore," she said. "He's too old for me. Is *he* in trouble?"

"Nothing for you to worry about, Tenecia."

"Okay, but I'm really not going to see him. You won't have to call again, will you? Sometimes my dad picks up my phone."

"You're fine, Tenecia."

"Thank you so much. Thank you."

Milo said, "Poor kid, we mighta scared her into celibacy."

"If she keeps away from Browning," I said, "we did our good deed for the day."

"Lowlife. Too bad he's not our guy."

He called in for messages. Gordon Beverly wanted to know if anything was new. Milo reached him, spent a few tortured minutes trying to be therapeutic.

Another try at Bradley Maisonette's parole officer produced a third burst of voice mail. Milo left an irate message and dialed Wilson Good's home number.

"No answer. Screw his flu, let's go bug the coach."

19

No cars behind the mesh gate at Wilson Good's house. No answer to the bell ring.

A call to St. Xavier confirmed that Coach Good was still out sick.

I said, "Maybe he went to the doctor."

Milo took in the sliver of view between the house and its northern neighbor. "Guy made a nice life for himself . . . okay, back to the gristmill."

Sean Binchy waved the Bentley key.

His presence in Milo's office meant no room to move and rapid oxygen depletion.

Milo said, "Heubel give it up easily?"

"Had to work on him a little, Loot. I figured telling him about Shonsky might do the trick but he got pretty freaked out, like 'Don't tell me stuff like that.' He didn't like the idea of the car being messed with but I got him to see it was important."

"Where's the car?"

"Across the street in the lot," said Sean. "Couple of uniforms saw me drive in, had all sorts of fun. It's an experience. Everyone stares."

I said, "I'm sure it caught Kat Shonsky's eye."

Binchy said, "A lot of girls would trust someone with wheels like that."

Milo said, "Okay, Sean, you get to be stared at all the way to the motor lab. I'll call and set up the paperwork."

Binchy grinned and rotated an imaginary steering wheel. "Anything else, Loot?"

"That's enough for the time being."

"Guess I opened a can of worms, huh? Calling you in the first place."

"It was obviously a can that needed to be opened, Sean."

"When you put it that way," said Binchy. "Weird, huh?"

"Without weird, life would be boring, Sean."

"Speaking of which, if I could possibly get in a position where I could return to Homicide, do you think that would be a good idea?"

"I think you should make yourself happy."

"So . . . you're not opposed to it."

"Why would I be?"

Binchy nodded and left.

"Maybe he's got a future," I said.

"What makes you say that?"

"Opening worm cans all by himself."

I drove home, walked Blanche, ate pizza with Robin, checked my e-mail.

Lots of urgent communication: six bogus stock tips, an offer to lengthen my penis, ads for two different kinds of organic Viagra, and Jason Blasco at DarkVisions.net wanting to know if I'd learned anything more about the Bright-Tranh murders and informing me he'd found pictures of one of the heads Jeffrey Dahmer had kept in his fridge (*"totally real don't ask me where i recieved it"*).

At the bottom was a message from Sheriff George Cardenas:

Dr. Delaware, doesn't look as if Ansell Bright ever owned property in California under that name or "Dale." His last known car registration was the year his parents died and his address was their home in San Francisco. I'll try to send you a jpg of his DMV photo tomorrow. The house was sold for $980,000 shortly after Mrs. Bright died and has changed hands twice. I managed to find the person who bought it the first time. The transaction was handled by agents and the buyer never met Ansell. He did confirm that Ansell was the seller, so we can assume Ansell got a nice chunk of money. Maybe he moved out of state to get more bang for his buck.

I haven't been able to access Social Security records without a warrant but maybe LAPD has more clout. The only other thing I could think of is what Mrs. Wembley said about Leonora telling her Ansell fed the homeless. I looked up various groups in San Francisco, talked to a few people but no one remembers Ansell or Dale Bright.

Best,

George Cardenas

Nine hundred eighty thousand was a serious motive. Well over a million if Ansell Bright's parents had left stocks, bonds, cash, or other real estate.

Tony Mancusi was set to become a millionaire as soon as his mother's will cleared.

That level of incentive, paying a hit man would be a terrific investment, if you put aside petty distractions like human decency.

How did Kat Shonsky's murder fit?

I worked that every way I could think of, concluded it didn't. If the same killer had gotten her, the motive had to be personal.

Young woman with hostile tendencies confronts a cross-dresser with a much darker secret than choice of wardrobe.

That brought me back to Tony Mancusi's effeminate mannerisms. Donald Bragen's description of Bright as "fluttering" over the phone.

Dale, an androgynous name.

A contract killer with a thing for chic French dresses meeting like-minded individuals and drumming up business?

Overtones . . .

If Tony led a secret life, surveillance of his apartment might eventually bear fruit. Finding Dale nine years after his sister's murder would be a lot tougher.

I got back on the computer, searched for soup kitchens and missions in L.A.

Fifteen minutes later, I'd printed three pages. Nice to know the city wasn't all about ego and tax brackets. I made a few calls. Most offices were closed until morning. The people I spoke to had never heard of Ansell or Dale Bright.

Just as I was about to pack it in, a new e-mail arrived.

> *Dr. Delaware, George again. I got back from a false raccoon call at Mavis's and that made me think about animal shelters. Leonora said Dale was cruel to animals but faked like he wasn't so wouldn't that be a perfect split personality thing? Anyway, I did find a group where he volunteered. Paws and Claws, the person in charge at the Berkeley branch remembers Bright because she used to work with him back when she was a volunteer. She said one day he just stopped coming in and when she called him the number was d.c.'d. She recalls this clearly as nine years ago, right after Easter, because someone dropped off abandoned bunnies and Bright took good care of them, then a few days later he went awol. That makes it a month before Leonora and Vicki Tranh were killed, so maybe he left to plan the crime. Or Mavis is wrong and he's just a normal guy who got tired of cleaning up animal crap. If you're interested, the informant's name is Shantee Moloney. Her number is 415 . . .*

Shantee Moloney said, "Whoa. That Mayberry cop said you might be calling but that was fast."

I said, "I appreciate your talking to me."

"I've gotta be honest, I'm not a big police person, when I was a student at Cal, law enforcement was tear gas and billy clubs. But I guess if Dale did something that bad—you really think he did? 'Cause part of me says that's impossible. Dale was so devoted and nonviolent."

"But," I said.

"But what?"

"Part of you . . ."

"Oh," said Shantee Moloney. "It was just strange the way he dropped out of sight without telling anyone."

"What was Dale like?"

"Devoted. Like I said. He said he was a vegan, didn't even wear leather."

"He said?"

"I really have no basis for doubting him."

"But you doubt him anyway."

"What are you, a mind reader?"

"Just a mere mortal trying to get some facts," I said. "Did Dale do something that made you wonder about his credibility?"

"No, nothing like that. I'm not sure it's even true."

I waited.

Shantee Moloney said, "I'm not a gossip."

"Sometimes it's hard to know what's petty and what's important."

Dead air.

"Ms. Moloney—"

"Okay, okay. After Dale stopped coming in, I mentioned to another volunteer that I'd tried to call him, got a disconnected number, was worried if he was okay. This other person said, 'Oh, he's fine, just saw him over at the Tadich Grill a couple of nights ago.' That's an old restaurant in San Francisco. I said, 'Well that's good, at least I know he's okay. But I'm still wondering why he suddenly stopped coming to the shelter.' And this other person laughs and says, 'Looked to me like Dale had a sudden conversion.' I say, 'What you mean?' And he tells me Dale was in a booth by himself eating a ginormous meal—huge platter of oysters, crab cocktail, then a honkin' shoulder of lamb. That floored me. I'm a vegetarian but I eat eggs and dairy. Dale claimed to be *total* vegan, used to go on about the ethical and health virtues of eliminating all animal matter. And now he's stuffing his face with flesh?"

"Faking it," I said.

"I guess he fooled me. If it's true. One thing he didn't fake was his dedication to the strays. No one could've cared for those animals with more tenderness."

"Bunnies."

"Someone's stupid idea of an Easter gift. I'm talking newborns, like big as your thumb. Dale stayed up all night nursing them with an eyedropper. When I left, he was *still* there."

"Why would the other volunteer make up that story?"

"Let's just say he and Dale weren't chummy."

"Could I have this person's name, please?"

"Brian Leary, but that won't help you, he's gone. AIDS, six years ago."

"Is there anyone else at the shelter who'd remember Dale?"

"No," she said. "It was just the three of us working the midnight shift. I'm a freelance embroiderer, my hours are flexible, and Brian was a nurse at UCSF, did the three to eleven and didn't need much sleep, so he'd come in after work."

"What about Dale?"

"Dale spent more time at the shelter than anyone. He never mentioned any job at all. I got the feeling there was family money."

"Why's that?"

"The way he dressed—wrinkled clothes but good quality? The way he carried himself? I'm pretty tuned in to class distinctions."

"What was the problem between him and Brian?"

"I really couldn't tell you. Brian mostly worked with the cats, he loved cats. Dale and I did anything else that needed to be done."

"Brian never said why he didn't like Dale?"

"No, I guess it was just bad chemistry. I was in the middle—I thought they were both good guys."

"Brian just happened to be at the Tadich Grill that night?"

"Was he stalking Dale? Not at all. Brian was out on a date, some doctor he'd been seeing."

"Do you recall a name?"

"You're kidding," she said. "First of all, Brian never gave me a name. Second of all, this was almost a decade ago."

I said, "Can't fault a guy for trying."

"I really can't imagine Dale doing anything criminal. Anyway, gotta go—"

"How'd Dale come to work at the shelter?"

"Walked in one night and volunteered. I was up to my elbows in abandoned puppies and it was a blessing. He got right to work, cleaning, feeding, checking for fleas. He was great."

"Can you describe him for me?"

"Big," said Shantee Moloney.

"Tall or heavy?"

"Both. At least six feet, probably taller. He wasn't really fat, more like . . . padded."

"What about his hair color?"

"Light—dirty blond, but it was dyed. He wore it long—shaggy, over his forehead. But it always looked clean and shiny. Real shiny. That's what I meant about carrying himself well. He wore hemp shoes and belt. But there was always a . . . I guess what I'm saying is he managed to look polished."

"Did he ever talk about his family?"

"Nope."

"No personal details at all?"

"The other cop asked the same thing and that made me realize Dale's family never came up. I'd call Dale a private person. But not cold. Just the opposite, friendly. And businesslike—really into doing the job efficiently."

"Any other physical details you can remember?"

"His beard was darker than his hair—medium brown."

First mention of facial hair. "Full beard or goatee?"

"It totally covered his face. Reminded me of that guy used to be on TV, that mountain man—Grizzly whatever—Adams. But Dale was no mountain man."

"Too polished."

She laughed. "You could say that."

"Gay?"

"A lot of us are. So where'd Dale end up?"

"That was going to be my next question."

"I'm supposed to know?" she said.

"Did he ever talk about traveling?"

"He did say he liked the great cities."

"Which ones?"

"Paris, Rome, London, New York. Maybe Madrid, I don't recall. The only reason I remember the conversation is he and Brian kind of got into it. Brian saying if you really loved animals you couldn't love cities, cities destroyed habitat, and Dale launched into this lecture about the cats of Rome and how they adapted and thrived. Then Brian said the whole urban thing was a cliché—April in Paris, et cetera— and Dale said some clichés persisted because they were valid, the great cities were called that because they were, and if Brian thought San Francisco was sophisticated, he was naive. It just kind of went on that way for a while, then they returned to work."

"Did Dale mention any other places he liked?"

"Not that I remember."

"No Grizzly Adams," I said.

"His nails were always clean and manicured and he wore after-shave. Couldn't tell you the brand, but it was something nice and citrus-ey."

"Anything more?"

"That's not enough? After all these years, I thought I was being pretty darn encyclopedic."

"You are. That's why I keep turning pages. So Dale was good with all the animals."

"Better than good," said Shantee Moloney. "Tender. Especially the little ones. Not just babies, anything small—he really had a thing for puppies and toy dogs. Nastiest little critter, he could calm it down. I got a sense he'd had experience with the teeny ones."

20

Ansell Dennond Bright's DMV photo came through at ten a.m. the following day.

Thirteen-year-old shot, when Bright was twenty-nine.

Six feet, two ten, blond and brown, needs corrective lenses.

Relaxed expression, nothing ominous in the eyes.

True to Shantee Moloney's description, lank, pale strands obscured Bright's brow, draping his ears and fanning his shoulders.

The beard was a broad, brown sheet, pelting his face from Adam's apple to the bottoms of his eye sockets.

Nothing to see *but* hair.

Art of the misdirect.

Did that explain Bright's lie about not eating animals? Manipulating Shantee Moloney, but to what end? Bright had never received a penny for his work at the shelter.

Love of the game or a need to feel virtuous?

Or both.

All that hair; nature's costume.

I thought of High Plains drifter duds. Plaid cap, old man's shuffle, conspicuous wheels. It all added up to clever theater.

In Kat Shonsky's situation, the Bentley would've been enough to lower her guard but I wondered if the killer had gone further.

Angry man with a thing for A-lines and heels, still seething at Kat's ridicule. What sweeter revenge than to stalk her in drag?

I pictured the big black car gliding by as she fretted in her Mustang. Passenger window sliding down, revealing a driver in a bouffant wig, designer dress, maybe a discreet string of pearls.

That extra touch.

A pretty, diaphanous *scarf*.

Kat's driver's license—the symbol of her identity—had been wedged in her private parts.

Some killers take souvenirs, other leave them. It's always about a message.

The message Kat's killer had delivered was *You're not the woman you think you are. Mock me at your own peril.*

Kat. An animal name.

Too perfect to resist.

Milo phoned just before two p.m., yawned a greeting followed by a bout of coughing.

I said, "Rock-and-roll pneumonia or boogie-woogie flu?"

"Oh, man, it's way too early for humor."

"It's the afternoon."

"Feels like daybreak . . . Jesus, you're right. Did a whole lot more nothing watching Tony, got home at six and crashed till an emergency call jolted me up at seven. Bradley Maisonette's parole officer. 'You sounded frantic, Lieutenant, so I thought I'd catch you early.' I'm on two cylinders, bastard's gloating. And what's the big news: Bradley's been *persona non show-uppa* for seven weeks. But not to worry, he's got a history of dropping out for stretches, always comes back."

"Addict's excursions," I said.

"Doesn't sound like a guy who digs art museums and thee*ay*ter. P.O. considers him low priority because he's got a long list of more violent guys who don't show up. Says Maisonette doesn't 'act out' unless he's exhausted legal avenues of income."

"He works?"

"Panhandles, sells his blood. P.O. diagnoses the basic problem as 'low self-esteem.' "

"Everyone's a therapist," I said.

"I finally got the idiot to agree to pretend to search for him. Thanks for Cardenas's e-mail. You get a chance to talk to the animal lady?"

I summarized the conversation with Shantee Moloney.

"Small dogs," he said. "As in Leonora's missing pooches?"

"If Dale was behind the Ojo Negro murders," I said, "it would be nice to think he took them as pets."

"Loves dogs, hates Sis."

"Wears hemp shoes and eats meat on the sly."

He sang the chorus of Lou Christie's "Two Faces Have I."

I said, "He's also the right size for Ella's killer, the cowboy, and Kat's cross-dresser."

"And size matters . . . loves the great cities, huh? Gets hold of major inheritance, travels the world, settles into L.A.?"

"Maybe it's the weather." I gave him my woman-with-a-scarf theory.

"Society lady in two hundred grand worth of car—why not? Now all we need is Dale to come waltzing through the door confessing."

"Short of that, how about this: One of the cities Bright mentioned to Moloney was New York. The chief's old turf. Why not start there and see if any black-car murders show up? Or if Bright left some kind of paper trail from San Francisco."

He didn't answer.

"There's a problem?"

"No," he said. "On the contrary. A chance for His Beneficence to demonstrate his commitment."

"You doubt him?"

"So far he's been as righteous as a politician can be, but I'm like that bumper sticker, *Question Authority*. New Yawk New Yawk . . . I was thinking Rome but my French is rusty. Okay, scan Bright's picture and send it over and I'll put a call in to Himself."

Three hours later, he was at my front door, freshly shaved, wearing a bright blue shirt under a coarse gray herringbone jacket, a green tie patterned with brown ukuleles, khakis, bubble-toe gray oxfords with red crepe soles.

Usually, he beelines for the kitchen. This time he stood in the door, eyes dancing, lips curled in a scary scimitar I knew to be a smile.

"His Excellency woke someone up and presto, we got records from the N.Y. Housing Department rolls. Mr. Dale Bright was never a property owner but his name does show up on a petition eight years ago. Converting an industrial building to condos."

"Pro or con?"

"Pro."

I said, "One year after he inherits, he's in his favorite American city, trying to break into the real estate market?"

He loped to my office, logged on to my computer, typed in *518 w. 35th st NY 10001*.

Six hits flashed, all culled from newspaper accounts, all variants on the same theme.

He called up the *New York Post*.

Vanished Couple Condo-Complexity?

The mysterious disappearance of a Manhattan couple involved in a long-term landlord-tenant dispute continues to baffle New York's finest. Three weeks ago, rent-controlniks Paul and Dorothy Safran left their apartment on 518 W. 35th Street to attend an off-off-Broadway production in lower Manhattan and haven't been seen or heard from since.

Paul, 47, a lithographer, and Dorothy, 44, a substitute teacher, had been embroiled in a yearlong struggle with their landlord over

*failure to provide heat and plans to convert the former warehouse that
served as their domicile to condominiums.*

*The three-story structure in the still-industrial 'hood had been
subdivided 22 years ago into Soho-style rental lofts and the Safrans
had lived there protected by rent-control provisions. Soon after the
building changed hands, the new owner, an Englewood, N.J.–based
developer named Roland Korvutz, announced plans for condo-
conversion. Under an agreement brokered between Korvutz and a
newly elected tenant board, residents were offered compensated relo-
cation or first dibs on the newly constructed units.*

*Most tenants opted for the payoff but the Safrans, claiming the
board was corrupt, refused to budge and brought suit against Korvutz
in Housing Court. For the past six months, the Safrans withheld rent
and tried to rally other tenants to their cause.*

*In a breaking story three days ago, The Post reported the claims of
Paul Safran's sister, Marjorie Bell, of Elmhurst, that shortly before the
dueling duo vanished they'd expressed fears for their safety because of
the conflict with Korvutz. Bell also criticized the police for not investigating Korvutz more thoroughly and alleged that Korvutz, an immi-
grant from Belarus, has a history of tenant intimidation.*

*When contacted yesterday by The Post for follow-up, Bell refused
comment.*

*Court records reveal eleven suits brought against Korvutz's com-
pany, RK Development, all settled before trial. Korvutz's attorney,
Bernard Ring, said, "Anyone attempting to beautify the city encounters that kind of thing. Call it the price of doing business in a litigious
society."*

*Repeated calls to Korvutz's home in Englewood and to RK Devel-
opment offices in Teterboro were not returned. Police sources describe
the investigation into the Safrans' whereabouts as "in progress."*

A five-year follow-up article reported no solve.

I said, "Dale signed the petition. He was living in the Safrans'
building when they disappeared."

"Dale was chairman of the tenant board."

"When he's around, some people's problems get solved, others stop breathing."

"If there was a money motive, it wasn't bargain real estate, Alex; Dale never bought a condo or any other residence in the city."

"Maybe he was paid to do a job," I said. "Wonder where his next stop was."

"By any chance," he said, "are you feeling some wanderlust?"

Finally, the inevitable foray to the fridge. Milo spread jam and butter on half a dozen pieces of bread, folded the first piece in half, pushed it into his mouth, and chewed slowly.

"Here's the situation," he said, gulping milk from the carton. "With two open cases and the need to stay on Antoine Beverly, I can't leave. Chief offered me Sean or another rookie D, but Sean's never flown further than Phoenix and I don't want to start breaking in a greenhorn. When I brought up your name to His Importance he thought that would be a peachy idea as long as you don't step 'outside the boundaries of departmental procedures and can adhere to departmental guidelines.' "

"What's the difference?"

"*Procedures* is don't get arrested. *Guidelines* is a discount flight on JetBlue, the subway not taxis, food vouchers that might cover Taco Bell twice a day, and hostelry that's a distant galaxy from that place you were gonna stay at a couple of years ago—the St. Regis."

Aborted vacation some time back with the woman I'd seen during the breakup. Through a mutual friend, I'd heard Allison was engaged . . .

"You can take Robin if you pay for her."

"She's in the middle of a big project."

He ate another slice of bread. "So when can you leave?"

CHAPTER

21

I booked the nine p.m. red-eye to Kennedy out of Burbank the following day. The flight was delayed an hour due to "factors in New York," and when the plane did arrive, the smiling woman behind the counter announced a refuel stop in Salt Lake City due to short runways at Bob Hope Airport and "wind issues."

We boarded ninety minutes later and for the next six and a half hours, I sat with my knees bent at an interesting angle, sharing a row with a young tattooed couple who made out audibly. I tried to kill time by watching the satellite TV screen on my seat back during the intermittent periods it functioned. Shows about gardening, competitive cooking, and serial killers made me drowsy and I drifted in and out of sleep, woke to loving murmurs and slurping tongues.

The final time I roused, touchdown was half an hour away and the screen was fuzzy. I took another look at the contents of the business-sized envelope.

Single sheet of paper, Milo's back-slanted cursive.

1. *Safran-Bright residence: 518 W. 35 now Lieber Braid and Trim. (bet. 9th and 10th)*
2. *Detective Samuel Polito (ret.) cell # 917 555 2396. Lunch at 1:30, call him for details*
3. *RK Developers new address: 420 Seventh Avenue (bet 32d and 33rd)*
4. *Roland Korvutz new address: 762 Park Avenue, 9A (bet 72d and 73rd)*
5. *Korvutz favorite restaurants:*
   a. *Lizabeth (breakfast), 996 Lexington (bet 71st and 72d)*
   b. *La Bella, 933 Madison (bet 74th and 75th)*
   c. *Brasserie Madison, 1068 Madison (81st)*
6. *Your hostelry: The Midtown Executive, 152 W. 48 (bet 6th and Broadway—give my regards to . . .)*

By nine a.m. I was presenting myself to a droopy-lidded clerk in the closet-sized lobby of the Midtown Executive Hotel. The space was eye-searing bright and beautified by a rack of postcards, maps, and miniature *I Love NY* pennants.

The clerk moved his lips while studying my reservation slip. "Bill's being paid by some kind of voucher . . ."

"L.A. Police Department."

"Whatever." He checked a card file. "Doesn't include incidentals."

"You've got room service?"

"Nah, the phone. Rates are a ripoff, I'd use a cell."

"Thanks for the tip."

"I need a credit card. Four thirteen. That's the fourth floor."

Cracking the door allowed me to squeeze into the room.

Eight by eight, with a lav half that size, all the charm of an MRI chamber.

A single mattress as thin as Tony Mancusi's Murphy bed was

wedged by a nightstand fashioned from a pink-blond mystery material. A nine-inch TV screwed to the wall fought for space with a snarl
of wires. Completing the décor were a bolted-down floor lamp and a
soiled watercolor of the Chrysler Building.

The sole window was stationary and double-paned, the glass thick
enough to mute the din of West Forty-eighth and Broadway to a per-
sistent, peevish grumble punctuated by random honks and clangs.
Drawing the lint-colored drapes turned the room into a tomb but did
nothing to lower the volume.

I stripped down, got under the covers, set the alarm on my watch
for two hours hence, closed my eyes.

An hour later, I was still wide awake, trying to synch my brain
waves with the urban soundtrack down below. Somehow I managed
to drop off only to be slapped awake at eleven by the alarm. I called
Detective Samuel Polito (ret.), got a canned female voice permitting
me to leave a message. During the time it took to shower and shave,
my phone registered a return call.

"Polito."

"Detective, this is Alex Delaware—"

"The shrink, how you doing? I got an appointment before you.
Where are you?"

I told him.

He said, "That place? We used to put witnesses up there, charac-
ters you needed to stick around to testify but they wouldn't unless you
babysat 'em. Used to give 'em a giant pizza, pay-per-view, and a good-
looking female A.D.A. to chaperone."

I said, "Zero out of three ain't bad."

"The Executive," he said. "Takes me back. Listen, I can't move up
seeing you earlier than half past one, you want a late breakfast by
yourself, go for it."

"Would've brought my Jell-O and oatmeal on the plane but security thought they might ignite."

"Got a sense of humor, huh? You'll need it. Okay, meet me at this place, Le Petit Grenouille, at half past. Seventy-ninth between Lex and Third, French, but friendly."

By noon, I was out on the street. The air was crisp and illogically fresh and the grumble had transformed to something rich and melodic. Ninety minutes remained until my lunch date; I used a third of it walking to Paul and Dorothy Safran's last known residence.

Commercial neighborhood, more trucks than cars. The three-story brick structure housing Lieber Braid and Trim was lined with rows of stingy, square windows. Wire-glass panes were crusted with grime.

Wondering what had prompted Roland Korvutz to abandon his plans to condo-convert, I turned around, picked up my pace, and headed for Fifth Avenue.

Being alone in a big alien city sometimes tweaks my brain in a strange way, setting off jolts of euphoria followed by a substrate of melancholy. Usually, it takes time to develop. This time, it was instantaneous and as I race-walked New York's bustling streets, I felt weightless and anonymous.

At Fifth and Forty-second, I got sucked up into the crowd near the public library, forged north dodging NASCAR pedestrians, handbill hawkers, window-gawkers, lithe pickpockets. Crossing Fifty-ninth took me past the construction project that had once been the Plaza Hotel. Hansom drivers waited for fares. The air was ripe with horseshit. I walked parallel with Central Park. The trees wore their fall colors with appropriate arrogance.

By one twenty-eight, I was sitting in a stiff wooden booth at Le Petit Grenouille, drinking water and red wine and eating acrid, oil-cured olives.

The place was set up with starched white linens, vintage tobacco posters, and rust-colored walls under a black tin ceiling. Half the booths were occupied by stylish people. A gilt-lettered window faced the energy of the street. Getting here had taken me past the mayor's graystone town house on Seventy-ninth. No different from any other billionaire's digs except for flint-eyed plainclothes cops guarding the front steps and fighting introspection.

A smiling waitress with chopped red hair and a sliver of torso brought a basket of rolls and a butter dish. I worked on my blood sugar and looked at my watch.

At one forty-seven, a blocky, blue-jawed man in his sixties entered the restaurant, said something to the host, flatfooted over.

"Sam Polito."

"Alex Delaware."

Polito's hand was hard and rough. The little hair he had left was white and fine. He wore a black windbreaker, gray ribbed turtleneck, charcoal slacks, black loafers with gold Gucci buckles that might have been real. Rosy cheeks contrasted with a lower face that would never looked shaved. His right eye was clear and brown. Its mate was a sagging remnant with a milky iris.

Polito said, "Hey, Monique," to the waitress. "Salmon wild today?"

"Oh yes."

"I'll have it. With the white asparagus, big glass of that Médoc wine, Château whatever."

"Potatoes?"

Polito contemplated. "What the heck, yeah. Easy on the oil."

"Bon. M'sieur?"

"Hanger steak, medium rare, salad, fries."

Polito watched her depart, aiming his face so his good eye had maximum coverage. "Red meat, huh? No cholesterol issues?"

"Not so far," I said.

The eye took me in. "Me, it's just the opposite. Everyone in my family croaks by sixty. I beat it by three years so far, had a stent when I was fifty-eight. Doctor says Lipitor, watch what I eat, drink the vino, there's a good chance I can set a record."

"Good for you."

"So," he said, "you got some kind of pull."

"With who?"

"Deputy chief calls me at home, I'm about to drive off to Lake George with the wife, he says, 'Sam, I want you to meet with someone.' Like I'm still obligated."

"Sorry for messing up your plans."

"Hey, it was my choice. He told me what it was, I'm more than happy." Snatching a roll from the basket, he broke it in two, watched the crumbs rain. "Even though we're not talking one of my triumphs."

"Tough case."

"Jimmy Hoffa'll be found before the Safrans will. Maybe in the same place."

"Under some building," I said. "Or in the East River."

"The former. The river, we'da found 'em. Damn thing runs both ways, all that agitation, bodies come up, I had more than my share of floaters." He reached for an olive, gnawed around the pit. "Trust me, the river, they'da shown up."

His wine arrived. He sniffed, swirled, sipped. "Elixir of life. That and the olive oil." Catching the waitress's eye, he mouthed "Oil" and mimicked pouring.

After he'd sopped up half the golden puddle with his bread, he said, "Work this city long enough, you get a taste for fine food. So tell me about these L.A. murders."

I summarized.

"That's it?"

"Unfortunately."

"So this Dale character, only reason you're here is guilt by association maybe, possibly, could-be."

"Yup."

"Fancy cars, huh? That's L.A., ain't it? They actually put you on a plane for that? LAPD must be getting modern, sending a shrink— sorry, a psychologist. How'd you get that kind of pull?"

"The Midtown Executive is pull?"

"You got a point."

The food came. Polito said, "Seriously, Doc, I'm curious, the whole psych bit. We got guys, but what they do is therapize when the brass thinks a guy's screwed up. You do that?"

I gave him a short-version account of my history and my role.

"Doing your own thing," he said. "If you can pull it off, that's the way to go. Anyway, the Safrans. Suspicion fell right away on Korvutz, because he was the only one they were known to have serious conflict with. Plus he had a history of what I'd call sneaky moves. Like bringing a demo crew in the middle of the night and taking down a building so the neighbors can't complain. Then, when everyone's got their panties in an uproar, his lawyers apologize, 'Oops, sorry, paperwork mess-up, we'll compensate you for any inconvenience.' Then it takes months to figure out what the inconvenience is, then more delays, then everyone forgets."

"The newspaper account I read said he'd been sued a lot."

"Price of doing business."

"That's what his lawyer called it."

"His lawyer was right, Doctor. This city, you sneeze upwind, you're in court. My son's finishing at Brooklyn Law. Did ten years in Brooklyn Robbery, saw where the bread was buttered." Smiling. "Olive-oiled."

His attention shifted to his plate and he began eating with obvious pleasure. My steak was great but my mind was elsewhere. I waited awhile before asking if there'd been suspects other than Korvutz.

"Nope. And it never went anywhere with Korvutz because we couldn't find any criminal connections. Despite the Russian thing. We got neighborhoods, Doctor, Brighton Beach, whatnot, you hear more Russian than English. Some of these guys came over in the first place to do no-good, we got Russian-speaking detectives keeping plenty busy. None of them and none of their informants ever heard of Korvutz. He wasn't from Moscow, Odessa, the places most of them are from."

"Belarus."

"Used to be called White Russia, it's its own country now," said

Polito. "The point I'm making is no matter how deep we dug, there was no dirt on Korvutz. Sure, he's in court a lot. So is every other developer. And each time he gets sued, he settles."

"Any of his other tenants disappear?"

Polito shook his head. "And no one he litigated with would talk trash about him 'cause that's the condition of the settlements. To be honest, Doc, only reason he was even considered was there was no one else on the radar. Now you're telling me about this Bright character."

"You remember him?"

"I got a vague memory, only because he was the head of that put-up tenant board."

"It was an obvious put-up?"

"Look," said Polito, "there's never any board before Korvutz buys the building, same goes for the first six months Korvutz owns it. Then he files for permission to convert and all of a sudden there's an election no one remembers too clearly and a board of three people, all of which are tenants who came on after Korvutz bought the building."

I said, "Bright plus two others."

"A distant cousin of Korvutz and the son of the plumber who services Korvutz's New Jersey buildings."

He produced a folded piece of lined paper, same size as Milo's pad. "I remembered the names."

"Appreciate it."

"Hey," he said, "D.C. calls, who'm I to say no." Slowly spreading smile. "Even if he is my wife's brother-in-law."

Neat typing on the sheet.

518 W. 35 Tenant Board Members
1. Dale Bright
2. Sonia Glusevitch
3. Lino Mercurio

I said, "Korvutz knew the other two before he bought the building. Any indication of a prior relationship with Bright?"

"Nope. And here's the thing, Doc: Even if the board was a puppet thing, it's no big deal legally. Landlord's not obligated to have a board, period. And none of the tenants gave a crap. Except for the Safrans. They screamed corruption."

I pocketed the paper.

Polito said, "Truth is, Doc, the Safrans had no leg to stand on, they were just making problems. Everyone else was happy with the deal Korvutz offered because it was better than what they had in that dump. We're not talking big lofts, like in Soho. This was a crappy place, used to be a shoe factory, that got divided into dinky units, real cheap construction. I'm talking singles and one-bedrooms, iffy plumbing and wiring, not to mention your basic rodent issues, because it's a commercial neighborhood, open garbage cans, whatnot. Korvutz makes an offer they can't refuse, no one refuses."

"Except the Safrans," I said.

Polito put down his fork. "I don't like bad-mouthing my vics but from what I could tell those two were *confrontative.* I'm talking hippie refugees from the sixties. He was at City College back when, radical SDS type. I was in uniform back then, did crowd control. For all I know he was one of those spoiled little bastards screaming at me."

"What about Dorothy?"

"Same thing."

"Rebels without a cause," I said. "Dorothy's sister said they'd felt threatened—"

"Margie Bell," he said. "Let me tell you about Margie. Long history of depression and whatnot. On all kinds of medication, plus she'd had two commitments to Bellevue. One year later, she hung herself."

"Definite suicide?"

"Her own kid found her in the bathroom with a note. Doc, the Safrans made a tempest out of a teapot. You get to live cheap in this city because of rent control, count your blessings and move on. I went through their apartment, tossed every inch trying to find a lead." Shaking his head. "Wouldn't let my dog live like that. They did, though. Let their dog. In one corner there was dirty newspapers spread out, urine stains, piles of dog dirt all dried up. These people weren't housekeepers—sorry if I ruined your steak. What I'm getting at is they were living like squatters, shoulda taken Korvutz up on his offer."

"Ever see the dog?"

"Nope, just what it left behind. Why?"

I told him about Leonora Bright's missing pets. Dale Bright's volunteering at Paws and Claws.

He twirled his wineglass. "This guy likes furry things but maybe he's not so nice to people?"

"It's been known to happen."

"You bet," he said. "Had one case, back when I started out, down on Ludlow Street, Lower East Side. Crazy junkie carves up his old lady, leaves her propped up, sitting at the kitchen table for two weeks. We're talking middle of the summer, tenement, no air-conditioning, you can imagine. Meanwhile, he's got a pit bull, everyone says it's a nice mutt, but you wouldn't catch me petting one of those. Anyway, this dog, this maniac pampers it, decides to up the protein in its diet. By the time we get there—sorry if *that* ruined your appetite."

"No sweat." I ate to demonstrate.

Polito said, "You really like Bright as your perp, huh?"

"He's associated with two violent deaths, one of which made him wealthy. If he was paid to dispatch the Safrans, that's two more with a financial incentive. And from what we can tell, after the Safrans vanished, so did he."

"Into thin air." He smiled. "That could mean something else, Doc."

"He got disappeared, too," I said.

Polito shrugged.

"Maybe," I said, "but right now, there's no one else on the screen. Anything you can tell me about him would be helpful."

"There ain't much. Even with my brother-in-law linking me up with his official big-shot brother-in-law computer." He snapped his fingers. "Just like you said, guy's nowhere. Once the building was vacated, no other address shows up. Can't find any sign he ever lived in the five boroughs or the entire state of New York. I'm talking no tax records, real estate deeds, driver's license, the works. All I *can* give you is a general physical description eight years ago and the fact that when I interviewed him, he was cooperative. And that's because if he wasn't cooperative, I'da recalled *that*. I talked to the guy exactly once—routine interview, same for all the tenants."

"What'd he look like?"

"Good-sized guy, beefy, bald."

"Clean-shaven?"

"Cue ball, no hair, period."

I fished out my copy of Ansell Bright's California license.

Polito's good eye squinted. "All that fur, you could make a coat . . . guess it could be the same guy, but I couldn't swear to it."

"Maybe that's the point," I said.

"A shape-shifter?"

"Was he gay?"

"He wasn't swishy. Your guy's like that?"

"Some people say he is."

"Some people . . . you're saying he fakes everything?"

I told him about the cowboy getup, the plaid-capped old man, a possible cross-dressing link, stolen luxury cars.

"Black cars," he said. "Maybe like a symbol of death." He pushed his plate away, touched his chest.

"You okay?"

"Reflux. This guy turns out to be the perp, I had him right there and he moved on to more bad things? Not a nice thought."

I said, "He could turn out clean."

"You thought he was clean, you wouldn't be here." He examined the photo some more, handed it back. "Nope, couldn't say it's him or not. And the Dale Bright I talked to acted normal. Absolutely nothing hinky about him."

He finished his wine. "I gotta say, Doc, talking to you is making

me realize how much I'd rather be on the lake. So let me give you the
rest of what I got and be on my way. First off, I went by Korvutz's
apartment this morning—that was the appointment I mentioned.
Schmoozed with the doorman, who happens to be ex-patrol. Don't
you bother him, it gets out he's talking about the residents, he's
screwed. What he told me is Korvutz is quiet, no problems, married
with a little kid, tips good at Christmas. Has dinner by himself twice a
week when the missus is out with her gal pals and lucky for you,
tonight's one of those. Creature of habit, goes to the same place, likes
Italiano."

"La Bella," I said. "It's on my list."

Polito smiled. "Who do you think made up the list? Anyway, Korvutz eats early, is likely to be there six, six thirty. The chance of him offering to share a plate of pasta is not a high probability, but you can fly
back to L.A., say you tried."

"Does he use bodyguards?"

"We're not talking Trump or Macklowe. This guy's small-time.
Relatively speaking, I mean. He still gets to live in a ten-room co-op in
a prewar on Park, bought in years ago."

"What does he develop nowadays?"

"He doesn't. Collects rent checks."

"Retired? How come?"

"Maybe 'cause he wants to be, or maybe 'cause he has to be."

"What do you mean?"

"To play in the city nowadays, you got to have big-time dough.
Starting with a B, not an M."

"Gotcha," I said. "What does he look like?"

"Sorry, no picture," he said. "Guy doesn't drive. What I can tell
you is that eight years ago he was fifty-three. Little guy, glasses, reddish brown hair. Your basic Russian Woody Allen."

"Thanks. I walked by the building on West Thirty-fifth. It's back
to being a factory."

"Strictly speaking, it's a warehouse, Doc. The braid's manufac-
tured in Queens, they store it on Thirty-fifth. So how come, after all

that rigamarole, Korvutz never built his condos? What I heard is he got caught in some kind of financial squeeze, leveraged himself, then the market dipped, he had to sell a bunch of properties at a loss, including that one. It's all about timing, Doc. The market's crazy again, crappy tenements getting gentrified in the Lower East Side, Hell's Kitchen's full of yuppies, got a new name, Clinton."

"The boom hasn't hit West Thirty-fifth."

"Those building's are worth plenty," he said. "Right now it pays to keep 'em commercial, but give it time. One of these days, the only people living on this island are gonna be the limousine bunch."

I waved the tenant board list. "Any problem with me contacting Glusevitch and Mercurio?"

"Not from my end," said Polito, "but you'll have problems on both counts. Mercurio's dead, got into trouble over a woman five years ago, ex-husband beat him to death, dumped the body in the Bronx. Nothing to do with Korvutz, the ex had a history of beating up boyfriends, only reason I found out is I noticed Lino's name on a vic list. Kid was a moron and a wiseass, one of those hair-gel guys wants to come across like a gangster. I can see him ticking someone off real bad. Him, I *woulda* liked as a suspect, I could picture him thinking he could make his bones by taking on a contract job. Problem is, he was alibied tight. Vacationing in Aruba with a girlfriend the week the Safrans disappeared."

"Convenient."

"But righteous, Doc. I checked hotel and airline records, Lino was definitely there. Maybe he paid for the trip with money Korvutz gave him for being on the board."

"Korvutz bribed the members to serve."

"Can't prove it, but why else would they want to bother?"

"And my second problem is Sonia Glusevitch is Korvutz's distant cousin, why should she cooperate."

He held up his palms.

I said, "Just in case, any idea where she is?"

"Let's see if we can find out." He pulled out his cell, dialed information, asked for listings for Sonia Glusevitch, came up empty, tried "initial S."

One hand flashed a Victory V. "Three forty-five East Ninety-third. You wanna try Sonia first, be my guest, but I think it would be a mistake. Better to use the element of surprise with Korvutz, don't risk Sonia alerting him."

"I agree. What was Sonia like?"

"Young, good-looking, had a thick accent," said Polito. "Bottle blonde but nice." Shaping generous, imaginary breasts.

Monique, the waitress, observed his pantomime and frowned.

Polito waved her over. "Delicious, the salmon. He'll take the check."

She glanced at me, left.

"I was you, Doc," said Polito, "I'd leave Monique a real generous tip. I come here from time to time."

CHAPTER

22

When Polito left at two forty-five, the restaurant had emptied.

Monique drank coffee at the bar. I paid the check and left a 30 percent tip. She thanked me with wide eyes and pretty teeth.

"Mind if I sit here for a few minutes?"

"I will bring you more wine."

I had over three hours before Roland Korvutz unfurled his napkin at La Bella. Killed some of it drinking a better Bordeaux than had come with lunch, and thinking about my conversation with the old detective.

Polito was troubled by the possibility that he might've had his prime suspect right in front of him and missed something crucial. But Dale's slipping under the radar was no discredit of Polito's skills; if Bright was a high-functioning psychopath, he'd have come across super-normal.

Shape-shifter.

If Bright's corpse wasn't embedded in the foundation of some

Manhattan high-rise, he was probably living under a new name and identity in L.A., toying with the boundaries of gender identity, getting off on the art of deception and worse.

I phoned in for messages, had three: Robin, Milo, and a lawyer chronically lax about paying his bills, and deluded that I'd want to talk to him.

Robin said, "I miss you but the big separation anxiety is Blanche. Not a single smile and she keeps sniffing around your office. Then she insists on going down to the pond, has to sit on the bench exactly where you do. When that doesn't work, she hops down and stares at the fish until I feed them. If I don't toss in enough, she lets out that girly little bark. I keep telling her Daddy's coming back soon, but the way she looks at me, she ain't buying it."

"Tell her I'll bring back a souvenir."

"She's no material girl, but sure. How's it going?"

"Nothing much so far."

"I checked the weather online. Sounds pretty."

"Gorgeous," I said. "One day we should go."

"Definitely. Got a nice hotel?"

I described the Midtown Executive.

She said, "One advantage, we'd be bumping into each other."

"I'll be back tomorrow, plenty of bump opportunities. How's work?"

"Picked up a couple of new jobs—easy repairs." Brief pause. "He called this morning, wanting to make sure I'll be in town when he's here. He sounded different."

"How so?"

"Distant—not brimming over with enthusiasm like he usually is. He claims he's really into the project but the tone didn't match the words."

"Buyer's remorse?" I said.

"Maybe he realized it's an awful lot of money when you can't play a note."

"Worse comes to worst, you sell them to someone else."

"I'm just wondering if he caught on that any amorous intentions are not going to be reciprocated. I have been avoiding small talk."

"If he had ulterior motives and drops out, you're lucky."

"For sure," she said.

Her tone didn't match her words.

I said, "You've put a lot of work into this and now it's complicated."

"Maybe just in my own mind."

"You've got good instincts, Rob."

"Not always . . . guess I'd better clear my head before turning on the band saw. See you tomorrow, love."

I told Milo about my meeting with Polito.

He said, "Deputy commissioner's brother-in-law, huh? And this particular D.C. also happens to be His Holiness's former driver."

"Takes a village to catch crooks," I said.

"And to breed 'em. So Bright didn't come across gay to Polito?"

"Combine that with dramatic changes in appearance, pretending to be a vegan, the Jekyll-Hyde pattern his sister described, and we can't be sure of anything about him."

"All the world's a stage."

"Bloody stage. Let's see what Roland Korvutz has to say about him."

"You're going to approach Korvutz directly?"

"Wasn't that the point of giving me his home address and his favorite haunts?"

"Yeah, but I woke up this morning with second thoughts. Why would Korvutz even talk to you?"

"If I can keep the emphasis on Dale Bright and off him, maybe he'll fancy *himself* a performer and let something interesting slip."

"If he paid Bright to do the Safrans, he'll give you the boot or worse."

"Why settle for pessimism when you can have fatalism?"

"You've been reading my diary. This guy could be big trouble, amigo, and I don't see any payoff in getting him nervous. Go back to your hotel, put quarters in the massage bed, get a good night's sleep."

"Aw, thanks. Mom."

"I'm serious."

"How're things on the home front?"

"Changing the subject doesn't alter reality."

"I'll watch my back. Anything new?"

"The home front is nada," he said. "Why settle for fatalism when I can have futility? Where were you planning to meet Korvutz?"

"Still am. La Bella."

"The Italian place."

"Upper East Side, we're not talking hefty guys drinking espresso in some social club."

"At best you're spinning your wheels, Alex. Why would Korvutz blink at you?"

"At one time or another, doesn't everyone want to be a star?" My neck tightened. "Just thought of something. If Dale's a wannabe Olivier, maybe that's what brought him to New York in the first place."

"Roar of the greasepaint," he said.

"The Safrans were headed for the theater the night they disappeared. Off-off-Broadway production downtown. What if Bright snared the Safrans by offering an olive branch? 'I'm doing a show, have your name on the comp list, would be honored if you'd come watch me chew the scenery. Afterward, we go out for drinks, bury the hatchet on the condo thing.' "

"And he brings a literal hatchet . . . that would be cold. Problem is we already ran every search we could think of on Bright and his name doesn't pop up in any productions. Or anywhere else."

"The show could've been too short-lived or obscure," I said. "Or he used a stage name. On my way over from Midtown I passed the main library. Maybe that was karma. I've got time before I try Korvutz. Let's see what the newspaper files have to offer."

"Good idea. You find something, forget Mr. Korvutz and come home."

"Now you're obsessing," I said.

"Pot and kettle."

I hurried back to Fifth, made my way through the afternoon crush, ran up the stairs to the library.

The Microfilm Reading Room was equipped with a dozen film-reading machines, twice that many multiformat readers, and a couple of microfiche viewers. Lots of studious researchers waiting for access, including a homeless guy who made it to the front, sat down, spooled randomly.

I located the theater guides for the week preceding the Safrans' disappearance in the *Times, Post, Daily News,* and *Village Voice,* waited for a free machine, got to work.

An hour later, I'd winnowed a long list down to nine downtown productions that seemed sufficiently obscure. A fifteen-minute wait got me a computer with Internet hookup. No mention of five of the shows. Of the remaining four, I found cast lists for three. Ansell/Dale Bright didn't appear on any of them, but I printed them and left the library.

The sky was blue-black. Fifth Avenue flashed copper and bronze and silver in the reflected glory of store displays. Vehicle traffic was a bumblebee swarm of yellow cabs and black livery cars. The pedestrian crowd had thickened to something purposeful and polymorphous and I felt like a tiny gear in a wonderful machine.

For variety, I took Madison north, catching glimpses of moonglow haloing sky-scratching towers. Development could be predatory, but man-made New York was as beautiful as anything Nature could conjure.

As I crossed from the sixties into the seventies, mega-designer flagships gave way to boutiques and cozy eateries whose glass fronts showcased pretty people.

Osteria La Bella was different, with a brick façade painted white and tiny beige letters whispering the restaurant's name over a glass door so festooned with gilt flourishes it might as well have been opaque.

Behind the glass, darkness. One of those places you'd have to know about.

I looked up the street, failed to spot anyone matching Roland Korvutz's description. Six twenty p.m. If he was in there already, I wanted him settled into a culinary routine. Resuming my walk, I continued all the way to East Ninetieth, picking up the pace to get some aerobic benefit from the gentle slope of Carnegie Hill. By seven ten, I was back at La Bella, with sweet lungs and a buzzing nervous system.

The glass panel opened to a glossy, deep green vestibule backed by a second door of solid black walnut. On the other side of the inner entrance, a small landing was announced by an engraved bronze *Please Watch Your Step* sign.

Three stairs down and a sharp left turn took me to a white marble maître d' stand. A tall, thick, tuxedoed man studied his reservation book in the amber light of a seashell Tiffany lamp. Low-volume opera supplied the soundtrack, some tenor moaning a sad story. My nostrils filled with alternating ribbons of ripe cheese, roasting meat, garlic, balsamic vinegar.

Behind Tuxedo, a wine rack stretched to the hand-plastered ceiling, obscuring the entire left side of the room. The wall to the right was covered by a mural. Happy peasants bringing in the grape harvest. The three tables in full view were round, covered in red linen, and unoccupied. Glass clink and the low murmur of conversation floated from behind the rack.

"May I help you, sir?"

"No reservation, but if you could accommodate one for dinner."

"One," he said, as if he'd never heard the word before.

"Thought I'd be spontaneous."

"We like spontaneous, sir." He ushered me to one of the empty tables, handed me a wine list and a menu, and told me about the osso buco special made with veal from serene Vermont calves allowed to enjoy their brief lives unfettered by pens.

His bulk blocked visual access to my fellow diners. As he described a medley of "artisanal vegetables," I feigned interest and glanced at the menu. Auction-gallery wines, white truffles, hand-netted fish from lakes I'd never heard of. The balsamic was older than most marriages.

Prices to match.

"Drink, sir?"

"Bottled water, bubbles."

"Very good."

He stepped aside, revealing two parties on the other side of the windowless room.

The first was a gorgeously dressed couple in their thirties clenching wineglasses and tilting toward each other like pugilists.

Tight jaws, parted lips, and rapt stares. Passion just short of coitus, or a poorly camouflaged argument.

To their right, a man sat with a child—a chubby, fair-haired girl. Her back was to me as she hunched over her plate. From her size, six or seven. The man leaned low to maintain eye contact, face melting into the shadows. He touched her cheek. She shook him off, kept eating. She had on a white sweater and a pink plaid skirt, white socks, red patent leather shoes. Except for the shoes, maybe a school uniform. His gray sport coat and brown shirt drabbed in comparison.

I could see enough of him to make out a small frame. That fit Polito's description of Roland Korvutz. So did his age—sixty or so—and having a child.

He broke a piece of bread and sat up to chew and I got a better look at his face. High, flat cheekbones, bulbous nose, narrow chin, steel-framed specs. If this was my quarry, the red-brown hair had faded to a sparse, gray comb-over.

He reached for his fork, curled pasta, offered some to the little girl. She shook her head emphatically.

He said something. If the girl answered, I couldn't hear it.

Black serge filled my visual field again. A large bottle of Aqua Minerale Primo Fiorentina and a chilled glass were set down gently. "Ready to order, sir?"

Still full from the late lunch, I opted for the lightest offering, a forty-four-dollar diver scallop salad. Before Tuxedo took away the menu, I checked the price of the water. Well over LAPD's daily food allowance, all by itself. Maybe it had been hand-drawn from artesian springs by highly educated, medically verified vestal virgins.

I drank. It tasted like water.

The little girl across the room said something that made the man in the gray sport coat raise his eyebrows.

Again, he spoke. She shook her head. Got off her chair. Her skirt had ridden up and he reached out to smooth it. Her hand got there first. She planted her feet, fluffed her hair. Turned.

Clear-skinned, blue-eyed, pug-nosed. The unmistakable visage of Down syndrome.

Older than I'd estimated; ten or eleven.

She noticed me. Smiled. Waved. Said, "Hel-lo," loud enough to override the opera.

"Hi."

"I'm going to the bathroom."

The man said, "Elena—"

The girl wagged a scolding finger. "I talk to the *man,* Daddy."

"Darling, if you have to go—"

The girl stomped a foot. "I *talk,* Daddy."

"I know that, darling. But—"

"Daddy," she said, stomping a foot. Then: "Daddy *sad?*" She grabbed his face with both hands, kissed his cheek, bounced happily to a door at the back of the restaurant.

Unmarked door; the kid was a veteran of hundred-dollar dinners.

The man shrugged and mouthed, "Sorry."

"She's adorable."

He resumed twirling pasta. Examined a diamond wristwatch. Put his fork down, checked the time again.

Tuxedo came over. "Everything okay, Mr. Korvutz?"

"Yeah, yeah, thanks, Gio."

"Nice to see Elena. Her cold's all better?"

"Finally."

"Smart girl, Mr. K. She like school?"

Korvutz nodded weakly.

"Some wine to go with the Diet Coke, Mr. K.?"

"No, I'm doing homework later, need to keep a clear head."

"Kids," said Gio.

Korvutz's face turned sad. "It's worth it."

Elena returned playing with the hem of her sweater. She stopped at my table, pointed a finger. "*He's* all alonely."

Roland Korvutz said, "Leave the gentleman alone."

"He's *alonely,* Daddy."

"I'm sure he'd just like to—"

"You're *alonely.* You can eat with *us.*"

"Elena—"

The girl pulled at my sleeve. "*Eat* with us!"

I said, "If it's okay with your dad."

Korvutz's face got hard.

Elena applauded. "Yay!"

"Elena, stop this. Let the gentleman—"

I got up and brought my water glass to their table.

"Yay!"

Korvutz said, "Sir, this is not necessary."

"I don't mind for a few minutes—"

"Yay!"

The intense couple glanced over. The woman whispered something to her companion. He shrugged.

"It's *really* not necessary," said Korvutz.

"It *is* nessery, Daddy!"

The hot-eyed couple smirked.

"Elena—"

"Nessery!"

"Shh, shh—"

"*Nesse—*"

"Elena! Shh! What do we say about La Bella?"

The child pouted.

Korvutz said, "In La Bella, we need to be . . . say it, darling."

A tear dripped from Elena's right eye.

Roland Korvutz dried it and kissed her cheek. "Darling, in La Bella we need to be *quiet.*"

"Darling darling," said Elena. "That's *Mommy.*"

"You're my darling, too."

"No!"

Korvutz colored. "Sir, sorry to bother you, you can go back—"

"He's a*lonely.* Ms. Price say be nice to alonely people."

"That's at school, Elena."

"Ms. Price say always be nice."

I said, "I can sit until my food comes."

"Elena, let this man be."

Korvutz's voice had risen. Elena's face crumpled. He muttered something in what sounded like Russian and reached for her. She jumped off her chair sobbing. The young woman at the next table rolled her eyes.

"Elena—"

The child ran to the rear door. "I *go,* again!"

Korvutz said, "Sir, I apologize. She is very friendly."

"I think she's adorable." Trying not to sound patronizing.

Korvutz's stare said I hadn't pulled it off.

I said, "I work with kids."

"Doing what?"

"Child psychologist."

"Okay," he said, with utter disinterest. "Have a nice dinner." Eyeing my table.

I fished out the brand-new LAPD consultant badge the chief had expressed to my house last night and placed it on the table in front of him. "When you have time, Mr. Korvutz."

His mouth dropped open. Gray eyes behind thick lenses bulged. Despite the sparse light, his pupils had constricted to pinpoints. "What the—"

I pocketed the badge. "We need to talk. Not about you. About Dale Bright."

He started to rise from his chair, thought better of it. Both hands clenched but remained on the table. "Get the hell out of—"

"I've come three thousand miles to talk to you. Dale Bright may have killed other people. Extremely messy murders."

"I don't know what the hell you're talking about."

I stood, shielding him from scrutiny by the neighboring couple or Gio. Kept a smile on my face to feign friendly conversation.

"Dale Bright. Former chairman of the tenant board on West Thirty-fifth."

Korvutz's shoulders crowded his neck. His fingers grazed a butter knife.

"You're not under suspicion. Bright is. What I need is details, anything that can help locate him."

Spittle collected at the corner of Korvutz's mouth. "I know nothing."

"Just a brief talk at your convenience—"

"Again they torment me."

"If you cooperate and help us find Bright, it'll end any—"

"I know *nothing*." Extruding the words through clenched lips.

"Even impressions. What he was like, his habits."

"Dry eye!" announced a voice behind us.

Elena danced to my side, wadded tissue in hand.

Roland Korvutz said, "This man needs to leave."

"*No,* Da—"

"*Yes!*"

"Daddy make me *sad*!"

Korvutz shot up and took her by the arm. "Life is sad. Even you can learn that."

He pulled the child, wailing, from the restaurant.

Puzzled, Gio watched the door slam.

The tenor on the soundtrack moaned.

The young woman said, "Bringing a kid to a place like this."

The young man smoothed a hand-stitched lapel. "Especially *that* kind of kid. Let's book."

CHAPTER

23

Elegant people walked refined dogs on Park Avenue.

Roland Korvutz's building, on the west side of the street, was ten stories of somber gray stone, each level one apartment wide.

Gleaming brass rods supported a spotless maroon awning. A carpet of some weather-resistant material that looked good enough for my house led to dead-bolted, brass-framed glass doors. The *All Visitors Must Be Announced* sign was the same gleaming metal. So was the call button.

Inside the lobby, a maroon-clad doorman relaxed in a carved chair and watched me watch him. Hispanic, mustachioed, too young to be the retired cop Polito had spoken to.

As I approached, he stayed put. Light from a crystal chandelier ambered the black-and-white marble checkerboard lobby floor. Dark wood panels glowed like melting chocolate.

The doorman didn't budge until I pushed the button. Even then, his movements were languid.

He opened the door a couple of inches. "Help you?"

"I'm here for Mr. Korvutz."

"He expecting you?"

"I sure hope so."

"Name?"

"Dr. Delaware."

He closed the door, got on a phone. I cooled my heels under the awning, braced for refusal, maybe a warning to cease and desist. Felt guilty about cutting Elena's dinner short, then thought about the Safrans and suppressed my regret.

The doorman hung up, cracked the door again. "He's comin' down."

Roland Korvutz emerged moments later in brown shirtsleeves, baggy gray pants, and white sneakers, cradling a tiny white Pomeranian.

I prepared for rage. His face was blank.

The doorman fulfilled his primary job description and Korvutz walked through. He pointed south, kept moving, still holding the dog.

Small man but he pumped his legs fast.

I caught up. The Pomeranian yapped happily. Licked my hand.

Korvutz said, "Everyone thinks you're a great guy." Small man with a big baritone. In the comparative quiet his accent was more pronounced.

"Kids and dogs," I said. "Sometimes they're good judges of character."

"Bullshit," said Korvutz. "I had rottweiler, love everyone, the worst scumbags."

"Maybe this dog's smarter."

"Gigi," said Korvutz. "That's her name." He fastened a pink leash to the dog's rhinestone collar, put her down.

"Like in the movie?"

"My wife like the movie." Shaking his head.

Gigi raced. We covered a block. Korvutz waited as Gigi explored a lamppost.

I said, "Thanks for seeing me."

No answer.

"Sorry for ruining your dinner."

"It not you, it woulda been something else. My daughter. She love the place, but she not ready for it."

"Too much pressure to be quiet."

"Sometime Elena get what they call overstimulated."

"I meant what I said. Cute kid by any standards."

Korvutz stared at me. "You really a shrink?"

"Want to see my license?"

He laughed. "She my only one. Got married late."

The dog pulled on the pink leash. Korvutz said, "Okay, okay," and allowed her to lead.

Ten steps later: "That guy Bright really kill someone?"

"Maybe a bunch of people."

"Crazy."

"You never suspected him for the Safrans?"

He held up a palm. "Eh-eh, them I don't talk about, no way. Brought me nothing but bullshit."

"All I'm concerned with is Bright—"

"Bright I meet twice? Okay? Only thing I remember is he's a big ass-kisser. Mr. K. this, Mr. K. that. Back then my buildings got four hundred fifty tenants, four seventy-five. I'm supposed to give a shit 'Mr. K.'?"

"What'd he ass-kiss about?"

"Trying to be my best friend, like I don't know when I'm being rimmed." Korvutz slowed, watched as the dog sniffed another post. Rearranged his eyeglasses. Gigi changed her mind. We resumed walking. "She take her time doing the business. C'mon, dog. I got homework to do."

I repeated my question.

Korvutz said, "Bright had ideas. My benefit. 'Have a *tenant* board, Mr. K., gonna make things smoother.' I thought it was bullshit."

"But you agreed."

"Someone wanna help, it's no skin off. I'm figuring Bright's gonna ask for something, I want, I say no. Turns out it was nothing."

"He never asked for anything?"

"Go figure."

"No break on the rent?"

"Hey," said Korvutz, "that I do before."

"How much of a discount did you give him?"

"Who remembers—maybe coupla thousand total."

"Goodness of your heart," I said.

Korvutz turned to me. "Like I said, I met him twice. He want to help out, why not? In the end, it don't help. Stupid tenant board."

"No help with the condo-conversion."

Scowling, he walked faster. "That building screwed me. Financed it with other properties, shoulda known better than to invest in that piece of shit. Then I got short, rates are getting worse, the banks not gonna lend unless they got you by the—the paperwork get all—crazy time it take this damn city to get something done. What the hell do you care? You want know about Dale Ass-kissey? That's the story. Period."

I said, "How'd he come to rent from you?"

"Referral."

"From who?"

"What's the difference?"

We walked until Gigi grew fascinated with the scents emanating from a trash can on the corner of Sixty-ninth.

"Go, already," said Korvutz. *"Dog."*

I said, "Who referred Bright to you?"

"Again?"

"What's the big secret?"

"I didn't even want new tenants. You convert, you need it *empty.* Bright get guaranteed no-hassle, I say what the hell, okay. That's my problem. Soft heart."

Gigi moved from the trash can. We covered another half a block before I said, "Who guaranteed him?"

"This is a big goddamn deal, huh?"

"Sonia Glusevitch?"

Korvutz licked his lips. "You know Sonia?"

"I know she's your cousin and she served on the board with Dale."

"Cousin," he said, as if learning a new word. "Her mother's second husband is nephew of one of my stepsisters."

"She knew Dale and recommended him."

Reluctant nod.

"Was she involved with him?"

"Sonia was married."

"Same question," I said.

"I don't nosy in other people's business."

"I'll take that as a yes."

"Look," said Korvutz, "Sonia come to me, say she got friend need a place. I say six months, tops."

"That could've fit Dale Bright's needs perfectly."

"What you mean?"

"He moves around," I said.

"Good for him."

"There's no record of him after he left your building. Any idea where he went?"

"I should know?"

"Where'd Sonia meet him?"

"That I know," said Korvutz. "Doing a show."

"What kind of show?"

"Sonia want to be actress. That time, she has terrible English, she a little better now. One year I'm here from Belarus, I'm talking perfect. Two years, I got the Puerto Rican Spanish, five years I'm talking to Chinese people. Hasta luego ying chang chung."

"Sonia has no gift for language."

"Sonia?" Chuckle. "What they say, not swiftest knife in pantry?"

"But she thought she could act."

"Wanna be big star."

"Movies or stage plays?"

"Even now," said Korvutz, "she go to classes at the New School. Paint pictures, make pots, ashtrays, candleholders."

"Artistic."

"Live off divorce money, you got time take lessons."

"Rich ex."

"Plastic surgeon. He do her boobies, like what he do, marry her, get to look at it all the time."

"What's his name?"

"Who remembers?"

"He marries your cousin and you don't remember?"

"Jewish guy," he said. "They get married in Anguilla, no one invited. Five years, she move to a big house in Lawrence, then divorce."

"She still gets alimony?"

"She live good."

"Where's this doctor's office?"

"Also the Five Towns."

"Which one?"

"Maybe Lawrence, maybe Cedarhurst."

"You don't remember his name."

"Jew name, some kind of Witz, maybe Markowitz, maybe Leibowitz—no, no, Lefkowitz. Bob *Lefkowitz*. Plays tennis." Miming a wide swing.

"So Sonia was seeing Dale Bright while she was married to Dr. Lefkowitz."

Silence.

I said, "You already told me she was."

"What I *say* is she tell me Bright needs apartment."

"Living with her husband but she kept an apartment on West Thirty-fifth?"

Korvutz looked away. The cords in his neck were miniature bridge struts. "I give her apartment, so what?"

Gigi beelined for another can.

Korvutz said, "Here we go again."

I said, "What show was Sonia in when she met Dale Bright?"

"Who remembers?"

"Did you see it?"

"She keep saying come. For free. Finally, I have to go. Some stupid place."

"Downtown?"

"East Village, no theater. Room over a Mexican restaurant, they set up chairs, piano, black drapes. Everyone dressed black, black bathrobes, black hoods. The whole time they run around chanting. At the end, someone throws up. Then you clap."

"What was the name of the show?"

"Maybe Black Bathrobes and Throwing Up?" Snickering at his own wit.

I pulled out the list I'd gotten from the newspaper files, began reading off titles.

"Yeah," said Korvutz. "That's the one, *Dark Nose Holiday*. What the hell does that mean, *Dark Nose*? I ask Sonia. She say it's climb into someone's brain. Like a tunnel here." Wiggling a nostril. "In here the truth." Laughing. "Achoo, eh? No more truth."

Gigi checked out the flower bed in a towering brick building. I examined the listings for *Dark Nose Holiday*. The *Times* was the only paper to capsulize the play. *"Neo-absurdist drama exploring mystical meta-motivations."* No cast or credits cited.

I said, "How many people were in the play?"

"This is important?"

"Could be."

"How many? Four? I don't know. Not a lot."

"Was Dale Bright one of the actors?"

"Maybe."

"Maybe?"

"I told you, hoods, the faces you don't see, maybe it was him, maybe Mickey Mouse."

"Sonia definitely said she'd met him at the production."

"Yeah, yeah."

"What else do you know about him?"

"Nothing."

"When the Safrans disappeared—"

"Uh-uh, no, no, I told you, we don't go there. They almost ruined my life."

"The Safrans?"

"The cops. Harassing, I try to do business, they come in the office with badges, bye-bye business. This Italian guy, look like a gangster. Harass 'cause I'm Belarusssian, want to know about smuggling, Moscow Mafia. Stupid."

"Prejudiced," I said.

"I keep telling him, look, you not going to find nothing 'cause there is nothing to find."

Gigi trotted to a discarded cardboard box and lifted her leg.

Korvutz saluted the air above his head. "Finally, dog."

I said, "The Safrans only interest me because—"

"Good night and good luck. Only reason I talk to you first place I don't want you bothering my kid no more. Also, I got nothing to hide. You gonna be back in L.A. soon?"

"Soon enough."

"Say hello to the palm trees."

"Talking about the Safrans really bothers you."

Keeping his mouth shut, he blew out air, ballooning the skin around his lips.

I said, "If you've got nothing to hide—"

The air escaped in a hiss. "Maybe they fly to the moon. Maybe Ass-kiss do something to them. Do I give a shit? Not even a little one—not even a Gigi shit."

"Good riddance to bad rubbish," I said.

"Hey," he said, "don't put words in. Why I gonna cry for them? They fight me just to fight me. I run away from all that."

"From fighting?"

"From *communism*—little slow dog, finish *finish* aready."

"The Safrans were communists."

"Bother someone else, mister."

"Is Sonia in town?"

"I should know?"

"Call her. If she can talk to me right now, I'm finished with you."

"You finished anyway."

"Call her."

"Why I do you a favor?"

"Your kid and your dog like me."

He glared. Laughed. "Why not, Sonia recommend stupid ass-kisser to me, I recommend *you* to *her.*"

He left me outside his building, handed the Pomeranian to the doorman, used the house phone. Brief chat; thumbs-up okay.

I mouthed, "Thanks." Korvutz gave no sign he'd noticed as he crossed the lobby.

The doorman followed. Impassive, as the dog licked his face.

24

Sonia Glusevitch lived in a fortress of yellow brick that
hogged a third of a block on East Ninety-third.

The doors to this lobby were wide open. Mirrored walls alter-
nated with panels of gold-flocked velvet. Ailing palms yearned for
something other than track lighting.

Two hatless doormen in white shirts sat behind a Formica counter
ignoring a bank of closed-circuit TVs. Sonia Glusevitch's name
evoked a wave-through as they continued to study an offtrack betting
brochure.

"Which apartment?"

Laborious consultation of a black plastic-bound book.

"Twenty-six eleven."

A metal-clad elevator griped all the way to the twenty-sixth floor.
The hallways were papered in shiny copper splotched to resemble
patina. Rust-colored carpeting had long lost its bounce.

I knocked on Sonia Glusevitch's door. The woman who opened
wore a lime-and-orange kimono and gold, high-heeled sandals.

Early forties, fleshy and pretty, with long too-black hair, tarantulous eyelashes, and crimson lips. Her face was coated with a fresh application of powder. Vanilla-laden perfume breezed out into the corridor.

"Ms. Glusevitch? Alex Delaware."

"Sonia." Two soft hands clasped mine. More vanilla as she kneaded my knuckles. "Come in, please."

Her living room was boxy, pale blue, set up with black velvet seating, white rugs, baroque gold-mirrored tables. Paris street scenes featuring too much pigment and not enough proportion hung on the walls. A black japanned console bore a collection of free-form ceramic mounds.

She perched on the edge of a love seat, pointed me to a chair that placed our knees inches apart. Undraped windows looked out to the East River and the night-glow of Queens.

"Thanks for seeing me."

Silk rustled as she crossed her legs. A gold-link necklace circled a soft white neck. Additional glint was provided by oversized hoop earrings, a cocktail ring set with a massive amethyst, a gold-and-diamond Lady Rolex.

"Ah-lex," she said. "That's a popular Russian nyame. You have Russian blood?"

"Not to my knowledge."

"Please." She pointed to a coffee table set with crackers, toothpicked cheese chunks, an open bottle of Riesling, two cut-glass goblets. Low lighting accentuated the river view and was kind to her complexion.

I poured wine for both of us. Her first sip didn't alter the fluid level. I drank less.

Both of us smiling and pretending to enjoy each other's company. Like a bad blind date.

She'd used the fifteen minutes it had taken me to walk from Korvutz's place on Park to put on her face and toss together a little spread.

I said, "Did Mr. Korvutz fill you in?"

"Oh, yes, of course." Tinkly voice, Slavic overtones. Show of small, white teeth as a crooked smile suggested a mischievous girl-hood. "Roland said you were very nyosy. He *didn't* say very hand-some."

She placed cheese on the cracker, nibbled. Played with the tooth-pick.

"You think maybe Dyale killed someone?"

"It's possible."

"Okay."

"That doesn't shock you?"

"Of course it shocks me. Cheese? It's good."

I'd paid for my forty-dollar salad at La Bella but had left before it arrived. Still, I had no appetite for anything but information.

I reached for a cracker. "Please tell me about Dale."

"What's to say?"

"What was he like?"

Sonia Glusevitch said, "Nice. Helpful. He liked to help people."

"He helped you?"

"Oh, yes."

"With what?"

"My lines, how I talked, doing the eyes. It's different."

"What is?"

"The myakeup for the theater. You must make a styatement."

"Dale told you that."

Nod.

I said, "Dale had experience with theatrical makeup."

"Experience, I don't knyow. He was very, very good. Artistic."

"Did the two of you meet doing *Dark Nose Holiday*?"

"Oh, yes. I was Neurona—a traveler in the brain—and Dyale was Sir Axon. He showed me how to use the light and the dyark." Touch-ing an eyelid. "To look mystyerious on styage. To make the face dra-matic."

Roland Korvutz had described actors completely shrouded by dark robes.

I said, "So the two of you became friends."

Sonia Glusevitch drank wine. "Dyale was a real friendly guy."

"You don't seem that surprised that he'd be a murder suspect."

"Everything can be a surprise. Or nothing, depends."

"On what?"

She cocked her head to one side. "If you trust people, you get surprised."

"You don't?"

"No more," she said. "Every day, my husband told me he loved me. Every single day, six thirty, first thing he woke up, even before the toothbrush. 'I love you, Sonny.' Covering his mouth so the bad breath didn't bother me." The hand drifted to her abdomen, continued to her knee. "He was a syurgeon. Every Friday, he gave me flowers, all the women were jealous. He worked so hard, plastic syurgeon, my Stevie. Long hours. Long long *long* hours." Flashing teeth. "He hired pretty little Puerto Rican nurses. Now he is married to one."

"Ah."

She recrossed her legs. Fabric shifted, revealing the flank of a meaty white thigh. A sandal bobbled.

I said, "You knew Dale when you were married."

"Oh, yes."

"What kind of relationship did the two of you have?"

Crooked grin. "You want to know did I sleep with him? A little, yes, it happened. Stevie was having his nurse fun. The rooster, why not the hen?"

"Only a little?" I said.

"I liked to do it. Dale not so much."

"No enthusiasm."

"Enthusiasm, yes," she said. "When he did it. And he was *able*. No problem with able, just problem with *often*."

"Any sign he was gay?"

"He told me no."

"You asked."

"It was a syad time for me." Her shoulders sagged. "I found a little Platinum American Express receipt in Stevie's jacket. Big, expensive dinner, at a place in the Hamptons I'd asked Stevie to take me. He nyever did."

"What a bum," I said.

"Oh, yes, Ah-lex. Big-time bum. So I was syad. I cried to Dyale, said please treat me like a woman. Instead, he was nice."

"Nice?"

"Like a gyirlfriend."

"Good listener?"

"The hand-hold, the listening, the hugs. The little kiss *here*." Tapping the tip of her nose. "The business? Nyo."

She shifted her weight, exposed more thigh.

I said, "Hard to believe he turned you down."

Her eyes moistened. "You are probably lying but I like it anyway."

She drank wine, looked up at the ceiling. Her chin quivered. She covered her thigh.

I said, "So you asked if he was gay and he said no."

"Right away, no."

"Did the question bother him?"

"Not at all," she said. "He laughed. Changed the subject."

"To what topic?"

" 'You are so beautiful, Sonny.' " Deep sigh.

"Was he effeminate?"

"Nyo," she said. "I'd say nyo."

"You're not sure."

"Yes, I'm sure, definite *nyo*. Dyale was not girly, just a sensitive guy."

"Helpful."

She winked. "Not like a nyormal man, eh?"

I laughed.

"Another way he was different," she said. "Very neat and clean, always smelled fresh. And no toys. I don't talk about sex toys, I mean fast car, big watches, big TV, big stereo. Stevie likes the toys."

"Dale didn't own any of that."

"Dyale had *nyothing*. Futon for sleeping, jeans and sweaters in the closet, nyo real food in the 'frigerator, just juice and water, a backpack, a locker."

"A locker?"

"A green locker. From the army."

"Dale told you he was a veteran?"

"Cyaptain, five years."

"Where'd he serve?"

"Germany. He fixed tanks."

"Mechanical."

"Good with his hands," she said. "One time he fixed my styove, the pilot light. Also, the toilet. Twice, the toilet."

"We're talking about your apartment on West Thirty-fifth."

She flicked a red nail against her goblet. "Ah-lex, I was very, very lonely in the big house, Stevie was working all the time with the little nurses. Roland had a nyew building, I was doing the play, why go back to Long Island every night?"

"You got yourself an apartment, then you got Dale one."

"I like to help, too." Smile. "I'm talking to you."

"I appreciate it. So—"

"How long are you going to be in the city, Ah-lex?"

"Leaving tomorrow."

She clucked her tongue. "You come back a lot?"

"From time to time."

"It's a good city," she said. "Always excitement."

"Where was Dale living before he moved into Roland's building?"

"Hotel."

"Do you remember a name?"

"Never knyew a name," she said. "Dyale told me it wasn't nice. I said, Guess what, I have a solution for you. I talk to Roland, Dyale moves in next to me."

"What else did he tell you about himself?"

"That's it."

"What about his family?"

"He said he didn't have a family."

"Why not?"

"The parents died. That's why he moved to the city."

"From California."

"California?" she said. "Washington, D.C."

"That's where he told you he was from?"

"He talked about the capital, all the politicians lying all the time. Maybe he was a politician, too, eh?"

"Before moving here, he lived in San Francisco."

"He never talked about California."

"Did he mention any sisters or brothers?"

"He said he was an only child." Smile. "Another tale?"

I nodded.

"Dyale, Dyale, Dyale," said Sonia Glusevitch. "See what I mean about trusting?"

"What else did he tell you?"

"I just said nothing else, Ah-lex. You didn't have cheese, it's good."

I bit off a corner of the cube. Rubbery and stiff around the edges. "There's nothing else you can tell me about Dale?"

"Mostly, I talked and Dyale listened. He was a good friend when I needed a good friend. And now maybe he killed someone? Who?"

"Could be several people."

She flinched. "I was alone with him so many times. He was always nyice."

"Helpful," I said.

"So helpful. The most helpful man I ever met."

She left to go to "the girl's room," returned moments later with her jewelry removed, less makeup, hair pinned up.

Looking plainer but younger. "You didn't move," she said, remaining on her feet. "Not an inch."

"Worried I'd steal the silver?"

She laughed. "You are leaving tomorrow? Morning or night?"

"Early-morning flight."

Eye flicker. "Have a good trip, Ah-lex."

Extending her hand.

I said, "If you don't mind, just a few more questions."

She sighed and sat. "Now you want to talk about the Safrans, right? Roland said you think Dyale killed them."

"Would that surprise you?"

"Those two," she said. "Who knows about people like that?"

"People like what?"

"Always like this." She made a sour face. "Sloppy, messy, like they don't wash. Dyale said they were like roaches."

"Pests," I said.

"Dirtying Roland's property, not being fair to Roland. The way they treat the dog."

"They were cruel to their dog?"

"Dyale said they never walked it, the dog made mess inside."

"Dale was inside the Safrans' apartment."

Her mouth slackened but her eyes got tight. "This is the fyirst time I think about that."

"Dale and the Safrans didn't get along," I said. "No reason for him to be there."

"Whatever," she said. "Roland *nyever* asked Dyale to help him, *nyever.*"

"Roland wanted to make sure you told me that."

"Roland is not some gangster. In Belarus he was a hospital clerk, helped old people get medicine."

"The night the Safrans disappeared, they went to a play downtown. Was *Dark Nose Holiday* still running?"

"Running." She giggled. "More like limping. We had four days."

"Did the Safrans attend?"

Slow nod.

I said, "Dale invited them."

"I say why, he say why not be nyice?"

"Did they enjoy the show?"

"Don't know."

"Did you see Dale with them after the show?"

"Don't know," she insisted. "I was taking off my makeup. It takes time."

"Dale had already left."

"Yes."

"Ever see the Safrans again?"

Long silence. Head shake. "My God. Dyale."

"Was Dale in any other productions after that?"

"Nyo."

"How'd he spend his time?"

"Mostly I was in Long Island. I use the apartment for when I don't want to drive back."

"Did Dale have a job?"

"He said he was going to look for one but not now, he had money. From the parents, just a little—that was a lie, too?"

"He inherited more than a little," I said. "Once he left Roland's building, there's no record of him working anywhere. What kind of work did he say he'd look for?"

"He didn't—ah, I think of something *else*. He said he was going to travel."

"Where?"

"The world. Like it is one place. I said, Dyale, trust me, the world is not one place, it is little boxes of people who hate each other and kill each other and no one likes anyone different. Do you want to go to Belarus and see why I left? He said, No, Sonny, I mean the great cyities. Paris, London, Rome. I asked why he never went to the great cyities when he was cyaptain in Germany. He said the army kept him too busy. But maybe he wasn't *in* Germany, eh?"

"That would be my guess," I said.

"All lies," she said. "Okay, so what else is new?"

"Do you have any pictures of him?"

"I don't kyeep souvenirs."

I asked for a physical description. The picture she painted—big, hefty, bald—matched everything Roland Korbutz had said.

"Brown eyes," she added. "Soft eyes. Sometimes he wore glasses, sometimes contacts."

"This may sound strange, but did he ever dress in women's clothing?"

"Not on the street."

"You're not surprised by the question?"

"At *Dark Nose,* one of the gyirls—she played Systema—was big, size sixteen, eighteen. Once in a while Dyale would joke around."

"About her size?"

"No, no, the clothes. He put it on, then a wig, talked in a high voice. Very funny."

"Goofing around."

"What, he is weird that way?"

I shrugged.

She said, "This is a weird sexy murder?"

"Hard to say what it is."

"Oh, boy . . . I guess I am lucky. Dyale was always nice to me, but who knows, eh? I am tired, now, Ah-lex. Too much talk."

She walked me to the door, leaned in, kissed my cheek in a cloud of vanilla.

I thanked her again.

"Why not?" she said. "Maybe one day I'll see California."

25

Did the chief get his money's worth?" I asked Milo.

"I'll let you know after I talk to him."

"When's that?"

"When the palace beckons."

Five p.m., gloomy skies, heavy air in L.A. We were in a coffee shop on Santa Monica Boulevard renowned for omelets the size of manhole covers. Coffee for me, coffee and a plate of cinnamon crullers for him. Two hours ago, he'd finished a late lunch at Café Moghul. An interesting mix of cumin and his digestive cigarillo lingered on his clothing.

Before going to bed last night, I'd left him a message, summarizing what I'd learned in New York. Hadn't heard back because he'd been surveilling Tony Mancusi until sunrise.

He rubbed his eyes. "Dale did the Safrans . . . okay, I got my money's worth, let me pay for your uneaten hundred-dollar plate of lettuce."

"Forty bucks," I said. "Lettuce and scallops."

"Whoopy doo."

I'd been back since noon. He'd remained unreachable until four p.m. Revisiting Gilbert Chacon at the Prestige rental lot and getting Chacon to admit that he'd arrived late for work, found the chain propped up but the lock missing, rushed to Rite Aid on Canon and bought the cheap drugstore version we'd seen.

"Think there's more to it?" I said.

"Someone bribed him to leave it off? Don't think so, he offered to take a poly, cared more about losing his job than aiding and abetting."

"However it happened, whoever picked the lock, kept it."

"Sentimental."

After leaving Chacon, he'd participated in a conference call with Texas authorities and detectives from six cities where Cuz Jackson claimed to have committed atrocities. Three dead ends, one unlikely, two possibles.

Plus Antoine Beverly, one big question mark.

The needle-and-gurney folk in the Lone Star State wanted to get things moving. The chief's office had asked Milo to push on Antoine but there was no lead to follow other than locating Antoine's boyhood friends.

No sign of either. "Hollywood unmarkeds been cruising by Wilson Good's house for the last forty-eight hours. Definitely no one home and St. Xavier's starting to worry."

I said, "Maybe he got really sick and ended up in the hospital."

"We looked into that. Zip."

"The coach has left the field," I said.

"Funny thing 'bout that, huh? Like I said, all the fool had to do was cooperate. Wouldn't that be something, Antoine coming down to some creepy kid-on-kid thing."

Thinking about that made me tired. Or maybe it was no sleep in the cell-like hotel room followed by a bone-fusing six-hour plane ride.

I swigged coffee. Milo tore open a packet of Splenda but didn't use it. "Good was Antoine's age at the time of the disappearance. You see a fifteen-year-old capable of something like that?"

"They're not myelinated."

"Who *what*?"

"Myelin," I said. "It's a substance that coats nerve cells and plays a role in logical processing. Teens don't have as much as adults. Some folks think that's a good reason not to execute young criminals."

"At what age does it turn normal?"

"Differs from person to person. Sometimes not till middle age."

"Bad living through chemistry," he said. "But we're not talking some low-impulse stupid homicide. Baby-gangbangers pull that off all the time. If Good's dirty for Antoine, we've got a teenager stealthy enough to murder his best buddy, smoothly cover it up, and go on living as an upstanding citizen. Serving as a pallbearer and crying his little eyes out."

"Seeing yourself as moral and living with something that evil would be a hell of a burden, but people pull it off. Or Good could be one of those highly functioning psychopaths who's managed to avoid trouble."

"And now trouble comes visiting," he said. "So he freaks out and splits."

"Or Antoine's death wasn't a calculated crime. Couple of kids horsing around and something went horribly wrong. Good panicked and hid Antoine's body. Now he's terrified."

"Maybe three kids. Antoine's other pal is a junkie and a career criminal. That could be self-punishment."

"Gordon Beverly said Maisonette had family problems, lived through a drive-by. Maybe his resources weren't as strong as Good's."

"Bradley sentences himself to a lousy life, Wilson gets the house in the hills. Maybe that makes Good the really cold one . . . hell, it *could've* been premeditated. The Goods told us Antoine sold more subscriptions than anyone. What if those little bastards wanted to pocket his dough and he wouldn't give it up?"

"The way those outfits generally operate, the kids hand in the forms and get paid later."

"Okay, but my nose is telling me something happened among

those three boys. Gotta find Mr. Good and start demolishing his illusions, but I can't lose track of Mancusi and Shonsky. Speaking of which, Tony called Jean Barone yesterday, wanting to know when Mama's will was going to be processed."

"What'd she tell him?"

"What I told her to say: The wheels of justice grind slowly. The Tonester hung up without as much as good-bye. Maybe cranking up the pressure will lead him to do something stupid. Like meeting with whoever Dale Bright's pretending to be."

Snatching a cruller, he bit down hard, created a spray of crumbs. "Thanks for taking the trip, Alex. You believe Korvutz about not setting up the Safrans?"

"He had no incentive, the building was going to be vacated with or without the Safrans' consent."

"So what was Bright's motive?"

"Killing's fun when you can frame it as altruism. Sonia Glusevitch said Bright was the most helpful man she'd ever met."

"The gal-pal," he said. "Credible?"

"I think so."

"Able but not often willing," he said. "But not gay."

"This guy defies classification."

He finished the cruller, took another. "Frolicks in frocks, good with makeup. No record of him living in Washington, D.C., Maryland, or Virginia. Same deal with military service in Germany."

"What a shock," I said.

"Reinvent yourself. Pastime of the new millennium. Why didn't he just run for office and save us all this grief."

"Politics would be a poor fit," I said. "He genuinely likes helping people."

He laughed so hard crumbs bounced off his belly.

I said, "Dale and Tony could've met at some cross-dresser get-together. Tony complains about money problems, how his mother lives in a nice Westwood house while he's forced to move to a dump because she's turned off the tap. Dale decides to put in a fix. Maybe

Tony has no idea what he's initiated but maybe after he hears the details—a killer in costume—he suspects something."

"The plaid cap," he said. "He talked about his father wearing one just like it. If that was one of Dale's little jokes, how'd he find out about Tony Senior's sartorial habits?"

"Tony gabs, Dale's a good listener. If Tony knows he's partially responsible for Dale butchering his mother, that would explain the emotion we saw."

"Barfing. But he doesn't turn Dale in because he's scared of being nabbed as an accessory."

"What interests me is that Dale acted with no worry about Tony giving him up. He understands Tony's psyche."

"Or he's biding his time."

"Tony's in jeopardy? I guess it's possible. Either way, if surveillance doesn't produce something soon, I'd think about confronting him directly."

He made his way through the second cruller. "You really think this is evil altruism, Dale doesn't get paid for his hits?"

"If we're right about the Ojo Negro killings, he murdered his sister and Vicky Tranh and got rich. But if money was his sole reason for eliminating Leonora, all he had to do was sit in the woods and pick her off with a rifle. Instead, he dressed up in costume, showed himself, stole a car, engaged in incredible savagery. To me that says there was psychosexual payoff. And that fits with what Leonora told Mavis Wembley about Dale: secretly cruel as a child."

"Tortures animals, volunteers at a shelter. He's all about irony, isn't he?"

"Irony and theater," I said. "Think what it took to pull off Kat Shonsky's murder: stealing a conspicuous car, stalking his prey, then abducting her, possibly in drag. Then returning the car to where it's sure to be found and leaving token blood on the seat. Leaving the scarf where it would be seen immediately if Kat's grave was unearthed."

"That grave would've definitely been unearthed," he said. "The permits for the sisters' swimming pool had just come through."

"Be interesting if Dale was aware of that."

His eyebrows arched. "Someone the sisters know . . . wonder if they're back from their cruise."

He motioned the waitress over, handed her some bills.

"That's way too much, Lieutenant."

"Caught me in a weak moment, Marissa."

"Honestly, Lieu—"

He placed a big hand over hers. "Take your kid to the movies."

"You're so sweet." She tiptoed to buss his cheek, just about skipped away.

I said, "Random acts of kindness."

"Me and Dale."

He brushed memos into the trash unread, searched Kat Shonsky's murder book for the names of the sisters who shared the burial lot.

"Susan Appel and Barbara Bruno . . . let's go alphabetically." Punching numbers so fast he hit the wrong button and had to try again.

"Mrs. Appel? Lieutenant Sturgis . . . I'm . . . yes, I know it was traumatic, ma'am, so sorry it was your . . . no, there'll be no need to do any further digging, that's not what I'm . . . absolutely, Mrs. Appel, and we do appreciate it, but I need to ask you one more question."

He hung up, rubbing his face. "Doesn't know anyone named Bright, Dale, Ansell, or otherwise. Would *never* know *anyone* capable of something so *terrible,* same goes for Sis because they have *exactly* the same social group."

"Close-knit," I said.

"They share real estate and haven't sued each other. Might as well be conjoined. Let me try Bruno, anyway . . . nope, voice mail, no sense leaving a message, Appel's bound to get to her first. Thanks for breakfast, I'm off to buy my Red Bull and sustenance, get ready for the wonders of Rodney Drive."

"You paid for breakfast."

"I was talking mental stimulation."

"Want company?"

"Robin's still busy on her project?"

"We're catching dinner at seven, then she's back to work."

"So play with the dog—thanks for the offer, Alex, but doing that forty-eight-hour N.Y. turnaround is already beyond the call. Plus hanging with me when I'm brain-dead is not amusing. And don't say you've already been there."

Dinner was lamb chops, salad, beer. By nine p.m. Robin was back to carving and I was stretched on the sofa in my office reading the paper. Blanche curled next to me pretending to be interested in current affairs. At ten thirty I snapped awake, feeling itchy and too large for my skin. Blanche snored with gusto. I put her to bed, walked out back to the studio.

Robin sat at her bench, tapping and carving. "Oh, no. Poor you."

"What?"

"You fell asleep and now you're wired."

"It's that obvious?"

She put her chisel down, touched my face. "The leather couch. You've got marks from the seams."

"Sherlocka," I said.

"Want me to go with you?"

"Where?"

"One of your drives."

"I wasn't planning on driving anywhere."

"No?" she said. "Okay, I'll stop and we can play Scrabble."

The fiddle-grain maple back of the dot-com guy's mandolin sat on the spotless bench. Neat pile of shavings on the floor. "I do not obstruct genius."

"Hardly," she said. "What are you going to do?"

"Maybe I'll join Milo. He's watching Tony Mancusi, may haul him in for questioning."

She smiled. "Now I know it's really you and not some alien clone. Give me a kiss and be off."

I phoned from the road.

He said, "Your myelin will wither."

"Probably have too much anyway."

"Mr. Mature."

"Not by choice."

He'd borrowed a dented brown Camaro from the police lot, was parked ten yards cars north of Tony Mancusi's building, positioned so streetlight glanced the rear of the car, avoided the driver's seat.

He saw me, unlocked the car.

The interior reeked of sweat, tobacco, and pork. Three cartons of short ribs gnawed to the bone shared the backseat with a tub specked with fried rice, a collection of little plastic cups emptied of sweet-and-sour sauce, grease-spotted napkins, used Wash'n Dris, a pair of broken chopsticks. Three Red Bull cans had been crushed to disks. In Milo's lap was a tartan-patterned thermos.

His face and body fused into a single dark mass. As my eyes adjusted, I saw that he'd changed into black velour sweats, a nylon shoulder holster housing his 9mm, and new-looking Keds.

"Spiffy."

He removed the earpieces from his iPod, clicked the machine off. "You say something?"

"Just hi."

"I'd offer you some grub, but."

"I ate."

"Another high-tax-bracket salad?"

"We cooked."

"Man of the people."

"What were you listening to?"

"Stereotype to the contrary, not Judy or Bette or Liza or Barbra. Guess."

"Doo-wop."

"Beethoven. *Eroica.*"

"What a classy guy," I said.

"Rick's iPod. I took it by accident."

We sat for an hour. Hollywood Patrol called in. No sign of Wilson Good.

By one thirty a.m., the tedium of surveillance started to hit me. I figured I'd give it another hour, return home to crash, get my time zones back in order.

Milo said, "Long as you're here. Punch me if anything happens." Pushing the bucket seat as far back as it would go, he lowered his head to the seat back. Twenty minutes later, he awoke with a frighteningly guttural start and wild eyes. "What time is it?"

"Ten to two."

"Wanna nap yourself?"

"No, thanks."

"Wanna split?"

"Maybe in a while."

"Tedious. Told you so," he said. "Nighty-night."

"Must be nice to be right once in a while," I said. "Emphasis on *once.*"

"My oh my, sleep deprivation brings out the vicious side—" Something to his left made him turn sharply.

I followed his glance, saw nothing. Then the front door to Tony Mancusi's building opened. As if Milo had smelled it.

A man stepped out to the street. Slumped, pudgy, shuffling gait.

Tony Mancusi walked south to his Toyota, got in, and drove toward Sunset.

Milo cranked down the driver's window and watched. Most of my view was obstructed by parked cars but I could see the twin dots of taillights twenty yards up.

Mancusi covered a block and rolled through a stop sign.

"First violation," said Milo, starting up his engine. "Hopefully, there'll be others."

The Toyota headed west on Sunset, passing Western Pediatric Medical Center and continuing through Hospital Row. At that hour, the boulevard was deserted until Vine, where the nightscape was peppered with drifters, addicts, minimum-wage workers waiting for buses.

Sparse traffic meant Milo had to stay well behind the Toyota but it also turned Mancusi's taillights into beacons. The signage of a big-box office supplies barn lit up a red-sauce stain blotching the corner of his mouth. Toss in the black hair and the gray skin and you had Dracula with a penchant for trans fat.

Mancusi caught a red light at Highland, backed up illegally, switched into the left-turn lane.

Milo muttered, "Tony, Tony," and stayed half a block behind.

The green arrow flashed, Mancusi turned into a darkened parking lot on the east side of the avenue. Headlights off as he rolled to a halt near a shuttered food stand.

Milo doused the Camaro's lights and watched from across Highland.

A huge painted sign on the roof of the stand starred an elated pig sporting a sombrero and a serape. *Gordito's Tacos.*

Mancusi stayed in his car. Ninety seconds later, three women emerged from the shadows.

Big hair, micro-skirts, stilt-heels, purses on chains.

Loose-hipped and sashaying as they strolled over to Mancusi's open driver's window.

Huddled conversation, heads thrown back in laughter.

Two of the women left. The one who remained had a teased platinum do, a big shelf of bust, skinny legs. A red wife-beater exposed flat belly above a minuscule lipstick-pink skirt—no, hot pants, let's hear it for tradition.

The blonde wiggled her way to the Toyota's passenger side, fussed with her hair, tugged at her top, got in.

"Guess Tony's not gay," I said.

Milo smiled.

Mancusi drove faster, taking Highland south to Sixth Street, turning left and speeding past Hancock Park and into Windsor Square, with its ancient trees, broad lawns, and landmark mansions.

A sudden turn took him north to Arden Boulevard, where he covered a block, stopped, parked in front of a mini-Tara.

Silent, dark street. Wide-open landscaping and a gap where a street tree had succumbed.

The Toyota's brake lights remained on. Ten seconds later, it pulled away, continued another block north, and parked again, this time facing a Georgian masterpiece nearly obscured by three monumental deodar cedars.

An equally massive sycamore on the parkway umbrellaed the car.

The lights went off.

The Toyota remained in place for ten minutes, then started up again and returned to Gordito's Tacos.

Mancusi idled at the curb as the blonde got out. She fooled with the waistband of her hot pants, leaned in, said something through the passenger window. Whipped out a cigarette and smoked as the Toyota drove away.

Milo jogged across the street, flashed the badge. The blonde punched her thigh. Milo spoke. The blonde laughed the way she had when approaching Mancusi. Milo pointed to her cigarette. She stubbed it out. He patted her down, took her purse.

Holding her by the elbow, he guided her across Highland and straight to the Camaro.

No expression on his face. Her eyes were wide with curiosity.

CHAPTER
27

Milo pulled a steel-handled straight razor out of the hooker's purse.

"Hands on the car."

"That's for protection, sir." Husky voice.

"On the car." Pocketing the knife, he stashed the purse in the trunk, put the hooker in back of the car, squeezed in next to her.

"Your turn to drive, pard."

I slid behind the wheel.

The hooker said, "I love company."

Next to Milo, she looked small and frail. Mid- to late thirties, hair stiff and shagged, platinum at the roots, copper at the tips. A hatchet face oatmealed by pimples gleamed through bronze pancake. Pert nose, plump lips, glitter-flecked cleavage, big hoop earrings.

Cobalt eyes under gritty half-inch lashes struggled not to bounce.

Below all that, a muscular neck. Pronounced Adam's apple.

She saw me looking at oversized hands and slipped them out of view.

Milo said, "This is Tasha LaBelle."

"Hi, Tasha."

"The pleasure's all mine, sir."

"Let's get moving," said Milo.

Tasha said, "Where we going?"

"Nowhere in particular."

"A few hours, Disneyland's gonna open."

"Fantasyland your thing?" said Milo.

No answer.

I pulled onto Highland, hit a pothole that rattled the car's suspension.

Tasha said, "Ouch. Such a teeny car for such big *men.*"

Gliding past Sunset and Hollywood Boulevard, I headed east on Franklin, drove past darkened apartment buildings, antique foliage. No people on the street. A solitary dog rooted near some hedges.

Tasha said, "What I done, you taking me for a ride?"

Milo said, "We like company. When we run your prints, what name's gonna come up?"

"Prints? I didn't do nothing." Tension kicked the voice a few frets higher.

"Your name for the record."

"Record of what?" A tinge of aggression lowered the timbre. Now I was hearing a nasal street guy, cornered and ready for fight or flight.

"Our investigation. There's also the issue of your little nail file."

"That's a antique, sir. Got it on eBay."

"What name were you born with?"

Sniffle. "I'm *me.*"

Milo said, "No doubt about that. Let's not make this a bigger deal than it needs to be."

"You don't understand, sir."

"I do. The past is the past," said Milo. "Right?"

Hushed "yessir."

"But sometimes history is important."

"What'd I *do,* you take me in this *car*?"

"Besides the blade, you were witnessed engaging in solicitation and prostitution. But you can be back at Gordito's in fifteen minutes instead of in lockup. Up to you."

"What're you investigating, sir?"

Milo's pen clicked. "First your given name. Not one of the monikers you use when you get busted."

"Sir, I have not been arrested in . . . thirty . . . eight—seven days. And that was in Burbank. And it was just shoplifting. And charges were dropped."

"Charges against who?"

Pause. "Mary Ellen Smithfield."

Milo said, "Like the ham."

"Huh?"

"What's on your birth certificate, Tasha?"

"You're not gonna arrest me?"

"That's up to you."

Long sigh. Near whisper: "Robert Gillaloy."

I heard Milo's pen scratching. "How old are you, Tasha?"

"Twenty-two."

Milo cleared his throat.

"Twenty-nine, sir." Breathy laughter. "And that's my final offer."

"Address?"

"Kenmore Avenue but it's temporary."

"Until?"

"I get my mansion in Bel Air."

"How long have you been in L.A.?"

"I'm a native Californian, sir."

"From where?"

"Fontana. My parents worked in chickens." Giggle. "Literally. I got tired of the feathers and the smell."

"When?"

"Something like thirteen years ago, sir."

I pictured a confused teenager making his way from the farmlands of San Bernardino County to Hollywood.

Milo said, "Phone number?"

"I'm in between numbers."

"You use prepaids?"

No answer.

"How do people reach you, Tasha?"

"Friends know where to find me."

"Friends like Tony Mancusi."

Silence.

"Tell us about Tony, Tasha."

"This is about Tony *Not*-Roma?"

"What d'you mean?"

"He don't look Eyetalian. More like pudding—that egg stuff—tapoca."

"He a regular, Tasha?"

"You're saying Tony's a badman?" A new vibrato twanged the voice. Back to girly and scared.

"Would that surprise you?"

"He's never a badman to me."

"But?"

"But nothing," said Tasha.

"How often do you see him?"

"No schedule," said Tasha. "Not a regular—a *un*regular."

"Tony circulates?"

"No, he likes *me* or he don't party. The issue is show me le money, honey."

"Tony's short on dough."

"He says."

"Complains about it a lot."

"Ain't complaining what men do, sir? The wife, the prostrate, the weather." Laughter. "The Dodgers. With Tony it's also his discus."

"His what?"

"The back discus. *This* hurts, *that* hurts. I'm like, poor *baby*. But no massage, these French tips are fragile."

"Putting up with all that bitching," said Milo, "you might as well get a husband."

"You're a nice, funny man, sir. What do *you* complain about?"

"Bad guys getting away," said Milo. "Where'd you meet Tony? And don't say 'around.' "

"Around. Hee hee—okay, okay, don't give me that evil look, I met him at a party. Wannaboo party up in the hills."

"What's a wannaboo?"

"A gentleman who pretends he's pretending."

"To be a girl," said Milo. "As opposed to your homegirls at Gordito's."

"My homegirls are *girls* no matter what the government say. My homegirls are la femme in the brain, where it counts."

"Wannaboos—"

"Wannaboos don't even try. For them the thing is *ugly.* Ugly *wigs,* ugly *dresses,* ugly ugly shaving bumps, square shoes. They don't got the bones. The deli-ca-cy. For the wannaboos it's Halloween Parade then back to the suit and tie on Monday."

"A costume party," said Milo.

"Not even, sir. They don't even try."

"Where in the hills was this party?"

"Some place near the Hollywood sign."

"Above Beachwood?"

"I don't know streets. It was a long time ago."

"How long?"

"Six months?" said Tasha. "Could be five? I talked to Tony but I went home with a lawyer. *That* was a house, all the way in Oxnard, by the water, to get there we drove and drove and the air smelled all salty. I won't give you his name no matter what you do because he was sweet. Sweet and old and lonely, his wife was sick in the hospital. Next morning he cooked waffles with fresh bananas and I watched the sun come up over the water."

"Also a wannaboo?"

"No, he was a straight."

"There were straights at the party, too."

"Girls, wannaboos, straights." Giggle. "Maybe kangaroos."

258 JONATHAN KELLERMAN
"What was Tony?"

"Straight. I thought he was the gardener or a plumber or something. Came to fix the toilet."

"He wore a uniform."

"Sloppy," said Tasha, as if it were a felony. "Wrinkled Dockers, sweatshirt that said *Aloha*. Very low-classy."

"How'd you end up at the party?"

"Some girl asked me. Germania, that's the only name I know. High-water but white, went back home a few months ago. Talked about her daddy having two wives in Utah, the stepmother was real accepting, but her own moth—"

"How many people were at the party?"

"Thirty? Fifty? People all over the house. The girls looking hot, the wannaboos like a buncha grammas, the straights trying to figure out what to do."

"Who owned the house?"

"Never found out."

"How'd you hook up with Tony?"

"He was sad."

"And . . ."

"Everyone else partying, he's sitting there complaining to this wannaboo. Wannaboo listens for a while then ups and leaves Tony all alone. Tony looks sad, I'm a nurturer so I sit down next to his poor self. He starts complaining to me, we take a walk. Up the road, but we heard coyotes. I got scared and we went back."

"No coyotes in Fontana?" said Milo.

"Lots of coyotes, that's why I got scared, sir. I seen what they done to the chickens."

"Tony was complaining about . . ."

"What I said, sir. Le mon*ee*. He used to live in a nice place then his back discus made him all messed up and his mama wasn't helping him no more, called him a bum."

"He said all that to the other wannaboo?"

"I heard the word 'money' before I sat down. That word *always* gets my ears unfolded. When we were walking he got into his mama mistreating him. Said she pulled the rug out, he was the only child, why would she do that."

"Angry?"

"More like sad. Depressed, even. I said you should try the Prozac or something. He didn't answer."

"When he complained to the wannaboo, did the wannaboo seem to be listening?"

"I guess . . . yeah, he was looking straight at Tony, nodding like *I hear you, bro*. Then all of a sudden he gets up, like he heard enough."

"Bored?"

"No, no, more like . . . like it was too sad."

"Describe the wannaboo?"

"Bigger than Tony. Not as big as you, sir."

"Heavyset?"

"Hard to tell with those clothes. I'm talking *tweed* and it was warm. Like . . . like . . . one a those movie gramma things, Gramma's a cold Waspy bitch? Stockings with *seams* up the middle."

"How old?"

"He was trying for biddy, all that makeup, the gray wig. Coulda been thirty, coulda been fifty. Lots of them do that, make like *Come to Gramma*. Like comfort food, you know? If having a gramma who don't shave her legs and got a face like a toilet lid gives you comfort— where are we, never been this far."

We'd traveled two miles east of her stroll.

As we approached Rodney, Milo said, "Pard, why don't you turn?"

I drove by Tony Mancusi's building. Milo watched Tasha's face. Tasha appeared to be sleeping.

Hooking a left on Sunset, I said, "It's kind of interesting, Tasha. Tony complains about his mother to a guy trying to look like a mother."

"Hey," said Tasha. "I didn't think a that."

Milo said, "What's this guy's name?"

"If I knew I'd tell you, sir, I truly would."

"Big, thirty to fifty. Give me more details."

"Ugly, sir. Puffy face, the red shiny nose like he's been drinking all day and all night . . . um um um . . . glasses. Pink plastic glasses. With the rhinestones. *Biddy* glasses—oh, yeah, natural nail polish."

"Eye color?"

"Don't know, sir. That long ago, all I really can remember is the ugly. Working at it, you know? Gray wig like a dishcloth, tweed two-piece, all baggy and heavy—green velvet trim." Retching sound. "Shoes you could step in mud no one's gonna notice. Like a *scarf's* gonna fix all that?"

"He wore a scarf," said Milo.

"Only pretty part of the whole *on*-sombel," said Tasha. "Purpley, gor-juss. Louie Vee-town. What a waste."

As I continued through East Hollywood, into Silver Lake and Echo Park, Milo pressed for more details on Tony Mancusi's confidant, got nothing. The lights of downtown came into view.

Tasha yawned.

Milo said, "Here's a picture of a guy we know."

"Hairy bear," said Tasha.

"Could he be the wannaboo?"

"Take a clippers to him, maybe I could tell you."

"Try to look past the hair."

"Sorry, sir, I want to be honest. Too much coiffure."

"Did you get a sense Tony and Tweed knew each other before the party?"

"Tweed, heh, yeah that should be his name. Never saw him or Tony before, never saw *him* after. Never went to another party up there. Because my sweet old lawyer told me not to. Wanted me all to himself when he's in town. Backed it up with le money. Still does."

"But you still have time for Tony."

"Too much free time's a bad thing, sir. Nothing's for free."

"What gets Tony off?"

"Being sorry."

"For himself?"

"That, too, sir, but I was talking apologies."

"For what?"

"Everything," said Tasha. "Taking up my time. Comes in wanting what he wants and then after he gets it, he's all Prozacky frowny-frown, says he shouldn't be doing it, he's really not like that."

"Denying he's gay."

"Tony's mind, he's *never* gay. You call him that, he gets cranky. He figures he likes me 'cause I'm a girl, he only likes girls. A lot of them are like that. Want to have it and eat it, too." Laughter.

"How often does he see you?"

"Most often was once a month, sir. Then it stopped. Tonight was the first time in like . . . three months? Could I go back? Please? I don't know this part of town, don't like being where I don't know."

Milo said, "Sure."

I found a driveway, did a turnaround.

"Thank you, sir. Can I have my little helper back?"

"Don't push it," said Milo. "So Tony's conflicted."

"Call it what you want, sir. Before they get what they want, they're all hungry. Then it's over slam bam wham and it's like a light's shining deep inside them and they're seeing something they don't like. A first-timer, you never know how they're gonna deal with that light. That's why I need my helper."

"Pretending only goes so far," said Milo.

"*There's* your Fantasyland. Tony really a badman?"

"Don't know yet."

"The *wannaboo* is a badman? You asking all those questions about him."

"Just collecting information, Tasha."

"Someone got killed? I'm on the street, I need to know, sir."

"Tony's mom."

"*No!* I noticed Tony was a little edged off tonight. But he didn't say nothing."

"Edged off how?"

"Looking around like enemies everywhere. Parking in a place no problem before then getting all paranoid it's too easy to see and moving to another place and he's still edged off. He coulda *done* that? To his *mama*?"

"What do you think?"

"I mean . . . I'm speechless, sir."

"His mother gets murdered, he never mentions it," said Milo.

"Nothing," said Tasha. "Edged off like I said, but then just the usual."

"Meaning?"

"Boom boom boom. Then getting all quiet. Then the *apologies*."

28

When we were two blocks north of Gordito's, Tasha said, "Drop me here, sir."

Milo returned her purse and we watched her sway along Highland. Another he-she loitering near a phone booth waved. Tasha gave a barely visible nod and kept going.

"Wannaboo," I said, driving away. "Must've missed that one."

"You didn't miss anything," said Milo. "She made it up. How much of her story do you believe?"

"If she wanted to lie, she didn't need to get into any of it."

"Tweed," he said. "Just being a helpful guy."

"If Korvutz was being righteous with me, he met Bright twice and Bright freelanced a double murder without being asked to. This is a prince who loves snipping off loose human ends."

"Tony's weak. Gotta start thinking about how to break him open. How do I get him to the office?"

"Ella collected service people's business cards. Tell him you've linked her murder to a gang of home-improvement scammers who prey on the elderly, have some mug shots for him to look at. At some point you could even show him Bright's DMV shot, let the name slip, see how he reacts."

"Creative . . . okay, let's aim for a planning session at nine—make it nine thirty. Once we finalize the script, I phone Tony, ask him to drop by the station. Guy never leaves before three p.m, we're ready by noon, we'll have him."

By nine fifteen the next morning I was drinking strong coffee in Milo's office as he shuffled a new pile of message slips.

The parole office hadn't been able to locate Bradley Maisonette and was "activating an investigation."

Wilson Good was still nowhere to be found and St. Xavier High was "extremely concerned." Good's assistant coach, a man named Pat Crohan, had tried to contact Andrea Good through her work number at a graphic design firm. Mrs. Good had abruptly resigned four days ago.

Milo said, "Hubby and wifey on a major rabbit."

"They have a dog," I said. "If they're gone for the long haul, they took it with them. If they're just in temporary seclusion, weighing options, they may have boarded it. Want me to try to find out?"

"Sure . . . damn case, sixteen years—two from Gordon Beverly, just checking in . . . chief's office wants a meet in three days on all pending matters."

He pulled out a panatela. "Let's talk about Tony."

The phone rang. "What? I'm busy—*who*? Do they have an appointment . . . okay, okay, no matter, bring 'em up—*what*? Fine. I'll come down."

He shot out of his seat, strode to the door, flung it open. "Stay right there."

Five minutes later, he was still gone. I used the time to look up canine-boarding facilities in the Hollywood area, found eight. Pretending to be a veterinarian named "Dr. Dichter," I began working my way through the list, inquiring about the health of my patient, "Indy Good," the acrobatic dachshund.

A pleasant woman at my fourth try, Critterland Pet Hotel said, "Oh, he's fine. Is Andy concerned about something?"

"She called my office to verify his shots." Whatever that meant.

"Oh. Well, Indy's feisty as ever and not playing well with others. Did Andy say when she planned to pick him up?"

"Not to me. She left it open-ended?"

"Oh, don't worry about that, Doctor, he'll be fine. Any idea how her husband's doing?"

"Something wrong with him?"

"That's why she boarded Indy. To take care of Mr. Good, some sort of bad flu. And you know how Indy gets."

"Feisty," I said.

"Needing all the attention."

"I assumed they were on vacation. Come to think of it, Andy didn't sound relaxed. Anyway, Indy's all caught up."

"Great. Andy's so nice. Never met her husband but he's lucky to have her."

Just as I hung up, an officer rapped the open door.

"Lieutenant's in Five, says you should join him."

I walked to the interview room. Milo had shoved the table out of the way and sat opposite two women.

"Ladies, this is Dr. Delaware, our psychological consultant. Doctor, Ms. Appel and Ms. Bruno."

One brunette, one blonde. Nervous smiles from both.

Each was in her forties and wore a cashmere crewneck, tailored jeans, large-carat ring, tennis bracelet, stud earrings. All the jewelry set with clean white diamonds.

The brunette plucked at her plum-colored sweater. She had a clear oval face, a toned body, blue eyes, dark hair cut in a boyish cap.

Her fair-haired companion was rounder, a bit younger, with painted eyebrows and sharp, brown eyes. Pumpkin cashmere, frosted locks. She held out her hand first. "Barb Bruno."

"Susan Appel," said the brunette, a few decibels softer.

"We're sisters."

Milo said, "Susan and Barb own the property where Kat Shonsky was—"

"Disaster," said Barb Bruno. "We got the call on the cruise ship. We're still traumatized."

Susan Appel said, "We were planning on building an Olympic pool for our families. To think . . ."

"Not that we'd ever change our minds, we can't let something hideous like this stop us from living. For us it's always been about family, our parents raised us that way. Do either of you remember the Circle F Ranch Market in Brentwood? That was our dad, Reuben Fleisher."

I'd never heard of the place. "Ah."

Susan Appel reached behind one ear, twisted a wisp of short dark hair. A look from her younger sister caused her hand to drop and I imagined a child's voice remonstrating.

Stop picking *at yourself.*

Barb Bruno said, "We're still not sure we did the right thing by coming in. You called Susan and she called me and we both agreed it was most probably nothing. Then we thought about it—*I* thought about it and I called Susan and we discussed it some more. We came to the conclusion that no matter what happens, it was our duty to call you."

Milo said, "We really appreciate it. Now, if you could tell us—"

"Which isn't to say our husbands are happy with us, they aren't," said Susan Appel, twisting her hair again and avoiding her sister's eyes.

Barb Bruno said, "They're both attorneys, head their own firms."

"Corporate litigation," said Susan Appel. "Both Hal and Mike will be the first to tell you they have no experience in criminal law, but they want to make sure we're protected."

Barb said, "Alpha dogs." Out of a suede weave bag came a folded sheet of legal-sized paper.

Milo read, put it down. "You want guaranteed confidentiality."

Barb said, "Doesn't seem too much to ask, seeing as how we've come forth voluntarily."

Susan said, "We're not even sure we know anything useful. Frankly we hope we don't. But just in case."

"We could be in danger," said Barb. "If we *have* hit upon something."

"Knowing the perp," said Sue. "Then ratting him out."

Milo said, "Ladies, this kind of citizen involvement is so important. But even if I signed this, it would be worthless because I don't have the authority to grant—"

"So who does?" said Barb.

"I really don't know, ma'am. It's never come up."

"Oh, c'mon. I see it all the time. *Law and Order, Crossing Jordan.*"

Milo said, "Sometimes on federal cases, there are grants of confiden—"

"See?" Barb swiveled hard and tapped her sister's knee. "That's exactly what Mike said."

Susan said, "Hal still thinks it could apply to a nonfederal case."

Barb rolled her eyes.

Milo said, "Ladies, I promise to do everything I can to ensure your utmost security. Your names will not be part of any public record unless there's a trial and a defense attorney requests—"

"That's *exactly* what Mike said."

"Hal's not denying that—"

"Ladies, if it gets to that point—and that's a big if—the suspect will be in custody."

"What about bail?" said Susan.

"Unlike on TV, murderers don't get bail, ma'am."

"Murderers," said Barb Bruno. "Hard to believe it happened to our property, so . . . degrading—you're saying you won't sign, Lieutenant?"

"I can sign it, but I'd be lying to you, ma'am. And if you do have relevant information, you really need to tell me."

Silence.

"Ladies, you know as well as I do that it's your obligation."

Barb said, "Seems as if we're being punished for doing our civic duty. If we hadn't come forward on our own, we wouldn't be in this position."

"That's true of any hero," said Milo.

Barb blushed. The color spread to her sister's face, as if by sibling osmosis.

Susan said, "We're not trying to be heroes, but . . ."

Barb said, "I guess in a sense we *are* heroes."

Milo folded the sheet and put it in his jacket pocket. "Please. Tell me why you're here."

Barb's turn to mess with her hair. Susan watched, fascinated.

The sisters looked at each other.

Barb said, "If you can't sign it, how about this: Once this whole mess dies down, we're going to build our pool. It's the obvious feng shui thing to do—the purifying nature of water. City codes have gotten totally bonkers, the zoning board's been literally driving us crazy because they can't grasp the concept of shared property and dual liability. They want to impose ridiculous limits on size, depth, are demanding ludicrous fencing even though all our kids are great swimmers and the whole point is building an Olympic-sized pool. Which will not impact the neighborhood because we have fabulous landscaping plans and our fence is right out of a Zen garden in Niigata, Japan."

I said, "Where the koi are bred."

She beamed. "Yes, exactly. We have a fabulous pond, show quality."

Susan said, "My daughter's on the Archer School swim team and needs the full lap length to work on her stroke."

Barb said, "Everyone is way past the age where drowning's an issue. We'll even work with the lot-tie affidavit requirement. Though we don't think it's necessary. But we would like for you to exert some influence here, and smooth the process."

"With the zoning commission," said Milo.

"One agency talks to another," said Susan. "That's what Hal says."

Barb said, "Have some big shot in your department or, better yet, the fire department because there's an abatement issue as well—have someone call the head of the building division and smooth things out for us. It's the least you can do."

"That," said Milo, "is feasible."

Susan said, "It is?"

Her sister shot her a sharp glance. "Of course it is. When there's a will."

Milo said, "I'll talk to the police chief personally. We're having a meeting soon."

"Fantastic," said Barb, shifting her body closer to him.

Milo said, "Go ahead, please."

Barb said, "Okay. When you called Sue and asked about that Bright person, she said she didn't know him. Because she doesn't. Neither of us do. But then we got to talking and we realized there *was* something that happened that we thought was a little creepy."

Holding her hand out to Susan.

Susan said, "There was this person who tried to get our husbands to invest with him. Took us out to dinner at Cut—that's Wolfgang's new place at the Beverly Wilshire. Spent a lot on wine, very hotsy-totsy."

"Four *Seasons* Beverly Wilshire," said Barb. "Now we've got two Four Seasons, a mile apart, must be so confusing for the tourists."

Susan said, "This person really laid on the sales pitch. Visited us at home. My house, because Barb's kitchen was being renovated and she and Mike and Lacey were eating all their meals with us. Our husbands were still considering his offer so when we had the cocktail party, he was invited."

"A benefit for MOCA," said Barb. "My sister and I planned the entire event. The lot was set up with a tent and a band, people had a great time."

"Everything was prepared in *my* kitchen," said Susan. "We moved the furniture, people had a choice to come upstairs and see the view from the living room."

"Great party," said Barb. "People were talking about it for weeks. The only creepy thing was *him*. Something he said to both of us and the crazy thing is we never knew that until yesterday when we compared notes."

Susan said, "So obviously it wasn't just a casual comment."

Milo said, "Obviously."

Barb said, "First, he asked about the lot, seemed really interested in it. But plenty of people are like that because nowadays who has open land in the middle of Bel Air? And no one can understand how Sue and I share so wonderfully. So that alone wouldn't have stood out. But then, after he found out the details—"

"About the pool," Susan broke in. "Even though I'd already told him, he had the same conversation with Barb—"

"Playing games, as if we'd never compare notes," said Barb.

"I guess we didn't," said Susan.

"Whatever. The point is, after talking about the pool, he gave this strange creepy smile."

"Lecherous, if you must know," said Barb. "I felt he'd been coming on to me all night."

"Me, too," said Susan.

"It was nothing you could call him on, Lieutenant, but you know—the handshake that lasts too long? The kiss on the cheek that moves a *leetle* too close to the lips?"

"Not too smart of him, seeing as he was chasing after Hal and Mike to invest with him. What did he think, we'd be turned on and work on the guys?"

"For a second I thought he was actually going to *plant* one on me," said Barb. "Instead he whispered in my ear, 'It would make a great family plot.' I said, 'Pardon?' And he said, 'A plot. For burial. Lots of wealthy families in Europe have them, it's a mark of aristocracy.' "

"As if that was supposed to impress us," said Susan. Blue eyes widened. "He told me the exact same thing, word for word."

"We both ignored him and never mentioned it to anyone," said Barb. "There was no need because Hal and Mike decided not to invest with him. They did some background checking, couldn't find any."

"Any background?" said Milo.

"Exactly. His excuse was he'd been living in Europe, all his projects were overseas. Mike said that sounded like four-plus bullshit."

"So did Hal. So there was no reason to think about what he said. He was off our list."

Barb said, "But now seeing as that poor girl *was* . . ."

Milo said, "What's this guy's name?"

Susan said, "Our identities will really be confidential unless there's a trial?"

"One hundred percent."

Another silent sisterly consultation.

Barb Bruno said, "He's a real smoothie. Drives a Bentley, wears nice suits. For all we know it's not even his real name."

Milo waited.

Susan Appel said, "Tell them."

Barb Bruno said, "He goes by Nick. Nicholas St. Heubel."

CHAPTER

29

Milo paced the interview room.

The sisters had just left, reminding him not to forget "our zoning issues."

He'd pressed them for details on the man they knew as Nicholas St. Heubel. Barb Bruno thought her rude guest played tennis. Susan Appel believed the game of choice to be golf. Both women admired his clothes, but thought him "way too smooth."

Both had discarded his address and phone number.

Milo cited the Brentwood street where we'd encountered Heubel and the Bentley and they said, "That's it," in unison.

He asked for their husbands' work numbers.

"Mike wants nothing to do with this."

"Same for Hal."

"Thanks, ladies, you really are heroes."

"Heubel." Working his shoulder and torturing his hair.

I said, "He's the right age and height. Thinner than the descriptions we've gotten of Bright but nothing a diet couldn't accomplish."

"Able to keep it off." One hand grazed his belt. "That alone makes him a goddamn criminal."

"Tasha described 'Tweed' as having a puffy face and Heubel has a pouchy mouth, as if someone's compressing his cheeks."

"Kissy-poo," he said.

"Kissing off the world," I said.

He slapped a wall hard enough to send vibrations through the floor. "Bastard called in the Bentley to stir it up face-to-face. He's that confident the cops are stupid."

"He's been getting away with serious bad deeds since childhood, thinks he's invincible."

"No more *St.* Heubel—what's that, another game? *I'm really not so pure?*"

"It's all about games," I said. "He played with the sisters' heads, returned months later and buried a body under their noses. The image of a backhoe churning up Kat's bones gave him serious jollies."

"Putting on the frightened-citizen act, I'm calming him down." Frown. "I was worried he might know the mayor."

"He might. Rosalynn Carter partied with John Gacy."

"Oh, man," he said.

Three more circuits.

"Asshole stalks Kat in his own wheels, spins a yarn about theft and recovery, leaves blood. All that just to jerk us around."

"Using his own wheels was the perfect cover," I said. "The Bentley's a conspicuous car, even at that hour he had to consider someone might see it. But so what? He'd be the last person to suspect. If he hadn't made the sisters nervous, he'd never have been connected to any of it."

"True," he said. "What *was* that family plot stuff about?"

"Arrogance."

"Why spook the sisters if he wanted their husbands to invest with him, Alex?"

"By that time he probably knew the husbands wouldn't bite, and taunting their wives was a subtle form of aggression. Or he just felt like being extra-naughty. What makes him a tough quarry is it's hard to say *what* he wants. I'm not sure *he* always knows."

"What do you mean?"

"I see his brain as a battlefield, with logic and compulsion constantly skirmishing. His lifestyle—his ability to adapt, to live simply when he needs to—says logic dominates. Then there are the times he needs to work off a little energy and people die."

"That *lifestyle* of his was grubstaked by slashing his way to a million-plus inheritance."

"Most psychopaths would've burned through the money quickly. He managed to parlay it into affluence. I wouldn't be surprised if he really does trade commodities. It's a loner job with high thrill capacity."

He rubbed his face. "Eight years between the Safrans and Kat is way *too* occasional."

"I agree. There're bound to be more bodies."

"No other black-car murders so far, but that means diddly," he said. "Lots of stuff never hits the news."

"The cars are props," I said, "not his signature. He uses them in locales where everyone drives. He's adaptable. Never registered a vehicle in New York."

"Walking the Safrans somewhere and doing them . . . then what, off to Europe? Something he actually told the truth about?"

"Good liars mix it up. He used his own name in New York but adopted a new identity when he returned to California. That could be covering his tracks for the bad deeds he pulled off during the interim."

"Nicko St. Heubel, continental naughty boy . . . wonder where he came up with the name."

"Could be the old-fashioned way."

He plugged *Heubel* into criminal databases, came up negative. A Web search proved no more fruitful.

"Okay," he said, "the *antiquated* way."

The chief's secretary said the boss was in Sacramento, smoking cigars with the governor, she'd pass on the message.

I called Sal Polito and he greased access to his brother-in-law the Manhattan deputy chief. The D.C.'s secretary took down the information and ten minutes later a clerk in Albany phoned.

Nicholas Heubel, born in Yonkers the same year as Ansell "Dale" Bright, had died of meningitis at the tender age of five. No Social Security number issued until twenty-five months ago.

Milo wrestled with the IRS for half an hour in order to learn that Heubel had filed tax returns for the last two years.

I said, "Six years he's out of the country. He comes back, goes the legal route."

"I'll get an Interpol thing going, but with the focus on terrorism, it's gonna take time. Meanwhile, Tricky Nicky's having leisurely breakfasts at the Brentwood Country Mart."

He stood, grabbed his jacket, checked the magazine of his gun, and holstered up.

He asked the watch commander for six officers in plainclothes and three unmarkeds. That took another forty-five minutes to put together and it was nearly two by the time we convoyed to Brentwood.

No SWAT team because that would've been too conspicuous in Nicholas Heubel's leafy, lovely neighborhood. But bulletproof vests for everyone, shotguns and rifles at the ready.

Milo had the other cars hold back a block, parked ten houses up from the vanilla house, told me to sit there and proceeded on foot.

Ambling, as if this were a casual visit.

He made it past six houses. Stopped. Pointed.

For Lease sign staked in the lawn of the vanilla house.

Taking out his weapon, he held it close to his pants. Dark pants, the gun was barely visible. Brief stop at the front door and a bell ring.

The inevitable silence. He walked around the side of the house. A similar foray last year had resulted in a date with a shotgun.

I sat there.

He reappeared, shaking his head. Weapon back in the holster.

Cell phone in his palm. He punched it hard enough to kill it.

Ten minutes later, a white Jaguar drove up to the house and a short, dark woman in an eggplant-colored pantsuit got out.

Milo greeted her. "Ms. Hamidpour?"

"I am Soraya. You are the lieutenant?" Straightening the *For Lease* sign.

"Lieutenant Sturgis, ma'am. Thanks for coming."

"You say there is a problem with the house, I come. What is the problem?"

"How long has it been for lease?"

"Two days."

"How long has it been vacant?"

"The owner doesn't know exactly. What is the problem?"

"When's the last time the owner heard from the tenant?"

"The owner doesn't hear from the tenant. It's a managed property."

"Your company."

"Now it is us."

"Who was it before?"

She named a competitor.

Milo said, "Owner's not happy with their performance."

"Not at all. The tenant left without giving notice. Two months' unpaid rent. At least he left it clean."

Milo rubbed his face. "Have you cleaned it further?"

"Yesterday," said Soraya Hamidpour. "The usual."

"Vacuuming?"

"Carpet shampoo, to make it look extra-good. It's scrubbed down pretty nice. Most of the rooms don't even look as if they were lived in."

"Who's the owner, ma'am?"

"He lives in Florida."

Out came the notepad. "Name, please."

Soraya Hamidpour scrunched her lips. "It's a little . . . tricky."

"How so?"

"The owner likes to stay private."

"Hermit?"

"Not exactly." She turned back to the sign, scraped something from a corner.

"Ma'am—"

"Do we need to get into that?"

"We really do, ma'am."

"The problem with the house is . . ."

"The tenant's not a nice person."

"I see . . . *my* problem is the owner . . . a certain type of exposure, he likes. But . . ."

"Loo?" A big, blond cop wearing an untucked denim shirt and jeans waved from ten feet away. As he got closer, the shirt's flap billowed, exposing his sidearm.

Soraya Hamidpour seemed entranced by the weapon.

Milo said, "What's up, Greg?"

"Sorry to bother you but calls are getting heavy and watch commander wants to know how long you'll need us."

"One car stays for right now, the rest of you go. Call for a crime scene team. We're going to tear this place apart."

"Tear?" said Hamidpour.

Greg said, "The warrant—"

"Signed, sealed, delivered." Wink wink hidden from the Realtor's view.

Greg grinned. "You got it, Loo." He hustled back to the convoy.

Soraya Hamidpour said, "You can't tear it up."

"This could be a crime scene, ma'am."

"Oh, no. Couldn't be, it's so clean—"

"We've got chemicals that go beyond the surface."

"But I already have someone interested—"

"We'll be as quick as possible, ma'am."

Soraya Hamidpour threw up her hands. "This is a disaster."

"Tell you what," said Milo. "If we could speak with the owner, get some details on the tenant, it might mean less of a—"

"The owner is—I can get you details but the owner doesn't like . . ." She took a deep breath. Recited the name of an A-list movie star.

Milo said, "Did he know Mr. Heubel?"

"No, no, never. It's managed. He lives in Florida." Cupping her hand around her mouth. "Something to do with community property. The last divorce. Also, he gets a place to park his airplane."

CHAPTER

30

A call to the company that had leased the house to Nicholas Heubel firmed up the details.

A-List Leading Man had owned the property for five years, purchasing it as part of a divorce settlement with his fourth wife. The plan had been for her to live there, but she'd changed her mind and moved to Colorado with a younger actor, where A-List bought her a ranch. Upon the advice of his business manager, the house had been converted to a rental.

Since then, three tenants had been in residence.

Two young families with "industry connections" and, for the past twenty-two months, Nicholas Heubel.

Heubel had cold-called the company, representing himself as a freelance investor, produced a bank account "more than substantial enough to qualify." He'd paid first and last months' rent plus a damage deposit with a twenty-four-thousand-dollar money order.

The leasing agent, still miffed about being fired, promised to fax over Heubel's rental application and any other paperwork in the file.

Milo said, "Time to talk to Tony Mancusi."

As we set out on the drive to Hollywood, he phoned Sean Binchy. "Forget the paint-and-chrome stuff. Here's something real you can do."

Spelling out the precise wording of a warrant for the vanilla house, he named a judge likely to speed things along. "See if you can get a current photo of Heubel. Asshole's a shape-shifter but maybe we can get a decent likeness . . . Yeah, it is weird. And all your fault, Sean . . . I'm *kidding*. You did good."

Tony Mancusi's Toyota remained where we'd last seen it.

No answer to the bell ring.

We squeezed through a cramped walk-space narrowed further by ragged planting and made our way to the back of the building. A slim rear door looked out to a Dumpster-lined alley. Garbage overflowed the containers and specks of trash had blown up the asphalt.

I said, "This reminds me of something. The back of Leonora Bright's salon."

"That so." He scrutinized the alley, stepped to the door.

Solid-core, hefty deadbolt.

Please Keep Locked at All Times sign affixed dead center.

The knob turned easily. The door swung open.

Mariachi music from somewhere upstairs was loud enough to sound-track the hallway. Bright white hallway, carelessly painted blue doors.

As we reached Tony Mancusi's apartment, a woman stepped out of another unit carrying two see-through plastic bags.

She shot us a look, continued toward the front door.

"Ma'am?"

She stopped.

The badge made her flinch. Fiftyish, short and solid, with nutmeg skin and black hair tied in a tight bun. The bags held party favors and bags of candy.

Milo pointed. *"¿Señor esta aqui?"*

She shook her head, left hurriedly.

Milo's knock on Mancusi's door fought the beat of the music. No reply. Harder rapping followed by "Mr. Mancusi, it's Lieutenant Sturgis," had all the effect of a foam hammer.

He put his ear to the door. "If he's in there, he's keeping it quiet."

The front door swung open and the woman with the bags came back in.

"¿Señora?" said Milo.

"I speak English," she said. "Sorry for not answering, but you scared me. How'd you get in?"

"Back door was unlocked, ma'am."

"Again. Just what we need."

"You've had problems with break-ins?"

"Someone upstairs got robbed a few weeks ago. I think they were drug dealers because they never called the police and right after they moved out. Before that, there were a couple more incidents. Every time I see the door open, I lock it. But other people don't bother."

Milo asked her name.

"Irma Duran."

"Looks like someone's having a party."

"My grandson's class. Reward for reading accomplishment. I'm a teacher's assistant at his school, on my way over there. Reason why I came back is someone else was looking for that guy. His mother, she seemed worried."

"His mother," said Milo. "When was she here?"

"When I came out to take my grandson to school—around six thirty. Raymond goes to a magnet in the Valley, we need to leave early. She asked the same thing you did—had I seen him. Said she was his mother and he hadn't called when he was supposed to. I told her I hadn't seen him and she looked concerned and left. Is he okay?"

"You know Mr. Mancusi?"

"I see him once in a while, we've said hello, that's about it. Mostly he keeps to himself."

"What did his mother look like, ma'am?"

"I really didn't get a good look at her, because I was busy with Raymond and his backpack, getting him to eat his sweet roll and drink his milk. She sounded worried, I felt sorry for her. That's why I came back. So you could contact her."

"Appreciate it, Ms. Duran. She didn't by any chance leave a number?"

"No, sorry."

"Do you remember anything about her appearance?"

"Um . . . tall. And she had a nice car. White Lexus, I saw her driving away. That was a little surprising."

"What was?"

"Her having money. Because he looks like he shops at a thrift store. Now that I think about it, she was just the opposite."

"Well dressed."

"Classy," said Irma Duran. "In an old-fashioned way. Like one of those women you see in old movies, all put together. Suit, stockings, shoes, big leather handbag. Like that Agatha Christie detective?"

"Miss Marple," he said.

"I love those books," said Irma Duran. "Exactly like that, conservative—sensible. Except for her scarf, that was different—really colorful. Big like a shawl, all kinds of wild colors. Is the son a drug dealer?"

"Why would you suspect that?"

"He doesn't *do* anything all day. Never had a visitor that I've seen—oh, I guess that means he isn't a dealer. At least not out of his apartment."

Milo said, "Mom's his first visitor."

"Moms care," said Irma Duran. "She seemed so . . . as if she'd been putting up with him for a while."

Milo kicked the door hard. The rip of splintering wood cut through trumpets and *guitarrón* but the panel remained shut. His second attempt broke it free of the frame.

We stood back.

Mancusi's Murphy bed listed from the wall at an acute angle, propped in place by a nightstand. A pair of arms extended from the sides of the mattress.

Gray mattress except where it was reddish brown.

Most of it, reddish brown.

Splotches the same color topped the nightstand, ran down the drawers, spread on the carpet.

One of the hands was missing two fingers. The severed digits sat in their own pool of blood, shriveled and white, desiccated grubs. A blood trail led to the shabby kitchenette.

Milo got closer to the threshold, kept his feet in the hall but stuck his head inside the apartment.

I heard a sharp intake of breath. Peered around him.

On the counter, next to a box of Advil, sat an empty half gallon of diet tonic water. To the left of the bottle sat a spherical thing on a dinner plate.

Thing with droopy yellow hair.

Tony Mancusi's eyes were open but his mouth was shut.

The plate made it worse. He'd been served up. A cannibal entrée.

Milo said, "Oh, Lord."

I had nothing to add.

CHAPTER

31

Milo gloved up, propped Mancusi's door in place, left the building, smoked, composed himself. Got the yellow tape out of his trunk.

A cloudbank cleared the sun. Rodney Drive almost looked pretty.

I sat on the curb, trying to clear my head. Waste of time; no trick of my trade was up to the task.

Tony Mancusi was Hollywood's first homicide of the year and Milo phoned Detective Petra Connor. She was on vacation in Greece and her partner, Raul Biro, summoned the crime scene crew and the coroner.

Biro was young, an Afghanistan vet, thoughtful, perceptive, with freakish stamina. He'd emerged from Mancusi's apartment expressionless, took notes as Milo summarized, tugging at a pale blue brocade tie that didn't need adjustment. Thick dark hair starting to gray prematurely was sprayed in place. His suit was navy, tailored, spotless. Paper booties protected spit-polished loafers.

When Milo finished, he said, "Let me frame this in my head:

You're figuring Bright, Heubel, whichever you want to call him, has been here before, knows the back's usually unlocked. Or he picks the lock, because he knows how to do that. Same deal for getting access to Mancusi's apartment. Once in, does his thing. On his way out, he encounters the neighbor, pretends to be looking for Mancusi, makes his getaway . . . sounds logical."

"But?"

"I'm thinking there could be another possibility, Loo. After Mancusi ditched the he-she, he met up with Bright and they returned here together."

Milo scratched the side of his nose. "Could be. Though Mancusi might've been wary of him."

Raul said, "If Bright and Mancusi were *real* good buddies before, Mancusi could've given Bright a key. Maybe Bright's been here out of drag. When I get back, I'll see if there's a recent photo, canvass the tenants."

"However Bright gained access, we've got a pretty good fix on the time frame. We saw Mancusi leave Gordito's around two forty-five, the neighbor saw Fake Mom here at six thirty. Almost four hours is time enough to do his thing, clean himself up."

"He stashes his tools in that big leather purse the neighbor described, slips out in broad daylight. No sweat because he's got a great cover."

Biro closed his pad. "Dowdy drag, except for the scarf. Lots of blood back there but I didn't see any impact spatter. How about you?"

Milo shook his head.

"So I'm thinking Mancusi was likely dead when he got cut up, Loo. Bright could've used the scarf to choke him out, got himself a passive corpse to dissect."

"For Shonsky, he used the scarf as a prop. Stabbed her to death. For all his victims we know of, the weapon was a knife. But he mixes it up identity-wise, so maybe he likes variety in his methods, too."

I said, "A stealth strangulation for Mancusi makes sense. Tony was a heavy man, making him harder to subdue. And wary, because he knew or suspected what Bright was capable of."

Biro said, "Sneak up behind, get the scarf around the neck, avoid a violent struggle. Keeping it quiet at three, four a.m."

He fooled with his tie again. "First Mama, now the son. He's got something against this family?"

"If only it was that simple, Raul."

"The psycho do-gooder thing, huh? In his mind, he's helping out, then he snaps?"

I said, "The do-gooder thing is a power play. He was a cruel kid, killed his own sister for big-time financial gain, developed a taste for playing God."

"Making the rules," said Biro. "He picks the who and the when and the how. But Mancusi got done because Bright was worried he'd talk."

Milo said, "That's how we see it."

"Serving it up on that plate. That's a whole different universe of bad."

Milo lit another cigarillo. Inhaled for a long time and blew smoke at the sky. "If he followed me when I was trailing Tony, saw me put Tasha in the car, that coulda been Tony's death warrant. Because Bright knew Tasha was at the party when Tony griped about his mother, figured too close for comfort."

I said, "If Bright was watching Tony, he'd already been thinking about snipping loose ends."

He grunted.

Biro said, "How we dividing the chores?"

"Mancusi's yours, the rest is my headache."

"You have any problems with this expanding?"

"To what?"

Another tug at the tie. "This many bodies over all these years, a suspect that psycho. Someone suggests a task force, I really don't see how we can stop it."

Milo said, "We take it wherever it goes, Raul."

Biro said, "Meanwhile, we work with what we've got. Starting with finding the he-she. You want me to get Vice over to Gordito's tonight?"

"Let me cover that, you concentrate on this."

Biro flipped through his pad. "So we know whodunit and maybe at least part of whydunit and howdunit. Now all we have to do is find this altruist."

A slow smile brightened his unlined face. "Rich old lady. Maybe I should start visiting some of those women's clubs—bridge, bingo, high tea, whatever."

"Bygone generation, Raul."

"Actually, Loo, they still do the tea bit out in Pasadena and San Marino."

"You grew up there?"

"Nope, East L.A." said Biro. "My mother cleaned rooms at the Huntington."

A crime scene tech emerged from the apartment in full hazmat suiting, unmasked, wiped sweat from his face. "Got the bathroom dark enough to luminol, Detectives. Lots of swipe marks and someone used granulated cleanser. But there's a whole lot of hemoglobin left. Tub, floor, sink, oodles in the shower."

"Oodles," said Milo.

"That's a technical term," said the tech. "This one's something, huh? Got a spare smoke?"

At three thirty p.m. we left the scene and cruised by Gordito's. Two rangy hookers, not even close to feminine, sat nibbling and drinking and gabbing. A trio of construction workers occupied a nearby table, everyone minding their own business.

Milo said, "Drive a little and circle back, we'll keep trying for a while. Once Tasha finds out Tony got sliced she's a sure rabbit."

His cell beeped. "What's up, Sean? . . . Any resemblance? . . .

Better than nothing, zip a copy over to Raul Biro . . . The smart one, worked with Petra . . . Yeah, him. Anything else? Good, get over to the house and be in charge while the techies do their thing . . . I don't care about that, Sean, if any of those chrome mavens have a problem, tell 'em to call me. Now read *everything* you've got, go slow and enunciate. I got old ears."

He listened for several minutes, worked his jaws, clicked off.

"Got a two-year-old DMV shot on Nicholas Heubel. Unfortunately, the photo shows him with a full gray beard and a shaved head and the address he listed is a P.O.B. in Brentwood that he only rented the month he applied for the lease on the house. He gave three references: Ansel D. Bright, San Francisco, Roland Korvutz, New York, and a Mel Dabson, here in L.A."

I said, "Establish a fake identify and back yourself up with your real name."

"Clever boy, huh? The leasing company says Bright's reference was 'glowing.' And the number they reached him at traces back to a prepaid cell. Korvutz never responded to the request. Unlike this Dabson character, who said he'd known Heubel for years, Nicky was upright, honest, and dependable. Two out of three plus twenty-four grand in cash was enough to close the deal."

I said, "Where in L.A. does Dabson live?"

He checked his notes. "Altair Terrace, zip code looks like . . . not too far from here, in the Hollywood Hills."

I said, "Wonder if you can see the sign from there."

I made several passes up and down Highland, drove over to Santa Monica where transsexual and male hookers share the stroll with varying degrees of harmony.

Milo looked for Tasha while he worked the phone. Trying for background on *Melvin* then *Mel Dabson*.

No such individual.

I said, "Could be another alter ego."

He ran AutoTracks and criminal searches using *Melford, Melrose, Meldrim,* and *Melnick,* sat back cursing.

A call to the state Franchise Tax Board on Dabson came up empty. But a brief chat with a helpful clerk at the county assessor brought a smile to his face.

"*Tram*mel Dabson. Been paying the property tax on Altair Terrace for twenty-one months."

A dive back into NCIC came up empty.

I said, " 'Trammel' means 'to hinder.' "

"Building word power every day." He phoned Sean to check on the toss of the Brentwood house.

Empty, clean, no cars in the garage.

As he shut his eyes and leaned back, something caught my eye at the edge of a strip mall near Orange Drive.

"Rise and shine." I pointed.

He jerked upright. "Pull over."

32

This time Tasha ran.

"Oh, great," said Milo, as she ducked off Santa Monica onto Orange and veered into an alley.

He jumped out of the car and I circled the block to Mansfield. When I got to the mouth of the alley, Tasha was racing toward me, skinny-legged sprint easily outstripping Milo's openmouthed lumber.

Shoes in hand, panty hose shredding.

Milo's arms churned air. His face was crimson.

Tasha looked back at him, picked up speed. Saw me. Looked back again. Stumbled.

She went down hard on her back, purse landing just out of reach from a splayed arm.

As she got to her feet, Milo caught up, sucking air. He flipped her over, did a quick frisk and cuff, snarled a command not to move. Snagging the purse, he dumped the contents. Tissues, condoms, cosmetics, and a packet of Oreos landed on the asphalt. Then a clatter as a pearl-handled straight razor slid out.

Still panting, Milo stomped the weapon hard, ground pearl into dust. Hauled Tasha up hard.

"Idiot," he said.

She grew limp in his grasp. Her face crumpled. Bits of gravel clung to her pancake veneer.

She began working up a smile.

Milo's snarl killed that. He put her in the back of the car, used the seat belt for further confinement.

This time he got in front.

Tasha jangled the cuffs. "You can take these off. I won't run, sir. I promise, sir."

"Open your mouth again"—pant pant—"and I'll hogtie you." To me: "Hollywood station."

"Sir, that's not necessary!"

Milo strained so hard for oxygen that his bulk rose off the seat.

I drove.

Tasha said, "Least it's a nice ride. Love these old Caddy-lackers. What was it, confiscated from some—"

"Shut the hell *up*."

"Sorry. Sir."

"Are you *deaf*?"

Five blocks from Wilcox Avenue: "Sir, don't get mad but you're still breathing hard. You sure you're okay?"

"Why the hell did you rabbit?"

"I got scared."

"Did we hurt you the first time?"

"No, but . . ."

"But *what*?"

Silence.

Milo said, "God forbid you should miss a trick. *Idiot*."

"A girl's got to make a living."

"You're not gonna *be* living if you don't stop acting like a moron. Guess who got cut right after he left you?"

"Someone got cut?"

"You really *are* deaf."

Long silence. "You're not saying Tony?"

"You're ready for *Jeopardy!*, genius."

"Tony got *cut*? Omigod is he all right?"

Milo said, "Quite the opposite."

"You mean—"

"We're talking one trick that won't be giving you any repeat business."

"Omigod, ohsweetlord—"

"It happened right after he saw you," said Milo. "We're figuring someone was watching besides us."

"Who who who?"

"What's that, your owl imitation?"

"Who, sir? Please!"

"Think ugly suit and seamed stockings."

"Him? Omigod no way!"

"You know something about him we don't?"

"No, sir, no . . ."

"But?"

"I just never knew someone who . . . did that."

"All those years on the street?" said Milo. "Spare me the innocence."

"I seen fights, sir. Seen a man beat another man to death over a wrong look. Seen people all doped up, losing their lives 'cause a . . . seen plenty of badmen, sir, but no, not that, never something like that . . ."

"Not what?"

"Something . . . all controlled."

"How do you know it was controlled?"

"Wannaboos," said Tasha. "It's all about the game. Tony didn't do nothing to nobody, right?"

"Why not?"

"Tony was weak, there was no anger in him, just sadness."

"You're right about one thing," said Milo. "This was *real* controlled."

"I don't wanna *know*, sir, please don't tell me *details*."

"Fine, but we *like* details. Let's hear everything you know about Tweed."

"Nothing else, I swear, nothing."

Milo turned to me: "This is not going well, pard."

Tasha said, "Just what I *told* you, sir, that's everything I *know*!"

"How many parties have you been to with Tweed?"

"Just that one."

"Why not more?"

Silence.

"What was the problem?" said Milo.

"It's not a place I gone to again."

"That's no answer."

Tasha said, "It's—to be honest, no one invited me."

When we got to the rear door at Hollywood station, she said, "You don't need to lock me up, I promise."

Milo whistled "Dixie."

"Sir, there's a problem, a real *problem,* usually they only got one girl cell free 'cause all the troublemakers are boys and if the girl room's all full, they put you in a boy room and it's *dangerous.*"

"You have equipment for the girl room?"

Silence.

"Do you?"

Barely audible: "Not yet, I'm saving up."

"Nothing I can do, then. You know the rules."

"I am human, sir, not plumbing."

"What can I say." Tough tone but his cheek muscles twitched.

"*Please,* sir. Other policemen are nice to me, I don't make trouble, they put me in the girl room. The girls like me there, ask anyone, I don't cause no problems, check your files."

"When's the last time you were here?"

"A year, sir. Maybe more. I swear. You put me in the right place and I'll do anything you—"

"Tell you what," said Milo. "You cooperate, I won't book you for the blade even though you were already warned. Or for resisting, even though you made me exercise."

"Yes, sure, of course . . . what does cooperate mean?"

"You're a material witness. I might even get you a snack."

"That is so kind, sir . . . you did lose my Oreos."

Hollywood Division obliged with an empty interview room where Milo stashed Tasha. He brought her a donut and a Coke, phoned Raul Biro at the murder scene on Rodney.

Biro was still waiting for access to the apartment, had some forensic guesses to pass along.

Tony Mancusi's head had been sawed off right beneath the chin, leaving most of the neck's internal structure intact. Care had been taken to sever vertebrae without breaking them.

Clean work; the coroner's investigator's guess was a large, extremely sharp, nonserrated blade, consistent with the weapon that had dispatched Ella Mancusi. The same weapon had probably been used on Tony's fingers. Exploratory cuts on the other hand suggested intent for a bilateral amputation.

"Maybe he got bored," said Biro. "Or ran out of time."

Final disposition was the coroner's purview but the C.I., a registered nurse with twenty years' experience, admitted off the record that the hyoid cartilage appeared ruptured. Pinpoint hemorrhages in the eyes could've been due to a number of causes but, combined with the neck injury, strangulation was a "decent possibility, let's see if the doc agrees."

Milo looked for the Altair Terrace address in a Thomas Guide, found a single block of curving, dead-end tributary off the northeastern edge of Beachwood Drive.

Not far from a rent-a-horse ranch where I used to ride when I worked at Western Pediatric. Walking distance from Franklin Avenue, but heavily wooded and freakishly quiet. I remembered how bends in the trail opened abruptly to dry, flat mesas. The vulgar message of the Hollywood sign.

Milo said, "I'm starved," and called out for four barbecued beef sandwiches from a place on Western. I had one, he ate two, he passed the last one to Tasha, who said, "Normally I stay away from red meat, but that smells yum."

By six forty the sky was felt-gray deepening to black and we put her back in the Seville.

She said, "I'm still tasting that lovely sauce."

Milo said, "Behave yourself and you can have dessert."

"So kind, sir. I do like this *car.*"

I drove up Beachwood, parked two blocks south of Altair Terrace.

Milo unbelted. "Time for a little hike."

"Sir, it's uphill, you sure you're okay?"

"Your concern is touching. Let's go."

"Is this guaranteed safe?"

"What are you worried about?"

"He could see me."

"What makes you think he's here?"

"You're taking me here."

"This is to jog your memory."

"I already told you, this is definitely the place."

"We're not on the street yet."

"This is it, I *feel* it."

"ESP?"

"I get feelings," she said. "In my hair, the roots get all tingly, means I'm getting a message."

"Out of the car."

One block later: "Can we at least go slow, sir? My poor little feet are so sore."

"I offered to get you some sneakers."

"With this dress? As if. Can we just go slow?"

Milo exhaled and shortened his steps.

Tasha winked at me.

Ebony night; no sidewalks or streetlights, wide spacing between the properties filled with unruly greenery and old-growth trees.

A world in silhouette.

Tasha said, "That's the party house, I'm sure. Let's go."

"*Whisper.*"

"Sorry. That's the party—"

"I heard you. Which one?"

"Um, we're not there yet."

"Forward march."

Ninety seconds later: "That's the one! All the way on top!"

"*Whisper,* dammit!"

"Sorry, sorry. That's it. For sure."

A long-nailed hand pointed to a low, pale box perched on the uppermost rim of the cul-de-sac.

Milo motioned us to stay in place, hiked past three houses, then four more. Stopped just short of the target. Waited. Hazarded a quick flashlight wash of the façade.

Blank but for a single shuttered window. Garage to the left, with a corrugated aluminum door.

The flashlight beam dipped to a cement walkway. Pines and eucalyptus towered behind the flat roof. Sparse vegetation in front: a spindly yucca plant and a stunted palm.

Milo padded back. "You're sure?"

Tasha said, "Absolutely, sir. That stupid spiky thing, got a run in my stocking. And over there's where if you step out in back you can see the sign and over there is where Tony—rest-his-soul—and me walked."

Tracing the curve of the cul-de-sac. "It's all coming back to me—

out *there* is where all the coyote screaming came from, I got so scared, sir, it was dark just like it is now. I hate the darkness, can we *go*?"

"Stay put with my partner." He retraced his climb, got closer to the pale house.

Tasha said, "All that climbing can't be good for him."

I didn't answer.

"He should work out . . . You don't say much, sir . . . It's too weird out here, real scary-quiet, know what I mean, like something's gonna jump out? Like something's gonna—quiet's basically an evil thing. The *devil* likes quiet. The *devil* likes you to think everything's nice and quiet then he jumps up and grabs you. This is a *bad* quiet. Even Fontana had a better quiet than this quiet. When the chickens were all sleeping you could hear the train. I liked to lie in bed listening to the train and wondering where it was going—okay, here he is again, maybe he seen enough and we can get outta here."

Milo said, "Can't be sure but looks like no one home."

Tasha said, "My hair says that's a message from God, let's get outta here, find us some noise."

As we descended Altair Terrace, Milo phoned in outlining a surveillance plan for later that night.

At Beachwood, Tasha said, "I'm feeling my appetite coming back. You can drop me at the Baskin-Robbins."

Before Milo could answer, headlights whitewashed us.

Single vehicle climbing from the south.

Milo pushed Tasha into the brush.

The headlights reached the intersection. VW bus, a dim color hard to make out in the darkness. Grinding noise as its tires turned left onto Altair.

Tasha said, "They need transmission fluid."

Milo stepped out, reached for the side of the bus just as it turned, tapped the passenger door.

One hand on his holstered gun, the other waving his badge.

The bus stopped short. Milo made a cranking motion.

The passenger window rolled down manually. The driver's hand remained on the handle as she leaned toward him.

Young woman, thirty or so, with wide, surprised eyes and short brown hair. The rear of the bus was piled high with cardboard boxes.

"Do you live on this street, ma'am?"

"Uh-huh. Something's wrong."

"Nothing to be alarmed about. Do you know the occupants of the house at the end of the road?"

"Not really."

"No?"

"I—they're not there."

"Not around much?"

Her eyes flicked to the rear of the bus. "Nope."

Milo said, "Everything okay, ma'am?"

"You surprised me. I have to go, Officer. Have a *child* to look after."

Biting her lip, she gunned the engine, ground the gears, lurched forward, nearly running over Milo's foot.

He fell back, barely held on to his balance.

We watched as the bus putt-putted up Altair.

Tasha said, "Maybe it's me, but that's one scared girl."

We stayed in the shadows, watched as the bus parked between the pale house and its nearest neighbor.

I said, "When you asked if she lived here, she said 'Something's wrong.' Statement, not a question."

Milo got on the phone again, whispered orders.

The van sat there for several minutes before the woman got out and unlatched the rear doors.

Shaking her head; as if responding to an unseen questioner.

A second figure emerged from the bus. Taller, short hair, shirt and pants.

Male.

He pointed at the woman and the two of them pulled something out of the van.

Rectangular; a carton, maybe four feet long.

The man straight-armed the woman away, completed the extrication, lowered the box to the ground.

The bump was audible.

The woman let out a high-pitched noise. The man's hand on her shoulder silenced her.

She reached for the box.

He slapped her hand away. Pointed again. She moved several feet away. Stood there. Hand to mouth.

The man began rocking the carton.

Let go of it.

The woman lunged forward, broke the fall, straightened the box.

The man placed his hands on his hips.

The sound of laughter filtered down Altair.

The woman tried to lift the carton, failed.

The man grasped one end and the two of them carried it toward the pale house.

Milo said, "Here goes aerobics," and took off on big, rubber-soled feet.

CHAPTER
34

I heard the scuffle before I saw it.

Tasha shivered, grabbed a branch for support. Leaves rattled.

I said, "Don't budge an inch."

"You don't have to convince me, sir."

I followed Milo's pathway up the street.

Twenty feet from the house, the details kicked in.

Milo's feet planted. Two-handing his 9mm. The weapon aimed at the smiling face of the man who called himself Nicholas Heubel.

Fast, uphill run, but not a trace of raspy breath.

Heubel wore a scooped-neck peasant blouse, white culottes that exposed hairy ankles, red Bakelite earrings, red lipstick. A two-day beard stubble and granny glasses rounded out the ensemble.

Bad joke, if not for the arm around the short-haired woman's neck, forcing her backward, so that her spine arched and her eyes watched the sky.

In Heubel's other hand, a little black pistol pressed against the top of the carton.

Seemed to be piercing the carton—embedded in a hole at the top.

The woman said, "Please let him go. He doesn't have much air."

Milo said, "Good idea, Dale."

Heubel didn't respond.

The woman said, "My baby," and Heubel put weight on the gun, drove it deeper into the box.

He said, "Maybe the merciful thing would be to blow his little tot brains out."

"Please!" howled the woman.

Lights went on in a house midway down Altair.

Heubel said, "Now look what you've done," and pushed the gun so deep the barrel disappeared into the box. Cardboard flexed. He kicked the carton. Noise leaked from within.

Muffled cries.

"Oh God, please, please, I beg you," said the woman.

Heubel choked off her voice with an arm twist.

Milo said, "Bad idea, Dale."

Heubel said, "I'm the idea guy," in a strange, vacant voice.

"I called for backup, Dale. The smart thing is defuse this now."

"Dale," said Heubel. "Who in the world is that?"

The cries from the box got louder.

Then: coughing.

The woman said, "He can't breathe!"

Heubel said, "Life is transitory. Makes us appreciate what we have."

"Please! He's only two!"

Milo took a step closer.

Heubel kicked the box again.

Milo edged nearer.

Heubel said, "Sneak up like that again and I'll bam-bam Bam Bam."

"Emilio," said the woman. "He's got a *name*."

"Let's just take it easy," said Milo.

"Good idea," said Heubel. "I'm as mellow as layer cake. Anyone for . . . anagrams?"

The woman whimpered.

Milo said, "They'll be here any moment, Dale."

Heubel said, "Don't insult my intelligence, I know it's only you and you don't have a radio."

"I called, Dale."

Quick arm twist. The woman gasped.

"Shush, now," said Heubel. "I believe in happy endings, don't you, chiquita?"

"Yes, yes, please let him go—"

"I guess my definition differs from yours."

Milo said, "The last thing I want to do is insult your intelligence, but—"

"Your *presence* insults my intelligence." Grinding the gun into the box.

Milo said, "Nice outfit. Who's your tailor?"

Heubel gave a start. The gun hand loosened for a second.

I jumped out, shouting.

"Freeze drop the gun drop it!" Or something like it, who remembers.

Heubel's head swiveled hard toward the intrusion, relaxing his choke hold long enough for the woman to twist her head lower.

She bit down on his arm.

He shook her off, said, "Bye-bye, Emilio."

Milo emptied his weapon.

Heubel stood there for an instant. Threw up his hands, as if surrendering. Fell.

One of his earrings flew off like a speck of hail.

The woman dove at the box, managed to keep it upright. Ripped the lid off, screaming.

Pulled out a sobbing flailing toddler and held him to her breast.

Heubel made an odd little squeaky noise.

When the child calmed down, the woman carried him over to Heubel's body. Kicked viciously.

CHAPTER

35

The woman's named was Felicia Torres and she was twenty-eight. Her husband, a landscaper studying biology at night, had been sent by the National Guard to Iraq three months ago. Without Stuart's income, the young family's savings depleted quickly and Felicia began looking for temp jobs. No computer skills limited her options for office work. She lowered her sights.

A couple of office-cleaning jobs downtown hadn't worked out because the babysitting money just about wiped out her salary.

The Craigslist ad for a "two-day house-straightening position" in Brentwood had seemed promising. Great neighborhood, "generous pay," and the man who answered at the number sounded friendly.

Generous pay translated to twenty dollars an hour, way more than Felicia had hoped for. When "Nick" readily agreed to let her bring Emilio along, that clinched it.

With her Hyundai in the shop, she'd needed to take the bus from her one-bedroom in Venice and walk a ways on Sunset, pushing Emilio in his stroller. The street was hard to find and there were no sidewalks, so the stroller bumped a lot but that helped put Emilio to sleep.

When she finally found the house, she knew she had a winner. Gorgeous and huge, like something out of *House & Garden.* Shiny white Lexus in front.

She knocked on the door and that same friendly voice said, "It's open, c'mon in."

Nick was just as nice in person, kind of lanky, real well built. Good-looking in that older-rich-guy way.

He handed her a hundred-dollar bill. "This is your advance, keep track of your hours and let me know when you're due for more."

The house was even huger than it looked from the outside, with cathedral ceilings and white walls. Real bright, even with the lights off. Probably cheery when furnished.

Now, to Felicia's surprise, it was totally empty. And really pretty clean-looking. But it was Nick's money and she liked the feel of that hundred in the pocket of her jeans.

Emilio was still snoozing away. Felicia looked for a place to park the stroller.

Nick smiled, whispered, "Cute," led her to a room at the back, where he'd set up a toddler gate and some toys. Unbelievable.

When she tried to thank him, he shrugged, took the stroller and wheeled it into a corner.

Sunlight glowing through a big, spotless window turned patches of oak floor gold. No glare on Emilio; Nick had put the stroller in a cool, shady corner—such a considerate man. Through the glass, Felicia saw a really lush tropical-type garden and a blue lap pool. She wondered what Stuart would think of the plantings. They looked okay to her but she wasn't picky.

Cute toys, some of them still in boxes. Nick grinned.

"I can't believe you took the time, sir."

"No big whoop, Felicia."

Using her name like they'd known each other for a long time.

She said, "To me, it sure is. This had to cost—"

Nick placed a finger on her lips. "The main thing is when he wakes up he'll get all jazzed."

"He will for sure, these are just what he likes—do you have kids, sir?"

"Not yet. I went over to Toyland, asked the salesgirl."

"That is so—"

"Felicia, if no one went the extra yard, the world would be a pretty sad place—c'mon, let me show you the gig. Anytime you need to tend to Little Man, feel free."

Felicia felt her eyes swell.

Maybe Nick sensed her emotion. "I like to help," he said. "Kind of selfish, really. Makes *me* feel good."

Emilio woke up in an okay mood. The toys overwhelmed him and he got hyper, but then he calmed down and focused on some plastic cars. Making that serious-old-man crunched-up face that reminded Felicia of her dad in Florida.

The only funny thing was, Emilio didn't seem to like Nick, got all whiny when Nick tried to talk to him. But her son was a shy boy, not used to strangers.

The main thing, he was occupied and Felicia could work steadily.

The "gig" was different; you couldn't ask for anything easier.

Felicia wondered why Nick was willing to pay someone to dry-mop every inch of wall and floor, scrub down granite counters and appliances in the clearly unused kitchen.

When Nick made her go over the walls a second, then a third time, gave her freshly shredded T-shirts and ammonia spray to "really get down" into the corners, she thought it was a little weird, but it was his money and the take-out Thai food he ordered from a place in the County Mart was delicious, not to mention the candy for Emilio.

Knowing, somehow, that she *loved* Thai.

She'd use a toothbrush and a magnifying glass if that's what he wanted.

While she cleaned, Nick kept busy in the master bedroom, emerged from time to time to inquire if she and Emilio were okay.

Between the second and the third go-rounds, when she made a joke about it being like one of those forensics shows on TV, cleaning up the evidence, Nick thought that was hilarious.

On the second day, the bus was late and so was she, but Nick was cool about it. He patted Emilio's head and had Felicia go over the dining room again. Then he showed her into the master bedroom, the only part of the house she hadn't been.

This was different.

Clothing was piled everywhere—on the bed, the floor, in the closet—except for one section where stacks of folded cardboard boxes stood ready to be assembled.

As if the contents of the entire house had been concentrated in one space.

"Please fold everything and pack, but not too tight," he told her. "If you can arrange it loosely by color, that would be great, but don't worry if it's not perfect. Do you know how to fold these sides to make the boxes?"

"Sure."

"Then you're all set." Big smile. "I'm going out for a while. I left drinks in the fridge and some snacks . . . it's really nice having you help me, Felicia."

"Me, too," she said. Boy, did *that* sound stupid. "Um, afterward— after the food is gone—do I need to scrub down the fridge again?"

Nick thought about that. "No. That won't be necessary."

It didn't take long to realize everything was for a woman. Big woman. Expensive stuff, a lot of it vintage.

Gowns and dresses, silk blouses and skirts. Tweed suits—a whole collection of those. Silky negligees and panty hose and real silk stockings you needed garters and clips for, she'd never actually seen those before. Lots of bras, size forty-four C.

On the bottom of one pile, she found a bunch of cute little leather boxes filled with costume jewelry. Tucked in a corner were cool old hatboxes, round and hexagonal, containing feathery cloches, felt derbies, berets, delicate straws with fake wooden cherries sticking out of the bands. One blue plaid cap that looked like a man's, but women with hat faces looked cute in them, too.

She tried that one on, tilted it at a jaunty angle, grinned at the mirror.

People had told her she had a hat face.

Parting two other stacks in the corner revealed a bunch of plastic bags containing tubes and jars of high-end cosmetics. Some of it all dried up, but she packed it anyway, Nick was the boss.

In a humongous plastic bag, she found a dozen wigs, with tissue paper between them. All different colors and styles. In a matching bag were the little foam dealies you put wigs on.

The *coolest* find was thirty-three of the nicest scarves Felicia had ever seen. Vuitton and Armani and Chanel and Escada and some others she'd never heard of. She counted them because she'd never seen so much gorgeous hand-painted silk in one place.

No men's stuff, not a single sock.

Felicia wondered if Nick was a costume designer. Or maybe married to an actress who traveled, needed all those changes.

Big woman, maybe a character actress. She conjured an image: tall, buxom, had to be a blonde. Big but firm and shapely, you had to give Nick credit for not insisting on an X-ray.

Felicia had once been a totally slim size six. She'd lost all her preg weight, but twenty-five months later was still a little poochy in front, favored baggy sweatshirts.

No competition for Nick's glamorous wife.

Stupid thought!

Like the fantasies that had begun filling her mind since last night.

Lying in bed, hoping Emilio would sleep through the night. Thinking about Stuart in Fallujah. It had been three weeks since she'd heard from him and no way would she listen to the news, all news did was make everything as horrible as possible.

Stuart's face faded from view.

Nick's took its place.

Felicia felt stupid and ashamed.

Fought the fantasy but it kept coming back and finally she gave in.

Her and Nick.

It starts off all friendly, totally innocent, they're both good people.

The two of them in that vanilla-colored house. Beautiful, warm sunny day.

She's mopping, dusting, sweeping stuff outside.

She goes outside, by the pool, to dustpan it up. It's so hot. She peels off her sweatshirt. Underneath is that skimpy black tank top. The one Stuart always asked her to put on when they . . .

For some reason, she'd worn it to work.

No bra.

She stretches. Bends down, accidentally flashes a full view of her dangling boobs.

That's okay, no one there.

Uh-oh; there *is*.

Nick. Lounging under a palm tree, reading a book.

Wearing swim trunks, nothing else. Nice body, not an ounce of fat.

He sees her, smiles.

She smiles back, shyly.

Her eyes drift to his swim trunks.

Uh-oh. *That's* kinda hard to miss.

Nick blushes. Tries to hide the evidence with a book.

She smiles. Walks over to him, real slow.

Both of them working at controlling themselves because they're good people.

But . . .

Remembering last night's fantasy, Felicia's cheeks burned. Her knees felt weak.

From the corner room with the toys, Emilio cried.

Thank God for the interruption.

. . .

At the end of the third day, Nick came home around five p.m., whistling and looking happy and carrying a big brown leather bag that could've been a purse or one of those things guys use.

Felicia said, "You want me to pack that, too?"

"Not necessary. Looks like you've made excellent progress, Felicia."

She had. Getting through most of the clothing, everything folded and organized perfectly by color and fabric.

She bragged about it. "Silk with silk, linen with linen."

Nick flashed his big, white smile. Removed his glasses and looked at her with clear brown eyes.

Felicia loved the fact that she could please someone. Her own happiness was an elusive thing, she knew Stuart wrote as often as he could but . . .

Nick said, "Why don't you take a break?"

Cool fingers grazed the nape of her neck. When had he moved close enough to do that?

Felicia drew back, feeling the scorch of her cheeks. Wondering if she'd done something to let him know what was flying through her head . . .

His smile turned crooked. "I'm going to look over these boxes, see if there's anything I want you to change."

"I hope there's more work," said Felicia. "You're a great boss."

Why had she said that?

Nick laughed. "Boss? We're two people who've reached an agreement. Take a break, Felicia. Go chill by the pool, drink something, you're sweating."

Running a finger along her arm.

She shivered. "Sure."

He closed the door to the master bedroom and she went to the kitchen, brought a Diet Peach Snapple outside, along with a carton of strawberries from the collection of luscious fresh fruit Nick had bought at the Country Mart this morning.

She stretched out in a lounge chair. The same one she'd imagined Nick in. Stretched and yawned and half a bottle of tea and seven berries later, the sun did a number on her head.

When she awoke, the sky was dark and her watch said she'd been out for thirty-five minutes.

Now she'd have to bus back later than she liked, walk those streets where gangbangers sometimes cruised.

Omigod, Emilio hadn't eaten dinner!

Then why wasn't he crying?

She hurried inside to the toy room.

No Emilio.

She called his name.

Heard a funny sound—like a bird when its wings were restrained.

From the master bedroom.

Rushing there, she found the door closed.

Opened it.

Nick had pushed boxes out of the way and created a narrow space where Emilio now sat in his stroller. Surrounded on three sides. Like her baby was being walled in.

He saw her and wailed, "Maaamaaa!"

Nick said, "Poor little guy, he woke up cranky."

She turned to him. Gaped.

Nick was dressed in a lavender satin ball gown, low-cut, something stuffed in the bodice to plump his chest up to cleavage.

Hairy cleavage.

He had on dangling violet-colored earrings, tacky purplish lipstick, real whore-y fake eyelashes. Combined with his short hair and beard stubble it was . . . it was . . .

Pivoting and cocking a hip, he wiggled his butt.

At her. Then at *Emilio*.

"Maaamaaa!"

"*Voilà*," said Nick. "*Très chic, non?*"

Emilio cried louder.

For some crazy reason, Felicia laughed.

She didn't know why. No matter how many times she'd try to figure it out she would never come up with why.

Because she *didn't* think it was funny, not *any* of it, what she did feel was *grossed out* and *freaked* out and—

What came out was *laughter*.

And that changed everything about Nick.

And he had a gun.

36

I spent most of the day after at Western Pediatric Medical Center, listening to Felicia Torres, guiding her through the hospital system. Observing Emilio.

The little boy clung to his mother, mute and tense.

Physically okay, according to Dr. Ruben Eagle, an old friend and head of the Outpatient Division. We agreed that Rochelle Kissler, a brilliant young psychologist who'd been my student, would be perfect for the long term.

I introduced both of them to Felicia, stayed with her after they left, and asked if there was anything else she wanted to talk about.

"No . . . I'm so tired."

"Is there someone who can stay with you?"

"My mom," she said. "She lives in Phoenix, but she'll come if I ask."

I dialed the number, sat there as she talked.

She hung up, smiling wearily. "She'll be here tomorrow."

"Do you need someone till then?"

"No, I'll be fine . . . this is so nice of you."

"We're all here to help you."

She began shaking.

"What is it?"

"The way you said that, Dr. Delaware. Being helpful. That's what *he* pretended. What kind of sick joke was that?"

I didn't answer.

"I never trusted him, Doctor. Not from the *minute* I met him."

Milo and I decompressed at a bar in Santa Monica. Eleven p.m.; he'd spent his day with Raul Biro and two other Hollywood detectives, going through the house on Altair Terrace.

One of the homes Dale Bright had bought as Nicholas Heubel. The other was a cabin near Palmdale, where he'd confined Felicia Torres in a bathroom. Forced her to imagine what he was doing to Emilio.

Mostly, he'd ignored the child. Letting him cry, then scream. No food or water. Then a quick drop into a shipping carton.

Airholes, to prolong the ordeal.

Milo said, "I know I'm supposed to have a reaction to shooting anyone. But, God help me, Alex, I wish I'd had more bullets."

Three of five rooms on Altair were filled with mementos. Nice view of the Hollywood sign from a corner of the deck. White Lexus in the garage.

The Bentley had been moved from the LAPD motor lab to the same department-sanctioned tow yard where Kat Shonsky's car had been ignored.

I said, "Maybe the chief can use it as his official ride."

Milo said, "Harness a couple of thoroughbreds to the front bumper, be perfect."

Ansell "Dale" Bright's medicine cabinet yielded nothing stronger than aspirin and over-the-counter sinus remedies.

Under the sink was a polished black-walnut box filled with ampules of synthetic testosterone. Its bird's-eye maple mate held plastic-sealed hypodermic needles.

"Pumping himself up?" said Milo. "To go with a dress?"

I threw up my hands.

He finished his Martini and told me about the passports under half a dozen aliases, the trove of documents that traced Bright's path from New York to London, then Paris, Lisbon, back to England, Ireland, Scotland. Final stop: Zurich.

Trammel Dabson was another pilfered identity. Same DOB as Bright and the unfortunate Nicholas Heubel.

The original owner of the identity, an infant buried in the Morton Hall Cemetery in Edinburgh.

Bright had done a gravestone rubbing, mounted it in a scrapbook.

One of fifteen scrapbooks.

Chronicle of a life lived in costume.

The souvenirs weren't limited to paper. In a small basement cut into the hillside behind the house, Milo discovered a trio of footlockers filled with firearms, knives, two acetylene blowtorches, stout rope, surgical gloves and tools, scalpels, probes, tissue spreaders, vials of poison.

Newspaper clippings from foreign papers created another chronology.

Unsolved murder of the landlord of a rooming house in the Eleventh Arrondissement of Paris.

Disappearance of an Oxford publican with a famously nasty disposition.

An article in Portuguese yet to be translated. But the grainy snapshot of a heavyset woman and the recurrent word *"assasinato"* said plenty.

The Brentwood house had served as a front and yielded nothing of forensic value. Upscale address for the social life Bright-as-Heubel had hoped to live as a financial advisor. Soraya Hamidpour had a client "from the industry" ready to move in.

Access to Bright's computer was easy. No encryption and his password was "Bright Guy."

His hard drive contained mostly financial files—algorithms for trading, performance histories, linkups to bourses around the world—and a scatter of sadistic pornography.

In a separate folder were five drafts of a prospectus "Nicholas St. Heubel, III" had composed and dated two years previous. Plans to start Hydro-Worth, a hedge fund emphasizing oil commodity trading. Bright had appended a puffed-up bio, lied about attending Eton, Harvard, and Wharton, termed himself "a brilliant tactician and financial soothsayer."

The boast had some basis in fact. Upon arrival in London from New York, he'd used fake credentials to get a job at a brokerage house in London. Learned to trade futures well enough to earn enormous performance bonuses and a letter of commendation from the managing director.

Within eighteen months, he'd quit, was investing for himself. Nine years after inheriting $1.36 million, his savings had grown to $7.1 million.

Not counting the Swiss bank account, which would take a while to access.

Something else from Switzerland: Mounted at the back of one of the scrapbooks was an elegantly handwritten receipt from a clinic in Lugano. Nothing itemized; the franc conversion translated to fifty-five thousand American dollars.

"Maybe a drug problem, one of those high-end rehab places," said Milo. "But except for the macho-juice, we didn't find anything iffy."

"Could've been successful rehab," I said. "If so, too bad for society."

"What do you mean?"

"He got his head clear enough to chop off other people's."

. . .

Despite Nicholas St. Heubel III's financial acumen, he'd picked up no clients and Hydro-Worth remained a scheme.

I said, "Superficially charming but maybe when they got to know him, he spooked them like he did the sisters."

"Too cute for his own good."

"The game was too much fun."

"Raul found something he wrote on a hard copy of the prospectus. 'Time for a frugal lifestyle, funnel in on what's important.' "

"Getting his priorities straight," I said.

He said, "Another too bad."

As we worked on our second round of drinks, Milo's phone vibrated on the bar.

Inaudible above the drone of bar-talk and an old football game on ESPN Classic.

He watched it jump like a Mexican bean, chewed his olive, swallowed, picked up

"Sturgis . . . *you're* up late, Doc . . . That so? Oh, man . . . I do appreciate it, anything else? True . . . I'll ask him, thanks for letting me know."

Emptying his glass, he waved for a refill.

I said, "Which doc was that?"

"Steinberg, at the coroner's. Ol' Dale's autopsy was prioritized, orders from the chief."

"All those bullet holes, an autopsy was necessary?"

"Police-involved shootings must be treated with utmost care," he pronounced as if talking about someone else.

His drink came. He sipped. Hummed something I couldn't make out.

I said, *"What?"*

He placed his glass on the bar, twirled the stem. "Turns out Dale–Nick–Mr. Bizarro had no balls. Literally. Surgically removed, nice neat job all healed over."

"The Swiss clinic."

"I hear money buys you anything there."

"He pays to get castrated," I said, "takes testosterone to stay masculine."

"No doubt, you've got an explanation based on your training and expertise."

Above us, on screen, someone made a thirty-yard run for a touchdown. Ancient history but some of the drinkers at the bar got excited.

I said, "I could theorize about the desire for total control. Regulating his dosage, enjoying the fluctuation."

"But?"

I snagged the bartender's attention. Pointed at Milo's glass.

Mouthed, "Me, too."

Two days after the rescue of Felicia and Emilio Torres, Milo was called to the chief's office for what he assumed was a pat on the back.

That morning, we'd both been at the coroner's and I stayed with him for the short ride to Parker Center.

The forensic pathologist had been asked to conduct a psychological autopsy and wanted my professional opinion on the psychological motivation behind Ansell "Dale" Bright's self-mutilation, hormonal manipulation, and fascination with "macabre altruism."

I'd rattled off a bunch of jargon that seemed to make everyone happy.

As Milo pulled into the headquarters staff lot, he said, "Why don't you come up, His Majesty would probably like to meet you."

"Probably?"

"He has his moods."

"Thanks anyway, I'll catch some air."

He went inside and I took a walk. Nothing much to see but the fall air was clean for downtown L.A. and the homeless guys I passed seemed tranquil.

Half an hour later, I was back in front of headquarters and Milo was pacing.

"Been here long, Big Guy?"

"Twenty minutes."

"Short meeting," I said.

"Cuz Jackson's other claimed bodies have frittered to nothing, the only thing holding Texas back from spiking the bastard is Antoine." Pointing his finger and beetling his brows. " 'Do something, Lieutenant.' "

"Not a word about Bright?"

" 'Cross-dressing bastard got what he deserved.' "

Back to the Hollywood Hills.

Watching Wilson Good's house after dark.

A night of nothing, followed by a day of the same. Hard to find shelter on the high, sunny street but Milo really wasn't hoping for much.

The second night, I offered to come along.

He said, "Too much free time?"

"Something like that."

Mr. Dot-com's executive secretary had phoned this morning, announcing her boss's "intention to visit his commission" in three days. Robin was working overtime to assemble the mandolin.

She said, "You're okay with being here?"

"Can I hold your tools?"

"When you get in a certain frame of mind, everything you say sounds suggestive."

"And the problem is . . ."

"Absolutely nothing."

I parked the Seville at the southern edge of Wilson Good's street. Close enough for a long view of the house and the electric mesh gate that caged its frontage. A couple of low-voltage spots created useless puddles of illumination. Most of the enclosure was dark.

I said, "Where's the Red Bull?"

Milo said, "Drank coffee all day."

We settled in for the long haul.

No need to; two minutes later, we both spotted movement behind the mesh.

The man was trapped. Slinking into a corner, he ignored Milo's command to show himself, huddled low, trying to look small.

Milo stood out of view, hand on gun. He'd used the weapon more this week than in months previous. "Out, pal. Let's have a look at you."

Freeway hum.

"Put your hands on your head and walk backward toward the sound of my voice. *Now.*"

The distant, bovine moan of a truck horn.

Milo repeated the order louder.

Nothing.

"Suit yourself, friend. One way or the other you're coming out."

Silence.

"You like fire hoses?"

Zoom zoom zoom from miles away.

He called for three Hollywood patrol cars and a locksmith. Five officers arrived under the tutelage of a sergeant who scoped out the situation and said, "Don't see what we can do."

The locksmith showed up ten minutes later, squinted at the gate from ten yards away. "He armed?"

"Don't know."

"What do you expect me to do? That's electric, anyway, I can't do anything with it."

"Any suggestions?"

"Use a tactical nuclear weapon."

"Gee, thanks."

"Welcome. Can I go now?"

Five more minutes of nothing before Milo called out, "You up for a climb, buddy?"

No answer.

"Pal, one way or the other, you're busted."

The sergeant said, "Maybe he's deaf. Central had a deaf guy last year, got shot, big trouble."

Milo continued his monologue. Alternating cajoling with threats.

When he said, "Okay, do the tear gas," a voice from behind the gate said, "I'll come out."

A figure stepped out to the center of the enclosure. The moon lit up half his face.

Thin, gaunt black man. Ragged hair, scruffy beard, sagging clothes.

"Hands on your head."

Scrawny arms shot up fast.

"Turn around and walk toward me. Back up so you're touching the gate."

The man said, "I know the drill."

Milo cuffed both his hands to the mesh gate.

"Thought you wanted me out of here, Officer. I climbed in, could climb out."

Milo turned to the sergeant. "There should be some kind of manual control over there, near the motor. Anyone in good shape?"

The sergeant said, "Someone feeling like Tarzan?"

A short, stocky female officer said, "I used to do gymnastics."

"Go for it, Officer Kylie."

After a couple of false starts, Kylie got a foothold on the mesh. Moments later, she'd scrambled up and over. "Here it is, right on the box."

Milo told the cuffed man: "Listen carefully: Gate's gonna swing open, just move with it, don't panic."

"I never panic," said the man.

"Unflappable."

"That, too."

Freed from the gate and recuffed, the man stared off into space.

Milo let the uniforms go, sat him on the curb.

"I finally get to meet you, Bradley."

Bradley Maisonette hung his head.

"Here to see your old pal, Will? Interesting way to visit."

"You know me?" said Maisonette. " 'Cause I don't know you."

"Been looking for you, sir."

The honorific gave Maisonette a start. He smiled. "You didn't find me for a while."

"Congratulations. Let's talk."

"How'd you do it?" said Maisonette. "Look for me, I mean. Like what's your technique? I was in plain sight, living the good life on Fourth Street."

"Tent City?"

Maisonette flashed rotten teeth. "We call it the Sidewalk Suburb. I'm in and out of there all the time, all you had to do was ask. Flash enough trash, some junkie would've sold me out."

Speaking softly, clearly. His clothes were in tatters but over the phone he'd sound like a refined man.

Milo said, "Your P.O. have any idea you crashed there?"

Bradley Maisonette laughed. "Those people? Never talk to them."

We took Maisonette back to Hollywood station.

He said, "What are the charges?"

Milo said, "Offhand I can think of trespassing, attempted burglary, resisting arrest. Give me some time and I'll come up with more."

"Small stuff. I'll cope."

"No need to if you talk to us."

"That simple, huh?"

"Why not?"

"Nothing ever is."

Maisonette ended up in the same room Tasha had marked with a flo-ral bouquet of perfume and lotions. He exuded the sour, unwashed reek that had filled the Seville on the drive over.

He sniffed, frowned, as if aware of his own odor for the first time.

Milo offered him something to drink.

Maisonette said, "I'll take a steak. Filet mignon, medium rare in-side, charred crisp on the outside, with some nice fried onions. Caesar salad to start, extra dressing. Red wine. I prefer California over French—Pinot Noir."

"Cooperate, Bradley, I can get you caviar."

"Hate that stuff. Tastes like bad pussy."

"Turn either down often?"

Maisonette smiled.

"Why were you trying to break into Wilson Good's crib?"

"No one was breaking in anywhere."

Under bright light, Maisonette's skin was sallow, scored, sun-spotted. Red-rimmed eyes drooped. Thirty-one years old, but he could've been his father's age. Crude tattoos brocading his arms did nothing to hide tortured veins and knotted track-smudges.

Milo said, "What were you doing there?"

"Trying to see Will."

"Why?"

"He called me."

"When?"

"Last week."

"You have a phone?"

"I stand corrected," said Maisonette. "He sent his *girlfriend* to Fourth Street and she invited me. Said Will and I needed to talk."

"About what?"

"She didn't say."

"You went over anyway."

"A week later."

Milo said, "She didn't have to spell it out. You knew."

Maisonette's eyes contemplated resistance.

He said, "What the hell." Gave a slow, weary nod.

"What was the topic?" said Milo.

"Twan," said Maisonette. "There's nothing else between Will and me."

"Good wanted to talk about Antoine Beverly."

"Just the opposite. The girlfriend said Will wanted to discuss *not* talking. He'd explain when I got there."

"Who's this girlfriend?"

"White girl, freckles, calls herself Andy."

I said, "That's his wife."

Maisonette grinned. "You believe everything you hear?"

"Why would she lie about that?" said Milo.

"Will's been stringing her along for ten years. Coaches at a church school, has to look all respectable, so he tells the priests he's married. But they never filed paper."

"Ten years, huh?"

"Will's one of those guys," said Maisonette. "Commitment-shy."

"The two of you have been in regular contact," said Milo.

"Not regular, intermittent."

"When was the last time?"

"While back, I don't keep a calendar."

"Years? Months?"

"Maybe a year," said Maisonette. "The topic was I needed a loan to get me on my feet."

"Will come through?"

"Sure did."

"Good friend."

"We go back."

Milo said, "Let's push things up to the present. Andrea the fake-wife came by to tell you Will would pay you not to talk about Twan."

"I didn't want to anyway," said Maisonette. "Talk. Called him, got no answer. Fine with me."

"Why was Will suddenly worried about you talking?"

Maisonette smiled. "Why ask questions you know the answer to?"

"I could use your answer."

"Because things were stirring up."

"Antoine's case was reopened."

Nod.

"After Andrea's visit, you rabbited."

Maisonette flashed a who-me look.

Milo said, "Bradley, I'm not as stupid as I look, been on Fourth Street plenty of times. Junkies said you were in the air."

Smooth lie; not a trace of tell.

Maisonette shrugged. "I wandered around a little. You didn't work hard enough."

"Well," said Milo, "at least you're here and we're having a great time. So what about Antoine worries Will?"

Maisonette scratched the crook of one ravaged arm. "You're not going to charge me, correct? Once you get hold of Will, he'll tell you straight-out I was invited to visit anytime, therefore no trespass and, for sure, no attempt 459."

Milo laughed. "You climbed his fence."

"Rang his bell first. I thought he was home."

"No one answers the bell, he's home?"

"Will can get like that."

"Like what?"

"Depressed, goes to bed for days, doesn't want to talk or see anyone. Last few years, he's been better, taking meds. Likes his job, doesn't want to rock any boats. But before—when we were in college—he'd miss a lot of classes, borrow my notes."

"You went to college together."

"Cal State Long Beach," said Maisonette. "One year, I studied electrical engineering. Will did a Mickey Mouse major." Flexing his hands. "P.E."

I said, "Will has a long history of depression."

"Ancient history."

"Did it start before Antoine's death, or after?"

Maisonette's eyes rose to the ceiling.

Milo said, "Is that a tough question, Bradley?"

Maisonette slid around in his chair. "I'll take some food now. And a Coke, real sugar, no Diet."

"Answer the question first."

Maisonette rubbed his palms together. Jammed his hands into his hair and yanked hard enough to shimmy his eyebrows.

I said, "Before or after?"

"After."

"Antoine stayed on Will's mind. Made dealing with life tough."

"You sound like a shrink."

"Happens sometimes. How did Antoine affect you?"

"Me? I'm cool."

"Not Will."

Maisonette hugged himself. "Cold in here, would you please turn down the A.C.?"

Milo said, "What preyed on Will? He did something to Twan? You and he did something together?"

Maisonette's head turned slowly. His eyes filled with tears. "You think *that*?"

"Mr. Maisonette, I've got a sixteen-year-old homicide all stirred up, like you said, and two supposed friends of the victim rabbiting."

"Supposed? Here are the facts: We were best friends. *Best*. I didn't do anything to Antoine, Will didn't do anything to Antoine."

"Antoine disappeared into thin air?"

"*We* didn't do it. Not Will or me."

"Who did?"

Maisonette worked his hands through his hair. Dandruff snowed on the table.

Milo slammed the table hard enough to twang the metal. "*Enough of this bullshit! What'd happened to Antoine?*"

Real rage. Maisonette parried it with long, cool stare. "Nothing."

Milo shot up to his feet. Leaned on the table, nearly upended it with his weight. "Sixteen *years,* Bradley. Antoine's parents living with the pain of not knowing. You and your so-called friend were at that funeral, pretending to be all torn up. Sixteen fucking *years.*"

Maisonette's skinny frame began to shake.

"*Say* it!"

Maisonette's head dropped. "Damn Will."

"Will did something."

"He swore me."

"To what?"

"Silence. Not 'cause we *did* something. Something got done to *him.*"

A beat.

"And to me."

CHAPTER

38

The man's name was Howard Ingles Zint.

Aka Floyd Cooper Zindt. Aka Zane Lee Cooper. Aka Howard Cooper Sayder.

Sixteen years ago, he'd been the "West Coast sales professional" for Youth In Action. The company, defunct for over a decade, had turned out to be a scam, taking cash for magazine subscriptions rarely delivered.

Zint arrived in L.A. in May, after a stint in Tucson, set about re-cruiting students from local schools. Concentrating on minority kids, using the racist logic that dark skin equaled poverty and poverty was a great motivator. When Antoine, Will, and Bradley met Zint, he was a smooth-talking thirty-five-year-old self-described "former college jock" able to sell anything.

Now he was a middle-aged inmate at the Supermax prison in Florence, Colorado.

The mug shot revealed a gaunt, white-bearded apparition with dead eyes.

Twenty-three hours a day in your cell could do that to you. Especially with ninety-two years left on a hundred-year sentence for abducting, beating, cutting, and molesting scores of boys.

Sixteen years ago, Zint hadn't yet progressed to violence, was content to seduce his prey with cash and promises of video games, running shoes, cool athletic gear. For the older boys, hookups with "hot babes."

It started off simply in L.A.: Zint picked the three laughing black boys up on a street corner, outlined their routes, collected them at the end of their shifts. Advanced them money, even though it was against the rules.

After trust was built up, he began pulling them off early, one at a time, where icy cans of beer, freshly rolled joints, and pills Zint assured them were just "for relaxation" awaited.

More cash was disbursed, then Zint played music from a boom box and watched, smiling, as the boys got all "hazy."

"What I mean by that," said Bradley Maisonette, "is even now I can't be sure it actually happened. Even though yes, I know it did. Maybe on my own I never would've come to that conclusion, I don't know, I really don't know."

I said, "But when Will told you . . ."

"After he tried to jump off the Long Beach pier, is when he told me. Second semester at college. I held him back, had to fight with him, he was always big. I said what the fuck you want to go and do that for? That's when he told me."

Deep breath.

"I saved his life, what does he do when he's finished talking? Hauls off and hits me." Rubbing his jaw. "I said, 'Man, what the hell is wrong with you?' He said, 'You messed me up, my life ain't worth saving.' "

Bradley Maisonette swiped at his eyes. "Big man, crying like a baby."

I said, "He told you what Zint did to him and you remembered."

"I always knew, I just kept it behind . . . some kind of curtain. Listening to Will woke up something in my mind—pushed the curtain aside. Like, what the *hell*."

I said, "Did you let Will know?"

"Not then, no way, it was too . . . overwhelming. This was finals week. Will was depressed the whole time we were there, borrowing my notes, cheating off my tests in English. Really looking bad. And yeah, the depression started *after* Twan, *right* after, I should've figured it out, but . . ."

"Eventually you did tell Will what happened to you."

"Yeah." Shaking his head. "We were both blasted on rock. Will didn't take to it. I did. He's cheating off my tests and *he* ends up getting all respectable." Throwing up his hands. "Here's me."

Milo said, "You're talking, now, Bradley. You're a good man."

"Yeah, I'm a saint."

"What happened to Twan?"

"What *happened*? He went with Zint, didn't come back. Went into Zint's van and the van drove off. Which was different, usually Zint parked on a quiet street, stayed in place to party. Like the van was his house—he had housekeeping stuff in there. Food, drinks, books, games, all kinds of shit."

"Zint changed his style that day and drove off."

"Don't ask me where, I've been asking myself that for sixteen years."

Maisonette sprang up, circled the room, wedged his head in a corner, stood that way for a while. When he returned to the table, he put his head down, closed his eyes.

His lips moved. After a while, sound came out. "First time."

I said, "It was the first time Twan went into the van?"

Nod; his hair scraped the table. "Twan didn't trust him. Twan was smarter than us. But that day . . ."

His eyes clenched. "Oh, God, this is so . . ." He flung one hand over his cheek.

Milo touched his shoulder. "You're doing the right thing."

Maisonette sat up, stared at something miles away. Sunken cheeks vibrated. His eyes were red and wet. "Twan went in there 'cause *we* said it was cool. Zint paid us fifty bucks to *convince* Twan it was cool. Will didn't want to admit what happened to him, same with me. We told Twan it was cool to go in there and he did and we never saw him again and now nobody's going to forgive me."

Howard Zint, diabetic, tubercular, HIV-positive, made the deal from a prison infirmary bed.

Two extra candy bars a month and no additional sentence.

He told the tale concisely, with no emotion.

Antoine Beverly had resisted Zint's overtures, tried to escape the van. Zint hit him in the face and Antoine's head snapped back, colliding against the edge of a miniature slot machine Zint had just purchased.

Zint drove to the undeveloped wilderness north of the La Cienega oil fields and buried the boy on a dune, somewhere on the eastern edge of what was now the Kenneth Hahn Recreational Area.

Sixteen years later, he drew a map.

Development had resected the land in some places, augmented others. It took a while to find the spot.

Bones.

The autopsy revealed no serious head injury but did highlight multiple cut-marks on Antoine's ribs.

Ever the con, Zint had reached for one more guilt-minimizing lie.

There was talk about negating the agreement and putting him on trial for murder.

Sharna and Gordon Beverly said, "Just give us Antoine and leave us alone."

The funeral was held on a beautiful autumn morning. Over two hundred friends, relatives, and well-wishers, the predictable sprinkle of politicians, journalists, and "community activists" trawling for photo ops.

Bradley Maisonette was nowhere to be found and neither was Wilson Good. Good and Andrea had been staying at a motel in Tarzana, picked up their dog the day before we'd found Maisonette, left town for parts unknown.

Milo said, "Hopefully someplace without a pier."

After the ceremony, we queued up to pay our respects.

Gordon Beverly clasped our hands, moved forward as if to embrace us, stopped himself.

Sharna Beverly pushed aside her veil. Her face was carved mahogany, her eyes clear and dry.

"You did it, Lieutenant."

Taking Milo's face in both hands, she kissed each cheek. Lowered the veil.

Turned away and waited for the next person in line.

39

R obin pulled an all-nighter and had the mandolin bound and varnished six hours before her patron was due to arrive.

She wrapped it in green velvet, carried it to the dining room table.

"Gorgeous," I said.

"He just called, definitely sounded off."

She'd showered, towel-dried her curls, avoided makeup, put on a brown knee-length dress I hadn't seen in years.

"I know," she said.

"Know what?"

"Not exactly something Audrey would wear."

Fooling with her hair.

I brewed coffee.

She said, "Decaf, right?"

I tried to occupy her with a guessing game.

What Kind of Car Will He Bring?

I'd looked up Dot-com on the Internet he'd helped develop. He was thirty-three, a Stanford grad and a bachelor, with a net worth of four hundred seventy-five million dollars.

Robin said, "I figured it was in that ballpark."

"So what kind of wheels?"

"Who knows?"

"How about you, Blondie?"

Blanche looked up and smiled.

Robin said, "Could be anything—one extreme or the other."

"Meaning?"

"Ferrari or hybrid."

I thought: *Bentley or VW bus.*

The coffee machine beeped. I fixed two cups. She took a sip, muttering, "I'm such a wimp," got up and parted the living room shutters.

"Nice day," she said. "Might as well wait outside."

"Want to take your coffee?"

"Pardon—oh, sure, thanks."

And the answer is: blue Ford Econoline van.

A large man in black jeans and T-shirt got out. Logo of Dot-com's company on the shirt.

He saw us on the terrace. Studied the house. Walked to the rear of the van.

"Muscle," I said. "In case you don't want to give up the goods."

"Not funny," said Robin. But she smiled.

Large Guy opened the van's rear doors. A ramp descended electrically. He reached in and guided out a wheelchair.

The figure in the chair was slight, pale, crew-cut, baby-faced.

Wearing a black sweatshirt with the same logo and blue jeans. Nothing much filled the jeans. As the chair rolled down the ramp, his body flopped. Held in place by a leather strap around his middle.

One of his fingers pushed a button. The chair rolled forward. Stopped.

He looked at the house, just as his driver had.

Taking in the steep, stone steps that lead to the terrace. On the other side, an acutely sloping grass and rock pathway.

Robin and I were attracted to the lot because of the slope. Joked about needing a lift when we get old.

The man in the chair smiled.

Robin rushed down.

She introduced me.

The man in the chair said, "Nice to meet you, Alex. Dave Simmons."

Not sure what do with my hand, I half extended it.

Dave Simmons winked.

Robin said, "Dave, I'm so sorry about the lack of access."

"Tom can always carry me."

Tom rumbled, "You bet."

"Just kidding, Tom. All I need is to see this masterwork."

"I'll bring it down." Robin ran up the stairs.

Dave Simmons said, "Careful, don't trip." To me: "I didn't want to shock her but I don't usually talk about it. Last time she saw me, I was weak but maintaining, she probably didn't notice. It comes and goes. Currently, it's coming."

"M.S.?"

"Something along those lines, but not exactly." Simmons smiled. His face was unlined, his eyes wide and blue and merry. "I've always had a thing about being different, so now . . . oh, wow, that's gorgeous."

Robin held the instrument out to Simmons.

"Can't," he said. "Hands too weak."

She moved it closer.

His breath caught. "Unbelievable, you're a wizard—or whatever the female version of that is. Could you please turn it over . . . look at that maple. One piece, or am I missing the seam?"

"One piece," said Robin.

"Must've been a great plank . . . got the fiddle-grain plus that vertical wave passing through it—like caramel."

Simmons's eyes closed briefly. When they opened, he strained, managed to get his head closer to the mirror-shiny surface. "Like a molten river flowing . . . where'd you find wood this spectacular?"

"An old violin maker retired. I've had it for years," said Robin. "It gets better as it ages."

"Sure, natural drying," said Simmons. "Can't replicate that with a kiln—I've been doing my research. It's amazing, Robin. Thanks for creating it and thanks especially for having it ready so soon. My idea is to give it to a deserving musician. Run a benefit for something, have a raffle. No charge for the tickets, to qualify you'd have to play a classic bluegrass song at a certain level. We'd use virtuoso judges. Maybe Grisman or Statman, someone of that caliber. What do you think?"

"It's a lovely idea, Dave."

"I think it's best, Robin. I really did intend to learn how to play, had a teacher all lined up." A flicker of arm movement stood in for a shrug. "Best-laid plans."

"I'm so sorry, Dave."

"Hey, stuff happens. Then it un-happens. I'm staying positive." He gave the mandolin another long, dreamy look. "Absolutely masterful, I'm blown away. Okay, Tom, we'd better get going. Nice to see you again, Robin. Keep it here until I get the details worked out. If you get any other ideas, let me know. Great to meet you, Alex."

Tom took hold of the chair and began pushing it toward the ramp.

Robin ran to catch up. Placed her hand on Simmons's arm.

He said, "Oh, one more thing. Could I ask when you see yourself finishing the rest of the quartet?"

"I'll start today on the mandola."

"Nine months seem reasonable?"

"Sooner, Dave."

Simmons grinned. "Sooner is better."